Praise for *The Tunnels of Buda*, Book 2 in the Soul Catcher Series

The Tunnels of Buda — the second instalment in Don Sawyer's Soul Catcher series — is a fabulous sequel to *The Burning Gem*. The novel's propulsive plot and mysterious settings — including a maze of shifting catacombs beneath the ancient palace of *Budavári Palota* — along with its wide cast of nuanced characters, make for an exhilarating ride as Zoltan and Barbara team up to attempt the overthrow once and for all of the tyrannical cabal known as The Company. Which will prevail: their belief in the power of love and freedom, or The Company's cynical doctrine that humans must be "managed" for their own good? *The Tunnels of Buda* makes this epic showdown — one very relevant to our own market-driven society — the centre of its compelling narrative.

—**Mark Morton**, broadcaster and author of *The Headmaster*

In this beautifully crafted page turner set in an imaginary world just beneath our feet, Don Sawyer has given us a deeply entertaining story of magic, ancient evil and the ability of love, courage and hope to overcome it. He reminds us of the power of imagination and fantasy to probe deeper questions of justice, sustainability, and belonging.

—**Frye Gaillard,** author of *The Cradle of Freedom*, winner of the Lillian Smith Book Award, *A Hard Rain*, named an NPR Great Read of 2018; and *The Southernization of America*, an NPR Best Book of 2022

The Tunnels of Buda is a real gripper. The plot races along with many a twist and turn, following the Tolkien strategy of suspense/refuge/suspense/refuge, which works so well. No question that if the stars aligned, this could be a movie bigger than *The Matrix*.

—**Tom Wayman**, author of *The Road to Appledore* and winner of the George Woodcock Award for Lifetime Achievement in the literary arts.

THE TUNNELS OF BUDA

BOOK 2 IN THE SOUL CATCHER SERIES

DON SAWYER

CASTLE BRIDGE MEDIA
DENVER, COLORADO, USA

CASTLE BRIDGE MEDIA
Denver, Colorado

Cover images by Les Richardson/Unsplash, Linus Sandvide/Unsplash
These images have been modified.

THE TUNNELS OF BUDA
©2025 Don Sawyer
All rights reserved.

ISBN: 979-8-9917855-3-2

For Jan

Acknowledgements

THIS BOOK AND ITS PREQUEL, *The Burning Gem*, began a long time ago in galaxy far, far away. They had their genesis as an exercise for a writing group in Fairhope, Alabama that was affiliated with the Fairhope Center for the Writing Arts (fairhopecenterforthewritingarts.org/), which provides a writer-in-residence program for authors from all over North America. I was fortunate to be there when Charlie Price was in residence. I joined Charlie and FCWA chair Skip Jones in the writers' group, and I will always appreciate their support, advice and for steering me in the right direction.

Thanks to Beta reader, Alpha friend and brother in arms Calvin White for a lifetime of shared battles and camaraderie. You've always had my back, each and every time. And to my long-time mentor and friend Tom Wayman. Without your encouragement and support, I would have never written my first book – or believed that I could.

Many others have contributed to this series, including the late great Jim Steel, imaginist and creative consultant Federico Holten-Anderson, my daughters Melissa and Farish, who have enriched my life in so many ways and continue to read their dad's manuscripts with a critical eye and loving support.

I want to thank my editors, Jennifer Day and especially Claire Ashgrove, who not only made this a better book, but also made me a better writer. To In Churl Yo and Jason Henderson of Castle Bridge Media, thanks for seeing the possibilities and enjoying the magic.

And finally, to Jan, my wife of 54 years, who always believed in me, even when I didn't. You typed my first manuscript 50 years ago because no one else could read my writing and haven't stopped being there for me ever since. So many miles together.

Chapter 1

ZOLTAN STOPPED TYPING AND LEANED back heavily in his chair. He stared blankly at the words on the screen then peered over the top of his rimless glasses at the room they were in. It was a back room in Mrs. Harlow's specialty jewelry store, windowless and spare except for the desk where he and Barbara sat, a scattering of chairs, and a round table covered in deep red velvet. And a simple wood tray holding eleven jewels.

The soft light from the glowing white walls played across the gem's facets, exploding in dazzling shades of blue, green, yellow, almost as if they were alive. Zoltan sat a dozen feet away, and even from that distance the jewels glowed with startling intensity.

His gaze fixed on a single small box made of what looked like lead but was in fact an alloy so dense it was impenetrable. It held, he knew, a simple black stone set in a gold ring, a stone of such power and evil it was hidden, locked in a container created especially to muzzle it, to arrest its dark emanations, a stone Zoltan knew he must destroy at any cost.

It had only been a few hours since they had met with Samantha and Pierre, Mrs. Harlow's molecular physics team, who, she claimed, were two of the most brilliant physicists in the world. Zoltan had no reason to doubt it. Here in the Market, located deep below the streets of New York in a gigantic subway terminal abandoned in 1873, there were many brilliant minds and talented artisans with arcane – some would say *supernatural* – skills and knowledge.

Two hours. Two hours since they had learned the terrible truth about the gems in the tray. Yes, and the black stone.

"You are hesitant," Barbara said from the chair next to him.

Zoltan brought his eyes to the woman sitting next to him, who was studying his profile.

"You are imagining an avalanche, poised on a mountain side, appearing stable, a face of snow and ice that when triggered sweeps everything in front of it to oblivion."

He glanced into the deep green eyes of the woman, a small smile on his face. Barbara's empathic skills had grown to the point that, at moments, it seemed as if she knew his thoughts and feelings better than he did. And in so short a time.

He thought back to the night—early morning, actually—when Barbara knocked on his apartment door, the first person to do so in years. How, against all of his instincts, he had invited her in, touched her, divulged his true name, abandoning DeAngelo, the name given to him by the *Mester* forever.

BAHr-ba-ra, he thought. *The woman from a foreign land, the Santeria goddess of fire, lightning, and thunder.*

How long ago was that? he wondered. *When she crashed into my life, when she forced me to open my eyes? A year? Month?* No, not that long. He counted the days in his head. The first night, and then Barbara's introduction to The Market. The day Mrs. Harlow agreed to make an unbreakable chain for Barbara's blazing red gem. The same day they met Caraldo and Zoltan learned the *Mester* knew he had violated his vows. The flight to Budapest, the nights with poor old Dezso. Reading of his murder, his head and hands severed and taken. Zoltan and Barbara's capture, and the tense flight to London and the *Mester's* compound. The near fatal confrontation there, Caraldo's death, Barbara chopping off the *Mester's* finger with the black-stoned ring and jamming the bloodless finger in her jeans. Scooping the agents' gems from the safe as they fled the carnage, escaping over the roof and finally back to the Market. Barbara's recovery of the flash drive from his apartment and barely eluding the *Mester's* agents.

And now, today the truth they had learned about the gems, the terrifying specter that they were far more than just beautiful stones, that they fed their owners a stream of darkness and despair, that they were connected to a powerful web of evil they were just beginning to comprehend.

So much in such a short time. How long has it been? Zoltan wondered once more.

"Eleven days," Barbara said quietly. "Since I came knocking on your door. Can you believe it?"

Zoltan looked at the woman and sighed. Her bright red hair fell across her face as she peered at the monitor. God, she could be so beautiful. And exasperating.

"Barbara, you are reading my mind."

"Sorry," she said absently, still peering at the message on the screen.

"So, Madam, are you now telepathic as well as an empath?"

Barbara glanced up from the screen. "I don't think so, but you're pretty transparent right now. By the way, you misspelled 'colleagues.' It has two 'l's."

He shook his head and smiled slightly. "I guess that happens when you turn one hundred and ten, no?"

When Zoltan had revealed his age that first night, she feared she had pursued not a man who could help her escape her empty life, not to mention her asshole of a husband, but a total lunatic. Only as she accepted the world she had walked into did she believe Zoltan's story of escaping Hungary after the First World War, of a failed academic career, and of his rapturous love for Rebecca, a love so profound, so passionate that her death in 1940 shattered him. And how his emptiness drove him into the hands of the *Mester* and gem making, which paid well and gave him extended life, but at a terrible cost.

"Probably," she agreed. "But as you say, you do pretty well for a guy your age." She looked up at him studying his angular features, his silver hair swept back at the temples. And his eyes, black as obsidian. "And you look *really* good."

"Thank you, madam. I am most flattered." He gestured at the message on the screen. "You approve?"

She nodded slowly.

"This is it, then," Zoltan said solemnly. "When I click the send icon, the game is on, yes?"

Barbara breathed deeply. "Yes. But then it has been on for some time, I guess."

"You are right," Zoltan replied. "For a very long time, it seems. But we were not paying attention, no?"

"No."

Zoltan's finger hovered over the mouse. Barbara's heart fluttered as his finger touched the mouse button. There was a slight swoosh. He took his hand off and stared at the screen. A banner at the top informed them that the message had been sent. Would they like to view it?

Barbara reached over and moved the cursor to View Message.

A solid black page appeared on the left-hand screen. Photos of the eleven jewels lying in the tray on the table appeared on the other. Barbara read the message in white letters on the black page.

I am Zoltan József, a gem maker like you. If you know me at all it will be as DeAngelo. You will be surprised to receive this message as we have been prohibited from communicating among ourselves. However, over many years I have obtained your personal contact information, which I am using to notify you about significant occurrences you should be aware of. After I learned of the Mester's intention to kill or re-educate me two weeks ago, I fled to Budapest, where I obtained important and disturbing information on the nature of the Mester's organization, of which we are all a part. Much of this evidence came from one of our colleagues, Bokor Dezső, who I regret to report was murdered and beheaded by Boris Zhukov. Victor Caraldo was sent to capture me. I was taken to the Mester's compound for interrogation and to be executed. In an attempt to save my life, Victor Caraldo died after being stabbed by Zhukov, who was himself killed by a bullet from Caraldo's gun. In the struggle, the Mester was blinded and sustained other injuries. During the chaos I retrieved twelve agent jewels he kept in his office safe. This included my own. I do not know which gems belong to which agents, so I am sending photographs of each of the gems I managed to seize. I regret that I could not save the remaining jewels, but I believe the potential for each agent to repossess his gem is a very real possibility if we collaborate. However, given the nature of the information I have uncovered, I am only asking each of the agents whose gem is pictured on the second page of this message to join me at a refuge site in the Market. You will, of course, be able to reclaim your jewels at that time. I will also share with you certain facts I have uncovered. Information on when and where to meet is attached in the "agent-only" encryption.

She turned to the second screen and studied the stones pictured. Each was stunning, even in a photograph. Tiny facets reflected shards of red and green light, hearts of yellow and orange burned in the center of shimmering blue and sparkling gold gems. Unset, they lay, brilliant, on the red velvet behind them. She sensed the tug of each through the screen and thought of her sense of loss even for the night her gem was being set. What would the agents, separated from their jewels except for short periods, feel when they viewed their stone?

"I am sorry you are removed from the account of events," Zoltan said seriously. "It is not because I do not fully appreciate…"

"Hush," Barbara said, shaking her head. "Sometimes you can be such an idiot."

Zoltan's eyes widened. "My apologies. I meant no offense, I assure you."

She turned to Zoltan, green eyes blazing. "Eleven men will be arriving in two days. We know little to nothing about them. Some may not be happy with this change of circumstances. Some may even be agents of the *Mester*." Barbara paused. "Or worse. Don't you think I know that? The last thing we need is to tip our hand."

"Tip our hand?"

Barbara waved impatiently. "Old saying. It means don't reveal more than we need to. Don't let our plans fall into the wrong hands."

Zoltan sat back in the chair, nodding slightly. "I see. You seem to understand the situation well, yes? So could I ask a question?"

"Of course."

"These plans of ours. Could you share them with me, perhaps?"

Now Barbara leaned backward, swiveling in her chair to face Zoltan. "You don't have a plan?"

Zoltan shrugged. "Do you?"

"Well, no. But I sort of thought that was your department."

"I am sorry to disappoint you."

Barbara stared into Zoltan's dark eyes, but they gave nothing away.

Zoltan folded his hands in his lap. "But perhaps we could review the situation. Something might occur to us, no?"

"That would be nice," Barbara remarked dryly.

"As you say, two days from now, this room we are sitting in will be filled with eleven of the *Mester's* agents. They will have travelled from all over the world. I will recognize most and know a few, but none well." He paused. "Indeed, none of us knows any other agent well. As you have quite perceptively pointed out, it is likely some may not approve of our recent encounters with the *Mester*. Or the outcomes."

"Approve?" Barbara cut in. "We didn't exactly beg to be kidnapped and nearly killed."

Zoltan held up his hand. "Nonetheless, our encounter has resulted in significant changes within the organization these men have been part of, many for a very long time. People do not like change. Especially when it threatens their finances, their way of life."

"But Zoltan, what sort of life has it been? They were forced to live lives of utter loneliness. You couldn't even share your name! You were little more than slaves to the *Mester*."

Zoltan's head moved from side to side slightly. "Perhaps. But we agreed to the enslavement. And were well paid for it."

"Well paid! Zoltan, are you crazy? The price you paid—happiness, love, companionship! And to keep you docile, any rebellion meant the threatened destruction of your jewels, of your very selves. And now you find out he's been manipulating you, injecting self-loathing directly into your unconscious. Compensation aside, that's hardly most people's idea of a great career and terrific working conditions."

Zoltan smiled slightly. "Indeed it is not. But you must remember, agents are not most people. Each of us was chosen because we were utterly alone. Orphans in every sense. We wished to leave the world we found ourselves in. For some, it was depression so dark we saw no spark to illuminate the deep caves we inhabited in our minds. For others, perhaps an illness that made us unable to live with others. Whatever it was, each of us stood at the brink, desperate to hit the reset button, yes? One way or another. And then, out of the blackness, The *Mester* appears, and he gives us something we never had before. He gave us power. Power we never dreamed of."

"Power?"

"Oh, yes. What could be more powerful than seizing a portion of someone's very soul? To encapsulate it in a sparkling stone that I created?" His eyes darted upwards. "To destroy it."

Barbara stared at him in silence.

"And in all the years, few, very few, ever complained."

"Yes," Barbara said. "And they are dead."

"True. But even fewer came to their aid."

Barbara gripped the arms of her chair in exasperation. "So what's your point? That you wish you still enjoyed that idyllic life? That you resent me prying you out of your cushy world filled with happiness and joy?"

Zoltan looked at her evenly. "No, madam, that is not what I am saying." He nodded formally. "I will forever be indebted. But the others arriving will not have had a green-eyed empath in their lives, at least not for a very, very long time."

Barbara's hands relaxed. "I'm sorry." She glanced down at the carpeted floor. "Sometimes, I think, I feel guilty for all of this. It was my unhappiness, not yours, that got you into this mess."

Zoltan leaned forward and covered her hand with his. His black eyes softened. "Please, do not say that. Do not even think it, for it is not true. You have given me the greatest gift one can receive, something I never thought I would experience again. You made me feel once more, to care." He sat back. "I want you to remember the gem maker that came to your home, not so very long ago. What sort of man was he?"

Her mind slipped back to their first meeting, the mild jewelry salesman at her door. And then later, the day he returned to create her jewel, the slightly stuffy, undistinguished gem maker fussing with his camera, his eyes dark and sad. His stories not of his loves or achievements, but of the customers whom he had served, and especially the tragedies of those whose arrangements had gone wrong. She remembered the timid, frightened man who opened his apartment door to her the night she had crept through the subway.

She stared into Zoltan's eyes. "You are not that man anymore."

"Perhaps," Zoltan agreed. "But who I was? That is who will be here in two days."

"And others," Barbara declared. "As I said, there will be agents of the *Mester*. I can sense it."

Zoltan looked at her quizzically.

"There are two, possibly three. They have another relationship with the *Mester*. I felt it in the stones. They work for him."

"We all work for him."

"Yes, but this is different. They are in contact. They are part of the circle somehow. Their allegiance is to him." She looked at the ceiling and thought about the tall figure in the brown robes Dezso told them about, the man who had enlisted the *Mester*. "And to his overlord, it would seem."

Zoltan sighed. "I suppose that was to be expected. But let me go on. They will arrive and we will have their stones, yes?"

Barbara nodded.

"We place the stones on a velvet-covered table in Mrs. Harlow's shop. As they arrive, they will enter the shop and find their gem."

"What if one of the agents chooses the wrong stone?"

Zoltan's hand dropped to the jewel in his vest pocket. One of the dozen gems Barbara had managed to scoop from the Mester's safe as they escaped his London compound had been his. After they returned to the Market, Mrs. Harlow had set Zoltan's magnificent gem, a gleaming sky-blue teardrop that contained a piece of his soul, in a simple gold hoop attached to a fine unbreakable chain. An unfamiliar warmth spread through his hand. "They will not, I assure you. They will select their gem. And then they will need time. It is quite overwhelming, to feel whole again."

Her hand pressed her stone between her breasts. "Yes. I think I understand."

"After all the agents have arrived and paired with their jewel, we will convene here." He nodded to the circular table in front of them. He stared silently at the empty chairs around the table.

"And then?"

"I will explain the events of the last few weeks. And then I will try to convince them to give up everything they have known for years and join me in a revolt against some mysterious *Ubermester* who, it seems, is headquartered in a yet-to-be-identified castle presumably in one of two dozen or so countries that can be reached from London by a jet helicopter in one night." Zoltan shrugged. "What could possibly go wrong?"

Aries are exciting, mercurial, daring, she thought. *We push until our flame can burn its brightest.* She snickered. *Of course, that works best if you don't die in the process.*

Chapter 2

AFTER THE HUSH OF MRS. Harlow's workshop, the Market's sounds and chaos struck her like a tsunami. A hundred stalls, small shops and cafes were spread around the perimeter of the gigantic dome. In front of her, crowds of people, most dressed in the red and black Market uniform, drifted across the great courtyard, which was paved in black and white marble tile. A few men and women in street clothes looked dazed as they took in the spectacle around them. They were "outsiders," she knew, sales agents and traders who took goods produced in the market for sale to exclusive shops in cities around the world. They came and left on the ancient Market train that left from an abandoned subway line and arrived at a station that did not officially exist.

In fact, none of this officially existed. The Market, a utopian syndicalist community buried deep below the city, populated with hundreds of men and women too strange and wonderful for the world above. And the train that brought supplies and traders, the ancient three-car train that veered onto an ancient subway spur to disappear down a long-forgotten tunnel to the Market station. There, the few specially chosen traders would disembark into a glittering, black and white world built in the shell of a terminal abandoned for a century.

And when they returned to their lives above ground, they would remember nothing of this place.

She smiled to herself, remembering the first time she had walked through the tiled arch entrance to the Market and stood in awe as her eyes swept over the crowd and the glowing dome that rose far overhead. No doubt she had gaped open-mouthed just like these outsiders.

The air was filled with chatter and laughter. Somewhere a bagpipe droned. Barbara heard the ping of a hammer on an anvil. The sharp bark of a dog cut through the din. The smell of baking bread and grilling meat wafted through the odorless filtered air.

She stood and stared at the turmoil, reluctant to leave the quiet oasis of Mrs. Harlow's shop. *The game is on*, she thought. *And I will be meeting the players very soon.*

"Barbara?"

She glanced at Zoltan, who looked back at her with concern.

"You seem very serious. How are you doing?"

Barbara thought about the web of evil, murder and magic she had wandered into, and smiled.

"Just peachy."

Zoltan looked at her quizzically but said nothing. He nodded across the bustling courtyard at a café with a small patio filled with tables covered with red-checked tablecloths and enclosed by a white picket fence.

"Will you join me for a cappuccino, madam? I do believe we have a good deal to discuss."

She looked at him coyly. "Are you propositioning me, sir?"

She had hoped to see a smile play across his full lips, perhaps a spark in those obsidian eyes. But his face remained dark and grim.

They stepped into the crowd and strode across the tiled floor, dodging the crowds that drifted around them. Her eyes strayed toward the ceiling of the dome that covered the Market, great concentric circles of multicolored tile that became lighter as they rose toward the center. There a yellow orb glowed brightly, providing light for the entire colony.

"The ball in the middle of the dome," Barbara mused as they walked. "You said it was like a miniature sun."

"Indeed. It is precisely that. And like the sun, it uses nuclear fusion. More efficient and no radioactivity."

She looked over at Zoltan. "Nuclear fusion? But that's just a theory. No one has created a workable fusion reactor."

"Yes. That is the story, no? But as you now realize, many things are not as they seem. The Market was founded by many extraordinary people, outcasts, eccentrics, geniuses. Two of those were among the leading physicists in the world. They came here in 1945. You see, they had been part of the Manhattan Project."

"The atomic bomb. Hiroshima and Nagasaki."

Zoltan nodded. "They could not go on above ground." He continued staring at the glowing sphere. "They did not mean for their work to be used so." He looked back atBarbara as they edged around a couple arguing loudly.

"So they came here, "Barbara finished. "And created a tiny sun."

"The Market, it is a place of hope, yes? Where gifts are used for the good of the community, not just to make a fortune." He was quiet for a moment. "They found peace here, I believe."

They had reached the café, and Zoltan pushed a low gate open for Barbara. She walked to a table in the far corner of the patio, the same table they had been at when Caraldo loomed out of the crowd and informed them that the *Mester* knew. Knew everything. About Barbara, about Zoltan's defiance. And that Caraldo had been sent to confirm what the *Mester* sensed about Zoltan.

And if necessary, destroy him.

Zoltan pulled the chair out for Barbara and sat down across from her. She stared over her shoulder at the crowd outside of the patio.

"I don't see as many Market police," she said. The break-in at Zoltan's apartment by two of the *Mester's* agents—while she hid on top of his bookshelf with the flash drive containing vital information on the gem makers—had triggered a full alarm. The entire police force, intimidating in their red helmets and black face masks, had been deployed for the first time in years.

Zoltan looked up absently. "Yes. Mrs. Harlow said the police had been ordered to stand down. But I am afraid it is not over. They were overbearing, yes? This is a community that depends on cooperation. They do not take the aggression of the police lightly."

After acknowledging the waiter with a quick smile and placing their order, Zoltan's eyes darkened, and his face returned to the grim expression he had worn since their meeting with Sam and Andre.

"Zoltan, are you alright?"

He glanced at her, his lips drawn in a thin line. "What was the expression you used? Just peachy?"

Barbara glared at him.

"Yes, madam. Everything is just fine." He gave a humorless laugh. "Why would it not be? As we have just heard, it appears that for the past fifty years I have been working for a force so wicked its sole purpose is to unconsciously turn men and women to evil, greed, hatred. To twist a world from compassion and kindness to one of selfishness and mutual destruction."

"We don't know that."

"Don't we, madam?" he asked, looking up from his coffee. "Perhaps you forgot our recent encounter with the *Mester*?"

"Of course I haven't, but we don't know if there is anything beyond his personal ambition and cruelty. He had been turned into a monster."

"Indeed he had." Zoltan ran his hand through his hair in agitation. "And then he was used by a force quite beyond his limited capacities, it would seem." He paused. "As was I."

"Zoltan," Barbara snapped. "You must stop this. You are nearing the edge of a very dark hole. You are letting guilt immobilize you." She reached over and covered his clenched hand with her own.

He closed his eyes, and she felt him consciously slow his breathing.

"You knew nothing of whatever plan you became part of. The *Mester* used your sadness. Your desperation. Not you. Not who you were or who you are at your core."

Zoltan continued to breathe deeply. "But I did not wish to look too closely, yes? To discover who I truly worked for or what my gems actually did."

"And why would you? How could you have known the extent of the web you had entered?"

She sensed him edging back from the abyss. "There, that's better," she said, withdrawing her hand.

Zoltan opened his eyes and looked into her face. "Madam, I am of the opinion that I have no privacy whatsoever."

Barbara shook her head. "It's not like that. I cannot look into your mind. I can just…" She paused. "I don't usually know exactly what you are thinking. I can only feel what you feel. And only when the emotions are strong."

He nodded. "And the reassurance you sent me now? The love and kindness when I felt none for myself?"

She pushed her hair back, flustered. "I don't know about that."

Zoltan nodded. "Thank you." He pulled his azure gem from the watch pocket of his green corduroy vest so that it rested in the palm of his hand. He peered at it as if he were trying to tell the time.

"It is bittersweet, yes?"

"To have your jewel back, at last, but to know…"

"To know that it is, what? Tainted? That it carries a black seed at its center?"

"That is not the case," Barbara said, almost angrily. "And you know it, sir. Your gem has had a receiver-transmitter placed inside it. You had no control over that. But the heart of your stone is still the clear blue of your soul. And, I might add," she said reproachfully, "with a pure *white* seed at its heart." She paused. "As does mine," she added softly. "And fortunately, whatever harm the receiver could have done has now been neutralized."

Zoltan took a sip of his coffee and nodded formally. "You are correct, madam. My apologies." He glanced down at the stone in his palm. "I do believe it is safe." He paused. "For now."

Barbara's voice softened. "And one day, the anomaly will be deactivated. Forever. Your stone will be fully yours." She felt his uncertainty. "I promise."

He waved his hand slightly. "Please, madam, do not promise what you cannot ensure."

Barbara extended her hand across the table, palm up. "Give me your hand."

Hesitantly, Zoltan reached out until his hand was in hers. She clasped it gently.

"Now, I want you to look into my eyes."

His eyes travelled uncertainly up to her face until he stared into her green, unblinking eyes. The two of them were silent, and the sounds of the

Market faded. A growing warmth in his hand slowly extended up his arm and through his chest until he felt lightheaded. Thoughts gave way to calm, to emptiness. And then he realized that he was looking at himself through Barbara's eyes.

His heart stuttered. The man he saw looked back at him with deep black eyes. Shallow lines etched his forehead. High cheekbones shadowed his cheeks. A strong jaw thrust upward slightly, and his lips were set, assured. Silver-grey hair swept back in waves. The man was handsome, timeless, neither old nor young.

Now the black eyes changed. He sensed Barbara there for a moment, and then he was peering deeply into his own eyes. He watched his hand close over the blue-green jewel in his palm, and a rush of strength swept through him, clarity, as if a dense fog had lifted to reveal rocks in the waves of a dark sea. A thought struck him hard, pushing his head backward slightly, and he knew it was more than a thought. It was a certainty.

He was a good man.

The thought started as a glow in the pit of his stomach then spread outward. It turned into trust. Her trust in him? Or his own? There was no room for fear. No need for it. Faith numbed it like a narcotic. Faith in what? Whom? And then he knew. Of course.

Slowly the perspective shifted, and Zoltan returned to gazing into Barbara's eyes. Sounds nibbled around the edges of his awareness, and then he was sitting at the table, one hand in Barbara's, the other around his jewel.

Barbara smiled at him. "See?"

Chapter 3

TWO DAYS LATER, BARBARA SAT at the desk with the two physicists and surveyed the group of gem makers around the table. It was an odd collection. Each was dressed elegantly, and though several were bald, those who were not wore their graying hair stylishly long, one in a long ponytail. They all seemed to be of some indeterminate but similar age, giving the meeting the feel of an elite prep school reunion.

So far, the gathering had gone as expected. Each agent had been met aboveground by delegates of the Market, who had escorted the eleven men through the labyrinth of stairways and forgotten subway stops directly to Mrs. Harlow's shop. Some came in twos, but most were alone. Barbara sat behind the counter unnoticed and watched the agents carefully as they arrived.

After the last agent had claimed his stone and proceeded down the hall to the waiting conference room, Barbara followed and slid into the seat next to Samantha and Pierre. Zoltan sat on the other side of the two scientists. He nodded at Barbara as she entered the room and stood up.

The low muttering quieted, but the room was thick with tension and raw anticipation.

"Gentlemen," Zoltan began, his voice calm and sure. "Thank you for coming on such short notice. You will have gathered from my message that there is some urgency to our meeting, yes? But first, shall we introduce ourselves? Some of us have never met. Others not for many years.

It wasn't much of an icebreaker, but the men grudgingly identified themselves and their base of operations. Barbara made mental notes.

The men said nothing, but their eyes were fixed on Zoltan. He scanned the semicircle of faces, slowly peering deeply into their eyes. "Each of us has been employed as a gem maker for many years, some of us for decades." Silence filled the room. "Each of us was carefully recruited, yes? When we were desperate, suicidal. Anguished. And since then, for all those years, have any of us known happiness? Have we found surcease from our sorrow, as Mr. Poe put it?"

The men shifted uncomfortably in their chairs, most dropping their eyes to the table.

"And have we not suspected, "Zoltan said, leaning forward slightly, "every single one of us, that we were part of something evil, debased?"

A few men began to raise their voices in protest, but Zoltan held up his hand, and they quieted. "There will be ample time for discussion, gentlemen, but before that, I wish to share information with you that I think is critical to any analysis of our situation."

He turned to Samantha and Pierre, who had discarded their usual black jeans and red collarless shirt for white lab coats for the occasion.

"I would like to introduce Dr.'s Samantha Langfeld and Pierre Najarian, two of the top research physicists in the world. Since we returned with your stones five days ago, they have conducted intense research on the composition of the gems. And their capacities. We just learned of the results of their investigation two days ago. Hence the short notice." He glanced once more at the semicircle of faces. "I have asked Dr.'s Langfeld and Najarian to share what they have found. I believe you will find their conclusions most informative."

He nodded at the physicists and sat down. Samantha and Pierre exchanged glances and Najarian began.

"Gentlemen, first I want to thank you for giving us the opportunity to share our research with you, those most affected by our findings." She nodded at Pierre.

"Essentially," he said, "we have found two anomalies in each of your stones. These anomalies are two molecular clusters that do not fit the normal crystal profile."

As the two physicists spoke, several men took out their jewels and examined them carefully.

"In fact, Samantha added, "they are not consistent with any molecular architecture ever recorded."

The men looked up at the physicists uneasily.

"One of those clusters is activated locally," Sam continued, "And appears to act as an accelerator that agitates the atoms around it. Based on what we have learned, it could serve to strengthen certain emanations from the bearer."

"Essentially," Pierre said, "it acts as a short-range receiver-transmitter that would pick up brain waves, enhance them, and re-transmit the strengthened waves to the gem holder's brain."

"It would accentuate what is already there," Samantha concluded.

Pierre nodded. "But the second cluster, well, that is something else entirely."

Over the next few minutes, Samantha and Pierre summarized what they had revealed to Barbara and Zoltan days before, starting with a review of brain waves, electrical communications between neurons similar to radio waves, that can be picked up by receivers tuned to the correct frequency. The second cluster in the agents' stones acted as a receiver. But not just any receiver: it was tuned to a single frequency so broad it was off the spectrum.

And there was yet another revelation. "While this cluster does indeed act as a receiver, it also appears to act as a transmitter," Samantha said. "We believe it is able to send the information it receives from an external transmitter to the gemholder's brain as infra-low brainwaves, which would most likely be received subconsciously."

"You said the receiver in our gems is tuned to a single frequency that is not on the known spectrum?" Zoltan broke in.

The physicists nodded.

"And that would mean almost certainly the signals come from a single transmitter, yes?"

"That is correct," Samantha said. She looked at Pierre and pulled out what looked like a small lead box from the pocket of his lab coat. He put it on the table in front of them and opened the lid to reveal the Mester's ring with its black stone.

"Yes," Samantha said. "And this is it."

The room erupted in a babble of voices. Finally Zoltan stood and the room quieted again.

"As Dr Langfeld and Najarian explained to us," he said, "energy is introduced into the core of this stone. The nucleus then produces electrons, electro-magnetic particles that travel at a wavelength only the receptors in the stones with this anomaly can receive." He paused. "Our stones."

The muttering began again. Then the agent with the ponytail spoke up. "What does it transmit?"

"Yes," Zoltan nodded. "A good question, for any powerful message could be fed into the transmitter," Zoltan gestured to the black stone, "which would be received by the receptor in our gems, and then delivered directly to our brains."

He glanced at Samantha, who closed the small case. "You will seal it now."

Samantha nodded and closed the box and stood to leave the room. At the doorway she turned and looked at the men.

"I regret revealing this information. It is undoubtedly highly upsetting to know that your jewels have been manipulated by the stone in this box." She extended it in her hand. "However, I wish to assure you that it is now inactivated. As long as it is in this case, it can neither receive nor send signals."

"But if it is stolen, opened and the stone is taken?" The questioner spoke in a thick South African accent.

"When it is sealed," Samatha replied, "it cannot be opened." She glanced at Barbara. "Except under singular circumstances."

She bowed slightly and walked through the door into the workshop beyond.

"So if this is all true, we would be programmed," the ponytailed man said quietly. "Fed like rats." His blue eyes flamed. "A mental IV of sadness, hopelessness, powerlessness!"

"Perhaps we are getting ahead of ourselves," another agent said.

"Agent Garripoli, you wish to comment?" Zoltan asked, still standing at the table.

Barbara recognized the man at once. When she sat behind the counter as the agents arrived, Barbara had watched as each of the men had found and retrieved his gem. From most she felt joy, laughter, relief at being reunited with their stones, their souls complete again. But not from Garripoli. He strode quickly to the tray of stones and seized a curiously dark gold stone and slid it into his vest pocket with hardly a glance at the spectacular gem. His handsome face had remained expressionless.

"Yes. Before we deal with the lies your lab-coated friends have presented, I for one would like to know how you acquired these gems." He looked fiercely at Zoltan. "As well as the *Mester's* ring."

Zoltan carefully reconstructed the events of the previous weeks, including what he had learned from Dezső about the *Mester's* background and his encounter with the tall, brown-cowled man. He finished with an account of their capture in Budapest, the final struggle in the *Mester's* office, and their escape.

"I do not know the extent of the *Mester's* injuries, or even if he is alive," Zoltan concluded.

The agents looked at each other, their faces displaying shock, disbelief, uncertainty.

"If he is not," Garripoli said coldly, "his blood is entirely on your hands."

Though there wasn't much of it, Barbara mused.

Garripoli's voice was not what Barbara expected. Somehow she had thought it would be sibilant, raspy, but instead it was a rich, deep baritone.

Now his light blue eyes were riveted on Zoltan, narrowing occasionally, but his face revealed nothing.

Zoltan showed no sign of surprise. He fixed his gaze on the man. "I see. Mr. Garripoli, you seem to have some later information, yes?"

The man gave a curt nod.

"Would you care to elaborate?"

"In due time, Mr. DeAngelo. In due time."

"Please. My name is Zoltan József, as I have said."

"Which in sharing is a violation of your contract, is it not?" Garripoli's gaze slowly travelled around the circle of faces. "A contract we have all signed and understand well."

Murmurs rose from the group. Several squirmed nervously in their chairs.

Zoltan nodded. "A contract I believe you will understand I felt was voided when our employer attempted to kill me."

His comment was met with a few smirks and soft laughter around the table.

Garripoli's eyes smoldered then shifted his glare toward Barbara. His gaze was piercing, like shards of ice. She held it, unflinching.

He swung his gaze to Zoltan. "Perhaps you should not have violated other clauses if you were so concerned for your health." His eyes swept the room again. "As I am sure the other agents here fully understand."

Zoltan remained standing, studying Garripoli, assessing the impact of his words on the men around the table.

"Perhaps. But as I have explained, the nature of the enterprise we are part of was not—how shall I put it?—fully explained by our employer at the time of our recruitment."

"You have regaled us with an entertaining story, Mr. DeAngelo, a fanciful tale of murder, eldritch beings, a conspiracy of evil on a scale"—Garripoli nodded stiffly at Zoltan—"which, with all due respect, quite strains credulity."

Zoltan eyed him calmly. "I have reported my findings as accurately and as thoroughly as I can, sir. My purpose is to share what I have learned so that my colleagues are fully conversant with the nature of their work, our work, and how they are being used, yes? How the gems we produce for clients are conduits for a power we do not understand, but whose primary purpose is to promote an ethos of animalistic urges toward domination, exploitation, detestation of the weak, selfishness. A lust for power above all things. An ethos…"

"This is all accomplished," Garripoli broke in, "through your mysterious transmitter/receivers in the stones we make, Mr. DeAngelo? Do you expect us to really believe that?"

Zoltan nodded at the two physicists sitting with Barbara. "I assume you were awake during the presentations by Drs. Najarian and Langfeld?"

Garripoli gave a dismissive wave of his hand. "You trot out two people in white coats and expect us to simply accept these absurd allegations?" He had been looking disgustedly at Zoltan, but now he turned to the group.

"This is a vendetta. An attack on our employer from an agent caught violating his contract." He glared at Barbara. "Too weak to honor his word and accept the consequences of his disobedience. Instead he covers up his betrayal with tales of 'molecular clusters' and deep conspiracies." He glared at the faces around him. "There is nothing to DeAngelo's claims, nothing!" He breathed deeply for a few moments. "We all know the jewels we make for our customers can enhance the natural abilities and tendencies of the owners. That is why our clients are—or become—corporate CEOs, politicians, generals, lawyers."

He sneered at Zoltan. "Mr. DeAngelo would have us believe there is something nefarious about all of this, some gigantic plot to turn the world evil. But we know better, do we not? Indeed, the world is a savage place populated by savages. It needs—no, *requires* strong leaders, warriors, to protect society from the chaos of the weak, to save us from the ascendancy of fools." He spread out his hands. "That is where we come in. We provide an essential service. We ensure stability against certain anarchy should the weak and vengeful prevail."

His voice rose as he spoke, passionate and convincing. After several moments of silence, Noyes, the agent from Johannesburg spoke up. "This is a fascinating discussion, to be sure, but perhaps one we should continue over wine?" Several men chuckled, and Noyes leaned back in his chair and nodded at Zoltan.

"But to be honest," Noyes continued, "while I appreciate Mr. DeAngelo returning my gem," he smiled at his colleagues at the table, "it seems its return has occurred at the expense of—how shall I put it—stability in our existing business model." He leaned back in his chair. "The damage—or should we call it a hostile takeover bid?—seems to have already taken place." He ran his hand over his prominent paunch. "What I really want to know is what this means to me. Who is paying my salary?"

A murmur of agreement arose until a voice, sharp, deep, and angry, cut through the babble. "I can't believe this."

Barbara turned to the speaker, who sat just to Zoltan's left. Brandon Friesen, the ponytailed man, she remembered, the only man who had introduced himself with first and last name. His face was gaunt, chiseled, and hard. He leaned over the table and glared first at Noyes, then at Garripoli.

"Have neither of you heard a word József has said? Do you not know what he has given us? And at what risk?" He stared angrily around the room. "Somewhere inside you know he is right. We all do. We are part of something dark. But it pays well, doesn't it?" He glowered at Noyes. "So let's just pretend. And what can we do anyway? The *Mester* has our stone. He could destroy us at any time. Best just to go along. Not to ask too many questions. To be content with the aloneness, the emptiness he requires."

Friesen reached into the breast pocket of his suede jacket and pulled out a glittering purple stone. The overhead light danced on the faces as Friesen held the gem between his thumb and finger.

"But no longer. We have our stones back." He paused. "We have regained our souls. Our freedom. Perhaps it is time for us to act like men again."

"Freedom?" A small plump man with thick round glasses looked at Friesen, a smirk twisting his meaty lips. He had introduced himself as Meijer from Cairo. "Freedom for what? Freedom from hunger, from want? From compromise with the world of the weak and detestable? That is what you have now, you imbecile."

"You are a dupe." Malik, a tall, striking man wearing a maroon turban leaned toward Meijer, who recoiled, sitting back abruptly in his chair. "Or worse. We have lived the life of an indentured servant. No decisions to make, no questions to ask." He raised his chin at Garripoli derisively. "Contract. Yes, we signed a contract. Out of desperation, hopelessness. A contract that binds us to a cruel master forever."

The room erupted in a babble of voices. Curses hurtled across the room. Shouts. Several men stood, talking heatedly. Another pounded on the table.

Suddenly, the room shook. A voice, deep like a clap of thunder filled the room.

"Gentlemen," it rumbled.

Chapter 4

A STUNNED PAUSE SWEPT THE room after the booming interjection. Finally, at the end of the table, Friesen rose to his feet. The disembodied voice seemed to have come from all sides. He gazed at the blank wall in front of him.

"Who are you?" he asked gravely.

"I am Justin."

The words hung in the air, commanding but ethereal. Friesen's head turned, searching for the source of the voice, but it was everywhere and seemed to come from nowhere.

The men were silent, waiting.

"And I want you all to know that I owe you an apology." The voice lowered in remorse. "The *Mester* was in my employ." There was an audible sigh of dismay. "It appears that he lost sight of our mission. He became overzealous, it would seem. Mistreatment of colleagues—especially those of your stature—is not a good business model. And it is not mine, I assure you." The voice warmed. "I prefer to work as part of a team."

The voice delivered the cant mellifluously, in a relaxed rhythm that seemed almost hypnotic. The men's eyes darted around the room, searching for the source. But there was none. The voice seemed to vibrate in the air, to emerge from the floor, filter down from the ceiling, radiate from the glowing walls.

"And now he has paid for his overreach, I am afraid." the voice continued with a sigh of regret. "A pity to have to neutralize an old associate. But perhaps these unfortunate events were for the best, my friends. We now have a chance to review our relationship, to tear up old contracts and negotiate new ones. New ones, that I assure you, will be most lucrative."

A low murmur arose from the agents.

"But these things are best discussed face to face, don't you agree? And so I am inviting you all to my office."

"In the castle," Zoltan said. "Yes?"

"Indeed, Mr. József. In the castle."

"And where would that be?" Zoltan continued.

Barbara thought she detected a slight hardening in the man's tone.

"That, I am afraid, I cannot divulge. But it will all become clear in due time."

Zoltan looked around the room. *How many knew this was coming,* he wondered.

Friesen remained standing and stared intently at the wall. "You are inviting us. Or are you ordering us?"

"Please, Mr. Friesen. Let us keep this amicable. I am inviting all of you to a friendly business meeting. I cannot force you to attend." The voice paused for a long moment. "But of course, if you decline my offer, there will be certain logical outcomes."

"Such as?" Friesen demanded.

Zoltan looked at the tall man, leaning forward menacingly. He saw in Friesen's fiery blue eyes that Zoltan's message had been like a bullet to the heart. Even while reading his account, he saw Friesen's face fall and then go hard. He could see that of all the agents, Friesen instantly knew it was all true. Like Zoltan, he had let his grief blind him to the evil Zoltan had revealed.

The hair on the back of Zoltan's neck stood on end. Clearly that evil had arrived in the room.

"I am afraid that your stones are very vulnerable still, Mr. Friesen. We will rectify that at our meeting. But for now, as much as I would regret doing so, if you no longer wish to continue in my employ, they will be—how should I put it?—deactivated."

A small gasp rose from the agents.

"And of course, your *camera obscura*, the gem creators, are not really your property at all, are they? No. They are on loan. You rent them. I am afraid that if you do not wish to join us, the devices will be gone when you return to your homes."

"I see," Friesen responded. "So, we agree to your 'invitation' or are ruined, possibly destroyed."

"Mr. Friesen, please. Why the unpleasantries? You are the core of a very important division in my operation. I do not wish to lose a single one of you. But clearly I have to protect my business interests as well."

Friesen turned from the wall and faced Zoltan. "You say you want to keep all of us as your agents. Does that include Mr. József?"

"But of course. Especially Mr. József. I'm afraid he had to suffer a great deal to bring the mismanagement of this branch to my attention. And for that I thank him."

Zoltan swiveled his chair to face the wall. "You are too kind, sir." He nodded toward Barbara. "And my associate. She too is welcome?"

Friesen and the rest of the men turned toward Barbara, who sat next to Zoltan her green eyes scanning the faces of the men in front of her. It was as if they had noticed her for the first time.

"Who the hell is she anyway?" Noyes blurted out. "What is she doing here?"

Now Zoltan stood. He focused his glittering black eyes on Noyes until the man dropped his gaze to the table.

"This is Barbara," Zoltan said simply. "She too is a gem holder. The holder of a most remarkable gem. One that is free of the --what is the term? Flaws, yes? The flaws that have contaminated our jewels." He leaned on the table. "And a woman of most extraordinary courage and powers."

The men moved uneasily in their chairs as Zoltan glared around the room.

"And the woman to whom each of you owe a great deal of gratitude, for it is *she* who recovered your gems from the Mester's safe. And at great peril to herself."

Some of the men smiled and nodded at Barbara, who inclined her head slightly in acknowledgement. At the same time, she saw Meijer's face sharpen with hatred. Next to him, Garripoli's lips drew into a thin line.

"Ah," the voice intoned at last. "I am afraid that is not possible. Despite Mrs. Steubenville's..."

Next to him, Barbara flinched in surprise.

"...uh, significant role in this matter, our meeting will be strictly business. It is only for agents in my employ." The voice chuckled slightly. "I assure you, Ms. Steubenville would be bored to death. And in any event, I don't believe you have much of a business background. Your husband, yes, a competent corporate lawyer, I've been told." The voice chilled. "Presently under investigation for murder, I understand."

Zoltan's expression did not change. "My colleague no longer goes by the name Steubenville, as you are no doubt aware. As I no longer go by the name DeAngelo, yes?"

He paused. The room thrummed with tension.

"But do not be too hasty, sir, for I believe I have something that once belonged to your former employee, yes? The stone Dr Langfeld just shared with us. But perhaps your absence here made it impossible for you to see?"

The room quieted. "It is something I believe is of the utmost interest to you. My colleague, Barbara, acquired it under it most unusual circumstances. Unfortunately, it required severing the *Mester's* finger to retrieve it."

The atmosphere in the room became suffocating. Zoltan heard short, heavy breathing.

"Go on."

"The Mester's stone is in our possession." He paused. "Or should I say in Barbara's possession," he continued. "It has been given to her for safekeeping in a container only she can open."

The silence stretched into seconds. "I see," the voice said at last, a grating, low statement. The tone lightened. "In that case, we may have our first female agent, gentlemen," the voice said brightly. "I believe we could negotiate a trade. Perhaps the item you mention for a new agent's jewel and gem creator for the lady?"

Barbara opened her mouth to protest, but Zoltan's eyes caught hers. He shook his head slightly and she quieted.

"Very well." Zoltan turned toward Barbara. "Madam?"

Barbara nodded and looked at the blank wall. "Thank you," she said. "I look forward to meeting you. In person."

"And the rest of you?" the voice asked.

Men leaned toward each other, whispering. Barbara heard a loud curse from across the room, and after a few moments, the room quieted. Friesen regained his feet, his expression dark and defiant.

"It doesn't seem that we have a choice."

"It's settled then. I am so delighted we will have the opportunity to continue working together," the voice said brightly. "I assure you, you will not regret it." The voice paused briefly. "And may I add that I believe you will find the gathering itself quite engaging. What is a successful business meeting without some entertainment?" He chuckled darkly.

The sonorous voice, vibrating with bonhomie and menace, laid out a simple plan: The agents would meet with the man behind the voice, who introduced himself as Justin, at the castle. They were to take the train from the Market that morning to the Bleecker Street station. They would be met outside the station by limousines, which would take them to a private plane. There would be no security or need for passports. They would be flown to an undisclosed destination, where another fleet of limousines would be waiting to take them to the castle.

The discussion was brief, the outcome a given. The voice seemed embedded in the air itself. Zoltan wondered if it was being transmitted through the agents' stones. But no—Barbara heard the voice as well.

"Good day, gentlemen. And lady. I will see you all very soon."

Then the voice disappeared. The aftermath was far more than the quiet after a speaker is disconnected or a microphone shut down. It was as if a presence had suddenly been sucked out of the room, or a mild spell had been lifted.

Where is this going? Zoltan wondered. He surveyed the room, studying the men standing or leaning forward in their chairs, silent, frozen in the position they'd been in when the voice thundered into the room. *Who's on what side?*

Slowly the paralysis dissipated. The men formed into small, uneasy groups, discussing the events in hushed voices. After several minutes, Garripoli turned from a foursome of agents who had been speaking quietly while standing against the curved wall opposite Barbara. He moved to the center of the room and looked around at the men seated and standing at the circular table.

"Gentlemen," he began. "I believe we have an important conference to attend. Justin has thoughtfully made our travel plans for us, but it requires an early train, I am afraid." He glanced at his watch. "I suggest we all meet at the Market subway platform at…" He glanced at Zoltan.

"The northbound train arrives at 4:27."

"Yes, thank you, Mr. DeAngelo. We shall meet at the platform at 4:25." He gave a curt nod to the group. "Perhaps you should get some sleep?" Garripoli walked toward the exit.

As he opened the door, he turned back to the agents and ran his ice-blue eyes over the men. "But do not sleep in. I assure you, you do not want to be late."

He pulled the door open and strode into the corridor.

Over the next few minutes, agents in small groups and singly, made their way out the door and through Mrs. Harlow's shop into the Market beyond.

#   #   #

The room cleared quickly until only Barbara and Zoltan were left. He had remained standing throughout the confrontation. Now he sat heavily into his chair and stared at the wall recently vacated by Justin's voice. Barbara took his hand and he turned toward her. She looked into his obsidian eyes.

"I see something new in those black eyes of yours, sir"

Zoltan managed a tight smile. "And what, my red-haired empath, might that be?

"I don't think I need to be an empath this time," she said softly. "We have met the enemy, haven't we?"

Zoltan looked over her shoulder, his gaze hard, his jaw set.

"Yes, madam. We have heard the voice of the enemy. One so formidable it can penetrate the defenses of the Market. So evil it can bend men and women to its will." He lowered his gaze and his eyes softened slightly. "This is indeed the end game."

Now she took both hands in hers. "This is where I want to be." She said it firmly, confidently. "This is what my life has been for. I know it now." She drew his hands to her lips and kissed the ends of his fingers. "And you are who I want to be with," she whispered. "I know that now as well."

Their eyes locked. "Madam…" he began.

Barbara lowered his hands and stood up. "I believe we have an early train to catch, no?"

Chapter 5

JÓZSEF SAT STIFFLY IN THE seat beside her as Barbara peered uselessly at the blacked-out window of the plane. Barbara sifted through the events of the past few hours, making sense of how they ended up on this sleek jet, silently hurtling through the night to a destination they only knew as the castle.

After Garripoli's exit, his warning ringing in their ears, agents in small groups and singly, made their way out the door and through Mrs. Harlow's shop into the Market beyond.

And, Barbara recalled ruefully, still staring at the black surface that should have been a plane window, no one *had* been late. After she and Zoltan parted, he went back to his apartment, now secured after the *Mester's* agents break-in and failed attempt to find the flash drive, and she returned to her room at Mrs. Harlow's shop. She slipped on a pair of black jeans over her blouse and wondered where she would be when she changed clothes again. Or if she would.

Well, I wanted to get out of the house.

Barbara and the twelve agents drifted onto the narrow platform over a period of half an hour before the train was scheduled to arrive. Another five merchants from the Market stood at the edge of the platform, talking softly, occasionally laughing. But the gem makers stood in the shadows, leaning against posts, talking little, shuffling uneasily. When the creaking old train slid to a stop, they dispersed among the three cars.

The plans unfolded exactly as described. A small fleet of limousines with mirrored windows swept them to a sleek executive where they filed silently up the fold-out stairs into the tube of the plane's interior. Even in the rapid transfer from the limousines to the waiting plane, she realized they were at Teteboro, the small airport they had used when travelling to Budapest. An airport, it seemed, where few questions were asked and fewer answered.

The seats on the plane were arranged so that the first three rows faced each other in clusters of four seats. The remaining ten rows had conventional seating, one on a side separated by a narrow aisle. Arriving in the first limousine, Zoltan nodded toward the rear, and he and Barbara made their way to the last two seats.

How long had they been in the air? The interior of the plane was almost black; there were no overhead or reading lights. Only a thin red illuminated strip ran the length of the plane. Barbara glanced at her watch and pushed the tiny button at the bottom right of the case. The face lit up dark blue. Almost four hours since they had taken off from Teteboro.

Barbara leaned across the narrow aisle. "Zoltan," she whispered. "Where are we going?"

Even for Zoltan, the face that turned to her was grim and set. "The castle."

"Yes, thank you," she hissed facetiously. "And where might that be? Somehow I don't think we're headed for Orlando."

Zoltan sighed deeply, closed his eyes, and leaned his head against the leather headrest. "I do not know."

"But you have your suspicions."

Zoltan opened one eye at her. "Perhaps."

"Not perhaps. You think you know where we are going."

"Madam, this prescience of yours is becoming annoying."

"Gee. And everything else has gone so smoothly."

The thin line of his lips seemed to relax at the corners. "I deserved that. My apologies, Madam."

"As I was saying…"

Zoltan opened both eyes and stared at the back of the seat in front of him. *"Budavári Palota,"* he said softly. "Buda Castle."

Barbara turned to the black window. "We are returning to Budapest."

"I believe so. I have had my suspicions for some time. The origins of *The Mester.* The Hungarian connections. The recruitment of Dezső and others from Budapest."

Zoltan had been speaking softly, but now his voice descended into a whisper, almost inaudible. "And there were other hints. Dark and sinister ghosts, ancient, evil. I felt them when we were last in the city."

"They live in the castle?"

Zoltan shrugged. "Who can know what lives in the castle? It has been built and destroyed six times, the new built on the sprawling cellars of the old. But that is just what we see. Even the first castle completed in 1265 was built upon caves so ancient the original inhabitants have long since disappeared. But their paintings, their statues—horses deep in the labyrinth, two-headed shamans—oh, those remain."

Zoltan fell into a brooding silence.

"You called it a labyrinth."

In the dark, Barbara saw his head nod slightly. "A labyrinth so vast, so deep it has never been fully explored. Seventy-five, a hundred miles of caves, dungeons, passageways, cellars. No one really knows. A maze where people have become lost and died wandering from one black tunnel to another. Only one kilometer is open. And beyond that…"

"What?"

"The labyrinth; it is a portal, a path between an unimaginably ancient world and ours. It has been used by humans for a half million years. And who knows what or who before that?"

In the silence and darkness, Barbara was aware of her breathing, in and out. Calm. She stared at the seat in front of her and cleared her mind. There was just the darkness and her quieted breath. Nothing more. Her eyes closed and she dozed uneasily. Then the images began crowding in. Stone arches lit by oil lamps. A stone figure in the middle of a dark cellar, its forehead carved in strange runes, its eyes malignant slits, and its long nose a chiseled triangle. It turned and looked at her. The rim of a stone cistern, water dripping into it from the arched ceiling, lined with skulls. Bones littered the passageway. And a wood door, arched and bound with iron. It throbbed as if a great force surged behind it, threatening to burst the heavy steel hinges. She reached for the handle and pulled her hand back with a shriek.

Zoltan reached across the aisle and gripped her shoulder. "Barbara, what is it?"

"The handle," she stammered. "It was hot. It burned my hand." She turned her palm upward. "It seared my palm. As if I was grasping a burning coal."

Her breathing quieted again.

"Barbara, what handle?"

"In the castle. On the door to the room where we are meeting. The room where Justin presides."

Chapter 6

A LINE OF LIMOUSINES MUCH like the one that had met them at the subway waited for the plane when it taxied to a halt. Barbara pushed the button on her watch: 7:24. From dark to dark.

A voice, startlingly perky, filled the plane.

"Good evening, gentlemen. And welcome to Budapest. I will be your guide tonight, and I do hope you enjoy your stay."

"He must work on a tour bus during the day," Barbara muttered.

"In a moment, the door will open. Please be careful as you descend the stairs. It is raining and they could be slippery. I strongly recommend using the railing to avoid injury. When you reach the bottom of the stairs, there are four limousines waiting. I ask that the first four proceed to the first limousine, the next four to the second, and so on. Mr. DeAngelo and Ms. Steubenville will take the final car. Our destination is about an hour away. Please relax and enjoy the ride. There is excellent scotch and some very fine wines in your limousines. Please do help yourselves."

He paused. "Oh, and one other thing. As you leave, a colleague will be standing at the bottom of the stairs beside a leather attaché case. Please deposit your cell phones or other electrical devices in the case. I'm sure I don't need to mention this, but please comply completely as you will be scanned as you depart the plane. Your devices will be returned to you on the return flight."

As he finished, the stairway swung down from the plane. A sliver of rain-slicked tarmac gleamed in the early evening gloom. The agents crouched in the low cabin and filed out one by one, each dropping phones and pagers into a brown leather briefcase. Zoltan turned to Barbara, and even in the semi-darkness she could see the shimmer in his obsidian eyes. He reached out and took both of her hands in his.

"We knew it would come—this time, this encounter, yes?"

Barbara nodded.

"I do not know what is to happen." He breathed deeply and squeezed her hands. "Or what we will face. I do not know if I will live through this. But…"

"Yes?"

"You said it to me last night." He breathed deeply. "Barbara, there is no one I would rather have at my side than you."

He raised his hands and cupped her face, staring into her emerald eyes. Then he leaned forward and kissed her on her lips.

Her heart jumped into her throat. She fought the urge to kiss him back, to wrap her arms around his neck and pull him to her. This was hardly the time.

"Come," he said, softly. "It is time to go."

The trip to the castle was blurred by rain dripping down the tinted windows. Barbara was vaguely aware of exiting a highway onto a four-lane road that paralleled the Danube on their right. The buildings thickened on both sides as they drove south into the city. Looking through the window, she saw the line of black limousines ahead turn west onto the entrance to a bridge.

"Margit Bridge," Zoltan said. "We are close now."

Barbara studied the river below them as they crossed. It is anything but blue, she thought, peering at the dark water swirling underneath them. The line of cars snaked through increasingly narrow streets and then swerved onto a cobbled road that ran steeply uphill.

"They are using the Porta di Vienna," Zoltan muttered.

"What?"

"We are entering *Varhegy,* Castle Hill. It is the oldest part of the city. There are several gates in the old fortifications. This is the north gate."

Through the streaked window, Barbara glimpsed an arched gateway in high stone walls as they passed, and then a church steeple sticking into the night sky. Ancient houses slipped by them, and then a square opened on their left, where they bore right onto a road edged by a long stone wall.

The limousine stopped.

"Look ahead. Can you see it?"

Barbara peered into the dark, but all she could make out was a dim barricade in front of them.

"On top of the arch. "

She shifted her gaze upward, squinting. "What is it?"

"The Raven Gate. The raven has a gold ring in its beak. It is said that such a bird fetched King Matthias back to Buda to save the royal Hungarian line. That was five hundred years ago."

"Five centuries," Barbara mused. "So long ago."

The car began to move forward again.

"That is but a brief moment in the history of this place," Zoltan whispered. "A half millennium shrivels when compared to a hundred thousand, two hundred thousand years, yes? A mere moment to the ancients who lived here before."

The cars swept down a service road and came to a stop at a small parking lot. The five limousines were lined up like train cars, bumpers hugging the bumper of the car in front.

The voice they had heard on the plane purred through speakers in the limo.

"It is a pleasure to welcome you to *Budavári Palota*. It is regrettable that you will not have the opportunity to fully enjoy this magnificent structure. But perhaps on another visit we can arrange a special tour," the voice ended chirpily. "But now I believe you have an important business meeting. We should waste no time.

"Ensuring the confidentiality of your deliberations is of the utmost importance. Therefore we have selected a meeting room where you will not be interrupted. It is also impossible to find your way in without a guide."

Or your way out, Barbara thought.

"You will be entering the great maze that stretches for many miles underneath the castle. We do not want to attract attention, so there will be no lights. As well, the area we will be visiting has no electricity. I will carry a single lantern. You must stay within the circle of light. You must not stray from the path I take. Should you do so, you will almost certainly wander these halls and tunnels until you die of starvation."

I have to admit, she thought, *he does have a way with words.*

Dressed entirely in black, the chauffeur, more an apparition than human, opened the limousine doors. After they exited and without signal, the column of black limousines drove silently up the service road and into the night. A cold wind whipped around the great dark bulk of the castle in front of her, and Barbara shivered. Zoltan put his hand on her shoulder and drew her to him. He was warm and solid, and the shudders subsided.

In front of them, the guide held a single yellow light aloft. They moved slowly toward it.

"Barbara, your watch."

"Yes?"

"It has a timer?"

"Yes."

"Set it."

She nodded and fumbled with the buttons as they moved toward the lantern.

"And you? Are we coordinating watches?"

Zoltan smiled and held up his wrist, the face of his watch a dull blue in the darkness.

"Done."

The lantern smelled of kerosene but was surprisingly bright. Shadowy forms joined them, all quietly walking toward the light like moths to a naked porch bulb. She stayed close to Zoltan and approached the man holding the lantern over his head.

Once they were near enough, Barbara inspected the man. He was hardly what she had expected. Surprisingly young, he smiled broadly, and his dark brown eyes danced in the kerosene light. The shadowy light revealed an aquiline nose and high cheekbones under short blond hair. There was no other word for it: he was strikingly handsome. His black leather jacket opened over a crisp blue-striped shirt tucked into a pair of tight jeans.

"Ah," he beamed, "it seems we are all here. Splendid. So, it is time to get started." He turned slightly and pointed to an unremarkable metal door set in the stone wall in front of them. "We will be entering through that door, and then we will descend into the caves and cellars below. All quite astonishing, but we do not have time to appreciate the workmanship, I am afraid." He grinned. "Another time."

He swung the lantern around and faced the castle. "Shall we?"

They crowded inside the entrance, and behind them Barbara heard the door close with a dull finality. They stood surrounded by blackness so deep it almost seemed solid, like some hideous gelatin they could touch, if they were foolish enough to reach outside the circle of light that bobbed and flickered around them as it led them swiftly forward. Barbara glimpsed massive arches as they passed through one bewildering passage after another. Sometimes stone steps led downward; black passages opened on both sides. In one echoing vaulted chamber, a tall stone column, intricately carved, rose into the darkness above them. Minutes later the outline of an animal, possibly a horse, was scratched onto a wall. They turned a corner and Barbara froze.

Zoltan took her hand. "What is it?" he asked quietly.

Barbara nodded at the stone statue mounted on a stone column in the middle of the circular room they had just entered. The flickering lantern turned the sculpture's empty eye slits into eyes of fire. Its long nose pointed at her like an accusing finger.

"It's the statue I saw. In my dream," she said.

"Yes," he said softly. "Yes. Come now."

Time ceased to have any meaning. They moved silently through ancient stone hallways and under broad archways. They passed through doors unlocked by the lantern carrier. Water dripped from the ceilings and walls into unseen pools.

Barbara moved forward numbly. She glanced at her watch. They had been walking these underground roads and paths for almost two hours.

The man with the lantern turned a corner ahead and the light stopped. They hurried forward until the twelve agents and Barbara, their faces streaked with sweat and fear, clustered around the young man. He turned to them, his lamp in front of his face.

"I do hope everyone is here," he smiled.

"Where is here?" someone questioned.

"Well, our meeting chamber, of course," the man beamed.

He turned and shone his light on the wall in front of them, illuminating an arched wood door with rusted iron straps. Barbara gasped.

In front of her was the door she had foreseen on the plane.

Chapter 7

THE HEAVY WOOD DOOR SWUNG open, and they entered a room the size of the nave of a small medieval church, twice as long as it was wide. Ancient stone arches rose from carved columns that lined the sides, soaring and branching overhead in a high arc. Torches sputtered in sconces at the top of each column, throwing dim, flickering light across the cobbled floor. At the front on the room on a raised stone dais, a man sat on a dark wood chair upholstered in red leather. As they entered, his head was bent forward, covered in a brown cowl attached to a simple robe tied with a simple white belt tied at his waist.

The man stood up, his face lost in the shadows of his cowl and the dim light of the room.

"Welcome!" he called. "Please, approach."

Barbara and Zoltan stood at the rear of the group. Unconsciously, she grasped Zoltan's hand. He squeezed it then withdrew, staring straight ahead, his face set.

They made their way forward slowly, the stone walls muffling their steps. As they neared the platform, they saw that twelve heavy wood chairs had been set in a semi-circle around the dais. A separate chair had been pushed against a wall behind the crescent of seats. They stopped behind the chairs and waited. The man grasped the front of his cowl and threw it back.

In the uncertain light, they looked into the smiling face of a handsome man, his blond hair cut close to his scalp. Even in the shadows, his eyes glowed a bright blue under arched blond eyebrows. An angular nose shaded prominent cheek bones. His full red lips opened just enough to show a line of sparkling white teeth.

"Ah, gentlemen," the man beamed. "It is so good of you to come, to give me a chance to speak with each of you personally." He motioned to the chairs. "Please, do sit down and make yourselves comfortable." His gaze flickered to Barbara. He nodded toward the chair against the wall. "And madam, a special seat for you?"

Barbara breathed deeply. So, she was to be shunted off to the side, marginalized again. She glared at the figure in front of her. Before she could respond, Zoltan turned to her and gave a small shake of his head. She turned and walked reluctantly to the single chair as the men settled into their seats.

The man studied each of the agents as they sat, his eyes bright in the gloom, his face fixed in a smile.

"First, let me introduce myself. I am Justin, the employer of your former manager, whom I believe you knew as the *Mester*. As I communicated to you earlier, I deeply regret the recent unpleasantries." The man shook his close-cropped blond head and sighed remorsefully. "I am afraid my employee made some grave errors." He raised two hands, their long, tapered fingers spread wide. "And I don't blame only the *Mester*. No, I too have to take some of the blame." He paused, looking solemnly into the face of each of the agents sitting in front of him.

"I am in charge of a very large operation," he continued, "and sometimes I do not monitor the various divisions as closely as I should." He glanced upward toward the arches above him. "A fault in my management style, I'm afraid." He spread his arms wide, embracing the twelve agents from his raised dais. "But the important thing is I want you all to know that those days are over." He looked at Zoltan and gave a brief nod.

"You all have your gems now, I believe, thanks to Mr. József?" he asked.

The men in front of him nodded or looked at each other uncertainly.

"Good, good. For that is how it should be. My associate, I am afraid, felt that fear was the best way to manage a team, and it was his decision to keep your stones from you, a decision on his part I very much regret."

Barbara sat back in her chair, leaning into the shadows of the column next to her. The grasping tentacles she had first felt back in the Market became stronger, more intrusive.

"You see, each of you was chosen to act as an agent for a reason. Yes, it is true the *Mester* conducted the interviews, but I put him in touch with each of you." He nodded slowly. "I have...peculiar powers, particularly when it comes to judging men. And I want to assure you, each of you is very special." He leaned forward slightly, the light illuminating the hollows around his eyes until they gleamed like blue fire.

"And powerful. You were before, of course, but now, now with your gems..." His chin jutted outward and his voice rose dramatically. "But now! You are more powerful than ever, more powerful than you can even know."

The men stared, transfixed. Only Zoltan, at the end of the row of chairs nearest to Barbara, continued sitting back in his chair, studying the man called Justin through his coal-black eyes.

"And I say to you today, you have always had such power in you, such influence. You were born to it! That is why I selected you. Unfortunately, in each case, society has stolen it away from you. But you're going to get it back. Remember this: Even if you look at the most important, the most powerful leaders, whether in business or politics, you are more powerful. Because you are stronger than those around you. And soon those others who you were meant to lead, to dominate, will believe this as well." His penetrating eyes glittered blue.

"But how can this be?" Justin asked rhetorically, his voice rising. He stood, his arms wide. "Why is it you have not felt this power before?" His deep voice echoed loudly in the stone room.

"That is because now you do not know how to *use* your power," the man thundered. "You must *learn* your power!"

The agents sat spellbound in their chairs. Then Garripoli leapt to his feet. "Yes!" He screamed, thrusting a clenched fist into the air. He turned from Justin to the men in front of him, his face contorted in excitement and fervor. "We will rule together!"

Other agents joined in, cheering and clapping. Barbara quickly scanned the chairs. Zoltan sat upright, his head back and face set. Friesen and Malik also kept their seats.

Justin smiled widely and held up his hands to quiet the group.

"I am promising you power beyond your wildest dreams! The money you realize from your gem sales will be all yours—no more secret accounts, no more cuts for the *Mester*."

Another cheer rose from the agents.

"But that is just a start, gentlemen," Justin went on, his voice lower. "With your gems, your independence, my support, ah!"—his hands flew outward—"there is no stopping you!"

Zoltan slowly rose from his chair and faced the man on the dais. The noise died down, and the men looked at Zoltan, then shifted their gaze back to Justin.

"Power? Is that what you are offering us, sir?"

Justin smiled broadly at Zoltan. "That's right, Mr. József. Power, as I said, beyond your wildest dreams."

"Or nightmares, perhaps?" Zoltan commented evenly. "This power, sir, how is it to be used? I have seen elements of your 'operation,' as you call it. It seems steeped in darkness, violence. It seems committed not to good, but to promoting ruthlessness, supremacy of a few; domination of many." He drew himself erect and narrowed his eyes slightly. Barbara could feel his stare cut through the murk of the room. "I believe, sir, that you are deceiving us. I believe that you have..."

"Good?" Justin shouted. He shook his head in exasperation. "Good," he said again, more quietly. "Mr. József, don't you get tired of these simplistic distinctions? You speak as if 'good' is some sort or absolute. A a morality passed down from heaven perhaps?" he asked derisively. "Or is it just the refuge of the weak?" He turned to the rest of the group. "You can see this, can you not? It is the nobles like us that are tasked with keeping order. Can you imagine the chaos if the weak, the stupid, should prevail?" He thumped his chest. "It is *we* who define what is good!"

He stopped and glared at the faces around him and pointed to each man individually. "You, you—all of you. I chose you all to be the nobles in a world without nobility. Without heroes." He leaned closer. "I want you to occupy your birthright. I want you to be happy!" He threw his hands above his shoulders, his eyes alight. "Have you been happy in your lives? No, you have not."

He leaned forward conspiratorially. "And do you know why?" he asked softly. "It is because of one simple truth." He paused again and smiled at the men, his blue eyes dancing. "Happiness increases only with power. That is all." He stood straight and his face became solemn. "Whatever makes you feel more powerful makes you happier." He nodded slightly. "You men know this. You know what I say is true. Now I give you a chance for unlimited happiness."

Zoltan was still on his feet. "I do not know this, nor do I believe it." He turned toward the men spread to his right. "Nor do you, my friends. In your heart, you know this is a lie. You know that a world without compassion, a world where only the powerful prosper is a..."

Justin gave a sharp nod in Zoltan's direction, and his voice froze in mid-sentence, and he stood rigid, unable to move. Only his eyes flashed frantically. Barbara's heart jumped and she silently pulled further into the shadows.

Friesen and Malik stood up, looking angrily at Justin. "What have you done to József?" Friesen demanded.

Justin glared at them, and they too froze, their voices muted.

Justin smiled and turned back to the rest of the men. He smiled broadly and shrugged. "Perhaps I misjudge occasionally."

Raucous laughter rose from a few of the men.

Garripoli strode to the dais and stood just to the right of the brown-robed man, who now sat in his red leather chair.

"Gentlemen," Garripoli began. "We have seen a vision, have we not? A vision of order, power, wealth and happiness." The men thrust their fists into the air and cheered. "And who do we have to thank?"

"Justin!" Meijer called out.

"Justin!" several men bellowed.

The brown-robed man beamed at the glistening faces in front of him. He nodded.

"Gentlemen, I believe we have an agreement, do we not?"

There was a roar of approval.

"Then may I propose a celebration? A little festival for you to get a taste of your new power." His mouth spread wide and his eyes shone. "I guarantee you will find it entertaining."

The men nodded eagerly, their faces flushed with eagerness.

"You will have to excuse the shift in time you are about to experience, but it cannot be helped. We are modern men, and though you will find the next moments exhilarating and exciting, an adventure you will not forget, we would not behave in this manner today."

His blue eyes sparkled. "And why is that? Certainly not because there is wrong in what we will do, quite the contrary."

The men looked upward, faces glistening with anticipation. They didn't know what was coming, but it seemed to offer pleasures beyond their imagining. From her shadowed corner, Barbara cringed in horror. Waves of raw lust, red with blood and fervor, swept around her.

"You see," Justin continued. "We have been restrained by moral and social obligations that interfere with our instincts, our desire for adventure and joy. Is that not true?"

Men nodded their heads and murmured agreement.

"So we must look to a time in the past to know what it was like to behave like the masters we are." Justin's voice rose in volume. "When warriors like us were supreme!" he shouted. "A time when we indulged in the pleasures and the control we deserve! And a time we can have again!" he thundered.

Several men stood up, cheering, their voices roars of animal anticipation.

The shrieks assaulted her. She squeezed her eyes shut to block the red claws of carnality that ripped at her.

"So," Justin said, "think of this as a taste of what it will mean to be a master again, a *man*! When our need to maintain order coincides with our morality, a morality based on our natural instincts. When we are able to eat to the bone! For this is what I am offering you."

"Justin! Justin!" some of the men began chanting.

Justin raised his hands on the arms of his chair. "Good. Now then, retake your seats if you will."

The agents settled back in their chairs, oblivious to the three men frozen like dark statues.

"Please. Relax. Now I want you to take your gem in your hand and close your fingers around it."

The men dug into their pockets eagerly, quickly finding their jewels and clasping them in their hands. Barbara considered grasping her own stone, warm between her breasts. Justin was using the receiver in the agents' stones. Hers had no such device, a fact she had been proud of. But now, without the receptor in the agents' gems, she doubted she would be able to receive whatever vile images Justin was about to project.

And here, if she did draw out her gem, what danger might there be to the stone itself? Could it be corrupted?

"Wonderful! Now, please close your eyes, gentlemen. I will do the rest." Justin sat back and his heavy eyelids shuddered shut.

And then there was silence. Barbara watched as the men quieted, slumping slightly in their seats as they sank into a deep trance. She rose to Zoltan's side and took his hand. It was cold, immobile, as if carved from wax. She looked at the men sitting in their chairs. Smiles were beginning to spread on their faces. Justin had begun his spell with his words. This debauchery, whatever it was, would finish it. The men would be Justin's, their corruption complete. She glanced at Zoltan next to her. And their fate would be sealed.

Justin was controlling the men's thoughts through their gems, and had been ever since they entered the room, very possibly long before that. Either she found a way to join them in their celebration and somehow intervene, or it was over.

Barbara reached for her jewel, now pulsing rapidly at her chest. She held it in her hand and closed her eyes. Redness throbbed in her head in rhythm to the pulsing. She opened her mind and felt darkness pushing at the edges of her consciousness, but there were no images, no celebration. It was as she feared: without the receptor she was excluded. Whatever game Justin was playing would play out unimpeded. What was left of the men's souls would be shattered forever.

It was desperate, she knew. Maybe impossible. But what choice did she have. It was their only chance.

Releasing her gem, she pushed her hand into her jeans pocket and felt the small metal box. It was why she was there—the *Mester's* stone. What would happen if she took it out of the box? Yes, it transmitted, but like the agent's stones, was it also a receiver? And here, opening the shielded box. What then?

Barbara pulled the box out and looked at it for a long moment in the torchlight. She placed her thumb on the slightly protruding edge and lifted.

The top swung up easily. She turned the box up and spilled the black sphere into the palm of her hand. The air seemed to ripple. Then she closed her eyes.

Chapter 8

BARBARA WASN'T SURE HOW SHE knew, but she understood she was now a man, sitting erect on a thin leather saddle, feeling the power of the horse between her legs as it pranced nervously. Barbara was surrounded by a group of men, nine of them, likewise mounted on snorting, impatient horses, black and brown. She scanned her companions. They were dressed in leather leggings, billowing shirts open to their waist. Black hoods were pulled over their heads, and she realized she was surveying the scene through holes in her own hood. The men wore swords strapped to their sides and excitement seemed to crackle in the air. She too felt it; the strength, the power. The lust. It started somewhere in her groin, spread up through her stomach and raced through her veins like fire.

"Gentlemen!" A voice cried out.

Barbara turned to a tall figure sitting on a black stallion, its reins made of carved black leather. The man was the only one of the group without a hood over his head. He wore a simple brown robe, its cowl pushed back. Justin's blond hair shone in the sun and his white teeth, visible through a mouth red and open in eager anticipation, lit up his face.

"The circus is about to begin!"

A raucous cheer rose from the mounted men, thrusting their gloved hands into the air.

"You see, my friends," Justin shouted, "I require your assistance. A peasant from the next village has defied me, defied us!"

Another roar arose from the group, this time tinged with anger, outrage. Barbara felt her own voice, now deep and raw, join the others.

Justin held up his hands for quiet. "He pushed my tax collector out of his hut," Justine continued. "Said his family was starving. Do we care about his wretched spawn! Is that *our* problem?"

The air filled with shouts of rage. Several men pulled their swords from their scabbards and raised the blades high into the air.

"What we *do* care about is order, my friends. The imperative of nature. *We* are order!"

Barbara's heart pounded loudly. She was shocked to hear her voice join the others in a full-throated bellow. These peasants! They cannot be allowed to defy us. That is the way to chaos. Justin understood that. We *all* understand it.

"We must re-establish order. Other villages must learn the price of defiance!"

Barbara's sword was in her hand now, thrust into the air over her head. She bellowed her agreement.

Justin's horse reared and neighed loudly. Justin unsheathed the black blade of his sword and pointed down the dust road. "The village is just beyond those trees. We will ride into it like the Valkyries! We will show no mercy."

He pointed to three men on his right with his blade. "You! The cur's hut is the first as we enter the village. You will dismount and drag him from his hut. You will slash his pants off with your sword then castrate him in front of his wife."

The men stood excitedly in their stirrups and howled assent.

Justin's eyes danced and his mouth curled in a broad smile. "Then hang him from the oak in the village courtyard!"

Barbara joined the rumble of approval, vaguely disappointed she had not been chosen for such a glorious mission.

"But my friends," Justin's voice dropped and he looked over the men, thirsty for action. "We are nobles. We shall *all* enjoy this while inflicting a necessary lesson. The rest of you will burn the village to the ground!"

Adrenaline surged through Barbara. A red haze fell over her eyes as she cheered.

"And you will rape the women, if possible in front of their husbands."

The cheer rose louder, higher pitched, a new note of animal hunger tinging the roar. Barbara felt a stirring between her legs.

"And what of the men?" a voice called out.

"Kill them all!" Justin thundered. He spurred his horse savagely. It rose on its hind legs, its head twisting madly, then leapt forward.

A shout went up from the men, and they stormed behind, pounding furiously toward the village ahead.

They rounded the curve in the road and swept into the village, their horses charging madly through the fleeing peasants, screaming in terror. One stupid man lunged at Barbara with a pitchfork. She reined her horse around and galloped furiously at the man, who dropped the fork and fled toward a low wall made of stones. Barbara raised her unsheathed sword and felt a thrill spurt up her arm and into her open mouth as her sword sliced cleanly through the back of the peasant's neck. She held her sword high, bloodied and shining. She galloped on as the peasant's head bounced into a clump of bushes and the torso collapsed into the dust.

Barbara wheeled around and charged back toward the village, the pleasure of her kill surging through her, the smell of blood in her nostrils. Around her, the other nobles had already set thatched roofs ablaze, hacking down children as they fled out of the burning homes. She grinned broadly with excitement, driving her sword into the back of a boy who dashed out of a flaming barn, noticing with pleasure how the boy struggled even though impaled. Ahead, men had dismounted and were dragging women from huts. He heard a woman scream as two of the nobles held her down while another pushed up her dress and dropped onto her. Barbara's loins burned, and she twisted in her saddle, scanning the turmoil around her.

She spotted a young woman with a baby in her arms. The woman ran up a cobbled street between two houses to Barbara's right, desperate to escape the smoke and mayhem. Barbara slipped quickly from her saddle and dashed after the fleeing woman. She fled up the narrow street but was slowed by the baby she carried, held to her chest. Barbara caught up quickly and grabbed the woman by the long red braid that swung wildly down her back and yanked her around. With her other hand, Barbara grabbed the collar of the young woman's linen shirt and ripped it downward, exposing one pink-tipped breast. She felt a prick rise inside her pants. Still holding the woman's head back by her hair, Barbara reached for her belt buckle.

The woman spit into Barbara's face, the spittle dripping off her cheek. A snarl of rage erupted from Barbara's chest. She had dropped her sword during the chase, but now she took the dagger from the sheath on her belt and raised the knife, imagining the pleasure she would feel as she plunged the knife into the woman's bared chest. She grasped the thick braid and yanked the woman's head back. But before she drove the dagger into her breast, she wanted to see the fear, the terror in the woman's eyes. Teeth bared, she thrust her head forward and stared into the woman's face.

Barbara froze. The face she looked into was her own. Green eyes glared at her, not with fear, but with defiance, hatred. Barbara heard the baby, still clutched in left arm of the red-haired woman, crying shrilly.

The air shimmered.

Barbara's eyes turned toward her right arm, raised to strike. She released the young woman's hair and looked over the village. A stench of burned thatch and charred flesh hung over the courtyard. The body of the man who had defied his overlords swung from a rope over an oak branch. Blood still pulsed down the dead man's legs into a pool on the cobblestones. Wounded peasants, some missing arms, cried out in agony. Men on their knees begged for mercy from grinning nobles. Women screamed in anguish and panicked goats, their slit irises wild, bleated madly. Barbara looked toward the woman who was being raped by the three nobles. One held her legs open while another, his leather pants at his ankles, thrust and grunted. The woman lay still on the ground, her face staring sightlessly at Barbara, tears dripping into the dust.

Barbara turned back to the woman who stood in front of her and dropped her right arm to her side. She turned away from the woman's burning green eyes—her own eyes—and sank to her knees. Revulsion spilled upward until she retched, over and over, onto the cobblestones. Sobs shook her body, and she pushed her face into her gloved hands in anguish. What had she done? Why? What madness had seized her?

Around her, a quiet grew. Barbara looked up from her knees. The rapists stood, looking dumbly at one another. A noble about to throw a torch onto a roof dropped the torch onto the ground. Faces twisted with lust and cruelty softened with uncertainty.

"Don't listen!" a thunderous voice boomed across the village courtyard. Justin, his brown cape open to its belt, blood streaking his chest, slick with sweat, sat on his black horse, which pranced uneasily in the dust.

"You have nothing to feel shame for! This is a festival! Pity is not for the strong, the noble. The powerful! We are warriors! This is our birthright! Do not let her weakness move you!"

Barbara felt the darkness swell again, the hunger building inside her. Power, domination. It filled her like a drug. She sensed the men around her returning to their rape, to their killing, but she could not. She would not. She raised the dagger again in her right hand, grabbing the front of her own shirt with her left hand to tear it aside and bare her chest to the dark blade.

"Do it!" Justin's shriek shook the ground.

The hand at her breast stopped over a small stone. It hung from a thin chain around her neck, throbbing as if alive, a tiny beating heart. Barbara's hand slipped between the buttons and clutched the gem.

The air shimmered again. She felt a shift.

She looked at a hooded man kneeling on the ground through the eyes of the young peasant woman. The man gripped a stone at his chest, his knife still raised but pointed toward his own breast.

There was a ripple, a rent in the air, and the two figures merged. Barbara stood, the fingers of her left hand wrapped around her gem at her breast. Her right hand with the knife trembled and the dagger shrank and was a hard knot in her palm. She opened the hand and looked at the black sphere, pulsating rhythmically.

She glanced up to see an obese man, his dark robes flapping behind him, break from a knot of men around Justin, running toward her with remarkable speed, almost as if he were flying. As he neared, the man's face melted, forming into a sharp nose flanked by yellow eyes. Black feathers appeared and the nose hardened into a yellow beak that opened, emitting terrifying screeches. Great black wings grew on each side and the raven head streaked toward her, its razor beak aimed at her eyes.

The hand clasping her gem at her breast opened slightly. A single shaft of red light leaked between her fingers. It stabbed upward into the darkness and pierced one of the man-bird's yellow eyes like a thin, burning blade. The creature gave a great shriek and beat its wings backward, its grotesque belly heaving in rage. The retreat left a small gap between them. She broadened the red shaft into a burst of red that filled the void. The beaked head screamed its fury as it was pushed farther and farther away, finally disappearing entirely. It was quiet.

Barbara stood in the stone room again. The agents sat, eyes still closed, in their chairs. Some twisted and muttered, but otherwise they were silent. Her eyes jumped to the chair on the carved dais. Justin leaned forward, his hands tightly gripping the red leather of the arms. The muscles in his jaw bulged and his teeth ground behind his red lips. His blue eyes were squeezed shut.

"Drop it," he muttered.

She opened her right hand. The black stone in her palm burned like a blazing coal. The skin around the black sphere began to peel, and the smell of burning flesh filled her nose. She screamed. The stone burned deeper into her hand, but she held it grimly. She closed her eyes in agony and screamed again.

Cries of pain rose up around her. She forced her eyes open. The men were writhing in their chairs, wailing in pain. Her pain. Some moaned; others twisted their heads back and forth in her anguish. She felt her own stone, which she still clutched to her chest, pulsing in her other hand. She turned it upward and opened her fingers until the brilliant red gem lay throbbing powerfully in her open palm. She lifted the gem and held it in front of her.

The light from the torch in the sconce behind her glowed through her stone and cast a brilliant red beam into the darkness. She took the stone in her fingers and focused the light onto the black sphere burning in her right palm. Instantly there was relief.

She closed her eyes again. *Focus,* she thought. *Focus on gentleness, on a memory of love.*

She was at the beach, her tiny hand in her father's gentle fingers. An errant wave washed over their feet, and he swept her up into the air, both of them laughing. She was filled with the joy of a child as her father swung her around in the air, safe and loved.

In front of her, some of the men began to blink their eyes, to move uncomfortably in their seats. She focused again. *Focus on humanity's goodness, the best we are capable of.*

She was with the choir. It must have been Christmas because they were singing the *Hallelujah* chorus. Her shoulders touched the women beside her and she heard her voice mingle with a hundred others, soaring, filling the hall with sound, sweeping each of them upward with the music so beautiful, so magnificent tears swelled in her eyes.

In front of her, Zoltan shook his head and blinked his eyes several times. He glanced at Justin, who moved erratically in his chair, his face contorted. Zoltan moved stiffly to Barbara's side. He pulled his stone from his vest pocket and a soft blue-green light joined Barbara's fierce red beam focused on the *Mester*'s stone burning in her right palm.

As Zoltan steadied his beam on the black sphere, he closed his eyes and focused his mind. He was staring into the grey eyes of a woman, who smiled at him with such tenderness that he flushed with warmth. They were naked on white sheets and he was so filled with love there was no space for anything more. The two of them entwined in each other's arms, and then she took him inside of her, and they were one. He no longer knew where he ended and she began, and they rocked gently together in an embrace he wished would last forever.

Friesen and Malik had also roused, and now they approached Barbara, their stones held in their hands. Friesen directed the purple beam from his jewel onto Barbara's hand, and then he too closed his eyes. He held a tiny baby that looked up at him with huge, trusting eyes. His breathing quickened as a surge of such love as he had never known swept through him, a knowledge he would gladly give his life for this child, so delicate in his great arms.

Malik held his amber stone between his thumb and finger, adding his light to the beams focused on Barbara's palm. When he closed his eyes, he sat by a small hospital bed. He looked down at a young girl, her smiling face turned toward him. She had no hair, but her eyes glowed with love as they looked into her father's face. The man rocked back and forth gently, her small hand between his. Then her eyes closed and the man's throat clamped shut. He kept rocking as tears streamed down his cheeks.

The room was astir. Most men were weeping openly. Some shook their heads as if awakening from a deep sleep. They looked at each other numbly.

Two other agents made their way toward Barbara and the group around her, training the glow from their gems on the sphere in Barbara's hand. Now six jewels shone rays of every color onto the black coal. The colors merged into a green corona around the orb, which began to vibrate. Barbara no longer felt pain; the light seemed to lift the ball off her palm, which healed as she watched.

The ebony sphere began pulsating more and more violently in her hand. The waves of color from the agents' gems washed over the *Mester*'s black stone with greater intensity, until it became harder to make out its shape or color through the green haze.

"NO!" The voice that erupted from Justin was not human. It shattered the air like a dull explosion.

Barbara kept her attention on the quivering black stone in her hand. She had hoped it would burst, shatter, willing to give her hand in the process, but it did not.

It simply disappeared.

Chapter 9

THE GREAT KEENING SCREAM DIED away into sepulchral silence. Barbara released her stone and braced herself on the chair in front of her with her left hand, still holding her damaged palm upward. Waves of darkness swept through her. Her knees gave way and she clutched the chair back to keep from falling.

Then Zoltan's arm was around her waist, holding her upright. She threw her head backward against his shoulder. A low moan climbed from her throat. She was so weary. She just wanted to let go, to collapse in Zoltan's arms and welcome the oblivion.

"You cannot," he whispered. "Not yet. It is not over."

She nodded and held onto the chair with her good hand and let Zoltan support her. She turned her gaze upward and looked into his face. He stared back, his dark eyes smoky and fierce. His lips were set and his jaw clenched so that his cheekbones stood out in the shadows of the crypt. His gaze was palpable, gently pushing her head backwards. Never had she seen such tenderness, such rage. She let go of the chair and drew his face to hers and crushed her cheek against his.

Around her she sensed the other men turning toward the front of the crypt. She turned away from Zoltan and looked at the ornate chair where Justin sat.

He stood, his hands grasping the carved arms of the chair. His handsome face was fixed, as if a mask, but something was different. The piercing blue eyes were changing, dilating, shifting colors. Red, a dark blue, yellow-green. The irises drew into vertical slits. As she watched, his face seemed to become unfocused, as if distorted by static. The image in front of Barbara melted, solidified like soft wax. The face reformed and the large red lips curved downward into a deep frown. Then the broad blood-red smile returned. A low buzzing surrounded the standing figure, soft then louder. The brown robe rustled and billowed as if blown by a strong wind.

Stiffly the figure returned to a sitting position. "To me!" he ordered. The man's lips seemed to barely move, but the voice shook the granite walls. Barbara shivered.

Barbara became aware of the agents in the room. While five stood around her, seven remained in their seats.

"You heard Lord Justin!" Garripoli snarled, his face full of fury and terror. "It is time to make your choice." He turned and strode to the right side of the dais. Meijer adjusted his round glasses and followed. A third figure stood. Barbara recognized him from the meeting in The Market as Jaromir, the agent from Riyadh. He looked toward the group around Barbara.

"A guy's got to eat." He shrugged and stepped forward to stand by Garripoli. A fourth man stood up, obese with jet black hair and an angular nose. He had said little since they met at the Market, but now he turned and looked directly at her. Barbara's heart jolted. As she watched, his eyes turned yellow and his hair swept back in fringe of raven feathers. His nose formed into a cruel yellow beak.

"What is it?" Zoltan asked softly.

The man gave a loud, croaking laugh and joined the men flanking Justin.

The three remaining men, including Noyes, sat in their chairs talking animatedly.

"Too late!" Justin bellowed. The cowled figure in the chair raised his chin.

The three men jerked upward until their heads struck the stone of the arched roof. They hung there for several seconds, screaming, their arms flailing helplessly. Abruptly they dropped three feet and jerked to a halt in midair. Their screams stopped. Barbara watched in horror as the bodies floated in front of her, their heads lolling loosely from their broken necks.

"You think you have stripped me of my power," Justin thundered from beneath his hood. His booming voice reverberated off the roof and walls until Barbara wanted to cover her ears with her hands.

"You are wrong," the voice hissed. The cowl moved back and forth. "You have no idea how wrong."

Barbara turned fully toward the front of the crypt where the three hanged men were suspended. She grasped her jewel, still clutched in her left hand, and sent a red beam stabbing across the room. She turned her stone to the right, severing the spell, and the bodies fell to the cobbled floor.

The figure in the chair cackled.

Zoltan and the four other men closed around Barbara in a semi-circle, each holding their jewels at arm's length.

"You think you are strong," the voice rasped. "But you do not *know* strength. I tried to give it to you, to show you what real power felt like, looked like. But you, you..." his voice gurgled into silence. "You spurned me. You showed yourself to be the weaklings you are."

Barbara whirled and looked upward as the voice ended. A large stone fell from the ceiling directly toward Friesen's head. Instinctively she pointed her gem at the rock and watched as it swerved backward, clattering loudly onto the floor.

It all took place in seconds. Friesen recoiled then looked at Barbara. He bowed.

The room fell utterly silent. Somewhere water dripped rhythmically.

He will bring the roof down. She knew this with absolute certainty and instantly imagined a dome.

The roar of crashing stones was deafening. Arches buckled as Barbara watched, pitching inward followed by a rush of squared blocks of granite from the crumbling ceiling. The room filled with dust and debris until she could not see beyond a few feet. Piles of rock formed at her feet, and then the quiet returned.

Barbara looked around her. She and the five men stood in a clear circle surrounded by a two-foot wall of fallen brick and broken stone. A light red haze arched around them.

It took several more seconds for the noise to subside, and then slowly the air cleared. The walls at the back of the room had completely collapsed, taking the torches with them so that their end of the chamber was utterly dark except for the glowing pink aura of the dome. At the front, still lit by a few sputtering lights, Barbara could see the four men crouching in terror against the far wall. The cowled figure sat motionless in his chair, his hands curled around the carved arm rest.

Next to her, Zoltan breathed deeply. "Let us go," he said to Justin. It was not a plea. There was menace and steel in the voice.

The figure cackled quietly. "And why would I do that, Mr. DeAngelo?"

"Because you cannot destroy us. Together we stood against you, yes? And won. You can break the necks of a few terrified, confused agents. But you cannot destroy us. And I assure you, sir, if you do not we will do everything we can to destroy you."

The cackle exploded into a full-throated roar of glee. "I see you still do not understand," the cowled-man said. "You're pathetic."

Barbara nodded at the dais. The chair Justin sat on burst into flame; great founts of orange and red fire licked the ceiling above the raised platform. She watched as Justin stood slowly, surrounded by flame, and moved aside. She could smell the scorched wool of his robe but only a few curls of smoke rose from the brown cassock.

Barbara cupped her jewel in her hand and the fire quickly expired. The red leather seat was blackened and cracked, and the carved wood of the chair back was charred and smoldering.

The man stood, weaving slightly back and forth, his hooded head turning as if he was trying to identify an odor.

"I have no need of you," he said at last. He waved his hand dismissively. "You cannot hurt me. But you are becoming a nuisance. Yes, I will let you go, though the chance of you finding your way out is nil."

For the first time something like hope stirred in Barbara's chest.

"But on one condition," the voice continued. "The woman stays."

Zoltan stood forward and threw a blue-green beam forward that lit the pale, leering face hiding under the cowl. The man turned his head sharply to escape the searing light.

"You are a coward," Zoltan rumbled. "I see *you* still do not understand. We will not leave without Barbara. And you will not leave with her."

The men closed around her, grim and determined. She felt their fierce loyalty. Barbara looked at each of the men and knew their goodness, their decency. Then she stared into Zoltan's face, dignified and chiseled with determination and bravery. Zoltan was right. They would all die to protect her.

She looked over Justin's shoulder into the darkness, and she knew that they would. All of them, including Zoltan would never leave here alive. Her future was less clear, but she could not let these men die.

"I will stay," she said. She had meant it as a bold declaration, but what she heard was a hushed voice filled with sorrow and resignation. "I will stay," she said more confidently. "But only when they are released and are out of this maze."

"Barbara, no!" Zoltan shouted, turning to her. His face was drawn in horror. "You cannot! I will not allow it!"

Barbara looked at Zoltan, smiling sadly. "You cannot stop me, sir."

Zoltan took her by the shoulders. "Please, Barbara." His eyes pleaded with her.

"I'm sorry, my love," she whispered. "I must."

Zoltan turned abruptly from her and faced the cowled man. "If she stays, I remain as well."

The man cackled again. "That is not part of the deal, DeAngelo. The woman stays. You go. Or die."

Zoltan held his gleaming blue gem at his chest. "Then die it must be."

Friesen was not a large man, but Barbara had already sensed his strength. Somehow she knew he had fought professionally. So when his fist crashed into Zoltan's temple, she knew he would collapse unconscious. She caught him as he toppled and laid him gently onto the floor.

Barbara looked up into Friesen's face, his eyes dark with regret.

"Thank you," she said. "There was no other way."

He nodded. "I want you to know that there is not a man here who would not stay and battle with you, you do know that?"

Gratitude swelled in her chest. Did she deserve such loyalty?

"I do." She looked at the anxious faces of the other men. "I do know that. And I thank you for it. But," she hesitated. "But when I look forward, there is only darkness here. For all of you."

"So be it," Malik said. "But know that we are not done. I promise you, we stand by our pledge: we will find a way out and then find you. Or we will die trying."

The four men bowed slightly to Barbara.

"So we vow," the turbaned man said softly.

"You are a seer," Friesen said, "among many other things. What happens when we leave? To you? To us?" "Is there a way out?"

Barbara shook her head. "It is not clear. I'm sorry."

She turned back to the cowled figure. "I will stay. You will open the door and the men will leave. You will have your guide take them out of the maze. Understood?"

The man slid his hands into the sleeves of his robe. "That was our bargain, was it not?"

The only thing Barbara knew for certain was that the man was lying.

Chapter 10

BARBARA HAD NO IDEA HOW long they walked through the labyrinth of caves, dark hallways hewn from live rock, and black spaces that might have been caverns or vast vaulted rooms. It might have been an hour, or several days. Her mind became numb, unable to concentrate, to calculate time or distance. She felt little, not even confusion. Was she simply exhausted? Or—was it possible?—perhaps she was dead? She tried to feel her feet on the stone floor, but while she had a sense of traveling forward, her legs seemed to barely move, her feet somehow floating along the passageway. She closed her eyes, letting the men grasping her arms guide her, and tried to focus. Slowly she began hearing muffled sounds. Then the noises were clearer. She realized she heard water gurgling from some underground spring. She breathed deeply with a pang of relief as she drew in the dank, stale air.

She was not dead.

But had she somehow been psychically invaded by Justin? She had felt no intrusion, no attempt to grasp control, but perhaps it was too late. Could he have seized her, numbed her when the doors crashed shut and the final stones of the crypt collapsed? She had spun inside the sheltering dome and it had taken several seconds for her to realize the men were gone and that she stood alone. From that point on, she had little memory of events, only a haze of shouts and distorted images. Had she let her guard down long enough for Justin to penetrate her defenses? With great effort, she tried to scan her body, to feel something.

There was a tingle of warmth at her throat, and she seized it, throwing what awareness she had into the growing kernel of heat. Slowly it caught and began to glow like a small candle sputtering alight, and she sensed a slight red tinge behind her closed eyes.

The heat grew and she knew it was her jewel, burning now, warming her chest, pushing the cold and numbness from her head.

Justin's black probe caught her by surprise. It jabbed upward just under the base of the skull. It was bitterly cold, like a blade made of hardened ice. She had just enough awareness to shift the growing warmth from her jewel upwards to the back of her head. She pitched forward as the heat met the icy thrust. She felt the blade stop, struggle and twist, and then slowly melt and disappear. Then she thrust the heat forward like a fireball. They had stopped. She slowly opened her eyes. In front of her she could make out Justin's hooded face turned toward her. It was as if she were looking at it through infrared binoculars—Justin was a faint red image surrounded by darkness but visible enough for Barbara to see his head jerk backward and his left forearm slash upward across his face. He hissed and turned his head away.

The silence was as vast as the cavern where they had stopped, but words came to her as clearly as if they had been shouted in her ear. *You're awake, I see. And strong. I like that. You will make a fine addition. I am sure I can find a use for you.* This was followed by the rasping cackle she had come to loathe.

If you have violated your agreement and killed my colleagues, I will know, she returned. *And you will wish you had never met me.*

She sensed Justin sneer, but there was also a tinge of uncertainty. *I have kept my vow. Your pitiful clutch of agents are free.* She heard him chuckle. *Free to wander in the caves until they die.*

Time returned. Barbara began to pay attention to the twists and turns, to the dozens of side passages they strode by, to the stalactites that jutted downward from the dripping ceiling like stone swords. She heard the labored breathing of the men on each side and knew who they were—Meijer walked on her left and Jaromir on her right. Their hands, Meijer's tense and tight, Jaromir's tentative and nervous, were locked on her upper arms. She extended the heat from her jewel down her arms and found some pleasure in the men's shriek of pain as they yanked their burning hands away from her skin.

Ahead of her, Justin's peals of shuddering laughter shook the cave walls. As the men dropped her arms, Barbara lifted her left wrist and pushed the button on her watch. She gasped. The elapsed time function read five hours and forty-one minutes.

Was it possible? Had all of this occurred in less than six hours?

Ms. Steubenville, she sensed Justin say to her. *Please come and join me on our stroll.*

The men beside her had obviously heard as well. They stood aside and Meijer shoved her forward. She stumbled by Garripoli, who glared at her. She regained her footing at Justin's side.

Ah, so nice to have you as a walking companion, Mrs. Steubenville.

"My name is Barbara," she said aloud. "And let's skip the mentalese, okay?"

She sensed Justin smile slightly. "As you wish, Barbara."

"You wanted to talk to me?"

Justin's brown cowl turned toward her slightly. "Well, I believe we have a good deal to talk about, don't you?"

"Do we?" Barbara asked. "Do jailers always converse with their prisoners?"

"Please, please." Justin waved his hand slightly. "Let's not be overly dramatic."

"Overly dramatic," Barbara said, her tone flat. "This from a man who just conjured up a vile scene of mayhem, of brutal rape, and the bloody murder of women and children for the enjoyment of a few potential recruits?"

"I regret your participation. I did not anticipate your joining our party." He shrugged. "I am sorry we got off on the wrong foot."

Despite her exhaustion, her loathing for the man next to her, she couldn't help it—she began to laugh. A laugh that built until she bent over and tears of mirth streamed from her eyes.

Even in the midst of her hysterics, Barbara could feel Justin bristle. He was becoming angry. Clearly few people laughed at Justin, and most likely only once. She was prepared when he sent the black blade at her temple and turned it away easily with a red halo from her jewel.

"Please," Barbara said, still chuckling. "I also don't much like being stabbed in the head."

Justin went silent and dark for several moments. Barbara realized that they were gradually descending and that the air was warming. She could not even guess how many miles they had walked. And what sort of route had they taken? Had Justin doubled back to obscure their trail, even if she could somehow reconstruct it? Were they even still in the cave system under the Buda Castle complex?

She could feel Justin begin to open up next to her like an old TV screen, the image blurry then clearing. "You are very special" he said. "I have to confess that I have not had good relations with women…"

Barbara began to laugh again but managed to limit herself to a few snorts. "I'll bet."

The anger flared again, but Justin quickly got it under control. "You are unusual. A female master, it seems. It does happen, but rarely. You were chosen. How?"

"I am hardly a 'master'," she said, gesturing over her shoulder with her head at the men behind her. "As you so like to describe your gang of sordid thugs."

"Please," Justin cut in. "You were chosen. Why?"

"I'm different I suppose; that is all." Barbara monitored the man's reaction. "Mine was hardly a magical childhood. Just a lonely one. A suburban one. At some point—I really don't recall exactly when—my mother checked out emotionally."

"Go on."

Barbara was surprised by his interest but realized it gave her the advantage. "Maybe I was nine or ten. I don't know what happened, but it had to do with my father. She never mentioned it, of course, but I think she caught him cheating, which, in retrospect, I imagine he was since he was rarely home."

Next to her, Justin walked and said nothing, but he was listening intently. She felt his guard weaken, and she began to probe his mind gently. If she could keep him engaged, what could she learn?

She continued, talking about her parents' constant arguing, shutting out their yelling by wrapping a pillow around her head and humming "Twinkle, Twinkle, Little Star." She told him about the night, when the yelling exploded into violence, her mother screaming in pain, her father slamming the door as he raged out of the house.

As they walked, a dim light had begun to glow above her and the rough-hewn walls and natural caves began to give way to hallways lined with cut stones. She paused.

"Continue," Justin said impatiently.

She resumed her story. The withdrawal of her parents from her and each other. The increased tension in the house. "I spent a lot of time in my room," she ended. "That's when I found the astrology books. So, you can imagine the mix. This lonely, unhappy kid discovering this mystical, arcane, ancient wisdom. I dove deeper and deeper."

"I see," Justin said. She was aware of the cowl nodding slightly. "You slipped your bond through those studies."

Now was the time; all his defenses were down.

"But enough about me. What was your childhood like?"

The image leapt across the space between the two: a boy, maybe five or six years old, lay in a narrow bed. He was thin, painfully thin, his face sallow. He stared out the single window in the room at a red brick wall only a few feet away. A nurse in a high white cap and white apron breezed into the room and took a bag of bloody tissues from the side of the bed. She closed it and left the room without saying a word. The boy looked up as she left, his face full of such loneliness that Barbara felt tears sting her eyes.

"Was it tuberculosis?" she asked, and as she did, his mind closed to her like the slamming of a door. The images ended as if a reel of film had suddenly snapped.

"It's not important," Justin hissed angrily. "That was many, many years ago."

"Yes, but do we ever escape them? The shaping experiences of our childhood? For you, you felt abandoned by your mother. Why had she left you there? Among the distant nurses, the white sheets, the months of isolation. The desolation, the bleakness, the impotence. It must have been terrible. Who could you trust? You closed off all your emotions and drew inward."

Even with his mind barred to her, Barbara sensed the seething emotions in the man next to her. There was an initial rush of anger, hatred toward her, and then it shifted immediately toward his mother. She felt him struggle to shut out the feelings that had escaped like monsters from a dark cellar. He stopped walking, and she watched his face writhe as he wrestled to seal the door again, to lock down once more.

He turned toward her, his face now contorted in rage. "It was nothing!" he screamed.

His mind was a mass of crawling things. Anger swept out of him like a bitter wind. She considered pushing him, goading, forcing him to react. But was it worth the risk? When dynamite explodes, all of those around are killed or maimed.

"I'm sorry," she said quickly. "Zoltan says I am an empath. I can't help it. I didn't mean to pry."

Slowly, the shuddering figure in front of her regained his composure.

"Thank you, Mrs. Freud," he said at last. She felt more than saw his fixed smile return. "But I find your attempts at psychoanalysis as infantile as they are amusing."

Justin began walking again, and Barbara fell in behind him.

The hallway widened. They walked on black slate paving stones, intricately fitted to create a nearly seamless glistening black road that ran straight for about a quarter mile. At the end stood what looked like a gigantic black semi-circle set in a rock face carved in a great arch. The hazy glow brightened slightly as they walked toward the end of the passageway.

The light was now bright enough for Barbara to study the party more closely. Meijer and Jaromir stood on each side of her, silent and awed by the nearing rock face that towered above them. Behind her to her left was the obese raven-man. Garripoli walked on his right. A yard in front, Justin slowed and stopped.

A stab cut through Barbara's left eye as if an ice shard had been pushed through her pupil and deep into her brain. She staggered and screamed in pain, steadying herself against the stone wall until the agony subsided. Jaromir heard her cry out and moved toward her as the rest of the party proceeded toward the door ahead of them.

"Are you all right?" Jaromir asked.

Barbara leaned against the wall, holding her hand over her eye. "Yes," she managed, panting hard. "What was that?"

"Justin. He's just letting you know he's not happy." Jaromir nodded toward the door and the rest of the party, which was now several yards ahead. "Come. We don't want to be left behind. If we are shut out, we are done. Being lost in these caves is a death sentence."

She nodded and followed Jaromir. As they neared, Barbara began to grasp the true size of the black gates that rose a hundred and fifty feet above her. The two of them caught up with the rest of the party, and she sensed that Justin's attention had turned away from her and the group and toward the rock face. Her head throbbed, anger rose inside of her. She stabbed forward, and then gave out a small cry as her thrust rebounded. Her body shook from the impact. His mind was utterly closed to her, as dark and impenetrable as black marble.

Suddenly the huge black disk began to part in the middle, receding into the rock archway on each side. It took only a few seconds for the massive door to part silently, and then they stepped forward.

Into what, she had no idea.

Chapter 11

ZOLTAN STIRRED, RAISING HIMSELF ON his elbow from the stone floor of the cave. An amber beam radiating from a jewel in Malik's hand lifted the darkness.

He looked groggily upward and made out the faces of the men who had stood with him and Barbara. The light grew brighter and he looked up at them, a circle of shadowy faces flickering in the glow from Malik's stone. They were outside the crypt. But how?

His head began to clear and he remembered. Barbara. She had agreed to go with Justin. He looked at the men around him. "Where is Barbara?" he asked desperately.

The men looked at each other uneasily. "She is still inside," Malik said carefully. "With Justin."

Zoltan looked up at the men's faces in horror. "What happened?

"She stayed to save us. She agreed to go with Justin," Friesen added. "It was the only way." He nodded at Zoltan. "Sorry about the punch."

Suddenly he remembered the blow to his temple. That explained the pulsing headache.

"We don't really know what happened," Malik continued. "We stood facing Justin and then we were here. The door crashed shut. He collapsed the entire entrance. The door is sealed forever."

Zoltan lay back on the damp rock for several moments and closed his eyes. Anger pushed through him. He had been betrayed. Anger was displaced with sickening loss as he thought of Barbara in Justin's hands. He should have done something. He should never have let her stay. But as he replayed the events, he realized any defiance on his part would have simply meant death. All hope for Barbara's release would have died with him. These men had saved him, and possibly Barbara.

He opened his eyes and looked into the four faces looking at him anxiously. "Thank you," Zoltan said simply. "Thank you all."

"No reason to thank us," Friesen rumbled in his deep voice. "It is you we should thank." The yellow light highlighted the angles of his face. "You saved our sorry asses." He paused. "You and Barbara."

His face pale, Zoltan turned his head and looked toward the deep pile of boulders that had buried the door.

One of the men—Zoltan was still groggy and his head felt like it was stuffed with cotton, but he thought the man's name was Maphaela—approached the rubble and clambered several feet up the slide, testing the rocks that filled the passage. He turned back to the group and shook his head.

"No way in," he said in a light South African accent. "It's solid and deep. It would take us days of blasting to get through. If we had the dynamite to do it with."

The fifth man, who had introduced himself at the meeting so long ago as Roger Kwan, ran his hand through his hair. "And even then, she wouldn't be inside. Or what's left of inside. They are long gone."

"She bought our freedom. At a high price," Friesen growled in frustration. He looked around the dank passageway. "Part of the deal was that we would be guided out of the tunnels. She knew it was the only chance to escape alive." He nodded grimly at the pile of rocks. "And find her."

Maphaela climbed down the rock face. "Well, we're not getting her out that way," he said, motioning with his head back at the boulders. "But we will not abandon her. Ever." His voice was steely, determined, and as he finished, the other men nodded in grim assent.

Malik directed his amber light from the dripping ceiling to the faces of the men, standing in a loose circle around him.

"I don't know how we will escape this place," he said, "but we will." His light brown eyes glittered in the amber light of his jewel. He carefully raised it and fit it into a gold setting at the center of his turban. "And when we do, we will find her."

Zoltan sat silently against the stone wall of the cave, staring blankly at the rockfall blocking the entrance. His mind swirled with loss, bleakness. He had failed Barbara. He had failed these men.

"Thank you, gentlemen," he said softly. "I appreciate your loyalty." He looked at the man who had just spoken. "Mr. Malik I know. Mr. Maphaela, is it?"

The man nodded. "Selick Maphaela."

"And for your commitment to Barbara. But when we escape these tunnels, if we can do so, I do not expect you to follow me in my search for Barbara. It will not be easy."

"Oh, please," Friesen rumbled, shaking his head. "Do you think any of us, after all of this," he motioned around the cavern, "and all we've endured over too many years of manipulation, lies and bullshit, that any of us are going to walk away from her? From you? Come on, give me a break.

"For the first time in way too many years I feel fully alive. And you know something? This isn't just about Barbara." He glared at the men. "I'm pissed, man. They've been fucking with my head. Using me, and I don't like it," he said angrily. "I owe both of you a great debt. I am Brendan Friesen, and live or die, I stand with you. As long as it takes."

The light in Malik's turban gave his face a golden glow, emphasizing his deep eyes and fine nose.

"My name is Joginder Singh Malik." He was a tall man, well over six feet, and now he drew himself erect, his maroon turban elevating him further.

"As you may know, *Singh* in Sanskrit means lion," he said. "I am of the *Nihang*, a Sikh warrior order." He stood expressionless. "We are also referred to as the *Akali*, immortals." A small smile creased his face. "We shall see. But one way or the other, I am with you to the end."

"Roger Kwan," the fourth man said. "I'm new here." Even in the darkness, his eyes glinted in amusement. "Only a few decades, and, it seems, willfully blind the entire time."

"Like the rest of us," Friesen added.

Kwan nodded. "But today, the scales fell off our eyes, didn't they?" He shook his head. "I was so consumed with my own grief I failed to see the scope and horror of what I was doing. God, what were we thinking? How did we let it get to this point?"

The men stared at the stone floor at their feet.

"But now it's atonement time. Whatever soul I've got left depends on what we do from here. No limits."

The blackness that had seized Zoltan only moments before began to lift, and something else stirred in him: bitterness, grim anger. And resolve.

"I am grateful." He took a deep breath and looked at the glowing faces in the circle of light. "We are all here because we have suffered terrible losses. We have been convinced of our weakness, our unworthiness. The hopelessness of our lives. But we glimpsed another possibility in the crypt, yes?" Zoltan looked at the blocked entrance, and tears welled in his eyes. "A way of being in the world that honors our humanity. That provides us with at least a hope for happiness."

Heads nodded around him.

"Now our task is to find our way from these caves and rescue..." Zoltan's throat closed, and he swallowed hard. "Rescue Barbara. And in so doing, perhaps, we will deal a blow to the forces who have used us so cynically for so long." Zoltan nodded toward Friesen. "We have become men again."

"We are indeed men, but also men who are lost," Friesen said somberly. "Men marooned in an endless maze of tunnels and caves with no idea of how to find our way out." He stopped. "If there is a way out."

"Mr. Friesen," Zoltan began.

"Brendan will do."

Zoltan smiled in embarrassment. "I know it is old-fashioned, but I did grow up a century ago. I prefer Mr. Friesen, if you do not mind."

Friesen gave a lopsided grin. "Whatever."

He looked around the circle. "As well as Mr. Malik, Mr. Maphaela, and Mr. Kwan. You each deserve my deepest respect."

"Thank you," Kwan said. "But back to Mr. Friesen's point. He is correct. Looked at objectively, our situation is quite hopeless."

The men looked at each other guardedly, knowing the truth of his statement.

"But then, we do have a few advantages," Zoltan said. "Do we not?"

He pulled on the gold chain attached to his blue-green jewel, which was glowing fiercely, and drew it from his vest pocket. As he did, the other men revealed their stones—Kwan's light green, Maphaela's bright orange, Friesen's purple. Malik directed his amber light to the center of the circle of men, where a great ball of brilliant light formed, illuminating the tunnels around them as if they were bathed in sunlight.

"I believe we will find a small open vault just around the corner of the passage," Zoltan said, nodding in in the direction they had come when entering crypt. "Shall we convene and discuss some plans?"

They walked to a barrel-domed chamber, its walls lined with cut stone and perhaps twenty feet long. A single doorway opened at the far end of the room. Lit brightly by the light from their gems, the atmosphere seemed almost cheery. One by one the men sat on the stone floor. Malik, regal in a deep red coat that fell below his knees, unwrapped a white silk scarf around his neck and folded it to sit on.

"We have little to go on," Zoltan began, "but here are a few facts. We are in the catacombs underneath *Budavári Palota*, the ancient Buda palace. I visited here as a child and know some of the tunnels nearer the main castle. This area I know nothing about.

"But consider this." He looked at the men around him. "We entered the tunnels two hours and twenty-seven minutes ago."

There was a collective gasp from the men.

"That cannot be correct," Kwan said. "Surely it has been far longer, days."

Zoltan held up his wristwatch. "Now two hours and twenty-eight minutes. And we entered the crypt itself just over two hours after we began our journey."

"All of what happened," said Kwan quietly, almost to himself, "in the crypt. All of that occurred in just a half an hour."

"An average walking pace," Zoltan went on, "is about three to four miles an hour, yes? So, in these circumstances, considering the darkness, the uneven floors, we are only a few miles from the entrance. I would guess less than six."

"That's the good news," Friesen muttered. "The bad news is we have no idea in which direction."

"True," acknowledged Zoltan. "But while I have never been this deep in the caves, I have some familiarity with them." He paused thoughtfully. "As a boy. My father was imprisoned here."

A quiet murmur arose from the men. "So I do have some idea of the construction, the elevations. Hopefully it will be of help. As well, the route out will be gradually upward—although there were four or five brief climbs, almost our entire walk in was a descent."

The men looked at Zoltan with something like hope in their eyes.

"And we will bear left, yes? Of the sixty-four turns we took at forks, forty-nine or fifty—I can't be completely certain—were to the right."

"You counted?" Friesen asked in astonishment.

Zoltan shrugged. "As best I could. I did not expect to be escorted back to the entrance."

"How much time do we have?" Maphaela asked. "We are without food."

"But we have plenty of water," Malik pointed out. "Without food, a human can survive for three weeks. Mahatma Gandhi fasted for twenty-one days without ill effects. Water, however, that is different. Without water we would last a week."

"Well, that is jolly news," Friesen said, his blue eyes dancing. "We may be extremely hungry, but we should be able to make if for two or three weeks without having to eat each other."

Malik started, shock on his face.

"I think he's kidding," Maphaela said, looking at Friesen. "But I could be wrong."

Friesen rolled his eyes crazily.

"I do not expect to reach our goal in one attempt," Zoltan said. "We will take wrong turns. We will have to retrace our steps as we run into dead ends."

"Hopefully not literally," Friesen said, smiling at the other four.

"We will have to trust our instincts, to use logic where we can." Zoltan looked seriously into the eyes of each man. "But if we stay together and use our combined resources, I believe we can find our way out."

Kwan stood and nodded at the door on the other end of the vault.

"We've only got twenty-one days left. Lead on, Macduff."

The men exited in single file with Malik in the lead, his amber gem lighting the way. Over and over they encountered forks, where they conferred. Other than that, the men hardly spoke. Even with the light from Malik's jewel, the darkness was just a few feet ahead, a few behind. Every sound was intensified in the rock passages.

After walking for thirty minutes, they came to a large room distinguished by its high, domed ceiling. Two routes led from it, one straight ahead and the other opening to the right. Zoltan stood at the center of the room, deep in thought, staring at the rock face to his left. *We should be finding passages to the left,* he thought. *But so far almost all have been to the right.*

"*Ahrey!*" Malik exclaimed, his voice booming in the stone room. "I am afraid I have left my *hajoori* behind"

"Your what?" Friesen asked.

"*Hajoori.* My scarf. I put it on the floor of the vault." He sighed. "It was quite lovely."

"Listen, it can't be that far back," Friesen said. "Just run on back and pick it up. We'll wait for you here."

Malik looked at him for a long moment. "I believe you are teasing. Is that right?"

All of the men chuckled, and Malik's face broke into a grin.

They decided on the arched entrance directly ahead of them and wandered back into the maze, scanning each meter for a familiar archway, or a pool they recalled from when they entered.

Zoltan changed places with Malik after another hour of walking, the light from his blue-green gem giving a twilight tinge to the cave walls around them. After fumbling their way forward, ducking low ceilings and stumbling on the slippery, broken pathway, Zoltan knew the men were fatigued, emotionally and physically exhausted. Ahead in the pale light from his gem, he could make out the outline of a doorway hewn from the stone that opened onto a room on the other side. He turned to the group behind him.

"There is a large chamber up ahead. We will stop there and talk, yes?"

He stepped forward, his jewel lighting the way, and ducked under the entranceway into the vaulted room. He had walked only a few yards before he stopped abruptly. He stood quietly and stared across the room. The other men entered and crowded around him.

"What is it?" Kwan asked.

Zoltan nodded to a shadowed wall on the far side of the room. A small white patch contrasted with the dark stone floor. He stared at the object in despair.

"I believe, Mr. Malik, you have not lost your *hajoori* after all."

Chapter 12

BARBARA WINCED, BLINDED BY A flood of dazzling light. The small party stood for several seconds inside the mammoth doors. They closed quietly behind her with a soft hiss. Her heart sank. Wherever they were, she was now sealed inside.

As her eyes adjusted, Barbara realized she was looking out onto an enormous square hall. Shiny dark grey walls rose two hundred feet above her to a roof that glowed a uniform, brilliant white. Offsetting the bright glow of the ceiling, a black floor, gleaming as if recently polished, extended to the walls, which were sharp, perfectly flat and symmetrical, as if sliced from a single block of grey granite with a giant knife. Around the top of the walls a banner of digital clocks slid from right to left, each carrying the time of one of forty time zones to the hundredth of a second. In front of her, brown-robed figures scurried through the central courtyard and along walkways that ran off into rows of cubicles that lined all the walls except the entranceway behind her. Some of the figures had hoods thrown back, but most had their faces buried in the shadows of deep cowls over their heads.

Justin swept into the hall, the others trailing behind, and strode toward a towering black cube set in the middle of the hall. It rose from the shining obsidian floor to the glowing roof. At first she thought it was a solid monolith carved from the same material as the floor, but as they neared Barbara realized it was a hollow column clad in black glass. Justin raised his hand, and a panel in the middle of the square column immediately rose upward.

Barbara hesitated, and Meijer grabbed her upper arm roughly and pushed her forward. As they entered the dark structure, the door whispered shut. The group stood in a perfectly square room. All four walls were vast glass sheets that rose to the ceiling above her. Only a square glass-sided shaft in the middle of the space interrupted her view of the courtyard outside, bustling with brown-robed figures hurrying from one line of cubicles to another.

Justin walked to the shaft in the middle of the room and turned back toward Barbara. Meijer shoved her forward again.

"Welcome to my home," Justin said, beaming. "This is the Company. Perhaps you've heard of it?" His red lips curled into a wide smile. "I do hope you will be happy here. I am anxious to discuss our business arrangement, but it has been a long day. I am sure you would like to freshen up." He nodded to Meijer and Jaromir. "These gentlemen will escort you to the guest deck. You will have the opportunity to shower." He frowned disapprovingly at Barbara's black jeans, which were stained and worn. "And new clothes will be provided."

He started forward and then turned back to Barbara. "I do look forward to our discussions." His smile slipped slightly. "But empath or not, there will be no more analysis." The sharp pain edged into her eye once more. "Is that clear?"

The psychic pick withdrew, and he turned abruptly and walked into the side of the glass shaft and seemingly disappeared. Garripoli and the Raven Man scuttled after him.

"You next," Meijer grunted, pushing Barbara forward.

She slipped through the wall as if it were a thin sheet of water and stepped to the center of the column, which soared above her to the ceiling, an unbroken glass rectangular tube.

Jaromir joined them at the center of the shaft. "Eight," he said.

Barbara's stomach lurched as they rose through the shaft as if they occupied an invisible, silent elevator. She looked giddily between her feet at the receding floor below them as they floated upward.

At the very top of the shaft, they slowed and glided to a halt. In front of them an opening appeared in the glass column.

"Step forward," Meijer ordered.

Barbara looked down at the shiny black floor of the shaft, now a small square beneath them. She took a deep breath and walked toward the portal, half expecting to plummet to the stone floor fifty yards below. But her feet struck a solid, if invisible, surface, and she strode forward, determined not to show the fear she felt. She passed through the doorway and into a brightly lit hallway. Portals glowed in the grey wall to her left, and the dark glass on the other side of the corridor opened onto a metal balcony that wrapped around the entire floor. Below that was the workspace, a vast cluster of cubicles, like the inside of an enormous beehive sliced open.

She surveyed the space below her teeming with workers. *The Company*, she thought.

"This way," Meijer said, nodding down the corridor.

Halfway down the hall, Meijer stopped in front of a rectangle outlined in red neon in the grey wall. "In here."

Barbara hesitated. "You can walk through," Jaromir said. "It took me a while to get used to it as well."

Her eyes shifted from the wall to Jaromir. He was sad. He wanted to apologize.

"Thank you," she said, nodding slightly.

He turned his head away.

Meijer frowned. "You cannot leave this floor," he said gruffly. "All exits are sealed. You have access to the balcony. There is food and amenities in the guest room. And a bed. One of us will be back tomorrow."

I can't wait, Barbara thought wearily. *And maybe then one of you can tell me where the fuck I am. And how I get out.*

Barbara scanned the time zones flickering around the ceiling. It was 8:35 in Budapest. If they were still in Hungary.

A long day. Yes.

#   #   #

The guest room was not large, but it was exquisitely appointed. Deep white carpet cushioned her feet; gentle music hummed soothingly from unseen speakers. An enormous bed with a white silk canopy covered one wall.

From the bedroom, a door led into a bathroom with a shower head protruding from the ceiling. There was no curtain, and no handles. Barbara wearily stripped off her clothes, wet and soiled, dropping them on the bedroom floor, and walked under the shower head. Instantly needles of hot water warmed her scalp, massaged her exhausted shoulders, and ran in rivulets around her jewel and between her breasts. The tension slowly dissolved and she began to relax until she almost collapsed as her legs began to fold under her.

She rested her hand against the tiles and steadied herself. She closed her eyes and let the soothing water wash over he for several minutes. Reluctantly, she finally stepped out of the shower and wrapped herself in a soft white towel. She walked back into to the bedroom where she had left her clothes and stared blankly at the floor. Her clothes were gone In their place, laid out on the white silk cover, was a dark red robe. She spun around, but she was alone. She had sensed nothing, no one in the room, no movement or noise. Her skin crawled as if unseen eyes were staring at her. She stood tall, covered one breast with an arm and grasped her gem with her hand. It pulsed reassuringly. She took the robe off the bed and slipped it on.

It fit as if it had been made for her, falling around her shoulders and gently cupping her breasts, tapering to her hips and folding around them like soft hands, then falling down her legs until the hem almost touched the carpet. A full mirror rose on the other side of the bed, and she gasped as she saw herself. Her hair hung in red ropes, like scarlet snakes, framing her face and folding across her shoulders. Steady, searing green eyes stared back at her. She had never thought herself beautiful, but this woman was stunning. She tugged the red hood over her head and smiled as her face glowed pink from within the silk cowl.

"Don't fuck with me," she said quietly to anyone listening. "Oh yeah," she added. "And I want my clothes back."

Chapter 13

ZOLTAN STOOD LOOKING AT THE *hajoori* on the floor as if it would explain what had just happened.

"We walked for two hours in a circle," Friesen remarked. "That's depressing."

Malik said nothing, but walked across the circular room and retrieved the scarf. He draped it over his shoulders so that the ends hung loosely down his maroon *jodhpuri*.

"There," he said. "That feels better."

Friesen shook his head slightly. "Listen, just don't leave your shoes this time, okay? I don't want to have to come back here again to pick *them* up."

The men chuckled, but there was nervousness to their laughter, and it subsided quickly.

"He's enchanted the caves," Maphaela stated. "He can alter the routes so they are never the same."

"Wait, wait," Kwan said. "Let's not let our imaginations get carried away."

"Yes," Malik agreed. "It is too soon. We did not expect to walk out the front door on our first attempt, did we?"

Zoltan fought off the hopelessness he felt when he spotted Malik's *hajoori*. What was Justin capable of? How had they managed to walk for hours and end up where they had started? He had to find the answer or they would not leave the catacombs alive.

Finally he turned from the wall. "Actually, I think Mr. Maphaela may be correct."

The uneasy silence of the men matched the deep quiet of the stone passages that led from the room into darkness blacker than night.

"Something is wrong; I knew it as we walked. How many left hands turns did we take?"

"I counted seven," Maphaela said. "Out of thirty-five or so."

Zoltan nodded.

"Please," he said. "Let us walk to the large room we found. The one, Mr. Malik, where you discovered the loss of your *hajoori*, yes?"

The men looked at one another blankly.

"If I had a better plan," Friesen said, "I'd be happy to provide an alternative."

The party exited the room again, but this time uncertainty, tinged with fear, replaced their earlier optimism.

They had little difficulty finding the room again, and the men felt some relief that at least they could retrace their steps, that the passageways weren't constantly fluid and shifting. They assembled in the middle of the large room and stood quietly.

Zoltan shone his gem on the rock wall to the left of the arch where they had entered. He was not wrong. Somehow, he knew, the path out led through the wall.

"It was here," he said. "Here I felt we should go left."

"Sounds like a plan, "Friesen remarked dryly, "except for that solid rock wall in our way."

The five men stood in a semicircle, the lights from their gems trained on the wall. Rivulets of water ran down its rough surface.

"Look!" Maphaela said, staring at the stones at the base of the wall. "The floor is worn by centuries of feet. There are faint trails."

Friesen stared downward. "I don't see what you're getting at. It's all the same slate flagstones."

Maphaela pointed toward the archway they had used when they exited the room the first time. "Do you see a faint pathway? Worn in the rocks?"

Friesen looked at the floor where Maphaela pointed. "Yeah," he said turning to his right. "I do. And there is another trail leading to the right toward that other archway. But I don't see how that helps us."

"Now look at the floor to your left," Maphaela said.

Underneath their feet, another stretch of worn rock, only discernible in the glare of the bright light of their gems, led directly into the wall.

Zoltan walked forward and studied the rock face.

"Perhaps there is a hidden doorway," he suggested. "Opened by a concealed trigger of some sort."

He took another step until he stood just inches away, his gem illuminating every detail of the surface. But there was nothing. Just an unrelieved expanse of ancient rock, roughly hewn by hands hundreds of years before. Zoltan knelt on the cold slate floor and examined the rock face where it met the floor of the passage, desperately looking for something, anything that would reveal a way out.

While he searched, the other three men spread along the wall, also looking for a secreted lever or protruding rock that would unlock the passage. If indeed there was a passage.

"Damn it," Friesen swore. He struck the wall with the side of his balled fist in frustration.

His arm disappeared into the rock up to his elbow. He gasped.

Zoltan turned as Friesen yanked his arm back in panic.

Facing the wall, Zoltan put both hands in front of him and pushed. They passed through the surface unimpeded. He stood at the wall, his hands seemingly swallowed by live rock as the other men watched in astonishment.

Zoltan took two steps and found himself on the other side of the rock face. He turned back and saw the archway into the room they had been in. He turned and strode back through the wall to the wide-eyed amazement of the others.

"It is an illusion," he said. "As Mr. Maphaela suggested, Justin has indeed enchanted these caves. But it is as I expected. He is not powerful enough to actually alter the stone, yes?"

"But what he can do," Kwan finished, "is create illusions. He cannot close passages, but he can make them invisible to us."

Zoltan nodded. "And I believe in so doing, he has given us a map out of this maze."

The men looked at him quizzically.

"Would he bother to block passageways that led nowhere? Would he expend the time and energy to arbitrarily create illusory walls? Or would he only block those passages that, if we took them, would lead us aboveground?"

"I see, yes!" Malik said. "We only need to find the blocked paths, the closed doorways, and we will follow the route we took when entering."

Friesen's face, usually set in a grim frown, lightened. He gave a gracious nod to Zoltan.

"I believe you are onto something there, Mr. József. However, I do have to point out that even if this theory proves correct, we will have to feel our way along the entire length of our exit."

"That is true," Maphaela said. "And I suggest that we get started."

He turned and walked through the wall.

Chapter 14

BARBARA SLEPT LONG AND DEEPLY, and awakened to the smell of bacon. A full breakfast, steaming as if it had been prepared five minutes before, awaited her on a table near the door to the room. She salivated as the rich odors wafted from a silver platter. How long had it been since she had eaten? Days? Weeks? She flung the deep down comforter to one side and slipped out of bed, almost tripping as she dashed for the table. She gulped down the orange juice and gobbled two pieces of bacon before she sat down. But then she stopped, pulled out the chair and sat still for several moments. She turned back to the eggs, ham and buttered toast, and ate slowly. This, she knew, could be another long day.

She tried to assess her situation. She had already realized that her powers as an empath, as a seer, were blocked by the walls of the Company. She was sealed inside this giant cube with no ability to contact Justin. Her heart sank. *If* he were still alive. She remembered the long walk through the tunnels, the agonizing attacks from Justin, his inaccessibility. She would only be tolerated by him as long as he thought she could be of some value to him. How long could she maintain that illusion?

She munched the toast. *How the hell am I going to get out of here?* she wondered.

Barbara was mildly surprised when she exited the room and simply walked through the glass onto the balcony. Doors in this place, it seemed, were optional. She placed both hands on the balcony railing and looked out over the vast floor below her.

From this height she had a much better view of the square. The great semi-circular door through which they had entered rose in the wall to her left. She guessed the wall was about five hundred feet long, and she had a feeling that the other three walls would not vary a thousandth of an inch. Except for the entrance, all the walls were lined with row after row of identical cubicles, obviously offices of some sort, each about ten yards square. She counted the rows—they were five deep with narrow walkways in between. Together they formed a broad U, opening to the central courtyard in front of the main doors. She processed the numbers: there would be nearly one hundred cubicles.

The tops of the cubicles were open, spreading out from the central tower on all sides. It was as if she were looking at a slice of some monstrous beehive, swarming with brown-cloaked figures hunched over flickering screens. From the balcony, she glanced at the ceiling, now only twenty or so yards above her. She squinted in its glaring white light, which glowed bright, sharp and cold.

Barbara turned as she heard a hiss behind her. Jaromir stepped out on the balcony and stood by her. He stared silently over the floor.

"Impressive, isn't it?"

Barbara looked at the side of his face. Lines of worry creased his forehead and his eyelids were slightly closed over grey, cloudy eyes. His thin lips drew downward in a permanent frown.

"You have been assigned to guard me?"

He shrugged. "I guess. Don't know why he bothers." He nodded toward the round doors. "That's the only way out."

"You've been here before?"

Jaromir nodded slowly. "Several times."

"Why you? Of all the jewel makers, why would Justin bring you here?"

"Wasn't just me. There were three of us."

Barbara turned back toward the courtyard. "You, Garripoli, and the Raven Man."

"Elrabol."

"You were his agents."

Jaromir shrugged again. "A guy's got to eat."

She turned back to study the man standing next to her. He glanced at her nervously out of the corner of his eyes. She wondered why her warden was so forthcoming.

"That's what you keep saying." She paused. "You are very anxious, Agent Jaromir. Why is that? I would think a senior aid to Justin would feel secure, at ease here. But you don't. Why is that?"

Jaromir turned to face her. His grey eyes had cleared and now burned fierce and bright. "You don't know me or what I am feeling," he said tightly. "Your guesses are irritating me."

Barbara met his gaze unblinking. She stared deeply into his eyes and saw the clouds swirling again like smoke from a dying fire.

"I apologize," she said quietly, looking away. She felt the turmoil boiling in Jaromir, and she knew she needed this man. To pursue his unease would simply force him to withdraw further. "I didn't mean to pry." She smiled, everything forgotten. "But perhaps you could help me understand what we are looking at here."

Jaromir barked a short laugh. "Sure, but you will have plenty of time to find out for yourself. You're not going anywhere." He paused. "Ever."

An unexpected chill caused Barbara to shudder.

"Humor me. For starters, everyone is wearing a brown cassock, most with the cowls up." She paused. "Like Justin."

"Standard issue for work. Justin, on the other hand, has quite a wardrobe."

She nodded down at the floor at a tall figure in a helmet and black robe walking beneath them "So in that case, what are they?"

As she spoke, almost as if it had heard her, the figure raised its head slowly and looked up at the balcony and directly at Barbara. Barbara unconsciously stepped backward as a shiver ran down her back. A shiny metal mask covered the face of the black-cowled figure. Two perfectly round holes, which seemed to be covered in a fine mesh screen, concealed the eyes. The mask tapered, noseless, to a silver oval grate where the mouth might be.

Jaromir snorted at Barbara's reaction, but she noticed him also cringe as the masked figure glared up at them.

"Better to look away," Jaromir said, fixing his eyes on the side of Barbara's head. "They're sort of like wild dogs; you don't want to challenge them."

She tore her eyes away and faced Jaromir, whose grey eyes flickered in fear.

"Who are they?"

"Or what. Those are the *Ceg Biztonság Milicia*, the CBM, known informally as the Company Berserkers." He smiled tightly. "Or just Berserkers for short."

Out of the corner of her eye, Barbara noticed the Berserker turn away and continue to pace slowly through the aisles. Her hand strayed to the jewel at her chest.

"They are guards?"

Jaromir shrugged. "Thugs. Executioners. Torturers. Enforcers. Sadists. Take your pick."

Barbara stared out over the floor as the tall figure strode through the walkways between offices. Workers who spotted the black figure coming quickly looked away and scuttled into a cubicle.

"Are they human?"

Jaromir shrugged. "Hard to say. No one I know has ever seen one outside of his uniform."

"Their eyes—can you see through the mesh? And what about their voices?"

"You can see movement, but the screen is too fine to make out any details. And when they speak—and you do not want them to speak to you—it is in a deafening, mechanical, uninflected voice."

As Jaromir spoke, Barbara scanned the floor noting two or three other Berserkers walking purposefully, almost at a march, through the maze of cubicles.

"How many are there?"

"Most I've ever seen at one time is about a dozen, I guess. At a riot up on the Pleasure Floor. They paralyzed thirty or forty workers. Didn't mean anything, just drunk, you know. But out they went into the killing cave. Most of them anyway."

Barbara stared at him blankly.

"They can't kill workers inside the complex, see? So they have a special cave just outside the main entrance. When the door goes up, and workers are taken out by the Berserkers, everyone knows they will not be coming back."

"And the Berserkers, they report directly to Justin?"

"Guess so. But if you look closely, and I don't advise it, you will notice that some of the mouth grids and earpieces are gold. They're the officers. I'm thinking three, four of them, tops. Maybe they're the only ones in direct contact. That would be my guess." He stopped speaking and glanced nervously over the floor.

Why is he telling me all of this? Barbara wondered. *Is this just a ploy to get me to trust him?* It would be just the kind of tactic that would appeal to Justin. But it didn't feel right. The man's fear was real, she was certain of it, and his cynicism too barbed, too bitter to be feigned.

"The earpieces let them pick up signals?"

"Look," Jaromir said, looking uncomfortable. "I've told you more than I should have already. Just take it from me—don't fuck with these guys. They can paralyze you with a look. I've seen them pick up a large man in one fist and hurl him against a wall."

Barbara turned away from the floor and leaned casually against the rail, looking at Jaromir. "So, let's start over again." Barbara peered across the massive floor. She could just see a few heads bobbing above the walls. "What's going on down there, Agent Jaromir?"

Jaromir repeated his humorless laugh. "What is going on down there. Now, isn't that the question?"

"You don't know?"

"Nobody knows it all, other than Justin. Possibly."

"Give me a hint." She raised her chin toward the floor below them. "There must be nearly a hundred cubicles down there."

"Exactly a hundred."

"Filled with people. What do they do?" She waved her hand across the floor, crowded with cowled figures crossing the courtyard, ducking into cubicles. "Look at them all."

"Yeah. Five hundred to be exact. We're not supposed to mix with the regular employees, so I don't know what they all do, but each is assigned a sector." He nodded behind him. "Somewhere along the back wall there is Commerce, Tribes, Religion, and Policy, or something like that." He nodded back toward the front. "I know Youth is over there somewhere."

"And the gem project. It is located in one of the offices on the floor?"

Jaromir shook his head. "Oh, no. That's Justin's baby. He kept it close by. Next to his office downstairs." He smiled wryly. "Well, not downstairs. I've never seen any stairs in this place. But several levels below us."

"Where he and Garripoli went when we arrived."

"Yeah. Along with Elrabol. His living quarters are down there. Quite extravagant I understand, but I've never seen them. He keeps apartments for his personal agents as well."

The unease she had felt from him turned into resentment. "But not you."

Jaromir shrugged. "Typically, I never made that grade."

Barbara had been watching Jaromir's face as he spoke, but now she looked back over the floor.

"You said the gem project is Justin's. He started it?"

"From what I understand, yes."

"And he brought in the *Mester* to run it?"

Jaromir shifted uncomfortably, his hands gripping and releasing the handrail. "Look, I don't really know that much about all of this, okay? And I usually don't talk about what I do know."

So why are you? She relaxed next to him. "Of course. I understand." She turned back to him, a slight smile on her lips. "I appreciate your orienting me. I really do."

Jaromir nodded slightly and Barbara looked at the activity on the floor spread out in front of her.

"Yes," Jaromir blurted, as if he'd made a sudden decision. "He used to come here monthly to meet with Justin and sometimes others. Agents, outsiders." He glanced down at the base of the elevator shaft. "We all met in Justin's personal boardroom. In his office." He paused. "You will see it when you're summoned."

"Thank you, Agent Jaromir," Barbara said softly. Her voice brightened. "Now what else should I know about what is going on below us?"

Jaromir took a deep breath and seemed relieved to change the subject.

He pointed to the far right-hand corner of the square. "You see that large group of offices over there? The ones with the dividers that extend to the roof?"

Barbara nodded. She had noticed the section set off by high walls and wondered about the offices inside.

"They handle media."

Her eyebrows drew together slightly. "Handle?"

Jaromir shrugged. "I don't know the details. I just get bits and pieces. Adjusting this. Inserting that. I don't really know. I just met a woman assigned there one time. In the pleasure rooms."

Barbara inhaled sharply. "Women? There are women here?"

"Some. Justin doesn't much like them." He barked another short laugh. "Says they're too hard to control. But he needs them."

"For what?"

"Sometimes he can't find a man with the skills he needs." Jaromir shrugged nervously. "And then there are the comfort women."

"Prostitutes."

Jaromir continued to stare out over the humming floor beneath them. "Aren't we all?"

Barbara said nothing, watching the cowled figures crouched over a thousand luminous screens.

"And then there have been a few like you," Jaromir continued.

"Like me?"

"Women with power." Jaromir paused. "It's all about power, isn't it? When he sees it he wants it. To possess it, to use it. Or to kill it."

His voice had taken on an edge of hardness. Remorse or conflict seemed to have resolved into bitterness.

She didn't know why, but the man was reaching out to her. Guilt, desperation—and hatred. They emanated from him like a dark aura. *I wonder what he would do…* Barbara's hand drifted slowly toward Jaromir until it rested on the arm of his coat. He flinched slightly but said nothing.

When she touched him, he let his guard down, and then she saw it. "One of these other women, like me. You loved her. Justin destroyed her."

Jaromir yanked his arm away, his face flushed with anger and pain.

"Leave me," he said. "You are indeed an empath. I saw you push Justin to the brink. We all did. But you must not probe too deeply. Please. It endangers us both."

Barbara withdrew her hand and placed it back on the railing. "Tell me about her."

Jaromir remained silent.

"This woman."

Jaromir continued looking out over the swirling activity beneath them. "Her name was…" he stopped. "Her name is Sibyl."

Barbara glanced over at the side of the man's face. "You said he destroyed her. Is she dead?"

Jaromir's eyes teared and his jaws clenched. "She might as well be."

"But she's alive. In some sort of prison. Here in the Company?"

Jaromir gave a slight nod, an acknowledgment.

She reached out gently and touched his arm again. "You loved her very much. You still do."

He turned on her fiercely. "He maimed her," Jaromir cried. "Turned her into a monster. Do you understand? The most beautiful woman I've ever seen made too hideous to look at." He leaned toward her as he spoke, his lips parted in in fury and his eyes blazing. "He destroyed us both."

"Yes, I see," Barbara said softly. "You know where she is, though."

Jaromir nodded. "But I cannot see her. I can't face what he's made of her."

Barbara looked back over the work area. "Does Justin know about you and Sibyl? Was he aware you were lovers?"

Jaromir lowered his head. "I don't know," he said miserably. "We were very careful. I don't think so. But maybe he does? Maybe he's toying with me? Torturing me." He gave a small shrug. "Who knows?"

"There were other women like me. Other than Sibyl. What happened to them?"

Jaromir scowled. "Listen, I hear stories, but I don't know what really goes on. Nobody does. I've been here ten , maybe a dozen times." He breathed deeply. "But at least I have a memory."

Barbara turned to him quizzically.

Jaromir glanced at her, one corner of his mouth turning up into a twisted smile. He drew the back of his hand across the square. "There are five hundred people down there. Another five hundred on leave."

Her head tilted slightly in confusion.

"Everyone works on twelve-hour shifts. The desks are always manned, twenty-four-seven."

"Of course. So there are actually a thousand employees in the complex."

Jaromir nodded. "Almost all of them work on two-year contracts. Make a ton of money and leave. But do you think Justin lets them walk out and discuss this little operation?" His head jerked back in amusement. "Section 12.14."

"Sorry?"

"Section 12.14. When they sign their contract, they agree to have their entire memory of the two years they spent here removed. When they reappear above, they have a lot of money in the bank and no recollection of what they did to get it. Neat, eh?"

Barbara stared thoughtfully at the far wall. "And I suppose orphans are preferred."

Jaromir nodded. "Sure. Not much family to notice. Just a few friends. Of course, workers are obligated to notify acquaintances they will be working in a foreign country for two years." Jaromir glanced around the square and snorted. "They got that right. And all the records are adjusted. So, *voila*—he gets their services, they never have to work again, and no one knows anything."

"But you're special," Barbara said. "As an agent, you come and go. Your memory isn't erased."

"Right. He needs us up above. To monitor. To inform. Can't do that with an empty head. And of course there are a few who stay longer than the usual two-year contract period. If he needs them, they stay."

"Whether they like it or not," Barbara whispered.

Jaromir shrugged.

"Back to the women, like Sibyl and me. Tell me what you know."

Jaromir's eyebrows rose slightly. "Not much. Some have stayed," he looked at Barbara. "She, Sibyl, even became part of the Committee. Some have left once he was done with them, memory removed. All of it in some cases, it seems. Some have died, I understand."

"How?"

Jaromir turned to her, his lowered eyelids hooding his deep grey eyes. "You will learn that asking too many questions here is not one of the practices of successful residents and employees."

"I don't plan on being successful."

Jaromir gave his usual shrug. "Suit yourself. But keep in mind while it can be very enjoyable here, dissent and disruptions are not tolerated." He paused. "Later you will meet Sibyl. In fact I've been ordered to take you there tomorrow."

"Sibyl?" Barbara said. "You will go with me?"

The man stared morosely to the floor far below him. "I will take you to her hut. But I will not go in." He shook his head sadly. "I cannot. I don't have the courage."

Barbara nodded slightly. "Of course." She breathed deeply, conscious of the mix of emotions he projected that were swirling inside of her—anger, hatred mixed with fear. "What was Sibyl's crime?"

"Defying Justin, of course. What else? But I don't really know the details. We didn't talk business much. They brought her in when things weren't going well, here at the Company. Don't know the issue, but she was recruited to sort things out. That much she told me." He stared blankly over the floor. "But once she understood the nature of the business, she confronted Justin."

Barbara looked into Jaromir's face. "And what is the nature of the business, Agent Jaromir?"

Jaromir's smiled sardonically. "Haven't you heard? We are committed to protecting and advancing human morality, culture, and stability by identifying and supporting those most able to rule wisely and well."

"And who would that be?"

The smile disappeared. "That's the problem, isn't it? It all sounds so…" Jaromir shrugged. "So logical, so laudable. Until you look behind the curtain. Who indeed? It didn't take Sibyl long to see through the charade. This is what the Company is: an ancient cabal dedicated to keeping an aristocratic elite in power." His rueful smile returned. "Oh, and keeping the rest of us in servitude."

Yes, Barbara thought. *The pep talk in the crypt.* She could still hear it thundering in her ears: *Nobles like us are tasked with keeping order. To make sure the weak, the stupid, should never prevail.* She recalled how the agents nodded.

"And she shared this with you?"

Jaromir shrugged. "Not all of it, but enough."

"How did the two of you meet? You and Sibyl?"

Jaromir sighed. "I really don't want to go into it."

"On the contrary. I think you do."

Jaromir's grip on the rail of the balcony tightened. "I've been a gem maker for a long time. Not as long as DeAngelo." He paused. "Zoltan. Sorry, that will take some getting used to. Anyway, they recruited me after my wife and son were killed in an automobile accident."

"I'm so sorry."

Jaromir clasped his hands in front of himself, leaning over the railing. "It was a long time ago, it's just a bad dream now. But then, then I was desperate, suicidal. A month after they died, I had carefully planned out my death. I had accumulated enough sleeping pills so that if I took them all I would just go to sleep and not wake up." His eyes clouded again. "So appealing. Just go to sleep. All the sadness, the bleakness would end. The guilt. Bang. Over."

"Yes, I see." Barbara paused. "But why guilt?"

Jaromir took a deep breath and began his story. He had been the vice president of a marketing firm, young and ambitious. He and his wife waited for him to secure his professional position before having children. Then they had a son. A few years after his birth, they knew something wrong. "We had noticed that his legs seemed to be weak. When he started walking, he could only take a few steps. It was heartbreaking," he said softly.

The boy was diagnosed with Duchenne muscular dystrophy, but Jaromir had refused to believe it. He buried himself in his work stayed away from home more and more. He refused to meet with the doctors. Finally he agreed to accompany his wife and child to see a specialist. He would take the train home and drive them all to the clinic

"I don't know," he said almost in a whisper. "Did I really have to stay at work or didn't I want to face it?"

"You didn't go home."

Jaromir shook his head slightly. "No. I called Dianne and said something had come up at work. That she'd have to go on her own. She was so angry. She called me a coward and slammed down the phone."

He stared quietly out over the floor for so long, Barbara began to wonder if he'd finished.

"An hour later I got the phone call. Dianne had tried to pass a car and apparently lost control. She ran head-on into a bridge abutment. They both died instantly."

"Jaromir..." she began.

"But here's the odd thing," Jaromir continued. "According to the police report, there were no skid marks, as if she didn't try to brake."

Jaromir's face sagged in sadness. His dark eyebrows arched up over his hooded, smoky gray eyes.

Barbara turned away from the man and looked blankly at the far wall. "And then he contacted you. The *Mester*."

"Yes. An ad in the newspaper. What did I have to lose? I was already dead inside."

"But there have been many agents. Why were you selected as his spy, his aide?"

"It was during the Fitz and Welser affair. Did Zoltan tell you about it?"

Barbara nodded. "When Victor killed the agents."

"Yes." He nodded but said nothing more.

"You are guilty over this. You are reluctant to tell me what happened."

Jaromir switched his gaze to Barbara and then turned back to stare across the floor.

"I didn't know Fitz that well, but Welser was different." He shrugged. "We were friends I guess, as friendly as you could get at our annual nightmare gatherings. I heard about Fitz being killed and that they were looking for Welser. Welser had been contacting the agents he knew. Wanted us to rebel." Jaromir shook his head slightly. "Silly bastard. He knew he was doomed from the start."

She recoiled as she realized the truth. "You're the one that tipped off Victor. Where Welser was hiding."

Jaromir said nothing, but Barbara felt him tumbling into darkness.

"Agent Jaromir," Barbara said sharply.

Jaromir turned to her in surprise.

"You can do nothing about your past, but you want to make amends."

Jaromir said nothing, but stared evenly into her eyes, which glistened with tears.

"Then let's start with Sibyl. You met on one of your visits."

"Yes." Jaromir nodded. "At a bar up on the Pleasure Floor."

Barbara glanced over the vast brightly lit space in front of them. "Of course. With a live-in workforce of a thousand, there has to be more to the complex than a warren of cubicles."

Jaromir nodded. "This is just the work floor. There are three tiers above us. Apartments for the workers, the Pleasure Floor above that, and above that the Garden." He gave a wry smile. "Wait until you see your apartment. It's beautiful." He shook his head. "I don't know what you've got, lady, but Justin wants it. Bad."

"You've seen it? My apartment?"

Jaromir turned away. "Yes. It was Sibyl's."

Barbara nodded slowly. "I see. I'm her replacement."

"It would seem so."

"You met in a bar. That doesn't sound very romantic."

"Well, it wasn't just any bar. The Aerie is in an upper room of the Pleasure Floor. Only top management personnel are allowed."

"And visiting agents."

"Yes," Jaromir nodded. "And visiting agents. When I saw her..." he stopped. "She was gorgeous."

"You mentioned that."

"Yes, but not just physically. She had an aura around her or something. When I sat down next to her she fixed me with these great, sad brown eyes." He glanced at her thoughtfully. "She was a lot like you. Somehow she got me talking. And, for the first time in many, many years, I felt something good, something kind."

"You fell in love."

"Yes. What's that old Bill Evans song? Stan Getz did it."

"I have a feeling that was before my time."

Jaromir smiled slightly. "Yes, I suppose so. It went, 'The two lonely people sit silently staring.' But then suddenly we weren't."

Barbara looked at him quizzically.

"Weren't lonely. We went back to her apartment." His eyes strayed to the roof. "To hold someone, to love her, after so many years." He glanced over at Barbara. "Do you know what that can mean?"

"I think so," she said softly. "But weren't you prohibited from touching anyone?"

"Hardly," Jaromir said. "We were part of the team. We were encouraged to take advantage of all the pleasures available."

"Including prostitutes."

"Among a bewildering array of other things, yes."

"And you were able to keep your relationship secret?"

"As I said, I believe so. Sibyl's status meant she had a secure apartment. Private access and protected from bugging. And we were very careful. And then while I was away—two years ago I guess—she challenged Justin at a meeting of the Committee."

"You mentioned the Committee before. Who are they?"

Jaromir glanced around nervously. "I know very little. Some people even question if it's real, but it is. I've been with Justin, as security, when he has met with them in various crypts in the caves. There are seven members plus Justin."

"Did you recognize the members?"

Jaromir shook his head. "No. Each was fully cloaked. I couldn't get close to them, even with my ring. They are all jewel owners. Sort of a board of directors of the Company."

Barbara looked up in surprise. "Like businessmen? Investors?"

Jaromir laughed mirthlessly. "Oh yes. This operation is not cheap. Money, and lots of it, is required. And the board represents a very wealthy set of investors who are used to getting a good return on their money." He paused. "And they do," he said quietly. "Servitude pays dividends to those who are served."

"Are they…like you? Do they have an extended life span?"

Jaromir raised his hands. "I know nothing more about them, and even Sibyl said very little."

"But she challenged Justin in front of them."

Jaromir nodded.

"And the Committee—they sided with Justin."

"As I said, I wasn't here then, but yes. That is what I understand."

"And he retaliated."

Jaromir nodded. "I only heard about it when I got back. It had all gone down shortly after I left. During the time I was gone, we could not communicate, so I knew nothing about it." Jaromir paused. "But when I got back she had been disfigured and isolated in her hut."

"Did you see her?"

He glanced at Barbara, shame in his smoky eyes. "No. I only heard what happened. After Justin denounced her, he had her paraded through the offices and then the Comfort Floor, tied to a throne, so everyone could see for themselves the result of defiance." He shuddered. "Most could only look for a few moments."

Jaromir looked back at Barbara. "We will talk more about this later. But I have been instructed to show you the full complex so you can become acquainted with all of our considerable amenities. As I said, there are many things about the Company that are quite captivating, appealing. Lovely even."

"I see." She turned from the rail, her back to the work floor and cocked her head at Jaromir. She smiled slightly. "So you were sent here to persuade me to join the club? Kind of a good cop, bad cop strategy."

Jaromir gave his noncommittal shrug once again.

Barbara raised her palm. "Don't say it," Barbara said. "A man's got to eat."

He chuckled uneasily. "Justin thought you would feel more comfortable seeing our establishment before he meets with you this afternoon."

"How very kind of him."

Jaromir looked at her sharply. "Isn't it though? He feels that you need a little time to get used to your new home."

Suddenly Jaromir's head drew back slightly, and Barbara sensed a shift in the still air around him, a tiny distortion. And another presence. She turned and faced Jaromir, moving closer to him, studying his face. The drooping eyelids drew open, revealing sparks of alarm in his smoky eyes.

"And he also regrets the circumstances of your meeting," Jaromir set mechanically. "He feels that you and he got off to an unfortunate start."

"Is something wrong, Agent Jaromir?"

Jaromir raised his hand as if to fend her off.

"Justin feels that you do not fully understand the nature and nobility of our undertaking here," Jaromir stammered, taking a small step backward. "He is confident that you will join us once you better comprehend our mission."

Barbara's jewel throbbed rhythmically at her throat. She probed the man in front of her, but only his fear leaked through a cloak she could not pierce, a cloak she sensed was not of Jaromir's making. Any hope, any power, was drained from him, leaving a sad and weakened man.

"And you, Agent Jaromir? Do you understand your noble mission?"

"Of course," Jaromir replied, with forced enthusiasm. "I have toiled loyally for the cause for more than sixty years," he said, regaining his composure. "I am fully committed to our great work here."

Barbara lowered her eyes and turned with her back to the work floor so that she was again leaning against the railing. "I am glad to hear that, Agent Jaromir. And I am sure Lord Justin is as well."

Jaromir swallowed nervously.

Another force had shrouded Jaromir, closing him to her but also filling him with terror. *We seem to have been joined by a virtual visitor,* she thought. *But who?*

"Thank you, Agent Jaromir, for your orientation. Now, I believe you were going to provide me with a guided tour of the Company complex, were you not?"

Chapter 15

THEY WALKED TO THE SHAFT they had used to ascend to the observation deck the day before, moving upward in the same unsettling manner, seemingly floating on thin air, until they again glided to a stop. This time Barbara stepped forward with slightly less apprehension, even though the floor far below her was now just a tiny black square. They stood in a broad hall that ran around the elevator shaft. At regular intervals, high-ceilinged hallways extended from the central landing in long lines.

"The residential floor," Jaromir informed Barbara. "Your apartment is at the far end of this hall." He nodded down a hallway that tapered to a blank wall a hundred yards away.

"Shall we?"

"Actually no," Jaromir said. "I want to show you the remaining floors. I will take you to your room on our way down. So you can prepare, I guess."

Barbara eyebrows arched. "And what is it I am preparing for?"

"For your conference this afternoon. With Justin."

"Ah," Barbara nodded slightly. "Justin."

"Yes."

Barbara turned from the empty hallway and faced Jaromir, whose eyes darted nervously from her gaze.

"What happened earlier? When we were talking on the balcony."

Jaromir's feet shifted uneasily. "I don't know what you mean."

"Oh, I think you do. It was me and you. And then it wasn't. Someone joined us." She sensed the panic rise in the man and waited, still looking him in the face, until it subsided.

"Was it Justin?"

Jaromir stared over her shoulder, his jaw rhythmically clenching and unclenching. "It has never happened here before."

"Was it Justin?" she repeated.

Jaromir shook his head. "No. He's too busy to bother with me right now."

"I see," Barbara said quietly. "Meijer?"

Jaromir gave a short, biter laugh. "That little swine. Hardly." He took a deep breath, in and out. "Garripoli. He's Justin's eyes and ears when Justin is preoccupied. Which he often is." A small smile played across his lips. "Especially after what you put him through."

"Ah. We got his attention, did we?"

"Not 'we.' You. He could have handled the others. He had it all worked out. How he would salvage the agents he could and kill the rest." Jaromir glanced at Barbara, something new in his grey eyes. "What he didn't plan on was you."

Barbara grasped the legs of her robe, nodded her head, and gave a slight curtsy. "Thank you. I guess."

"You were something." Now the look was unmistakable. He gazed at Barbara with respect verging on awe.

Barbara waved her hand at him playfully. "I bet you say that to all the girls."

Jaromir looked away, his face set. "And despite what he says, make no mistake: when you destroyed the black stone, you weakened him."

"I'm glad to hear it."

"I don't know how long Justin has been here, but he started the gemstone project. And you have effectively killed it. He invested a lot of his power into that stone, and he had entrusted it to the *Mester*. When you took it, Justin was enraged. I heard that his shrieking rang through the entire Company for an hour. The next day he confronted what was left of the Ugly Master. Justin killed him. Cut off his head."

"So he is dead? Garripoli said he's alive. You heard him, right?"

"Like the rest of them, Garripoli is a fucking liar," Justin said evenly. "The *Mester* is dead. His head is preserved in Justin's office. Meijer saw it."

Barbara stared at the empty elevator entrance.

"That seems like a popular interior decorating item around here."

Jaromir snorted. "Just make sure yours isn't next. I'm sure he'd love to have your head in a jar, your red hair floating across your face."

Barbara shivered slightly. "Okay, so back to our conversation on the balcony. We were talking and Garripoli jumped in. You felt him, and so did I. You changed your tune pretty quickly. Had he heard the rest of what you said?"

"I don't know." His voice was low, shaking. "I hope not. Things are bad enough."

"Can they hear us now?"

Jaromir shrugged. "They can, of course. They can hear anyone anywhere. But I don't think they're listening. I can usually feel it." He raised his left hand. A blue stone, set in a heavy gold ring, glowed dully.

"Your stone," Barbara said. "It is ice blue."

Jaromir raised his hand and stared at the jewel. "It's beautiful, isn't it?"

"It is. And does it freeze water at a touch?"

Jaromir looked at her, startled. "How could you know that?"

Her eyes narrowed. "I am a woman of mystery," she said in an unidentifiable accent, possibly Eastern European. "A necromancer with preternatural empathic powers."

Jaromir's eyes opened wider.

Barbara laughed. "Actually, nothing that exotic. Zoltan told me how different stones had different powers, abilities, related to their color. He mentioned how one agent's ice blue stone could freeze a bottle of water solid in seconds."

Jaromir gave a small smile. "I see. Very handy if you are short ice cubes. But no, I don't sense that they are listening. Besides, they have other things on their mind."

"Such as?"

"Barbara, I still don't think you understand the damage you've done to Justin's little operation here." Jaromir looked uneasily around the landing.

"Let's go up to the next level."

"The Pleasure Floor?"

Jaromir nodded. "Where your most fantastic wishes are realized."

"I doubt it," Barbara said. "Don't imagine they offer escaping the prison."

They turned back toward the shaft and walked back to the center and stood still.

"Barbara," Jaromir said falteringly as they began to drift upward. She realized he had used her name for the first time. "There is no escape. Believe me. The only way out of here is the main gate. And if somehow you could get through that unnoticed, which you can't, you are faced with an impossible maze of caves and tunnels that he shifts at his will."

"There is no other way?"

"None," he said as they glided to a halt.

"Maybe," she said in a whisper. "Maybe not."

They stepped into a wall of music punctuated by the shouts and screams of people milling around the central landing. The smells of popcorn, marijuana and something sweet she couldn't put her finger on overwhelmed her. Neon signs glared garishly along wide streets. The red outline of a naked woman blinked off and on. On the other side of the street, a naked man winked back in bright blue. Glowing cocktail glasses tilted over doors into bars. Above several other entrances, giant red lips opened in a broad smile, the tip of a tongue moving sensually from side to side. A gold and silver opium pipe glittered from a signboard standing outside a pulsing entranceway. A gaping archway on her right opened onto an acre of slot machines, roulette wheels, and craps tables, all crowded with figures talking animatedly, laughing.

Barbara stood staring at the scene, riveted. It was about as far from the hum and efficiency of the work floor as she could imagine. With a start, Barbara realized the crowd of people surging around them wore khakis, plaid shirts, baggy shorts. Three women swayed together down a street, two were dressed in identical skintight silver leggings and sheer pink tops. The other wore nothing.

"I see the dress code is somewhat looser up here," she commented.

A man wearing aviator sunglasses, his long blond hair tied back in a ponytail lurched toward the elevator. He stumbled and careened into Barbara before righting himself.

"Fuck you," he muttered thickly, staggering toward the elevator entrance.

She stared at the back of his Hawaiian shirt as he pitched headfirst into the elevator and descended softly to the floor below.

"Boy's night out," she commented.

"You want to see more? We have time to walk down some of the streets. It's not all as bad as this." He nodded to the area on the other side of the elevator shaft. "There are some great restaurants over there, and even a gym."

Barbara's gaze raked the scene in front of her. She gave a quick shake of her head. "I think I get it." She turned and walked back to the elevator, followed by Jaromir, and walked in.

"Up," she said.

If the Pleasure Floor was unsettling, the Garden was a crushing disappointment. Barbara had pictured an underground grotto, ferns and moss growing from deep caves, stone pathways winding among tropical plants, wooden park benches, the sound of gently rushing water and the damp smell of life. Instead, the Garden turned out to be a series of five small theme parks, each with an entranceway that opened from a central courtyard. You could take your pick: a simulated walk through the jungle, a virtual reality tour of the Himalayas, or a float down through the Grand Canyon. Then there was an electronic redwood forest, which seemed pretty real until your hand went through the illusion, and an English garden, studded with topiaries of rabbits and deer, the flagstone path lined by perfectly trimmed hedges and beds of violets and tulips. It was only when Barbara realized there were no smells, not a trace of heavy lily fragrance or the faintest scent of roses, that she realized it was a sophisticated hologram.

While the Disneyland-like illusions were of little interest to Barbara, the fountain in the main courtyard was very real. A semi-circular chromium railing ran around a deep pool fed by a brass culvert six feet in diameter that emerged some four feet below them from a plain stone wall. A great gout of water gushed from the glistening pipe into the pool, which was lit with shifting multi-colored lights shining from the bottom.

"Our water supply," Jaromir said, nodding at the fountain.

Barbara stood by the railing and watched the water rushing out of the huge brass pipe. She gazed at it silently for several moments. She had already realized that whatever her emerging powers as an empath were, they were confined here to the precise dimensions of the Company compound. She could sense nothing outside of the walls surrounding her, as if no world existed outside of this place, a giant cube encased in lead.

But here, here she felt something, a slight softening, a tiny crack in the thick metal walls.

"What is it?" Jaromir asked.

Barbara looked away from the spouting water.

"Sorry," she said. "Just got lost in the water. Soothing."

"I guess so," Jaromir replied. He fidgeted with his ring nervously. "But we have to go. You cannot be late."

She saw the worry and fear in his eyes.

"You're right. I should go." She smiled. "And get prepared."

But for what exactly? she wondered.

Chapter 16

THE MEN'S PROGRESS WAS FRUSTRATINGLY slow. As Friesen pointed out, looking for hidden passageways meant they had to painstakingly feel their way along every foot of the cave walls, on both sides, to ensure they didn't miss an obscured doorway. Even armed with the knowledge that their way out relied on discovering passages they could not see, again and again they found themselves at junctions where two or more very real tunnels connected with no clear way to determine which to take. While they initially stayed left when in doubt, too many times they would travel an hour or more and find no hidden passage, which generally meant they had taken the wrong fork. They had to make their way back along the track they had followed and then try other routes.

On Maphaela's advice, they built simple three-stone cairns at each intersection to make sure they were able to retrace their steps after deciding they had taken a wrong turn.

"Nature can occasionally place one rock on another," he said. "But never three."

Zoltan monitored the time. It had been nearly twelve hours since they had left the vaulted chamber for the second time. Exhaustion was catching up with them all.

As they entered the next gallery, a large round room lined with carved rock, Zoltan called the group to a halt.

"Gentlemen," he said, his quiet voice echoing in the domed chamber.

"It is late afternoon. None of us has had any sleep for thirty-six hours. We must rest."

The other men looked at him wearily.

"Damn," Friesen said. "And I went off and forgot my sleeping bag. What was I thinking?"

Malik looked at Friesen. "I would be happy to cover you in my *hajoori* if you are cold."

Friesen looked up in surprise, and then smiled slowly. "Malik, is there a word in Punjabi for sarcasm?"

Malik looked upward, concentrating.

"Yes, I think so: *Tirasamā* I believe is quite close in meaning." He looked quizzically at Friesen. "Why do you ask?"

Friesen threw up his hands and laughed aloud.

Relief coursed through Zoltan. At least spirits were still high.

"Shall we sleep for four hours?" he asked.

Kwan and Maphaela had already slid down the walls and were sitting on the stone floor, their eyelids drooping.

"And I believe I have an idea that may help us reduce the time we are spending taking wrong turns."

All three men looked at him, their exhaustion forgotten for the moment.

"We have found that our gems are receivers. Tuned, it seems, to a narrow frequency used by the *Mester* and, as we have learned, Justin, yes? To transmit messages and images to us through the black stone that we destroyed in the crypt."

The men nodded as he spoke.

"With that stone removed, that frequency we share is clear. We are free of those transmissions, but can we use our gems to communicate amongst ourselves?"

Friesen rolled his powerful shoulders. "Even if we could," he asked. "What good would it do?"

"If we can reliably send messages to each other, when we are faced with passageway choices, we can break into two teams and explore two routes simultaneously. When one team finds a hidden door, they report back and we all join them."

"We could cover twice as much ground," Malik observed.

"Hopefully, that would be the case," Zoltan agreed, pulling his turquoise gem from his vest pocket. "But can we establish a network?"

Friesen raised his hand and made it into a fist so that his purple jewel, mounted in a platinum ring, pointed toward the group. "Worth a try."

Malik's amber jewel, set in his maroon turban, had proven to provide the best light for illuminating their routes. He broadened the beam to enclose the small group in a circle of light.

Kwan held up his chartreuse stone, attached to a fine gold chain around his neck. Maphaela drew his orange gem, attached to an intricately woven leather thong and glowing brightly like a tiny torch, from inside his shirt.

"In the crypt," Zoltan said, "Justin used our own gems to insinuate his illusion into our minds."

Next to him, Friesen stirred angrily at the memory.

"But also, Barbara, she called us to imagine other images, yes? Did you not all feel it, hear it?"

"Yes," Malik said quietly. "She bid us to feel. To remember who we truly were."

Zoltan nodded. "Please, gentlemen, close your eyes while grasping your gems. And attempt, if you will, to empty your minds. I ask you to concentrate. If you hear or see a message from me, please do not shout it out, yes?"

The men remained upbeat on the surface, but he knew they were worn out. It was only a matter of time before emotional strain and the physical hardship would lead to despair. Or worse. He didn't know if the experiment was doomed or a stroke of brilliance, but he was pretty sure that their survival depended on it working. He took a breath and the domed gallery became utterly quiet. Only the faint dripping of water in one of the passages disturbed the silence.

Malik raised his head sharply and Kwan and Friesen nodded.

"Let's open our eyes now," Zoltan said. "Gentlemen?"

"It always seems impossible until it's done." Malik said solemnly. "Is that correct?"

"Exactly!" Maphaela exclaimed. Kwan smiled, and Friesen nodded in agreement.

Zoltan smiled broadly. "Yes."

"Nelson Mandela, is it not?" Maphaela asked.

"Indeed. And he should know, yes?"

But I didn't hear it," Maphaela said. "Or read it. I just knew your thought."

Zoltan beamed. "Wonderful. I think we have discovered a power of great value. But I believe we should practice a bit before bed, yes?"

Over the next thirty minutes, the men explored the communication capacities of their rings. Zoltan picked up thoughts from greater distances and with greater clarity, and his transmissions, along with those from Maphaela and Kwan, were stronger than those of Malik and Friesen. Their experiments showed that images from Maphaela, Zoltan and Kwan were detectable from at least one hundred yards, no matter how many twists and turns they took. For the other two, their communications were received up to about a hundred and fifty feet, and less if they were deeper in the caves.

"Gentlemen," Zoltan said as the men congregated in the vaulted chamber. "I think we can sleep knowing we will be able to explore in teams of two. Friesen and Maphaela have already discovered a hidden passage. Tomorrow we will start there."

Kwan slumped against a wall. "When we reach a fork and cannot determine the correct route," Zoltan continued, "Maphaela and Friesen will take one branch, and Malik and Kwan the other. I will remain at the junction and receive and retransmit messages, yes?"

He looked over the group. Friesen nodded wearily. Maphaela was already asleep on the floor.

"I will stand guard," Malik declared.

Zoltan's knees weakened, and he held himself upright by leaning against the side of the cave. He had to stay awake. He fought to keep his eyes open, but his eyelids didn't seem to get the message.

"No, no," he protested, holding up his wrist. "I have the watch." He rallied and forced his eyes open wide.

"That is easy to fix, Mr. DeAngelo," Malik smiled, extending his hand.

"But you..." Zoltan's words slurred slightly. What had he meant to say?

"I believe I can determine how to operate a watch, Mr. DeAngelo." Malik held his palm flat. "Please remove the watch and give it to me."

Zoltan fumbled with the leather strap at his wrist, his eyes closed. *I wonder what the odds are of escaping?* he wondered. *A hundred to one?* He handed the watch over, barely aware when Malik took it gently from his hand. *And then rescuing Barbara? A thousand to one?*

He only vaguely remembered sinking onto the stone floor and rolling against the wall before falling asleep.

Chapter 17

JAROMIR TOOK BARBARA DOWN THE two floors to the residential section and led her to her apartment. At the entranceway, a large rectangle outlined in glowing red, he pushed a sequence of buttons, and the door slid upward. "I will not be taking you to Justin's office," he said. "Meijer will come for you…" he looked at the watch on his wrist. "In exactly forty-seven minutes."

Meijer, Barbara thought. *Perfect. One son-of-a-bitch escorts me to see an even bigger one.* As she entered the apartment, Jaromir touched her tentatively, carefully on her shoulder. She looked into his drawn, ashen face.

"Please, don't be late." He hesitated. "And beware of Meijer. He is a cruel man."

Barbara tilted her head slightly. "Thank you."

Jaromir stood awkwardly.

"Is there something else?"

"Just…" he stammered. "Just be careful of Justin. He can be very persuasive."

She smiled. "Thank you for your concern, Agent Jaromir. I will keep that in mind."

Jaromir nodded uncertainly. "I will see you tomorrow."

"For our visit to Sibyl."

"Yes. Well, have a nice day."

He turned and walked swiftly along the corridor toward the elevator.

A nice day, Barbara thought ruefully. *I'm heading into a face-to-face confrontation with a man whose lust for dominance is boundless. Who views rape and brutality as entertainment. Whose powers are beyond my imagining.* The door slid shut with a hiss. *Getting out alive is about the best I can hope for.*

As Jaromir had promised, the apartment was sumptuous. At first, though she knew it made no sense, she thought the broad picture windows in the living area opened onto a rolling meadow, glowing with wildflowers nodding in a breeze and lit by a warm, glowing sun. It wasn't until she looked closely at the dial underneath that she realized she could choose one of twenty-five settings, from seashore to mountains. Her bedroom had two shuttered windows. When she drew the shutters open, birds chirped from a forest that extended as far as she could see. A warm shower was already running in the enormous bathroom that opened off the bedroom. A table filled with covered dishes was set next to the bed. She smelled ham and something more delicate, possibly lobster.

She stared at the food and recalled reading somewhere that Louis XVI had been given a sumptuous meal the night before he was beheaded. If she remembered right, it included chicken, beef, pastries, pureed turnips and lots of wine. *I get the wine,* she thought, *but turnips?*

Her clothes had been freshly laundered and folded carefully on the bed. Barbara took a warm shower and slipped gratefully into her black jeans and hoodie. Whatever was coming, at least she was dressed for the occasion. She pulled a white leather chair from the living room, turned it toward the doorway and pulled her jewel from underneath her hoodie and grasped it in her right hand. Clearing her mind and concentrating her power, she formed an invisible protective aura around her.

Barbara focused her gaze on the door to the apartment, letting her eyes close slightly as she breathed deeply. Her heart rate slowed and she sank further into a state of calm and relaxation. Without warning, the door slid upward and Meijer stepped into the apartment. He saw her staring at him and took a step back. Barbara enjoyed the look of confusion that flashed across his face.

"Next time, Mr. Meijer, it would be courteous of you to knock first."

Meijer quickly regained his composure. "Come on," he said impatiently, jerking his head toward the open doorway. "He's waiting."

Barbara had expected to be led to the elevator shaft and ascend to some penthouse, but instead once they stepped inside the tube, they plummeted downward. The black floor rushed toward her, and Barbara found herself squeezing her eyes shut as they hurtled toward it. But there was no crash or hideous collision with the floor. Instead, they passed silently through the tiles and kept descending. The glassed sides of the shaft gave way to gleaming steel walls. They slowed and glided toward a solid metal floor. She could almost hear a clank as they settled to a stop. In front of them, they faced a single white doorway, about three yards high.

Meijer gave a curt nod, and Barbara walked slowly forward. As she exited the elevator, the door in front of her turned light green and then disappeared, revealing a short corridor with two doors on each side. Meijer stepped inside and motioned her forward. As she entered, the door to the elevator shaft reappeared behind her, solid white like dense porcelain. Meijer walked ahead and stopped at the second door on the right of the hallway and waited impatiently for her. When she reached his side, Meijer stood at attention and nodded. The door glided upwards.

Inside, Justin leaned back in a green leather upholstered office chair, beaming.

"Come in, come in," he said jovially, looking as if their visit was an unexpected pleasure.

Justin rose from behind the desk and waved to a small round table in the wood-paneled office. Behind him a wood fireplace crackled invitingly. He strode over to the table and pulled out one of the chairs.

"Please, do sit down."

Barbara stood just inside the entrance and examined the man in front of her. He wore a dark blue business suit and a red silk tie, every inch the corporate CEO. His broad smile and twinkling blue eyes contrasted darkly with the twisted face she remembered in the crypt. *Would the real Justin please stand up?* she thought.

He turned the chair out a bit more from the table, welcoming her into the office. "I think it's time we talk, don't you?" His eyes crinkled at the corners. "Strictly business, I assure you."

Barbara raised her chin slightly, disdaining his overture, and walked forward. She ignored the proffered chair and went to the far side of table. She drew out a chair and sat, never moving her eyes from Justin's face.

Justin's eyes flickered, but his smile didn't waver. "Suit yourself." He turned to Meijer. "You can go now. Ms. Steubenville and I have a great deal to talk about. Just the two of us."

Meijer nodded and backed out through the door.

"My name is Barbara," she said. "Ms. Steubenville doesn't live here anymore."

"Ah, yes," Justin nodded, his smile broadening. "As you pointed out in the caves."

"And may I call you Justin?"

"Of course," Justin said, shaking his head in embarrassment. "My apologies." He reached across the table. "We haven't been properly introduced, have we?"

Barbara looked at the proffered hand and then shifted her eyes to his face. Her left hand covered her jewel under her sweatshirt. She studied him as she took his hand.

She remembered the blinding rage that had swept through Justin in the caves. She wondered if she could induce it again. She didn't have many advantages, but being able to exploit his rage and fragile ego might at least throw him off his game.

Justin's smile broadened as they shook hands. He tried to withdraw but Barbara effortlessly held his grasp firmly. Confusion froze the grin on his face, and then she felt the red haze of anger surge through his hand. His blazing blue eyes dilated and stretched oblong.

He threw his head back and laughed, his pupils returning to normal. "Touché," he said.

Barbara released his hand. "As I said, my name is Barbara. I'd like to say it's a pleasure to meet you, but it isn't."

Justin settled back into his chair, still chuckling, his eyes bright and smiling.

"I do hope you change your mind. I think we could have a good deal of fun together."

"I doubt it."

Justin sat in the empty chair he had pulled out for Barbara and leaned back, his hands clasped behind his head. "I believe my assistant, Jaromir, has passed on my apologies, has he not? It is so unfortunate we got off to such a poor start."

Barbara folded her hands in front of her on the table and leaned forward, concentrating on remaining mentally blank. She felt the man probing, looking for weakness, chinks. He was uncertain. Cautious. She could read his thoughts as clearly as if he spoke them: *What do I have here?*

"What do you want with me?" Barbara asked.

Justin took a deep breath. "I run an extensive business out of the Company compound here, as you have no doubt observed. Like any business, it requires a great deal of energy, new ideas, new blood. And like any good businessman, I am always on the lookout for men"—his eyes twinkled again—"and women who have the knowledge, skills, and power to help me carry out our mission."

"I see. And what exactly would that mission be?" She returned his smile. "To promote global misery? Evil for fun and profit? To encourage and justify corruption?"

"Oh, please…Barbara," he said, his eyes dancing with mirth. "Don't be such a child. You misunderstand. You have been fed the usual line of virtuous platitudes and lies I am afraid." He sighed deeply. "But I don't blame you."

He leaned forward and propped his chin in his hands, jutting his chin out slightly, assessing her. "I think you can best understand our enterprise as a very large service organization."

"I see. Sort of like a big Rotary Club."

"Precisely. In fact we have a number of prominent Rotarians on our Board of Directors."

"Is it the truth? Fair to all concerned? Build friendships and be beneficial to all? That sort of thing?"

Justin beamed. "Something like that, yes."

"But your agenda is somewhat narrower, it would appear."

"Not at all. It might appear that way, but actually we are deeply committed to many of the same goals: building a better world through the promotion of peace, good governance and a global meritocracy." He sat straight up in his chair, his hands flat on the table. "We are part of an overall movement working to enrich and stabilize society." He opened both hands. "Look at the chaos that is enveloping the globe. What can be done?"

"Hmm. Reinstitute rape and pillage as a means of governance?" Goading him was rather entertaining. More importantly she could sense his growing annoyance.

Justin lifted his left hand and rubbed his forehead in exasperation. "I have already explained, have I not? That was simply a bit of theatre. Some entertainment for the agents." He leaned forward with an air of confidentiality. "Perhaps it was a mistake. But that is irrelevant.

"What we are doing here is nothing short of saving humankind. Ours is a grand and noble mission. We identify and develop natural leaders, regardless of race, class or gender." His red lips curled in a sheepish grin. "Though we are admittedly somewhat weak in the latter category." His face became serious and he spoke clearly and emphatically. "But our goal is as simple is at is profound: we seek out those whose inborn courage, intelligence and loftiness of soul sets them apart from lesser beings. We strive to create a new society built by and for the most gifted of humanity, to build a meritocracy that will rule for a thousand years." As he spoke, his voice rose dramatically, and Barbara sensed fervor growing inside him that matched his voice.

"And this meritocracy you are creating. It would rule, brutally if necessary, over the rest of us?" Barbara asked evenly. "Those of us not so gifted?"

"Please!" Justin spat. "You must stop thinking of yourself as one of *them*, of a member of the horde with its mediocrity, foolishness; its stupidity and cupidity; its weakness and hesitancy!" he thundered. He breathed hard as contempt swept from him in such waves of revulsion that she recoiled, sickened by the man's dark, roiling hatred.

His breathing slowed. His hands, clenched on the table in tight fists, relaxed. He opened them flat as he sat back and swiveled in his chair toward a blank wall behind him.

"I'm afraid I am not doing an adequate job of explaining our great mission,' Justin said, almost apologetically. "May I share with you a brief presentation that will provide you a bit more about our enterprise."

"Do I have a choice?" Barbara asked evenly.

The wall in front of them became a three-dimensional screen. Across it, knights in armor, pendants flying from their lances, rode sedately across a landscape of wheat fields, peasants in the background threshing the grain and stacking the straw in shocks.

"From time immemorial," a deep, mellifluous male voice intoned as the picture shifted to a group of men dressed in robes of various colors sitting on stone risers around a man in a flowing white toga and wearing a bronze helmet with a burgundy crest. The man raised his hands to his listeners as the voiceover continued. "The times of stability and greatest human development, whether in ancient Athens..." the picture shifted to a group of Chinese men sitting at tables in a great hall writing with brushes on rolls of white paper "...or seventh-century China, were when systems were carefully constructed to identify and promote the worthiest to positions of government and economic leadership."

She could feel her mind slowing; a barely detectable quiescence crept over her as if she had been drugged. She slid her hand to her gem under her hoody and felt the warmth extend upward and clear her head.

The picture shifted to a scene from a medieval community, the villagers dancing merrily to in the square to a simple bagpipe, flute and fiddle. "During these times there was peace, prosperity and good government." The knights reappeared, riding among the villagers, who waved and saluted them. "The masters of these times ruled sagely and provided security for all." Now the statue of David appeared, the camera sweeping around his perfect body, and then to the ceiling of the Sistine Chapel. "Man's noblest ideas, and greatest achievements whether in art or philosophy," Aristotle appeared, lecturing a group of young men clustered at his feet, "occurred during these periods when the *aristoi* held power."

Barbara stared transfixed as the wall exploded in machine gun fire and the screams of men dying in trenches as shells rained around them. A mushroom cloud swept upward in a great gout of fire followed by photos of bodies charred and blackened. The voice became melancholy. "The golden eras ended not with the failure of the rulers," a mob appeared in what might have been Moscow, bellowing their hatred and carrying red banners, "but when those ruled displaced their masters. Sometimes these revolts were political and sometimes economic." A parade of men and women on strike swelled down a nineteenth-century avenue carrying placards. "But in all cases," the voice said darkly, "the results were the same." Clips of starving children, too hungry to cry; boats of refugees overturned, their passengers crying out as they drowned; sickening scenes of children bleeding in a school massacre; an apartment building under a barrage of bombs. One after another, the horrors flashed, the blood real, the screams ringing through the room.

Barbara sat, shaken and horrified but unable to look away. Finally the screams and explosions stopped, replaced by a sun rising above a green hill. Silhouetted against the clear blue sky, a knight rode over the hills directly toward Barbara, his visor open to reveal a strong, handsome face with a short reddish beard. "We at the Company are committed to returning the world to sanity, to prosperity…" the voice swelled, "To a new era where those most fit to rule are reinstated to their rightful place." The knight had stopped, seemingly only a few yards in front of Barbara. He smiled warmly at her, the horse switching its tail and snorting quietly.

"We invite you to join us," the deep voice concluded, "in this greatest of human and social endeavors, the success of which will determine the very survival of our species."

The knight nodded and his visor fell in front of his face. He turned his snorting steed and charged back up the road. Words, written in deep blue, scrolled upward as the knight departed. "Welcome to The Company," the words read, "and we hope you will help us achieve our mission." The knight disappeared over the hill and the screen changed to black.

Words appeared as if branded in red:

Our Mission: To advance human development and contribute to global stability through the identification, training and elevation of outstanding leaders in all fields and to support this great enterprise by influencing public opinion and creating formal and informal institutions favorable to the creation of a New Golden Age.

Barbara sat silently, staring at the mission statement emblazoned on the wall. Slowly it faded, and the wall returned to white. The spectacle had been mesmerizing. She knew that an emotional manipulation strand had been woven into the presentation and had resisted it, but she still felt as if she were returning from a dream so real that her ears rang with the screams of the dying and still smelled the sweat of the horse.

"*Aristoi*," Justin said, breaking the silence. "Do you know what it means?"

Barbara said nothing.

"It means the best. The best in terms of birth, rank, morality. It is the origin of the word aristocracy, The rule of the best. Like the great civilizations of the past, that is what we are building, here, now."

Justin sat back nodding. "Yes, the best. The most noble, the most creative. The best humans. The best and brightest. Five percent. And the rest who lived in those societies, which we all recognize as the pinnacle of human social achievement? They were commoners with no rights. Laborers, women, foreigners, and yes, slaves. Many slaves, who understood that their owners were superior in every way and that the rule of the *aristoi* was good for all concerned—the slave, the master, the community."

Justin's eyes glittered brightly again. "The great philosophers understood this. Aristotle widely taught that slaves were clearly and inalterably inferior. How could they compete with the bloodlines and rich education of the nobility? They were born to serve; the nobility to rule."

Barbara turned her gaze away from the blank wall and looked at Justin. She realized her hand still covered her jewel. She breathed deeply. Slowly the spell broke, shattering as she concentrated on the warmth of her gem, as she strove to emerge from the trance Justin had woven. She knew enough about hypnosis to realize that an external oscillation mechanism had established confluence with her own brain, pushing it deep into the theta and gamma bands where he could feed her unconscious without resistance.

"Born to rule," She said dully. "Bloodlines." Barbara's gaze dropped toward the table as she spoke. She sat quietly, studying her long fingers. How remarkable, these fingers of mine, she thought. They can manipulate, caress, strangle. Craft beautiful things. They can touch gently, lovingly. Or they can strike and claw with hatred, anger, inflict pain.

Justin's probe was hardly noticeable, like an EEG sensor. How had she reacted? Had the oscillator fully overcome her conscious mind? Had the presentation worked its magic? Had she recognized her true nobility?

Barbara looked up at the glowing white ceiling. "Thank you for that. It really does help me better understand your operation."

Justin gave a cautious smile.

She gestured around the room. "This is quite a complex you have here. I wouldn't have thought you would need such a system if, as you say, the nobility naturally rises to the top, the losers to the bottom." She paused and gave a small shrug. "I guess they just need a little help along the way?"

Puzzlement flashed across Justin's face.

"Isn't that what you do here? I noted that you have an education division. I've been in those schools," she said. "I saw how they work, making the rich think they succeed because of merit, the poor fail because of their stupidity, their inferiority." She looked up into Justin's face. "I just didn't know why, or who it all served. Now I do."

She held Justin's flickering gaze.

"But that's just for starters, isn't it? You encourage churches that preach that the elect are divinely intended to rule, that the wealthy are smiled on by deities. You make laws that ensure money is shifted from generation to generation and sell the myth that the rich have gained their status through hard work and talent."

Justin's full lips curled upward in a broad smile, showing off his perfect white teeth. "By George, I think she's got it."

She nodded. "But there's more. When you open your eyes, you see the Company's, uh, work all over the place. Like promoting caste and color as sources of pride or shame. Oh, and convincing us that tribal affiliations are what make us safe and others are not to be trusted. And of course you really sell the idea that workers are helpless without the leadership of owners and direction of bosses and the more we have the happier we will be, right? That thinking too much causes wear and tear on the brain best filled with fun and games."

Justin's eyes glinted in amusement. "You must visit our entertainment division. Brilliant."

"But most importantly you convince us that the world is hard and immutable and can never be remade in any other model." She gave him a small smile. "Am I on the right track?"

Justin shook his head in mock admiration. "I knew it," he said, his voice a mixture of sarcasm and amusement at her naiveté. "You're a natural! Yes, Mrs. Steubenville, all of that and more, much more, and in so doing we keep this fragile world of ours stable and ensure that the best and brightest rule."

"And in constant fear of each other," Barbara said. "Because that's what you really promote, isn't it?"

Justin tilted his handsome head quizzically.

"Fear. Fear," she repeated. "Fear of power. Fear of not *having* power." She paused. "What other fears do you cultivate? Death? Insecurity? Hunger? Change?" She gave Justin a broad smile. "Which keeps the rest of us from kicking your *aristoi* asses to the side of the road while we create a new society in the shell of the old."

Once more she felt the fury building in Justin. His eyes flashed dangerously and his angular jaw clenched and unclenched. *Do I dare push him any further?* She wondered. *And what happens if I do?*

"Power doesn't corrupt," she said. "Does it? You know that. No, power simply reveals the character of the person who has it." She gazed deeply into his eyes. "And I see who you are, who you truly are." She paused. "And it is a sad, hideous, malignant thing."

He erupted from his chair in an explosion of fury that caught Barbara by surprise. The wave of pure rage pushed her back into her chair like a cruel slap, softened only by the light protection maintained by her gem. He stood across from her, his hands braced on the table, his eyes blue flames.

Barbara's heart raced as she pushed back against the assault. Her hand closed around her necklace, and she rocked gently in her chair for a few moments until her breathing steadied.

Justin laughed aloud. He settled back into his chair. "Well said," Mrs. Steubenville, well said." He continued to chuckle in amusement. "I wouldn't have expected anything less. But I do hope you will give me a chance to better inform you of our operation here and that you will assist me in its administration." His voice hardened. "For you see, there is no way out without me."

A cold fist clenched in her stomach.

"You will work with me or you will spend the rest of your life in your apartment. You will rot there. I would much prefer that you join me in what I believe you will come to see as a truly noble cause, but at least with you here you can pose no threat. Oh," he added. "About 'no way out.' That is not entirely correct." His lips curled into an amicable smile. "You can take your own life."

Barbara looked at him with a steady gaze. *What was this about?*

"You see, normally we can't afford disgruntled employees to terminate their contracts prematurely. I'm sure you understand. After investing in their recruitment, orientation, training, well, it would be bad for business, wouldn't it? So suicide is impossible here." He paused, still grinning. "But in your case, I can make an exception."

He reached into his inside coat pocket and drew out a gold ring. A small round cylinder with a tiny clasped lid mounted on the band. He pulled the lid open gently. Inside there was a black pill encased in red velvet.

"It would be most unfortunate, but if you cannot come to my way of thinking, you could become a burden, and I don't need another example of what happens when one defies me. Sibyl is quite enough." His smile slipped slightly. "But you will have a chance to see for yourself. You on the other hand could prove troublesome. If you cannot abide our company any longer, you merely need to take this, and you will die."

Barbara studied the man's face as he spoke. She recognized the detachment in his eyes and the brutal heartlessness in his voice. Years ago she had heard the word: *bedlamite.*

"In that case, why not simply kill me?" She paused, staring directly into his eyes. "Or try. I would think you would be quite good at that."

"That is true, outside of the Company. But I cannot kill people inside." He sighed. "As much as I'd like to sometimes."

"I'm surprised. Why is that?"

"It's simply against the rules. Can you imagine if we started to kill each other? Come, come. No, and we cannot injure each other here. Well, except for our security force, of course." His smile broadened. "We want to create a safe work environment for our personnel. It greatly enhances productivity. But outside, as you witnessed in the crypt, that is quite another matter."

"And you?" Barbara asked.

Justin cocked his head inquiringly.

"Where can you be killed?" she asked mildly.

Justin laughed, a sort of gurgling cackle.

"Let us say I have a wider circle of protection than other employees." His face slipped into a wrathful mask and he leaned across the table at Barbara. "No place you will ever see," he snarled.

He pushed the ring across the table toward Barbara. "Put it on. I do believe it will fit you perfectly."

Chapter 18

IT TOOK A LONG TIME for Zoltan to awaken. Dreams of crows beating enormous black wings against his head gave way to confusion. The floor. Was he on the floor of his bedroom in the big house in Budapest? No, so many years ago. Then where?

His eyes blinked open. Underground. He could smell the must and dampness. He groaned as he rolled over. A sharp pain shot through his lower back. He sat up groggily against the cave wall.

Barbara, where was she? How long had she been gone?

He looked around the domed room. Malik sat cross-legged in the center of the chamber, looking at him waiting for something from him. To rouse and lead them in another day of wandering?

Zoltan drew his hand over his face and squeezed his eyes shut.

"Malik," he said, his voice still husky from sleep. "What time is it?"

"It is 23:45," Malik replied.

"Are you sure? We stopped around 4:00 in the afternoon."

As they spoke, the other men, lying around the edges of the room, began to stir.

"And that would mean we have slept for more than seven hours."

"Yes."

"What's going on?" Friesen called out, propping himself up on one elbow.

"I think we slept in," Kwan said.

"Malik, did you get some sleep?" Zoltan asked.

Malik stood up and peered down at the men around the room. "I need very little sleep."

"So you stayed up all night while we slept?" Friesen asked, his voice deeper even than usual.

"May I remind you it is just after midnight, so I did not stay up all night. I stayed up all evening. It was quite pleasant."

Zoltan stared at the tall man. "Thank you, sir."

Malik bowed slightly.

"Did you hear anything?" Friesen asked. "Or see anything?"

"Nothing. The drip of water. An occasional bat. That is all."

"A bat?" Kwan asked excitedly. "You actually saw a bat?"

"That is correct."

Kwan beamed. "Bats need to have access to the outside to access insects at this time of year. I have never heard of bats roosting more than a half mile from an opening to the outside."

"You mean, we could be less than a mile from the entrance?" Maphaela asked.

Kwan nodded. "Or another outlet. It could, of course, be a small break in the cave wall that leads to the surface. Bats can squeeze through an opening just a few centimeters wide."

As the men talked, Zoltan walked over to a pool of water that had formed at the base of the chamber. He splashed water on his face, cupped water in his hands, and drank deeply.

"Is it safe?" Kwan asked. "I mean to drink?"

"We are deep below the surface," Zoltan replied, "and I believe any water that makes it this far will either be from a pure aquifer or filtered until it's safe."

"Of course he could be wrong," Friesen said. "Might be loaded with bacteria, mercury, viruses. One sip and he could be dead." He smiled at Zoltan. "Mind if we sit here a while and watch?"

Malik turned angrily toward Friesen, who held up his hands in mock defense. "Kidding, just kidding."

"Zoltan is almost certainly right," Maphaela added quickly. "I worked in mines for many years. Water at this level should be okay."

"I might point out, sir," Malik said, still glowering at Friesen, "that if we do *not* drink we will all *certainly* die in a matter of days."

Malik strode to the pool and drank deeply. One by one, the others followed.

The pool was in the middle of a round room with two passageways forward, one directly on their left and the other leading to the right. The five men stood and looked at the entrances wearily. How many times had they confronted this choice? How many times more? And would they ever really find a route out, or would they wander in these dark, dank catacombs until they died?

Zoltan seemed to sense the growing despair.

"Mr. Kwan, will you and Mr. Malik be so good to examine the left route. And Mr. Friesen and Mr. Maphaela please proceed to the right." He smiled encouragingly. "I look forward to your reports."

As the men's footsteps died away and their shadows flickered and disappeared into the black tunnels, the quiet of the underground room closed around Zoltan like a blanket. He gently returned his jewel to his vest pocket. And there was only darkness.

He sat still for several minutes, focusing on his breath, letting the thoughts of Barbara arise but then letting them go. He could do nothing until they were out of the catacombs.

His meditation was broken by a sudden flash from Kwan—of excitement perhaps. Or panic?

What is it? he directed to Kwan.

Not sure. Maybe nothing. But coming in, didn't we pass a wall painting of a horse?

I believe so. On the left as we entered. Going out it should be on the right-hand wall.

A rush of hope and joy burst from Kwan with such strength that Friesen and Maphaela received it deep in the other tunnel.

What's going on? Friesen asked.

Not sure yet, but please return to the pool. Mr. Kwan may have found something.

Zoltan felt the surge of anticipation as the two men rushed back toward him, and he fervently hoped their new optimism would not be dashed.

The sound of Friesen and Maphaela's footsteps grew louder, echoing hollowly as they neared the entrance to the gallery. They burst into the room, eager to follow Kwan and Malik. Zoltan had drawn his blue stone, and with it lighting the way, they entered the left-hand tunnel.

Within minutes Zoltan saw the pale green of Kwan's jewel lighting a large square room. They almost ran the final few yards until they entered the chamber and joined Kwan and Malik, who stood staring at the wall to their right. Malik shone a bright amber beam onto the stone surface.

"The horse!" Maphaela cried. "I saw it on our way in. I remember it because it's not carved, you see? It is scratched into the surface and then rubbed with ochre to give it color."

A wave of relief swept through Zoltan. They were near now.

"Yes," he said. "I too remember the horse. We had been walking for only fifteen or twenty minutes after entering." He turned to his left and stared at the wall across from the horse.

"I believe you will find an arched entrance right there," he said, nodding at the middle of the far wall. "It will lead us into a circle with a very old statue in the middle, yes?"

Friesen dashed to the area Zoltan had indicated and pushed. Instantly his arms disappeared. He turned back to the group, his angular face creased in a smile.

"Yes!"

The men all but tumbled through the doorway, and when, sixty feet further, they burst into the round chamber, the ancient statue on its stone column staring at them through empty eye slits, a cheer rang the tiled ceiling. They knew they were still a distance from the entrance, maybe several hundred yards, but they were near, and they knew now, with certainty, that they had already negotiated this section on the way in.

Friesen dashed to the wall to the left of the entranceway and eagerly ran his hands over the rough wall. Suddenly, his left hand sank deeply into the rock.

"This way!" he shouted, sliding through the illusion.

Zoltan hesitated, looking at a broad passageway that led straight ahead. He felt certain they were closer to the castle than the group realized and that the tunnel in front of them would lead to the underground gated entrance. But could he be sure? Was it worth countermanding Friesen's decision?

Kwan stopped, half way through the illusionary door, and looked back at Zoltan uncertainly.

Zoltan took one more look up the tunnel and turned toward the hidden archway. "Coming."

There were still frustrating forks, but now the path was more worn and sloped steadily upward. Oddly, the cloaked doorways disappeared. The team simply stayed to the left and were rarely wrong in their choices of passages as they recognized the path on which they had descended.

"You notice the passages are all clear?" *Friesen called out.* "Why would he have abandoned the illusions?"

"I do not think he thought we would ever get this far," Malik suggested. "I believe he has underestimated us."

Or, thought Zoltan, *we took the wrong route and there is no need to confound us.*

Twenty minutes after leaving the statue, Malik, who was in the lead, stopped, his jewel illuminating a broad arch in front of them. The others hurried forward and joined him. They stared at the metal door they had entered. After coming so far, enduring so much, now they stood in a semi-circle staring at the heavy door through which they had entered. The door was massive, impenetrable. They stared at it in silence as if now, so close to freedom, no one wanted to make the next move.

Finally, Zoltan stepped forward. He grasped the large round handle and yanked.

The door did not budge.

Malik moved to Zoltan's side and placed both of his huge hands on top of Zoltan's. He braced his right foot on the stone doorjamb, and nodded. Together, they pulled until blood vessels in Malik's neck stood out like ropes. But there was not the slightest movement, not a whisper of the door grating open.

Malik rose and faced the men, breathing hard.

"It is locked, I fear, from the outside. It will not open."

Maphaela held his orange jewel he had pulled from inside his tunic. "May I?" he asked

The other men moved behind him as he directed. He concentrated his orange beam like a laser on the round handle. In seconds it began to glow until it was bright red, a small curl of acrid smoke rising from its surface. After several minutes, he shut off the beam and slid the jewel down the front of his shirt. He walked forward and gave the door a sharp kick.

He might as well have kicked one of the rock cave walls. The door didn't even shudder. Maphaela stepped back, hopping slightly on his other foot.

Kwan looked uncertainly at the door. "Shall we try combining our beams, as we did in the crypt?"

"I do not believe it will work," Zoltan said. "Barbara's gem made the difference, I am afraid. As well, Mr. Maphaela's gem provides the hottest beam." He nodded at the heavy metal panel in front of them. "This is no ordinary door."

Zoltan looked at his watch.

"It is 6:30 in the morning. The castle opens to tourists at 8:00."

Friesen looked at Zoltan blankly. "I'll remember that when I visit next time. Get here early and beat the rush."

Zoltan smiled slightly.

"Part of the cave system is open to tour groups. We are near the entrance. I am nearly certain I know the route from the statue. That is why I hesitated in the statue chamber."

"Why didn't you say something?" Friesen asked.

"I was not sure. But now, yes. From the statue room we can walk to the gate into the castle complex. Guards will open it at 8:00, and I believe we will be able to walk out of the castle through the exit and onto the castle grounds."

There was a long silence.

"Will the sun be shining?" Friesen asked.

Turning back into the labyrinth of dark tunnels was agonizing. The door might have been locked, impregnable, but at least they knew that only a yard away there was night air, stars.

Zoltan led them quickly back to the statue, and then, with unaccustomed confidence, through several tunnels that became steadily broader. Soon electric lights, though still unlit, were wired into the cave walls.

They turned a corner and stood in front of a broad, arched gate made of iron rods topped with cast spearheads. The two sides were locked together with a chain, but through the openings in the gate, they caught a tantalizing glimpse of stairs and handrails.

"Let us extinguish our light," Zoltan said quietly. "We do not wish to give the guard any reason to advance into the tunnel."

The group drew back into the passageway and waited.

The sound of men chatting, though faint at first, was shocking after the quiet of the caves. In the dim light from the inside of the castle, they could see two uniformed guards standing at the top of the stairway that led down to the gate. One guard said something in Hungarian, and the other roared in laughter.

The five men shrank against the wall as one of the guards walked noisily down the stairway and fumbled with a set of keys. He found the key and turned it in the lock.

The tunnel burst into light.

Instinctively, all five men dropped to the floor, out of the blinding lights lining the passageway. Even lying on the tiled surface, they were still visible, but the guard, his head turned, was still talking to the other man at the head of the stairs and didn't notice them. The guard removed the chain and hung it on a hook on the wall. He turned back up the stairs.

The five men lay silent on the cave floor until the voices disappeared. Zoltan rose to a crouch and walked carefully forward. At the gate, he pushed his index finger through the bars and lifted the iron latch. He grasped the right-hand gate and gently pulled. The hinges gave a sharp squeak, and Zoltan froze. But he heard nothing. He carefully pulled the gate further open and slid through. The other men were right behind him. Zoltan carefully closed the gate behind them and latched it.

He nodded up the stairs.

They emerged into a gift shop, stopping warily at the top of the stairs and scanning the empty room. They saw no one. A broad hallway opened to their left and right. Zoltan nodded right and led them through rows of postcards and tea towels with an image of the castle. In front of them, a great wooden door filled with a dozen panels of stained glass led outside.

"Állj! Mit keresel itt?"

Zoltan turned around. The guard who had unlocked the gate ran toward them, his hand on the gun at his side. Panic rose in Zoltan like a flame.

Friesen brushed by Zoltan and calmly walked toward the guard. Friesen threw up his hands, a gigantic grin across his lean face.

"Goll-ly," he drawled. "Am I ever glad to see you, *sir*! You are a *sight* for sore eyes! I mean, we got let off by our tour bus and were just wanderin' around, lost as a coonhound in a Wal-Mart, and Billy over there," he raised his chin at Zoltan, "he's from Indiana, ya know. Do you have any relatives in Indiana? Well, Billy, he says, ah think we're supposed to meet the rest of the bunch in heah. Now ah didn't…"

The guard stopped and squinted at Friesen, noting his striped dress shirt, wet and torn, his blond hair matted and his eyes flickering bright blue.

"…course ah didn't want to say nothing 'cause Billy is my third cousin, but…"

"Elég!" the guard said waving his hand. He pointed at the door. *"Most te, mész!"* he shouted.

Friesen looked hurt. "Well now, sir. There's no reason to get sore. Ah mean…"

"Friesen," Zoltan hissed. He nodded toward the door.

Friesen tugged at the front of his hair.

"Mahty nice to have met you, sir." The big grin creased his face again. "Now if y'all ever get to Kentucky, you know you've got a friend there."

Malik grabbed him by the sleeve and yanked him down the aisle. He pushed the door open and held it as the other men exited, then shut it quietly behind them. And then they looked at the sky.

Chapter 19

WHEN THE DOOR TO HER apartment slid open the next morning, Barbara was relieved to see only Jaromir standing in the doorway. Meijer had told her to be ready at 8:00, and she had expected him to barge in, crude and aggressive. She had prepared herself and now sat in the white leather chair facing the door. Jaromir seemed shaken to see her eyeing him coolly.

"Next time knock," Barbara said.

"I'm sorry," Jaromir stammered.

"I guess a doorbell would be out of the question."

Jaromir stood still, his face drawn. His eyes blinked rapidly in agitation. Desperation leaked out of the man like air from a deflating balloon.

"What is it?" She asked.

"I need to talk."

Barbara nodded to the living area. "Have a chair."

"Not here. While we are walking."

She got up silently and strode toward the door, noting it slid closed as she passed through into the hallway.

She said nothing as they walked down the long corridor, lined with identical glowing portals.

"Sibyl," Jaromir said at last. "You are to see Sibyl."

"Yes, that's what I understand." They neared the elevator shaft. "Why is he so insistent on my meeting Sibyl?"

Jaromir looked distractedly at the elevator door opening and stepped into the middle of the shaft.

"Jaromir? Did you hear me?"

His eyes, grey like ashes, turned to her. "Did you say something?"

"I asked why Justin is so insistent that I meet Sibyl."

Jaromir turned back to staring out the clear elevator shaft sides as they ascended. "As an example to you," he said. "And to me," he added quietly.

"An example of what?"

"Of what happens if you defy Justin."

"And what is that?"

"He turns you into a monster."

The elevator slid to a stop. "Garden," Jaromir said distractedly.

"The Garden?"

"Yes. She lives in a hut in the Jungle Garden."

"Cute."

They exited the elevator into the courtyard, and Barbara took a deep breath. Below them, the water rushing from the rock face splashed into the pool, leaving the cavern dank and musty, like an old cellar she remembered discovering under an abandoned farmhouse when she was a girl. The sound of the crashing stream was not soothing; it hissed and spurt, taut and angry like a giant firehose.

"You are in great despair," Barbara said at last.

Jaromir walked silently around the pool toward the wall on the far side of the elevator. "There is an old story, supposedly an American Indian fable. Perhaps you've heard it."

Barbara carefully matched the slow pace of Jaromir's footsteps. "Go on."

"A grandfather is talking to his young grandson. 'Like all of us,' he says. 'I have two wolves fighting inside of me. One wants me to be kind, compassionate and generous. The other wants me to be cruel, hateful and arrogant. It is a fight to the death.'"

They had reached the end of the walkway along the pool and stopped. Jaromir leaned against the chromium railing and stared into the water.

"The grandson is very upset about this. He thinks for a few moments and asks, 'Grandfather, which wolf will win?'"

Jaromir turned to Barbara with cinder eyes. "Do you know how the grandfather answered?"

Barbara shook her head.

"He said, 'The one I feed.' "

He turned quickly away, but not before Barbara saw tears welling from his eyes.

"And I have been feeding the wrong wolf for far too long."

Jaromir's sadness and grief nearly overwhelmed Barbara. Her breath became shallow and ragged and tears streamed down her cheeks. She grasped the railing with one hand and her jewel with the other until the blackness subsided.

"I think we have all done that," she managed, her voice still tight with emotion. "Fed the wrong wolf."

Jaromir managed a small smile. "No doubt. But here there is a difference. A different wolf. This is a wolf that ravages whole worlds. That consumes the souls of those who feed it."

Barbara's breathing returned to normal, but she said nothing. Instead she stared at the churning water pouring out of the brass pipe protruding from the rock.

"I cannot do it anymore," Jaromir said softly. "I am done."

"What is it you can't do?"

"Feed the wolf."

"And the other wolf. Can you not feed it instead?"

Jaromir looked up at her with such sadness, such desolation, that tears stung her eyes again.

"That wolf does not live here," he said.

"No," she said softly. "But it lives in you. I felt it even in the crypt."

Barbara eased the defenses around her mind and guardedly opened to Jaromir. She knew Justin could be using him as bait, waiting for the chance for a thrust she could not parry.

But there was only sadness so intense she had to choke back tears again.

"There is more, isn't there? I see no future for you here." She paused. "And none outside of here."

Jaromir peered blankly into the water. "It is as I feared. I cannot leave."

"Go on."

"Garripoli told me yesterday. I cannot go above. With the chaos in the jewel section, he says Justin needs me to sort it out, to maintain contact with the gem holders. That I am to stay here."

"How long?"

Jaromir paused. "He says two years, but I wonder. I don't think they will ever let me go. Garripoli no longer trusts me outside. He reported to Justin that I did not support him strongly enough at the meeting at the Market."

Barbara looked at the side of the man's face. It could be a trap, she knew. Why should she trust this man? After all, he had to eat.

"Jaromir," she said. "Turn toward me."

He turned, his hooded grey eyes showing misery mixed with fear.

"Give me your ring."

Jaromir hesitated then raised his hand with the ring toward her. She took his hand, grasped the ring, and closed her eyes, holding her own gem with her other hand.

Her jewel glowed red and she and Jaromir were standing in a void. There was no pond, no splashing water. No dark tentacles testing the zone she had created. Just the two of them. His jewel glowed blue on his finger and transmitted only sorrow and choking sadness.

She gently unclasped his hand and let it drop to Jaromir's side.

"I see," she nodded. "But it is not over yet."

"Lady, Barbara," Jaromir said fiercely. "Don't you get it? There is no help." He spoke in a low voice, but shook with anger. "There is no hope in this cursed place."

"Jaromir, did you expect to live to be a hundred and twenty? To turn people's souls into gems? To watch colleagues raised from the ground and snapped to their death? Did you expect a woman to stop the most powerful man you have ever met in his tracks? To see men willing to die for me and for each other?"

Jaromir shook his head slightly and turned back to the pool.

"Look at me," Barbara commanded.

Jaromir looked over his shoulder.

"The world is too full of possibilities to give up hope," she said. "We are far from powerless. We are two jewel carriers. And there is a way out. I can feel it."

Jaromir's eyes fixed on Barbara's. The smoke swirled, thinned, and cleared.

"My, Agent Jaromir," Barbara said, more cheerily than she felt. "What lovely grey eyes you have."

Jaromir turned to face her fully. With his eyes not leaving hers, he bowed to one knee and offered his ringed blue jewel to Barbara.

Her first response was embarrassment, and she started to order him to his feet, to laugh at his gesture. But she didn't. She took his hand.

Jaromir rose. "I don't believe you, I cannot. But you make me want to try." He nodded his head sharply, a salute. "I will do whatever you say."

Barbara smiled. "Thank you, Jaromir," she said simply. "I believe we have a meeting scheduled, do we not?"

Jaromir took a deep breath and nodded. As he did so Barbara realized that while she had thought of him as medium height, he was actually a head taller than she.

Jaromir pointed to the opening of the Jungle walk. "Please, come with me."

Chapter 20

FROM THE MAIN WALKWAY, JAROMIR led Barbara onto a side trail and into a theme park version of an African village. Round thatched huts made of clay brick were arranged in a broad circle around a central clearing. Barbara stopped in her tracks as women, piles of firewood and five-gallon buckets of water on their heads, crisscrossed the opening. She stopped, aghast, until she saw one figure after another disappear into a digital void.

"Very convincing," she muttered to Jaromir.

"Yes," Jaromir agreed. "But Sibyl, I'm afraid, is quite real."

He led them across the circular opening. Barbara flinched slightly as a hologram woman passed through her and kept walking.

They approached a large hut at the far end of the circle. Something about the structure told Barbara this was no Styrofoam imitation, no electronic trick. This was a substantial, almost formidable building. The structure was heavily cloaked from the inside, but she felt a core of heat, almost radioactive, deep in the building.

They stood outside a massive wood door bound with riveted iron.

"Do I knock?"

Jaromir nodded.

She looked at him. "Are you coming in?"

He stood straight, his eyes staring over her shoulder.

Jaromir hesitated. "I cannot." He glanced back at Barbara, a flicker of self-loathing and shame in his smoky eyes. "I told you. A year ago Justin paraded her through the Comfort Floor, tied to a throne, so everyone could see for themselves the result of defiance." He stopped. "Most had to look away."

"So you said. But you were not here. You did not see her."

He nodded and swallowed hard. "That is true. But I have talked to many who did."

"I see. And I am here for the same lesson, is that right? To see for myself what can happen if I challenge the Leader."

Jaromir gazed evenly at Barbara.

She nodded. "And to you as well it would seem."

Jaromir said nothing, but the muscles of his jaw clenched.

"And why here?" Barbara looked around the village, noticing a hologram lion lurking behind a nearby tree. "Why did Justin bring her to this ridiculous African movie set?"

"Justin thought it would be amusing to have his vanquished African rival returned to her rightful primitiveness. Just another exotic animal in the park."

"She is African?"

Jaromir nodded. "Ghanaian. Garripoli recruited her. He's been trying to make it up to Justin ever since."

"Recruited? For what purpose?"

Jaromir shrugged, and Barbara smiled.

"I've done something amusing?"

"I'm glad to see you're back to normal."

Jaromir started to shrug, and then laughed. "Nervous habit, I guess."

"Go on."

"I have always been on the edge of the inner circle here. I don't know the specifics. Even when we were lovers, Sibyl was very careful about what she said. Mainly for my own protection. But from what she did tell me, they brought her in to be co-chair of the Committee."

"The Committee. Our shadowy hedge fund investors." She looked at Jaromir with a wry smile. "In fact, he offered to make me a member."

"Yes," Jaromir said bitterly. "I'm sure he did."

Barbara turned toward the hut. *And what awaits inside?* She wondered.

She hesitated, her hand poised to knock, and then rapped sharply on the heavy wood door.

Chapter 21

AFTER EXITING THE SOUVENIR SHOP, the five men made their way down the steep steps of Castle Hill to the bus stop *Budai Also,* the main road along the western banks of the Danube. Zoltan was vaguely surprised to find his wallet still in the front pocket of his khakis. He looked at the Euros he removed for their fare, wondering which world he was in.

The men remained silent on the trip, following Zoltan as they transferred to another bus once they had crossed the *Szabadsag* Bridge to the Pest side of the city. The second bus drove leisurely up the treed *Ansdrassy Ut.* Zoltan pulled the buzzer and the bus stopped at a circle. The men exited and followed Zoltan along another block lined with ancient mansions. At the corner he stopped in front of his former home. He gazed at the crumbling but still lovely structure, remembering his last visit. With Barbara. And their encounter with the magnificent Caraldo. So long ago. A lifetime.

He led them along the route he and Barbara had taken, entering the old house from the back garden.

The house had changed little since he had last been there. A little grimier, perhaps. A bit more mold along the window sill. But the ancient piano was still a grey shape under a rotting sheet and the red velvet chair Caraldo had sat in remained in the center of the room. Zoltan recalled that encounter, Caraldo's gun pointed at Zoltan and Barbara, the tensions thick as the dust on the furniture. Then the nightmare flight to London, the assault in the *Mester's* office, Caraldo's death and their desperate escape. It seemed like a lifetime ago.

The men stood uncertainly in the curtained darkness, just a few shafts of light peeking through the thick drapes.

"Welcome, gentlemen, to my childhood home," Zoltan's said, his soft voice hushed by the air heavy with dust and years of silence.

"Nice place," Friesen commented, looking at the boarded windows and stained wallpaper. "But where's the kitchen?" Chan chuckled. "We made it three days without food," Friesen continued. "Wouldn't want to test my cannibalistic instincts much further."

Malik looked at him disapprovingly.

"Of course," Zoltan said. "We are all ravenous. Would takeaway be acceptable?"

Malik and Zoltan left the other men and walked to a restaurant down the street Zoltan remembered from his childhood. They returned with two whole roast geese, pork shoulder *paprikash* and a case of *Egri Bikavér*. To Zoltan's surprise, when they returned, the others had found plates stacked in the kitchen cupboards, and a dozen crystal wine glasses, filled with dust, underneath a sheet covering an ornate china cabinet. These had been washed as well as cold water allowed and were set grandly on the dining table. But the veneer of civility evaporated as soon as Zoltan and Malik slid the food onto platters.

Unfortunately, they had discovered no silverware, so the men tore into the pork and goose with bare hands while simultaneously bolting down glasses of wine, the red liquid splashing down their chins and staining their shirts.

"The Ottomans would be terrified once again," he remarked.

Friesen looked up, a goose leg in one hand, a glass of red wine in the other. "I presume there is a story there?"

Zoltan laughed. "*Egri Bikavér* means bull's blood. Supposedly, during the one of the many battles with the Ottomans, some Turkish spies snuck up on a bunch of Hungarian soldiers, roaring drunk, wine dripping from their beards, running down their throats, bloodshot eyes. So they hurried back and reported that the Hungarians were too fierce to deal with."

"Ah," Friesen said smiling, his teeth stained red. "Don't fuck with guys who drink bulls' blood."

"Couldn't have put it better myself, Mr. Friesen."

Friesen drained his glass, wine dribbling out of the corners of his mouth. He grinned more broadly. "I like it."

They had uncovered enough chairs for all of them to sit around the walnut table in the dining room. There had been no debate about their next move: find Barbara. But agreeing on a strategy was more difficult.

From the outset, Friesen had been adamant: their only chance was to re-enter the caves under the castle and retrace their steps to the crypt, and then try to determine the route Justin had taken.

Zoltan felt a shudder around the table at the thought of returning to the maze of tunnels, and an uncomfortable silence followed Friesen's proposal. Then Maphaela raised the idea of radio frequencies.

"Look, we know our jewels are transmitting at a certain frequency, right?"

Zoltan nodded. "As explained by Pierre and Samantha, the physicists, back in the Market."

Maphaela nodded. "And Barbara's is transmitting as well. She just has no receiver, so we are unable to contact her. However, if we can devise a receiver that will pick up her signal, we should be able to use triangulation to identify the origin of the transmitter—her jewel."

"And Barbara," Zoltan said quietly.

Friesen shook his head. "First of all, we would need a damned electronics genius to set up a receiver able to pick up her signal, and that's assuming she is able to transmit from whatever godforsaken place they've taken her to. And then, even if we pick up her signal, she's presumably still underground in the bloody caves. How are we going to get to her? Dig?"

Maphaela looked steadily at Friesen. "We all have pasts, Mr. Friesen, and skills acquired before our being drafted into the gem game. I was an electrical engineer, working in the mines in South Africa. Not to brag," he added, smiling modestly, "but I was regarded as something of an electronics whiz kid in my day."

"No offense," Kwan said with a grin. "But your day was, I imagine, some time ago."

Maphaela raised his eyebrows, conceding the point. "But the principles remain the same. If we can determine the frequency range Barbara is likely to be transmitting at, we should be able to find an antenna and receiver capable of catching the signal—and pinpointing its source."

"And how would we do that, sir?" Malik asked. "From the report of the physicists, the signal band width is an anomaly, not even on conventional scales."

Maphaela nodded. "You're right. But remember, they also told us that all the gems are fixed to receive a single signal. In other words, if we can ascertain the frequency of our gems' transmissions, we should know Barbara's as well."

"There are a lot of 'shoulds' and 'maybes' in there," Friesen muttered. "How would we even start to figure out our frequency?"

"Not as hard as you might think," Kwan offered. "I am a biologist, not a physicist, but I do know that there are frequency counters."

"That's right," Maphaela agreed. "Quite simple really. The machine compares an unknown frequency --that would be us—well, our jewels, actually—with the harmonics of a known frequency. By generating a known complementary through the use of a frequency generator, then using a harmonic generator and mixer, the counter can fairly accurately measure the frequency of the originating transmitter. There can be problems with stability…"

Friesen held up his hands. "Okay, okay. I get it. Sort of. But as I said, what if a) she does get a signal out, b) we do manage to pick it up, and c) we're actually able to isolate the location of the transmission, how do we get to it?"

"All good questions," Zoltan said. "But it is possible that she has been taken outside of the cave complex and is above ground. Also, if she is still underground, we can at least identify the general area of the caves where she is being held, can we not?"

Maphaela nodded his head. "Theoretically."

"Theoretically?" Friesen asked in exasperation.

"Yes," Maphaela replied more confidently. "Although the signal will be detected at the surface, we should be able to triangulate the data to give us a more specific location of its origin underground."

"Should be," Friesen muttered. "Okay," he agreed. "Looks like I'm outnumbered. I'll go with this as plan A. But how many days do we give it? While we are huddled over a radio up here, she could be carried to another continent. Or worse."

Zoltan shared Friesen's fears. But the idea of returning to the tunnels, at least before trying other tactics, was unbearable. "Thank you for your concern, Mr. Friesen." Zoltan looked at Maphaela. "A week, Mr. Maphaela?"

"We'll do our best." He looked at Kwan. "Looks like it's up to us, Mr. Kwan. Can you make a note of what we're going to need?"

Kwan nodded and grabbed a pen and small notebook that had survived their trip in and out of the caves.

"For starters, we need an absorption wavemeter, and then a high frequency receiver—I'd really like an Icom IC-R8500, but we can probably get away with a Watkins Johnson. And a good directional antenna." He thought as Kwan wrote. "The key may be the GPS. Let's see if we can find a Garmin Nuvi 3597LMTHD, Mr. Kwan. And we'll need a vehicle."

"Vehicle?" Friesen asked.

"Once we pick up the signal…"

"If we pick it up," Friesen muttered to himself.

"We should have enough time to place the site and enter the coordinates into the GPS. Hopefully we can reach it by car."

"And start digging," Friesen said.

Chapter 22

SOMEHOW, SHE HAD EXPECTED A deep voice to invite her in, but instead, the dark wood door slid silently upward moments after she knocked as if the person inside had been waiting for her. Barbara took a deep breath and walked through the doorway. Instantly it shut with the wheeze of a closing freezer door. Barbara glanced around her in the reddish gloom. The structure was far larger than it looked on the outside.

A woman sat in the dark at the far side of the circular building with her back to Barbara, her long legs crossed under her. The figure's back was straight and the hood of her robe hung over her shoulders, revealing waves of glossy black hair.

"So, you found me, eh?" the woman asked, her voice light, almost jovial. "Well, come on in and close the door. You'll let the mosquitoes in."

Barbara turned toward the entrance, confused. They were a half mile underground.

She heard a snort and laughter.

Barbara turned back to the teasing voice, her forehead creased. "Are you Sibyl?"

"No, no. There are hundreds of women here at the Company, all of whom are hideously disfigured and made to live in isolation in some stupid colonial stereotype of an African village. Of course I'm Sibyl!"

Barbara stood still, not knowing what to say, staring at the back of the woman, who continued to sit upright, facing the wall.

"I'm sorry," Barbara said. "I guess that *was* a pretty stupid question."

"Right up there with 'Dr Livingston, I presume.'"

"Listen, I need to talk to you," Barbara said, beginning to feel annoyed.

"So talk away, honey. Nice to hear another voice. Not many people drop by."

"But I want to be able to see your face," Barbara continued. "To look you in your eyes."

The woman was silent for a long moment. "You sure? They say it's pretty horrible."

Barbara hesitated. "You don't know what you look like?"

"You see any mirrors in here? Not really interested."

"Well, I am," Barbara said firmly.

"Huh. Okay, Sweetie. Prepare yourself."

The ceiling began to glow brighter and brighter until a warm yellow light illuminated the entire hall. Intricately woven tapestries in deep primary colors covered the walls. Sibyl sat on a round cushion at the far end of the room, which was still partially darkened. A low carved wood table stood between Barbara and the woman.

As the room brightened, Barbara saw that rather than the general issue brown robe, Sibyl wore a wrap printed in a pattern of flowers and birds, green, yellow, red. But while that was extraordinary enough in this place of gleaming steel drab uniforms, Barbara's eye grew wide as she watched the pattern move. The flowers grew, turning to an unseen sun. Birds flew slowly across a woven blue sky. Leaves twined in intricate patterns as they twisted upward.

"You ready, honey?"

Barbara took a deep breath and held her jewel against her chest. The round cushion Sibyl sat on began to turn. Her face remained shadowed in the half light. Then the figure nodded, and a beam shone down from the ceiling, fully lighting her face.

Barbara gasped.

"Huh. That bad, eh?"

Barbara stood silent, staring at one of the most beautiful women she had ever seen. Her skin was a deep brown, like polished mahogany.

Underneath her high forehead, perfect eyebrows arched over closed eyes, lined with long, curling eyelashes. A fine nose flared slightly above full, sensual lips, which curved slightly upwards in what Barbara suspected was a permanent smile. High cheekbones rose over sculpted cheeks that rounded into a delicate chin. Even from a distance, Barbara could see her skin was smooth, soft, unblemished.

"Well, you're the one who wanted to talk face to face," Sibyl said, lifting her head back proudly. "If I'm that horrible, you know where the door is."

"You..." Barbara stammered.

"Well, spit it out."

"You're beautiful."

Sibyl's head tilted upward until her closed eyes were level with Barbara's

"Well, well, well."

"I'm sorry?"

"Describe my face."

"You want me to tell you what you look like?"

"No, I want you to tell me what you see."

Barbara stepped forward and carefully studied the woman's face, relating what she observed—her glowing dark skin, magnificent lips, shaped cheekbones a model would die for. A delicate nose that rose into arched eyebrows.

"And your eyelashes! They're gorgeous," Barbara enthused. "They look too long to be real but they're too magnificent not to be."

As Barbara spoke, Sibyl's smile broadened until her lips parted.

"Oh," Barbara added. "And fantastic teeth, too!"

Sibyl laughed a hearty, welling laugh that began deep inside of her, erupting as if she had not laughed in a very long time and was just remembering how good it felt.

"Girl, you just made my day. No, I take that back. You just made my *year*."

Now Barbara laughed, too, thinking how ridiculous they would look if someone happened through the door, which she knew was highly unlikely.

After a few moments, they got their laughter under control. Barbara cocked her head at the gorgeous woman still chuckling in front or her. "Sibyl, you have some explaining to do. Everyone I've met says you are hideously ugly. What's going on?"

Sibyl was quiet for a long moment. "Well, well, well."

"You've already said that. What does 'well, well, well' mean?"

"It means that Justin doesn't control your perception, honey. That you can still see clearly, even in this place. That he cannot shove his ugliness into your heart." She shook her head. "Haven't seen anybody like you here for a *long* time."

"You mean he didn't really disfigure you? He only makes people see you that way?"

"Uh, huh, that's about it. But for everyone here, it doesn't matter. He wants them to see me as an old hag, so that's what they see."

Barbara suddenly felt exhausted. She looked around the circular room. "Would it be okay if I sat down?"

"Of course, honey." Sibyl glanced toward a round leather ottoman near the door. "Pull that up here to the table and sit yourself down."

Barbara slid the ottoman forward and sat, and as she did so, a pot of steaming tea, two small cups to the side of the pot, appeared on the table.

"I'm not even going to ask you how you did that," Barbara said.

Sibyl laughed lustily. "Girl, you ain't seen nothing yet."

"I don't know how much time we have," Barbara began. "I was sent here to learn a lesson."

"Ah, yes. 'This can happen to you if you cross the Big Man.' Something like that?"

Barbara nodded and sipped her tea.

"Is that right?" Sibyl repeated.

"Yes," Barbara said. "That is exactly right."

"He will not expect you to stay long, and he may have his antennae up. But don't worry, girl. I'm not going anyplace soon." She laughed, not so deeply this time. "And neither are you, I suspect."

"Okay. Just a few things. First, I understand you and Justin had a falling out."

Sibyl nearly fell backward in hysterics, her laughter just as loud as before, but this time sharper, tinged with bitterness.

"Yeah, honey. Oh, yeah. You could say that. That man wanted me dead so bad it drove him crazy." Sibyl stopped chuckling. "Or crazier."

"So, okay, I don't understand it, but it seems it's against the rules for him to kill anyone here. Seems like he sometimes takes them out and has it done outside, but not in here, right?"

"You're a quick learner, honey."

"So if he wanted you dead, why didn't he send you outside and have you murdered up there? Seems like there's no shortage of killers for hire."

"Uh, huh. But you see, I wouldn't leave. And he couldn't send me out because of our contract."

"Contract?"

"Later. So the next best thing was to mutilate this beautiful woman, to humiliate her. To force her into isolation. To destroy her."

Barbara's eyes tilted upward toward the ceiling. "Okay, but he didn't mutilate you. He just makes people think you're hideous. They see his image of you. Why didn't he really do it?"

"I may not look it, honey, but I'm not exactly helpless. I got some juju of my own, you know. Why do you think I was here in the first place? He didn't want to take me on, you see. He might have been able to win, but it would have been a hell of a battle. Besides, if I wasn't actually disfigured, maybe I'd get desperate enough to be sent outside, to take my chances. I have a standing offer, you see."

Barbara nodded. "Bastard."

Sibyl laughed. "Yes, ma'am. You got that boy *all* figured out."

"So you've been holed up here for, what? Two years?"

"More or less. Kind of hard to keep track of time up here."

"You never tried to escape?"

Sibyl rocked back and forth slowly. "Haven't you heard? There is no way to escape this place." She chuckled as if to herself. "Easy place to get into. Devil to get out of."

"Yes, I've heard that. Over and over. Meijer. Justin again and again." She paused. "Jaromir."

Sibyl's lips grew taut. "Jaromir," she repeated. "You've seen him?"

"Yes. Actually, we have become quite close. But they all agree: The only way in and out is the great door. And beyond that a maze of tunnels Justin constantly changes and shifts." She stared at Sibyl, rocked gently back and forth.

"But it's not true, is it? You know another way."

Sibyl stopped rocking and sat still on her cushion, her lips set.

"You know another way. I can feel it too, but not the route. That is closed to me. But not to you. Why did you never try?"

Sibyl slowly opened her eyelids. Barbara's heart jumped. She stared into eyeballs that were dull white and sightless.

"Because I am blind, sweetie." She laughed again. "Justin thought it was funny, you see. A seer that couldn't see."

Barbara stared into the beautiful face and empty eyes for several seconds. "Sibyl," she said gently. "I am so sorry." She paused. "I would like to invite someone in to join us."

Sibyl's blank eyes widened. "In here?" She hesitated. "I don't know. Not sure I can stand the screams of horror. Really hard on a woman's self-esteem."

"You might be surprised. Besides, I think we will need him."

"Honey, in my experience, men are more trouble than they're worth."

"Perhaps," Barbara agreed. "But let's give this one a chance. He's just outside. Could you unlock the door please?"

Sibyl sat motionless, and then sighed. "Guess I don't have much to lose." She nodded at the door and it gave a soft wheeze as it unsealed. Barbara stood up from her seat and exited the hut. The door slid shut behind her.

Jaromir stood a few yards away under an artificial palm tree, his face drawn and anxious. Barbara crooked a finger toward him and he walked forward hesitantly until he stood a few feet away from her.

"What is it?" he asked. "Is she okay?"

"Oh, yes. Quite okay. In fact, I think she would very much like to say hello."

Jaromir's face fell, his ashen eyes filling with terror. "Please," he begged, his voice shaking, "I can't."

"Actually, I think you can. And I think you should. A few minutes ago, you said you would do what I asked, yes?"

Damn, now I'm starting to talk like Zoltan.

Jaromir nodded miserably.

"Then I am asking you to join me."

He took a deep, shuddering breath and gave a curt nod.

"Good." She turned back to the wooden door of the hut and knocked again. The door opened immediately and the two entered with Barbara in the lead. She noticed Jaromir start as the heavy door hissed as it resealed.

Sibyl again sat with her back to them, her long hair tumbling down the back of her robe. "Do forgive me, but I am not accustomed to so much company," she said cheerfully to the wall. "My hostess skills are a little rusty. But please, do come in."

Jaromir stood awkwardly inside the door as Barbara retook her seat to Sibyl's left.

"I have brought an old friend of yours," Barbara said "It's been several years, I understand, and he would like to greet you. To your face. Isn't that the case, Jaromir?"

Sibyl stiffened and Barbara heard a sharp intake of breath that sounded like a hiss.

"It's been a long time," Sibyl said after several moments. "A very long time."

The room was so quiet Barbara could hear Jaromir's shallow, labored breathing. The silence stretched on uncomfortably.

"Too long," Jaromir said finally. "Far too long." He paused. "To my shame."

Barbara sensed Sibyl relax slightly.

"I was a coward," Jaromir said quietly. "I couldn't bear seeing what he had done to you."

Sibyl sat, her back rigid, facing the far wall. "It was cowardice then? I never knew, you see. Whether you had betrayed me. Or," her voice faltered. "or if you were dead."

"I am sorry. So very sorry," Jaromir stammered, tears welling in his eyes.

"Well," Sibyl said breezily. "No matter."

"No, you are wrong. It does matter."

Barbara felt Sibyl fight back tears. "What matters is that you're here now."

"Yes, and as in love with you as I was two years ago. That never changed." He stopped. "And I want to tell you that to your face."

"Are you sure?" Sibyl asked.

"I am sure," Jaromir said firmly.

Sibyl said nothing, but in a few seconds her cushion began to turn. Barbara glanced at Jaromir. He had his eyes closed.

The cushion completed its rotation and Sibyl looked toward Jaromir, her eyes shut. He took a deep breath and opened his eyes.

"Sibyl," he whispered, moving forward. "Sibyl," he repeated.

Sibyl stared upward toward him. "The same," she said.

"Yes," Jaromir said. "The same. As beautiful as ever." Tears streamed down his cheeks. "They said…"

"That I was hideous, huh? Disfigured. But you never bothered to come and see for yourself, did you?" Her voice was even, casual, but behind it Barbara felt the hurt and betrayal.

Jaromir strode forward and sank to his knees so that his head was level with hers. He reached out and took her face gently in his hands. Slowly, she brought her hands up until they were touching his face, feeling along his cheek bones, sliding her long fingers along his lips. And then she opened her eyes, and Jaromir gasped.

"What has he done?" Jaromir demanded angrily.

"He blinded me," Sibyl said. "That much he could do. And turn me into a monster."

"But how…" Jaromir stammered. "I talked to dozens of people here. They all saw you. They said it was horrible what he had done to your face. Disfigured it beyond recognition."

"That's because they could only see what he wanted them to see," Barbara said. "They could not see beyond the illusion. But you, you can see through the mask he created to the person behind it, to Sibyl's heart."

Jaromir turned slightly toward Barbara. "Did you know?" he asked.

Barbara shook her head. "I wasn't sure. But I felt the love in you. If I could see through the illusion, I was pretty sure you could too."

"Thank you," he said, and then turned back to Sibyl.

Sibyl smiled broadly. "Yes, thank you."

She brought his face close to hers and kissed him on the lips.

Chapter 23

BARBARA WALKED THOUGHTFULLY NEXT TO Jaromir toward the pool, where she stopped, staring down at the huge brass pipe spewing water two or three yards to crash into the artificial pond. Her visit with Sibyl had renewed her hope of escaping. And somehow the brass culvert was the key. Jaromir stood silently by her side.

"Jaromir, can you arrange another meeting with Justin?"

"I think so, through Garripoli. He is expecting a report."

Barbara nodded. "Mention that I seemed quite shaken by my encounter with Sibyl."

"Okay."

"Tell me something."

"If I can, of course."

"The communications section you pointed out from the balcony. Their walls continue right to the ceiling, the only office that does so. Do you know why?"

"As I said, I don't really know a lot, but from my friend I gather that the enclosure contains a narrow shaft that extends up through all three floors and then through a hole bored through rock to the surface. An antenna that extends from the communication complex to the surface is able to transmit and receive satellite signals." He hesitated. "But Barbara, any shaft would be only five or six inches wide. There's no way you could escape through it."

Barbara laughed and shook her head. "No, I wasn't planning on escaping through it."

Jaromir turned toward her. "What then?"

"If Zoltan and the other men escaped the catacombs, they will be looking for me."

Jaromir shook his head miserably. "Barbara, please."

"Ah, ah," she said, raising her hand to stop him. "Remember, the world is too full of possibilities to give up hope."

"Little Miss Sunshine," he said.

"No. I am far from that. But we must consider all possibilities if we are going to get out of here. You would agree?"

"I haven't even agreed we *can* get out of here," Jaromir said. "But go on."

She glared at Jaromir in mock annoyance, "As I was saying, *when* Zoltan escapes, he will be looking for me. They'd have to be mad—which they're not—to simply re-enter the caves in a random search, no matter how well equipped. They will wait for some indication of where they should search."

Jaromir kept his eyes on Barbara, wondering where this was going.

"So how can we let them know I'm alive? And about where I am?"

Jaromir gave a wry smile. "I don't know. Cell phone connection down here is terrible."

Barbara grinned. "And so is my jewel connection. I can't receive any impulses from outside these walls, and I am almost sure mine get no further as well. But what if I could get near the transmission shaft? Get access to the antenna that leads outside. Would I be able to use my gem to at least send out a signal that could be picked up by Zoltan?"

Jaromir frowned. "The broadcast and reception equipment they have is astonishingly powerful. Would your jewel impulse be strong enough to penetrate to the surface? And even if you could get a signal out, how would they pick it up? They're probably miles from here."

"All true, but remember the men's jewels are meant to receive signals from a great distance." Barbara brought her palm to her chest and covered her jewel. Underneath her hand, the gem pulsed gently. "And mine has shown some capacities of its own, would you not agree?"

"Of course, but you are talking about transmitting a signal without direct contact with the antenna through a half mile of rock and then hope the men, assuming they escaped the tunnels, have identified your gem's wave frequency and devised a way of receiving it from a location that could be twenty or thirty miles away." Jaromir gave one of his characteristic shrugs. "Do you really think it could work?"

Barbara turned from the pool and walked toward the elevator. "Don't know, Agent Jaromir. But if I can finagle a way down to the floor, we may get a chance to find out."

#   #   #

The call to meet Justin came in the form of Meijer striding through Barbara's front entrance. As the door whispered upward, a sheet of blue and red flame shot up from the floor like an acetylene torch. Typically, Meijer had barged in head first. He screamed as the flame singed his eyebrows and burned his broad forehead and then lurched backwards, his round glasses clattering to the floor.

"Goddamn it," Meijer swore, pawing at his eyes.

"I believe the last time you visited," Barbara said, "I asked you to knock first, did I not?"

Meijer kicked at the doorway angrily, triggering another gout of flame. The acrid smell of rubber filled the room, and Meijer drew his foot back with a screech.

"What the fuck is this?" he roared, hopping on one leg.

"Mr. Meijer, you don't think I'm here because I am utterly without skills of my own, do you?" she asked tilting her head coyly. "Now, let's see. If you agree to knock in the future when visiting, perhaps I can remove the barrier you find so vexing. Deal?"

"If you don't…" Meijer snarled.

"Now, now, Mr. Meijer. I don't think you have the right attitude."

Suddenly the flame erupted from the floor again with a dramatic whooshing noise.

"Okay, okay," he screamed. "Just put it out!"

She felt vaguely guilty for enjoying the man's discomfort, but Jaromir was right. Meijer was a cruel man. She remembered his rough hands clenched painfully around her upper arm when they were in the caves. "Very well, Mr. Meijer, but I do hope you will try to be more courteous."

A final blast of fire erupted that caused Meijer to cover his face with his hands and cry out.

"Dear, dear," Barbara said, shaking her head. "Wrong way."

Meijer collapsed to the floor, panting, as the flame slowly extinguished and disappeared into the floor.

Barbara walked to the doorway and stared down at Meijer, who kneeled in the carpeted entranceway, running his hands across his blistered face.

"If I'm not mistaken, we have a date with Justin," she said, motioning toward the door. "Shall we?"

Meijer pulled himself up from the floor glaring at Barbara, his eyes, even more beady than usual without eyebrows, lit equally with hate and fear.

"And please, Mr. Meijer, don't forget your glasses," she reminded him helpfully.

As they hurtled downward in the elevator, Barbara wondered why this time the ride to Justin's office felt so different. She was somewhat ashamed to admit it, but having Meijer standing as far from her as possible and smelling of singed hair didn't hurt. When the elevator swished to a stop, she walked out and through the white door on her own. She strode to the end of the hall and stood in front of the wood doorway. She nodded slightly, and the door flew open, crashing against the wall.

To her delight, Justin pitched back in his chair in alarm, his eyes flickering with fear. She walked casually to the conference table and sat down, and then motioned to a chair across from her. "Join me?" she asked, smiling.

Justin stood up, glaring at the door just as Meijer rushed in rubbing what was left of his scorched eyebrows.

"Sorry, sir," he began, stammering in fear as Justin's blazing blue eyes turned toward him.

"What the hell happened to you?" he demanded, eyeing Meijer's blackened shirt collar and singed hair. He glanced at Barbara, who sat demurely at the table. Justin took a breath and waved the back of his hand dismissively. "Never mind, Meijer. Just close the door when you leave."

Meijer grabbed the door and tried to pull it shut, but Barbara inserted a doorstop, and he kept slamming the door desperately, over and over. Barbara watched fury surge in Justin's face. She nodded almost imperceptibly toward the door, and it whispered shut.

Justin stood behind his desk, breathing hard. He slowly turned toward Barbara sitting quietly at the table.

"Do you have any coffee?" she asked.

Barbara had expected the black stabs to her forehead, but they still pressed her back into her chair. She shook her head sadly. "Guess not."

Barbara focused on his eyes, which were once again dilating from round to oval. As they shifted, the jabs of fury became stronger but less focused, slashing around her harmlessly. She counterthrust, watching as his head pitched back as if struck with a blow to the forehead. He staggered several steps backward.

Barbara settled into her chair.

Justin regained his balance and struggled to control his anger. His pupils became round again and his attacks slackened. They faced each other across the room in absolute silence.

"Quite an entrance," Justin said at last, his voice tight but controlled. "Very entertaining."

Barbara said nothing and held his stare unblinkingly.

"It seems you have been honing your skills since I saw you last." He dropped his eyes and walked to the table. He pulled out a chair and sat across from Barbara, his face wary. "I believe you asked for this meeting?"

"I have been thinking about our last discussion," Barbara began.

Justin nodded knowingly. "Ah, yes. You have seen Sibyl."

Barbara rocked gently in her chair. "Yes, I have. A charming woman."

Justin smiled cruelly. "And a rather ugly one, wouldn't you agree?"

Barbara shrugged slightly. "On the outside, perhaps, but quite lovely inside." She returned his smile. "The opposite of you."

Justin's smile drooped and his full lips drew into a tight line.

"And as for the hideous exterior," Barbara went on, "that's what you would have people believe, isn't it? But actually it's simply an illusion."

Justin pulled out a chair and sat down, looking at her evenly.

"In fact, I'd say that's what you are: A master of illusion. You take what's ugly and hateful and make it seem attractive, palatable, and even moral." Barbara leaned her elbows on the polished wood top of the conference table. "And twist the beautiful and kind to make them seem repulsive and weak."

Barbara sensed the confusion and knew it would take very little to push him into another frenzy.

"So yes, I saw Sibyl. In all her interior and exterior beauty."

Justin continued to glare at her but said nothing.

"We talked for some time." Barbara fixed Justin with a steady gaze. "And I am here to bargain, for my future and hers."

Justin's defenses weakened slightly as he considered her comments, letting Barbara slide in an impulse of belief and sincerity in the form of a small red wedge.

"Go on," he said.

Barbara sat back in her chair. "I am not going to sit here and rot. By now you know that I can create utter chaos for you. And I am not oblivious to your ability to respond. So I have a proposal for you."

Now was the time. Her plan, such as it was, demanded mobility and access to both the communications center and to Sibyl. It was a high-stakes bluff, and to work she had to convince Justin of her sincerity, that accepting her proposition would be a win for him.

Justin had reestablished his guard, and his eyes narrowed slightly. "I'm listening."

"You have imprisoned Sibyl for nearly two years. You have taken her sight. And you have created an illusion that makes her appear hideous to viewers you influence. I believe you have exacted the revenge you sought."

A slight smile returned to Justin's lips. "My object was not simply revenge. It was to remind those that might challenge me that there are consequences." His eyes grew hard like chips of ice. "Serious consequences."

"But you are not rid of her, are you? She refuses to leave for fear that you will have her killed if she leaves the Company compound. She sits in her hut and bides her time. And now there's me," Barbara said, smiling sweetly.

"You don't know what to do with me either. For some reason, your suicide solution just isn't all that attractive. So you're stuck with both of us."

Barbara mentally circled Justin, monitoring his fluctuating emotions—anger, frustration, hatred and, she was pleased to note, a touch of fear.

"So why not get rid of two birds with one stone?" Barbara asked leaning forward on the table again. "Here's the deal. For six months, I will work on restructuring the gem program that is, I fear, in some disarray. During that time I will promise not to directly challenge you or your authority."

"And at the end of six months?"

"You will free both Sibyl and me and return us to the surface. You will be done with us forever."

"And why wouldn't I simply kill you both once you were released?"

"Because it wouldn't be that easy, would it? We would not take to being murdered kindly. Together we would be a formidable force."

Justin stared at her across the table. She felt the tumult in him, the uncertainty.

"But I could not have that, could I? A hostile, as you put it, formidable force working outside to upend my work here, derail the critical mission to which we are committed."

"No. And that's why Sibyl and I will agree to have our memories of this place erased, just as you do with your regular employees."

Justin tilted his handsome head, intrigued. His thoughts were so clear Barbara could almost hear them in her head. *What a relief that would be,* he thought. *Done with the two of them. And once I had them outside of the Company, I would kill them.*

Justin's eyes flickered. "I see."

He stared silently at her, wondering, Barbara sensed once again, what he had on his hands with her. Questioning the wisdom of bringing her to the complex. How and if he could still use her. Whether her offer was a trap.

His eyes softened. "As you know, I welcomed you to my organization because of my confidence that you could make some very positive contributions. I regret that we have not been able to find a role for you here."

Justin looked at her for a long time, Barbara felt him probing, attempting to determine her sincerity. Barbara held his gaze for a long moment then dropped her eyes to the table.

What do you have to lose? She projected to him. *She'd be monitored the whole time. At least it would shut her up. Maybe she could be useful there. Better that than making trouble out of boredom and resentment.*

"I don't trust you," Justin said affably. "Any time you spend on the work floor, every minute, you will be supervised."

"Nor do I trust you," Barbara replied. "But that doesn't mean we can't find a confluence of interests, does it?"

Justin stared at her, still and quiet. Only the pupils of his eyes moved, narrowing and darkening, as he studied the woman in front of him. "I will give you a trial," he said at last, "but I will keep you close at hand. As I believe you know, the gem project is located across the hall. Tomorrow you will be taken to the project headquarters and oriented." His eyes hardened again. "You will be escorted to the office and back. You are not to be on this level unsupervised. Is that clear?"

Barbara gave a slight nod. Now, to ensure access to Sibyl. "I was quite taken with your amenities here," she said, trying to curl her lips in a modest leer. "Am I free to visit the other floors?"

Justin gave her a wide smile. "The Pleasure Floor, yes." His eyes darted from her face and chest to her hands folded in her lap. "I imagine you will find some entertainment to your liking. You will be tracked at all times. You are not to enter the work floor or Gardens without a member of the team accompanying you. Is that clear?"

This was not what she'd hoped for.

Barbara nodded meekly. "I have a feeling Mr. Meijer would pass on that duty," she said. "Besides, he is a bore."

"Indeed," Justin said, visibly relaxing. "But it's so hard to get good help these days."

"Perhaps Mr. Garripoli or Mr. Jaromir?" Barbara suggested, calculating that Garripoli was too valuable to squander on chaperoning a mere woman, no matter how potentially valuable.

"I believe we could spare Jaromir for a few hours a day." He stood up, signifying the discussion was over. "I will give Jaromir instructions. Now, if you will excuse me. I have much work to do, and quite frankly, you have wasted too much of my time already."

Barbara said nothing. She pushed her chair back and began to walk to the door. She felt his anger, distrust and caution stalking her.

"One more thing," he said.

Barbara turned, expecting some warning, but when it came, even though she was ready, it still staggered her. Great black wings beat around her shoulders, trying to crush her, smother her. She stood still until the shrieking dark winds blew out around her and disappeared.

"Don't fuck with me, Mrs. Steubenville."

Chapter 24

THE DAY AFTER BARBARA'S ENCOUNTER with Justin, Jaromir escorted her back to the Garden and another visit with Sibyl to report, with Justin's blessing, the bargain she had negotiated.

"You're sure we can't be overheard?" Jaromir asked, eyeing the curved walls of Sibyl's hut.

Sibyl smiled. "For two years I've heard that man beating around my house, trying to get in. Big bad wolf. But, honey, I am electric." As she spoke, a green, humming aura curled around her head. "Not only is this place impenetrable, he got some nasty shocks for poking around. He's not going to fool with me."

Jaromir stood just inside the door. Even from a distance Barbara could see the uncertainty still clouding his grey eyes. "Agent Jaromir," she said. "Relax. You are in good hands. He cannot get you here."

"Now, Barbara," Sibyl said. "I see you've been busy."

She was finally getting used to Sibyl's reference to sight, and turning her blank eyes on Barbara as if they were making perfectly normal eye contact.

"My meeting with Justin *was* rather eventful," admitted Barbara.

"Eventful!" Jaromir exclaimed. "Meijer came back to the compound utterly terrified with skin peeling off his nose and no eyebrows!"

Sibyl cocked her head.

"Small disagreement around entry etiquette," Barbara explained.

"And Justin?"

"Oh, you know him. Gets so angry when you drop in unannounced."

"Yeah," Jaromir added. "And blow the doors off his private office."

Sibyl rocked back and forth slightly, smiling. "Uh, uh. Wish I could have seen *that*."

"We struck a deal," Barbara said. "Sort of."

"A deal with the devil?"

"More of a feint to buy time. You were a big help. He figured after seeing the horrible consequences of defying him I had seen the error of my ways and was coming around."

"So glad I could be of assistance," Sibyl smiled.

"Yes, but not in that way. I told him I saw through his illusion. That you were beautiful. On the inside, opposite of him."

"Huh," Sibyl said. "How did he react to that?"

"The way I wanted him to, I think: He realized I am more powerful than he thought. That I am largely immune to his mind control. That gave me leverage. Like I said, I cut a deal with him. You see, I am going to help him reconstruct the gem-making project. Then he is going to release you and me."

She explained how the plan bought them time and gave her access to the work floor. "He doesn't trust me, of course, so he has assigned Jaromir to be my chaperone."

Jaromir looked at her aghast. "He bought that?"

Barbara smiled. "With a little persuasion. I convinced Justin that he was better off keeping me busy. The bargain is that I would work on the gem project for six months. After that he will take Sibyl and me above ground and release us."

"What?" Jaromir cried. "And you believed him?"

Barbara rolled her eyes. "Of course not. I told him that we would allow our memories to be scrubbed, but his intention is to neutralize me while I'm here and then take us to ground level and kill us." She smiled broadly at Sibyl. "I think the idea of getting rid of you once and for all was what sold him. He's still scared to death of you."

"Um. That's nice to hear."

"So, tomorrow I get my introduction to the gem project. Later I will be able to visit the other floors. I'm on my own on the Pleasure Floor."

"Keep you stoned and happy," Sibyl commented.

"And on the work and garden floors, but only under the strict supervision of Agent Jaromir." She grinned broadly at him. "And under his scrutiny, while looking around the work floor, I will try to get to the communication complex and get a signal out." She paused. "And hope someone is listening."

"Justin said it was just fine for you to drop in on the communication hub. Just to say hello?" Jaromir said.

"Actually, no. He said the complex is strictly off limits. That I was not to even approach it. So that's where you fit in."

Jaromir looked at her quizzically.

"He's tracking me, so I can't be too blatant. But after two or three visits to the Gem Project offices, we will stroll around the work floor to see the extent of the operation. With your help, I will get as close to the complex as I can. If I can't get inside, hopefully I can send a transmission through the wall and then up through their antenna to the surface." She nodded at Jaromir. "You will stand watch for me and let me know if anyone is approaching."

Jaromir shrugged. "Great. If it's a berserker, I'll be sure to warn you before it tears your head off."

"I thought they couldn't kill inside the Company compound."

"True. They just make you wish you were dead." He paused. "Even if you do get close enough, I figure you have one chance, at best. If Justin sees you're hanging around the communication complex, I suspect your pass will be cancelled." He looked at her, his face grim. "Or worse."

"Look, it was the best I could do on short notice," Barbara said, an edge of irritation in her voice.

"In any event," Sibyl broke in, "we can't depend on anyone outside to save us. Whether Barbara gets the signal out, or whether her friends are able to receive it or have enough time to track it, well, that we have no control over. It is up to us to get out of here."

Barbara nodded and leaned forward eagerly. "You're right, of course. Please, tell us your plan."

Sibyl turned toward Barbara. "Honey, I don't have any plans."

"But you said you know another way out," Barbara protested.

"Knowing there is another way out and knowing how to use it are two very different things." She looked toward Jaromir, her eyes still shut. "As Jaromir knows, the Committee brought me on four years ago. It seems they had lost confidence in Justin. They were not getting the return they wanted. Environmental concerns were leading to demands for stricter industrial controls. Governments willing to tax the rich were getting elected. Détente was breaking out. There were calls for less military spending. The boys were getting scared."

Barbara looked into Sibyl's beautiful face, dismayed. "And you agreed to help them?"

Sibyl raised her hands. "Now, don't get carried away, girl. I was young, ambitious. I had risen through corporate ranks but knew I'd hit the ceiling. How far do you think a black woman gets in this system?"

Barbra looked at her dubiously. "Go on."

"And everyone knew there was something odd about me."

"And that was?"

"I am telekinetic. I had known it since I started mentally pushing cats off sofas where I wanted to sit when I was three. I tried to hide it, but it got stronger as I got older. I stopped a semi from slamming into a stalled car at an intersection while I was sitting in my car. Just stopped it. The media called it a miracle, but I never came forward. A mugger attacked me in New Orleans one night. Gun pointed at my head. Made me really mad, so I slammed that pistol into that son-of-a-bitch's head so hard it fractured his skull."

"Okay, so you were different and frustrated with your corporate advancement. Boo Hoo. What the hell does that have to do with joining up with the Company of barbarians?"

"Girl, I may be blind, but I know when I'm being judged mighty harshly. You just back off a bit now."

Barbara took a few deep breaths and tried to soften her forehead and loosen her jaw.

"That's better. I was recruited. By some very nice young men. Very rich nice young men. They were headhunters, they said."

"Literally," Barbara muttered.

"They were interested in both my outstanding administrative skills and additional powers they had heard about."

"Your telekinesis. How did they know?"

"Honey, these things get around in certain circles. They literally made me an offer I couldn't refuse. Autonomy, money, bonuses…"

"Power," Jaromir said softly.

"Yes," Sibyl admitted. "And power. To make a *Kwange* in the world. To ensure there was stability and good government. That noble, genuine leaders were identified, selected and placed in positions of influence. To combine my extraordinary skills and knowledge with other outstanding Company personnel to contribute toward global survival during such turbulent times."

"To make the world run as it should," Barbara said.

Sibyl chuckled softly. "Exactly."

"How long did it take you to figure out what was really going on?" Barbara asked.

"About two days," Sibyl gave a snort. "By then it was too late. I had signed a five-year contract. Which included a no-exit clause." Sibyl shook her head in amusement. "Literally."

"But you continued working for the Company," Barbara said disbelievingly, "even after you saw the vileness of their ideology? Of the product they *really* sold?"

"What could I do, girl? Couldn't leave. Couldn't stay. At first I tried to see if I could influence direction. I asked to convene the Committee to review our mission statement." She laughed. "You can imagine how that went over. So then I just bided my time. Tried to get as much information on the operation as possible. Stayed out of Justin's way and did the best I could to find allies on the Committee. And when I couldn't take it anymore, I confronted Justin at a Committee meeting."

Barbara noticed that the woman's usually expressive face became set and her breathing short and shallow.

"I lost," she said.

"Your eyes?"

"Uhm. I kept my mind closed but my eyes open. It felt like two ice daggers plunging into my sockets."

"I'm sorry," Barbara murmured.

The three sat quietly for a long time.

Sibyl's face softened and her breath became normal again. "And now you are here," she finished, smiling broadly.

Sibyl nodded to a small ebony-wood trunk against the wall where Barbara was sitting. "Honey, you mind opening that box over there and pulling out the long brass tube?"

Barbara leaned over and lifted the heavy lid. It smelled of dust mixed with wood and old brass. The tube lay on the bottom, covered in papers, books and elaborate landscape sketches Barbara knew were Sibyl's. She handed the tube up to Sibyl sitting upright on her large round cushion. She expertly unscrewed the end cap and pulled out a roll of yellowing papers. She leaned forward and spread them across the low table in front of her.

Barbara and Jaromir stared down at diagrams of what looked like a system of mine shafts; sketches of a large underground lake; more diagrams, these of mining elevators; and what appeared to be a map.

After a long minute of shuffling through the papers, Jaromir asked, "What are we looking at here?"

"Our way out," Sibyl said. "If there is one."

"I know you don't have a plan," Barbara said. "But I do hope you have a bit more explanation."

"Are you looking at the sketch?"

Barbara unrolled the drawing of the lake. It had been drawn in ink and was finely detailed. "Yes."

"That, my friends, is the Company's water supply."

Jaromir frowned thoughtfully. "So the pipe that empties into the pool…"

"Draws its water from the underground lake you are looking at."

"Just behind the walls," Jaromir said.

"Yep. The sides of the Company complex are carved from the natural rock and then lined with a copper, nickel, zinc alloy. Provides total shielding from radio and electromagnetic waves."

"Noted," Barbara said.

"But at the pool…"

"There would be only a wall separating the pool area from the reservoir on the other side," Jaromir said.

Sibyl beamed. "You're a quick learner, Jaromir dear."

Barbara shook her head. "Okay, so I guess I am a *slow* learner. What does this have to do with anything?"

Jaromir pointed to the picture of the lake. "The lake acts as a reservoir for the complex."

Barbara nodded. "Okay."

"So the wall behind the pool isn't solid rock." He pointed to the far left end of the sketched lake. "There is only the barrier, which acts as a dam, between the cavern and the Gardens."

Barbara nodded. "That's why I felt the weakening by the pool. If we could get through the barrier, we'd be in the cavern." She turned to Sibyl. "But isn't that sort of like being out of the fire and into the frying pan?"

"Except for one thing," Sibyl said in her rich voice. "Elevators."

"That's handy," Barbara commented. "They installed elevators for us."

Sibyl laughed. "Not for us. For coal miners two hundred years ago."

"Come again?"

"The whole Company complex was built here because the cavern had been discovered over a hundred and fifty years ago when a coal shaft broke through. The lake is about two miles long and the mine elevators are on the north side, if we can find them."

Jaromir frowned. "But even if we could find a way through the barrier, we could come up at the bottom of the lake."

Sibyl nodded. "We could but we won't. One thing I learned is that there are more ways than one to see. I had the skills—I knew that—but when I lost my sight, I began to understand them better, to develop them. So now I can see—sometimes in the oddest ways." She paused. "It's hard to explain. I can walk around the gardens without striking a thing. I don't see what's around me, but I sense obstacles. Like I'm operating on radar-driven autopilot."

She looked at Jaromir. "And I can see you have a good heart, troubled as it is." The she turned to Barbara. "And you, girl. Um, um. You are *red*!"

Barbara looked at Sibyl in surprise. "Is that good?"

Sibyl rocked back and forth, laughing. "Honey, you have *juju* to spare. No wonder Justin wanted you so bad. Course now he doesn't quite know what to do with you."

She stopped chuckling and opened her opaque eyes to stare at Barbara. "Did he give you a suicide pill?"

Barbara fingered the ring uneasily.

"Thought so." Sibyl raised her right hand, showing a duplicate of the ring Barbara wore. "Be careful. He will play with your mind." She closed her eyes again and leaned backward. "Came close lots of times." Her deep voice softened. "Lots of times."

"Sibyl, Barbara," Jaromir said. "We don't have much time. The longer we're here the more likely we are to be discovered. They will tail us. Find some way of listening in. We may get away with this meeting and one or two others, but at some point…"

Sibyl nodded. "You're right. So here's the point: When I was on The Committee and realized I was trapped, I used my time to explore the history of the place, to see if I could find an escape route." She nodded at the papers on the table. "That's when I found and copied these. After my, uh, disagreement with Justin, I became desperate. I explored every possibility." She nodded at the papers spread in front of them. "I realized that other than the main entrance, this is the only way out. So I sat outside on the bench by the pool and let that radar sight thing have a look at what was between me and the reservoir."

Barbara and Jaromir leaned forward slightly.

"There was good news and bad news. The good news was that the lake level is just a few feet above the water pipe on this side of the wall. On the other side, the water stretches for about sixty feet along the wall. But if I could get through the wall, there is about twenty feet or so of shoreline all the way to the far end of the cavern. If I punched a hole through in the right place, I'd be on the lake shore high and dry."

"And the bad news?" Barbara asked.

"I couldn't get through. At some point, maybe a hundred years ago when they first built this place, they reinforced the dam and inserted the pipe into the pool on this side to provide water for the complex. Then they built a stone wall and lined it with the same impermeable covering they used in the rest of the complex. The wall alone is six feet thick, at least, and made from limestone blocks quarried inside the cavern and fit into a waterproof wall.

With no mortar. Quite a feat."

Barbara tilted her head. "But if you couldn't get through then, how can we do it now? What's different?"

"You, honey. That's what's different."

Chapter 25

WITH ZOLTAN'S KNOWLEDGE OF THE city and Hungarian, it had taken Maphaela and Kwan less than a day to locate the equipment they needed and set it up in the bedroom. Using their gems, they began scanning the transmission frequency.

"Would you mind having a look?" Maphaela asked.

Kwan moved to the man's side, watching the numbers flicker on the receiver's LED display.

"What's the frequency range now?"

"Between 375 and 500 GHz. P Band."

"Jesus, I didn't even know there *was* a P Band. Or that anything transmitted at that high of a frequency."

"No one uses it anymore." Maphaela tuned the antenna for maximum directional scanning. "Old radar frequency, really. But that's what our stones are working at." He sat back in the cheap folding chair. "I just hope Barbara's is set to the same band."

"Or that she can transmit at all." Both men turned to Friesen, who was standing behind them.

"Not sure what else we can do," Kwan said.

"We can go back in the caves and find her," Friesen growled. He waved his hand at the equipment they had purchased. "This is a fucking long shot at best."

Zoltan entered the bedroom they were using for their radio equipment and walked toward the men. He put his hand on Friesen's shoulder.

"I understand your impatience. And your courage, my friend," he said. "But we have agreed to try this, yes? No one wants to find Barbara more than I." He thought about his sleepless nights, his mind filled with images of Barbara standing proud and defiant saying to Justin, "I will stay, but only when they are released and are out of this maze."

Friesen looked at Zoltan and dropped his eyes.

"So, let's give this a few days, yes?"

Friesen nodded. "I'm sorry."

"No need for that," Zoltan smiled. "We've been through too much together to apologize. I share your frustration." He nodded at the Kwan and Maphaela, their faces set and determined. "We all do."

"Let's get started then," Maphaela said. "Now that we have the frequency isolated…"

"Hopefully," Friesen added.

Maphaela ignored the comment. "We can set our receptor to receive any transmission sent on that frequency."

The men watched in awe as Maphaela set to work. Using some tools and wiring acquired from a rather run-down electronics store they had found in a side street deep in the Jewish Quarter, he connected the receiver to a roll of insulated wire and tossed the wire outside through the open window. He leaned an ancient wood ladder that had been stored against the side of the house against a utility pole that held a power running down the alley behind the mansion. He climbed up the ladder with a pair of wire cutters and the roll of insulated wire over his shoulder.

"You're going to splice directly into the line?" Friesen called as he held the ladder. "That's two-twenty, you know. That can kill you."

"True," Maphaela called down. "The trick is not to ground it. Like birds on a wire."

Friesen squeezed his eyes shut.

By late evening, the receiver, attached wirelessly to a rotating directional antenna on the utility pole outside, was operational, its green LED display flickering numbers that meant nothing to anyone other than Maphaela.

And then they waited.

Chapter 26

FOR THE NEXT TWO DAYS Barbara contented herself with daily visits to the gem project offices. Jaromir would pick her up and they sank directly down the elevator to the bottom floor. The project was located on the other side of the wide ceramic hall from Justin's office: double doors opening onto a space the size of a small gymnasium. The area was divided carefully into sectors, including a long laboratory that ran along the right wall when they entered. A few workers in lab coats stared at screens and hovered over elaborate control panels. Along the far wall, a sealed workshop contained various gem machines, housed in old wood cameras, in various stages of completion. Several technicians worked on the units, adjusting dials and monitoring responses with handheld computers. A line of workstations ran down the center of the space connecting the two labs.

But most of the cubicles were empty. Most of the staff of twenty or so were huddled around a bank of monitors that covered most of the wall behind them. Mathematical data that Barbara could not understand flowed across the screen like a tickertape. A hologram map of the world turned slowly underneath, tiny red, yellow, and green lights blinking uncertainly. A young man glanced away from the screen as Barbara and Jaromir entered and stood inside the doorway.

The man looked at them anxiously and hurried over, his hand extended. "Agent Jaromir. And you must be Mrs. Steubenville."

Barbara looked at the man coolly. He couldn't have been more than forty, she figured, his long brown hair brushed over his scalp in a desperate attempt to hide his baldness. She wondered idly if his carefully trimmed goatee was an attempt to compensate.

"Barbara," she corrected. "Just Barbara."

"Of course," the man said, smiling broadly. "First name basis. Let's cut to the chase, eh?"

"Barbara," Jaromir said. "This is Dr. Matthews. He is a molecular physicist on the project."

Matthews waved his hand. "Dan," he said. "Dr. Dan will do." He smiled his wide toothy smile again, motioning to a door to the right of the entranceway. "Please. Do come into my office."

As Barbara had expected, the entire operation was in chaos. Even Dr. Dan seemed to know little about what had occurred above ground. They had hardly sat down across from Matthews' large desk before he began asking questions. They had lost contact with the gem makers. They could no longer monitor their activities or send them client contact information. What was going on? The data they had collected had been erased. Where was it? Had three of the agents really been killed? Workers were not even sure if the project would continue.

Aware that every word she uttered would be monitored, Barbara agreed to update the team on what she knew about recent events. But she also pointed out that she had been assigned to the project mainly there to observe. She was not equipped to provide any direct assistance. But she knew Justin was working on a recovery plan he would soon introduce.

Barbara gave the team a minimal explanation: the black stone had been destroyed, three gem carriers had been killed in an unfortunate accident, she had no idea what the future held.

After the initial interest, Barbara showed she had little to offer and just generally stayed out of the way as the gem project team continued to operate in a vacuum.

Of more interest to Barbara was their quick visit to the work floor. On the way back from the Gem Project lab, she and Jaromir strolled along the passageways through the aisles of cubicles, Barbara calculating how she could best access the communication complex. The second day they tried to approach the communication center directly, Jaromir leading her down a passage between units toward the communication center entrance. As they neared the intersection with a walkway in front of the communication unit, Jaromir stopped suddenly. In front of her a Berserker stood, his massive arms folded over his chest, clearly guarding the entrance to the complex.

They backed up quickly to avoid being spotted.

"Guess he really didn't trust me," she muttered to Jaromir as they returned to the elevator.

That night they devised a plan. The next day when returning from the Gem Project, Jaromir went ahead of Barbara and walked to the entrance of the communication center. The guard stopped him, and Jaromir engaged the Berserker by insisting he be allowed inside to visit his associate.

From around the corner, Barbara heard the Berserker's voice, inflectionless and threatening.

"No one is allowed in without authorization," the Berserker rasped.

"But I have an associate working here," Jaromir protested. "I just want to let her know I'm back."

While they argued, Barbara slipped down the passageway to the far corner of the towering wall that separated the complex from the rest of the work floor. She pressed up against the metal barrier and closed her eyes.

She immediately sensed that the partition was permeable, a dense but thin wall her gem could easily penetrate. She felt more than heard the voices inside the unit, feeling the flow of energy upward as if it were being sucked up by a giant vacuum. She yanked her gem out of her blouse and held it against the wall. She concentrated on the glowing red jewel, focusing it, strengthening its conduction. It warmed in her hand and she felt the energy from her stone being pulled through the wall and coursing upward like an electrical current, joining a thousand other transmissions.

She knew she only had a few minutes. She pressed against the hard wall, her eyes shut.

Suddenly she heard Jaromir yell, "Alright then. I'm leaving!"—their signal that he could not stall any longer—and she quickly pulled back into the maze of cubicles.

"Jaromir," she called out quietly as he strode angrily down the walkway.

"I'm here."

Jaromir looked briefly over his shoulder to make sure the Berserker wasn't watching and then quickly veered into the passageway and joined Barbara.

"Could you transmit?" he whispered as they walked back toward the elevator.

Barbara kept her eyes focused straight ahead. "I think so," she replied. "Yes. Now the question I guess is are they listening."

"I hope so," Jaromir said as they entered the dark glass rectangle that housed the elevator, "because I doubt we'll have another chance. They must suspect something." He looked out the glass elevator shaft nervously. "Too much going on. I've never seen security at the Media Center so tight."

They had intentionally stayed away from Sibyl, but after getting the transmission out, Barbara knew they were quickly running out of time. She wouldn't be able to keep up the charade much longer, and if Zoltan did pick up her signal, they would be looking for her. How long could they sustain a search on the basis of a single transmission?

Once in the elevator, Barbara moved close to Jaromir. "Don't stop at the residential floor," she whispered. "We have to see Sibyl. We have to make our move soon or it will be too late."

Jaromir nodded grimly.

They continued on to the Garden Floor and made their way toward Sibyl's hut.

Chapter 27

"JESUS CHRIST, IT'S HER!" MAPHAELA shouted from the radio room.

Malik sprang from his chair in the living room and rushed to Maphaela's side. The other men were dozing fitfully on dusty carpets under a few cheap blankets they had bought. As one, they rolled from under their covers and stumbled toward the chirping of the receiver.

"Malik," Maphaela ordered. "Bring the car to the front of the house. Go!"

Malik turned and sprinted to the back entrance.

"What's going on?" Friesen asked groggily.

"Shut up!" Maphaela barked, desperately turning dials and watching numbers flicker on the display until the chirping became a steady buzz.

"Kwan, write these down. Now!"

Kwan rushed to the table and grabbed the clipboard next to Maphaela's elbow. He snapped a pen from his breast pocket. "Go."

"Longitude: *one nine point zero one six six three nine west,*" Maphaela called out loudly, enunciating each number. "Latitude: *four seven point four eight one seven five zero north.* "Maphaela picked up the glowing Garmin GPS in his left hand and tossed it to Friesen. "Enter this." He turned back to the screen and nodded to Kwan. "Repeat!"

Kwan read the numbers back clearly. "Got it!" Maphaela shouted. "Map!"

Friesen finished tapping in the coordinates. "What?"

"Map!" Maphaela repeated. "Map, man. Tap the map."

Maphaela kept his eyes on the screen in front of him, writing down the numbers himself to be sure while the other men huddled around the map that appeared on the GPS Friesen held. A red pin sprang onto the screen.

"Distance?" Maphaela asked.

"11.83 miles," Kwan called back. "Can you believe that? Practically under our nose."

Zoltan had been studying the map over Friesen's shoulder. "I know this place," he said. "It is in District twelve just southwest of us. Near *Sashegyi*—Eagle Mountain Park." He nodded. "Of course. The park is riddled with caves. This place is a preserved wilderness area."

Suddenly the loud buzzing that had been droning from the receiver stopped, leaving a menacing quiet. "We've lost her." Maphaela grabbed the coordinates he had written on his own pad and pushed his chair back. "Let's go."

The men sprinted through the kitchen and out the back door then around the old house to the black SUV waiting at the curb. Bright blue lights flashed from the inside dash, and the heavy traffic made its way warily around the SUV, glancing nervously at the tall turbaned figure sitting at attention in the driver's seat.

The men clambered into the car, and Malik pulled away as the last door shut.

Friesen nodded at the blue light, still oscillating on the dash. "Nice touch."

Malik ignored him. "Directions?"

"West on *Andrassy*," Zoltan said. "But at *József Atilla*, bear right. We'll take the *Szczesny* Bridge over the river. Less traffic."

The flashing blue light helped clear traffic as Malik wove through the crush of cars on the wide boulevard. He veered right as instructed and flew across the ancient chain suspension bridge and onto the broad road that passed just north of the Buda Castle, which loomed ominously on their left.

"Go left on *Mészáros*. You'll cross over the railroad tracks. Then take *Hegyalja út*. Just stay on it. It will wind through the hills and get us into the area." He looked to Maphaela, who now held the Garmon GPS in his hands, studying the map on the screen. "Then it's up to you."

The SUV rumbled over the tracks and sped through a mixed industrial area. Almost immediately they were in a dry, rolling country. Even with the city visible behind them, they had entered farming country with a scattering of small villages. Soon the fields gave way to rocky terrain covered in scrub trees and bushes. Bare limestone outcroppings poked through dry grass and wildflowers.

"Stay to the left up here," Maphaela ordered. "We want *Bod Péter ut*. Take it to the end. Then it looks like the road is blocked. We'll have to walk."

Malik guided the car arounda few houses and skirted a series of high hills on their right. The road became a dirt track as it wandered upward through low trees. They rounded a sharp curve and almost ran into a yellow metal gate set in old stone posts. The remains of an ancient wood fence trailed away into the woods on each side.

"Out," Maphaela said. "We're about 500 yards from the signal coordinate." He nodded up the overgrown ruts on the other side of the gate. "Up we go."

With Maphaela in the lead, the men jogged up the old road. At a fork, Maphaela veered to the right on a steep path that wound through low pines and boulders the size of a car. They hurried up the last few feet of trail over a ridge and burst into a clearing that covered the top of the hill. Broken rock and scrub trees were scattered across the field.

"Over here," Zoltan called, running toward a cluster of trees at the edge of the clearing. "I can feel it."

"Bingo," Maphaela said, looking at the GPS screen.

Zoltan reached the thicket and stopped, his eyes closed. He opened them and strode toward a small cairn of rocks. Just behind the cairn a solid metal rod about the thickness of Zoltan's thumb, almost indistinguishable among the stones and brush, jutted three feet into the air.

Maphaela rushed up behind Zoltan. "That's it," he said, switching off the GPS.

Friesen and the other two men crowded around the rod. Friesen looked around the rocky terrain and then back at the rod. "Okay," he said. "Who brought the shovels?"

The five men sat in a semi-circle facing the rod in front of them. "Can you hear it?" Zoltan asked.

Kwan squinted, concentrating. "A buzz."

Maphaela nodded. "Like hornets, louder then quieter."

Friesen pointed at the rod. "So what is it?"

"It's an antenna of some sort," Maphaela said. He examined the rod carefully. "Some sort of silver alloy would be my guess protected by anodized titanium."

"Silver?" Malik asked.

Maphaela nodded. "Best conductor on earth. It only has one valence electron. Moves around with little resistance. But from the strength and volume of the signals I'm picking up, it must be alloyed with something else. Even pure silver couldn't carry this conductivity weight." He shook his head. "This signal is what you'd expect from a major mast transmitter."

"I didn't mean what is it made of," Friesen said testily. "I mean 'What the fuck is it?' What does it do? Where does it go?"

Zoltan stared at the rod. "I believe it is a transmission and reception antenna attached to a broadcast system."

Friesen's forehead wrinkled. "Underground?"

Zoltan nodded. "The Company."

Kwan looked at Zoltan. "Sorry?"

"I heard stories. From other agents. They spoke of rumors that the *Mester* was part of something larger, more sinister—the Company. I paid little attention. I did not know if it was a place or an organization or even if it was real." He paused. "Nor did I care. But our late associate Dezső convinced that me that it is all of those." He paused, his eyes fixed on the ground in front of them. "And it is located directly underneath us."

"Where Justin took Barbara," Friesen said quietly.

Zoltan nodded again.

Friesen glanced over the broken landscape, tumbling down from the hilltop in a rocky slope studded with clusters of trees, sharp rock outcroppings and narrow valleys. A cool wind blew through the trees, rustling the leaves. He shivered. "How do we get down there?"

The men stared at the barren terrain and said nothing.

"It is possible," Zoltan said, "that there is an entrance. Perhaps a cave opening lower down, yes?"

"Possible, but not likely," Friesen said glumly. "Why would they go to all this trouble to put in a hidden antenna and then install a front door nearby? My guess is they are deep in the caves, and that we will only find this place by going back in." He kicked at a pebble and watched it tumble down the hill. "As I have said all along."

Malik raised his head. "You may yet prove to be right, Mr. Friesen. But we could not free her until we knew where she was." He nodded at the ground. "Now we know. But we are here now. I see no reason to leave without exploring the area." He looked at Zoltan. "Mr. József often senses things we cannot, I believe."

Maphaela stood up, dusting a few brown leaves from the seat of his jeans. "I agree." He looked around, scanning the space from the hilltop. "Based on the transmissions, if there is an entranceway, it would be within this area." He pointed at the edge of the roughly circular circumference of the hill below them, about two miles in diameter, which then spread into a treed plain, dotted in the distance with fields and a few houses.

Friesen got to his feet. "Okay, let's do it."

Zoltan stood and looked out over the broken terrain. The wind riffled his grey hair. "She is down there," he said, almost to himself. The four men looked at him but said nothing.

Zoltan smiled. "Gentlemen, you are good and loyal friends."

Friesen cleared his throat and looked away from the group.

"And if we find anything, anything at all, we will signal with our gems, yes?"

Malik stood high on a rock at the very top of the hill, scanning the landscape. "This is a large area to survey, Mr. József, and there will be this hill between us."

Zoltan looked up at the figure, silhouetted against the late summer sun. "Yes?"

"I do not believe we will be able to communicate directly, as we found in the caves." He jumped off the rock and looked at Zoltan. "I do not think you will like this, but you must stay and monitor signals."

Zoltan felt sick with despair. "No, please!" Zoltan protested. "I cannot sit here while you search. I must be looking too." He looked around at the men. "I *must* do something."

"Mr. Malik is right," Kwan said. "We need you here to relay messages."

"But…"

Maphaela put his hand on Zoltan's shoulder. "We know your desperation. We share it. But you can best contribute by staying here."

Zoltan looked morosely at the gravel at his feet.

"Come on, Zoltan," Friesen said, shifting his feet impatiently. "You know you're the best at receiving and sending. You gotta stay here." He glanced at Maphaela. "Can we go now?"

Maphaela nodded. "Let's take sections," Maphaela said. "Like pie slices." He spread his arms about two yards apart. "Stand next to me in a circle around the top of the hill and hold out your hands until we've covered the entire area."

Zoltan stood aside. Agony churned inside of him. He knew as certain as he breathed that Barbara was near them, deep beneath the ground perhaps, but almost connected to him by the thin metal rod protruding from the rocky soil. And he was to sit while the other men searched for an entrance that likely wasn't there.

The other four men arranged themselves in a ring until their arms encompassed the circumference. "Find markers at the bottom. Each of us will be responsible for that sector within our arms."

"It looks like I am to be left behind," Zoltan said grimly. "But you must promise that if you see anything, *anything* at all—a cave entrance or even a small breach in the rock—you will signal me immediately, yes?"

"Yes, Yes. Off we go," Friesen said, moving down the hillside.

The men quickly dispersed through the dry brush and rocks while Zoltan sat on the boulder Malik had vacated. He looked at the sun, calculating the hours of light they had left, and sat cross-legged on the rough surface of boulder. He pulled the chain attached to his jewel and drew out his blue-green gem from his vest pocket. He placed it in his palm and lay his other hand on top and waited, listening to the breeze blow uncertainly through the trees.

Chapter 28

BARBARA NOTICED THE BERSERKER FIRST. He stood in the shadows of the entrance to the African Garden as she and Jaromir approached. She started in surprise and felt her heartrate leap as the black figure moved toward them.

"Mr. Jaromir," it said in a voice so cold, so mechanical that Barbara wondered again if the thing was human.

Jaromir stopped and turned his hooded grey eyes on the approaching figure. If he is afraid, Barbara thought, he sure isn't showing it.

"Yes."

"Officer Garripoli wants you."

By this time the Berserker stood only a few feet away. Barbara stared up into the dull metal mask and shuddered. The voice seemed to come from the silver oval where the mouth should be, but she could see nothing through the grid. Behind the fine protective screens that covered the two round eye holes, dark eyes moved alertly, darting between Barbara and Jaromir. The pupils seemed to cover the entire eye, like two polished obsidian beads.

Barbara sensed Jaromir pull himself to his full height. He tilted his head back slightly to look the Berserker in the eye. "As you can see," he nodded toward Barbara, "I am presently engaged."

"Well, disengage," the voice rasped, flat and menacing. "He wants you now."

How much does Garripoli know? Barbara wondered. *Can I still use my position to buy us some time?* She turned toward the figure, which loomed over her. "You are a member of the CBM, I understand. A very important branch of the Company operation."

The Berserker turned his attention toward her, the black eyes shifting behind the round screens. "That's correct."

Barbara held out her hand. "I've been hoping to fit you into my fact-finding schedule. As you no doubt know, I have recently joined the Company and Justin has encouraged me to learn as much about the operations as possible."

The mention of Justin had the desired effect. The metal mask drew back slightly. He glanced at Barbara's hand and uncertainly held out his own.

Barbara had expected the huge hand to be cold, maybe covered in some sort of mail, but it felt entirely human, the strength in the fingers nearly crushing her hand as the Berserker folded them around hers. She closed her eyes.

The being had been modified, but it was human, that much she was sure of. She felt the blood pulsing slowly, regularly through the palm of its hand, but somehow the man had been gutted, anything unnecessary to function in its capacity as Company enforcer removed, and refitted with brute physical power unhampered by fear or compassion.

Barbara probed behind the mask and encountered the blankness of the dull, smooth exterior. The silver earpieces on each side of the mask contained receptors that routed commands directly into the neocortex, bypassing inhibitory circuits. These were beings designed to act on command, without judgment, ethics, or questions.

She opened her eyes and stared into the eyeholes. *You have delivered your message. Agent Jaromir is on an important mission sanctioned by Justin. You will return to Officer Garripoli and report that Agent Jaromir will report to the Compound as soon as he has taken the woman to her apartment. That is all.*

The Berserker took a step back and looked at Jaromir. "I will report to Officer Garripoli that you will report to the Compound as soon as you have taken the woman to her apartment."

Jaromir shot a glance at Barbara. "Very good," he said. "I will join

Officer Garripoli shortly."

The tall figure strode toward the elevator.

"How the hell did you do that?" Jaromir whispered.

"Never mind. We have to move now. They're on to us. We break out now or…" She didn't need to finish.

"But we don't even have a plan," Jaromir protested.

"True, but how much time do you think we have before they're swarming up here in force? And do you think Garripoli just wanted to have a little chat?"

"Not long and no, in that order," Jaromir replied.

"Right. Run and get Sibyl."

Jaromir nodded and sprinted to the entranceway of the hut. The door whispered open. "We must leave. Now," he called to Sibyl.

Sibyl made no protest. Within seconds, she emerged from the doorway and grasped Jaromir's outstretched hand. Together they hurried to Barbara's side, and the trio rushed back along the trail to the central pool.

The pool was a rectangle about one hundred feet long. A railing ran across the front and then along both sides for forty feet to the blank wall. Twenty-foot-wide promenades ran along both sides of the pool, forming a shallow U. On the left side of the pool, the elevator opened onto the promenade, but on the right, the walkway simply ended at the blank face of the wall. It rose twenty feet to the ceiling, which extended over the gardens. Barbara hurried along the railing to the right side of the pool and stood in front of the solid wall in front of her. On her left and about six feet below her, she heard the water pouring from the brass pipe into the pool. She studied the dull white wall in front of her.

It was covered with the same alloy as the rest of the complex, but behind this section, she knew from Sibyl's drawings, instead of solid rock there was a wall made of limestone blocks. They would need to cut through the thick covering and then, somehow, move enough blocks out of the way to enter the cavern beyond. She glanced at the angle of the brass cylinder gushing below her and guessed from the diagram that the intake on the other side would only be a few feet higher than the water level in the pool. That meant if they got through the wall, they would probably be three or four feet above the lake shore. Probably.

She sensed Jaromir and Sibyl hurrying up behind her.

"Girl, you could have at least given me time to pack," Sibyl said.

"Sorry for the inconvenience," Barbara said, not turning around. "How the hell are we going to do this?"

"Can you cut through the sheathing with your jewel?" Jaromir asked.

Barbara pulled her jewel out from her shirt and looked at it resting in her hand, giving off a soft rose glow. "I think so."

"And Sibyl, can you move the blocks with your telekinesis?"

Sibyl stood next to Barbara, mentally examining the barrier in front of them. "I don't know," she said. "I can move loose objects. Not sure if it's in a solid wall."

Barbara glanced at her over her shoulder. "Thanks for sharing that with us."

"Hey, girl!" Sibyl protested. "I didn't know we were going to dash out here and jump through the wall. I thought we'd at least have a dry run."

"Okay. That's enough," Jaromir said. "None of us knew we'd be here now. But we are."

All three turned to the wheeze of the elevator arriving at the other side of the pool. Eight Berserkers emerged from the doorway and cautiously made their way onto the Garden Floor landing. Even from their distance, Barbara could see that the mouth pieces of two of the tall, black-robed figures were gold, gleaming against the smooth metal mask.

"Shit," Jaromir muttered.

"They haven't seen us yet," Barbara whispered, crouching behind the metal bars of the barrier fencing.

"They're not sure we're up here," Jaromir said. "Or there would be more of them."

One of the officers with the gold mouthpiece stood in front of the group; his black-hooded head swept deliberately around the perimeter of the Garden. Slowly the round eyes turned their way.

Barbara jumped as the huge redwood standing outside the entrance to the Forest Garden crashed suddenly onto the group of Berserkers in front of the elevator. To her horror, Barbara watched as three of the figures casually caught the massive trunk in their hands and tossed it aside. She turned back to Sibyl, who was crouching, her eyes closed, facing the melee on the other side of the pond.

Clear of the tree trunk, the lead Berserker charged inside the entrance to the Forest Garden, the others following behind.

"Way to go," Barbara said admiringly.

Sibyl put her hand to her lovely neck. "*Moi*?" She asked modestly. "You think I might have had something to do with that?"

"We only have a few minutes," Jaromir whispered urgently. "Whatever we are going to do, we need to do it now."

Barbara stood and moved closer to the wall until she stood only three feet away. She raised her gem and closed her eyes. As the other two watched, the jewel burned brighter until it became a glowing red coal in Barbara's fingers. Barbara concentrated the energy into a red shaft the size of a pencil.

"Get ready," Sibyl said. "All hell is going to break loose when she breaches that wall."

Her eyes still closed, Barbara quickly drew a glowing red square on the wall with the beam. As it travelled along the surface, a tiny plume of black smoke curled upward.

They had all expected some response when she cut through the outer covering, but none of them was prepared for the mind-numbing screech that filled the hall. She had set off an alarm no one had mentioned, an alarm so powerful it could deafen in minutes.

Barbara pulled her attention away from the wall and saw Sibyl and Jaromir on their knees, palms over their ears. She cast a noise-reducing netting and dropped it around them, reducing the frequency they detected from 20,000 Hz to nothing. They stood up, shaking, and Barbara returned to the wall.

She completed the burn through the wall covering in seconds. Then, holding her jewel like an Exacto knife went over the outline again. She had expected the square to fall out and onto the floor, but nothing happened. It stayed firmly in place. Damn, what if she couldn't penetrate the material after all? Why had she been so confident?

"Fuck!" she cried, kicking the square in frustration.

The square, still smoking along the edges, promptly tilted and fell to the floor at Barbara's feet.

The piece she removed was thicker than she had expected, about eight inches deep. Now she looked through the six-foot hole she had carved. Just as Sibyl had promised, she stared at a wall of limestone blocks, each about three feet square.

"Sibyl!" she called.

Jaromir tapped Barbara on her back and motioned to his ears.

Barbara quickly lightened the netting. "Can you hear me?" Barbara asked.

Jaromir nodded.

"But not the siren?"

He nodded again.

"Sibyl!" Barbara yelled again.

Sibyl hurried up behind her. "Thanks for the earplugs, honey."

"Can you move those blocks?"

"Trouble!" Jaromir shouted behind her.

Barbara turned quickly and saw the Berserkers pouring out of the Forest Garden entrance. One of the officers held a pistol with a wide barrel in his hand as he ran at the three of them.

"What is that?" Barbara asked.

"You don't want to know," Jaromir said, crouching. "It won't kill you, but it will make you wish you were dead."

The lead officer dropped to one knee and aimed carefully, giving Barbara just enough time to thicken the netting into a gauzy red shield around them as a gout of flame shot from the muzzle. The fiery beam struck the protective canopy and spread quickly around its circumference, blazing angrily.

Barbara was vaguely aware of Sibyl cursing behind her and turned back toward the wall. She leaned against the rough surface of the stone block, her eyes squeezed shut.

"God damn it," she muttered, shaking her head.

"What is it, Sibyl?"

"I can't move it, honey. I was afraid of that. I can move an elephant if it's loose, but these blocks are solid, fit together like gears on a clock. Can you burn through them?"

Barbara still held her gem in her hand and again fused the light into a thin laser. She trained the beam on the rocks, but it barely penetrated, just etching an outline in the limestone surface.

"Oh shit!" Jaromir cried behind her.

She turned to see the elevator door opening, disgorging Garripoli and Elrabol. Between them stood Justin, his ice blue eyes raking the scene. He pivoted until he looked directly over the pool at Barbara, Jaromir, and Sibyl. A black vector slammed against the protective barrier, ballooning it inward and tearing a small rent.

"I can't hold him off for long," Barbara gritted. "Jaromir, your gem. Freeze the block!"

"Freeze the block?" Jaromir asked, facing Justin with his ring outstretched. "What good will that do?"

"Just freeze the fucking block, love," Sibyl said calmly.

Jaromir turned to the rock face and brought his ring up until it touched the center of the limestone slab. He closed his eyes, and a blue haze instantly spread across the limestone.

"Now move back, Jaromir," Barbara called as another bolt from Justin struck the shield, shaking it like a tent in a windstorm.

Barbara held her gem in front of her concentrating on the tiny embracing arms of the necklace. They lit up like miniature butane torch flames, brighter and brighter, and then Barbara directed them toward the frozen stone.

The fire that burst from Barbara's necklace struck the wall like a flaming clenched fist. The stone exploded like a bomb, sending chunks of limestone high into the air and covering the protective netting with grey dust. Behind her, Sibyl had pulled a column of water from the pool and battered the three oncoming men, knocking them to their feet. Justin's scream of rage shattered the air, causing Sibyl to recoil in pain, even with her reduced hearing.

They turned to the wall as the dust settled and looked at a gaping four-foot square of darkness where the limestone blocks had been.

"Go!" Barbara yelled. "Now, hurry, hurry!"

Sibyl brushed by Jaromir and leapt head first through the hole.

"Jaromir!" she called from the other side of the wall. "It's a two-foot drop to the shore. Come on!"

Justin had formed his men into a wedge. He stood in the middle, flanked by Elrabol on one side and Meijer on the other. The Berserker officers were on each side, their faceless troops spread behind them. The first attack was a coordinated slashing salvo that tattered the shield Barbara had erected, and she barely had enough time to repair it before the second barrage billowed the curtain inward within inches of her head.

Jaromir hesitated. "You first!" he shouted.

Barbara leaned toward the charging men, her jewel in front of her, and sent a flight of sharp red darts. The Berserkers grabbed at their throats, and Meijer and the Raven Man staggered, holding their temples. Justin fixed his glittering blue eyes on her, and Barbara looked away quickly.

"Jaromir," she ordered. "Go now!"

Jaromir nodded, turned, and disappeared through the hole. A black barb tore through the shroud, forcing Barbara to duck as she backed toward the wall. When she struck the limestone wall with her outstretched hand, she turned and dove through the opening as she felt the protective shield disintegrate behind her.

Despite Sibyl's assurances, relief flooded through Barbara when her shoulder crunched against a sandy beach after a fall of only a few feet. She quickly stood and faced the wall through which they had just escaped. It was a square of light, like a window in a nearby house in the dead of night.

She tried to throw a protective shield over the opening, but already Justin had secured the space, and dark tendrils were inching into the opening, searching.

Barbara screamed as the gap in the wall slammed shut with a crash. She looked blankly at the dark wall.

Beside her, Sibyl breathed hard. "Damn, couldn't do a thing with it in the wall. Least I could do was close it up again."

Barbara turned toward the voice but could see nothing. They stood on the shore of the underground lake in utter darkness.

Chapter 29

FRIESEN TOOK THE NORTHEAST SECTOR bounded at the bottom by their SUV on the right and a tall pine on his left, two miles apart. Off the trail, the terrain was rough, and the precipitous slopes and loose rocks make walking difficult. The leaves on some of the shrubs were beginning to turn a dark red as summer gave way to fall, hiding crevasses and cracks on the steep hillside. He didn't hold out much hope of finding an entrance, but when he agreed to a task, he did it with as much thoroughness as he could. This meant traversing the hillside almost meter by meter, back and forth, looking behind each stone, studying every cleft. After more than an hour he had only worked his way halfway down the hill. He glanced at the sun, which was moving over the hilltop. He knew he only had another hour of good light until the sun would be blocked by the jagged cliff above him.

He rounded a clump of stunted fir on the eastern limits of his sector and began across the face of the hill. His feet suddenly slid underneath him on the gravelly slope, and he fell hard on his hip, sliding downward ten or twelve feet and stopping at a stone outcropping. He got up slowly, painfully, and felt his side. At least everything seemed to still work—no broken hip, but he would have some dandy bruises.

He glanced back up the scree slope he'd slid down, wondering how he could manage to climb up to the ridge again. The route he'd been taking wound along the base of the cliff. As he looked upward, he saw a sharp cut in the rocky face at the far end of the cliff, a narrow opening hidden by fallen rocks he had walked by. It wasn't a cave entrance—more of a notch—but looking at it from below, Friesen could see it opened into a narrow chasm.

Grimacing at the pain in his hip, he scrambled up on all fours back to the ridge and pulled himself onto the rocky path. He walked back down the ridge to the gap he had seen from below. When he got to the rocks that hid the entrance, he slipped between two boulders and found himself on a narrow trail between two steep rock faces. He wound along the path and then stopped. The trail widened and then opened onto a small box canyon, closed at the far end by the cliff face. He stood some twenty yards from the end of the gorge, his eyes adjusting to the shade after the bright sun of the hillside.

He started. In the middle of the rock face in front of him was a large arched entranceway made of limestone blocks. Thick rusty bars stretched from the canyon floor to of the top of the archway.

Chapter 30

"IT'S DARK AS A TOMB in here." Jaromir's voice echoed in the silent cavern, and even though Barbara sensed he was only a few feet away, he was invisible in the blackness.

"Might want to think of another simile, love," Sibyl commented.

Barbara gently tugged her gem out of her shirt and directed a red flare upwards. It struck the roof overhead and spread a dull red light across the top and down the sides of the grotto. Arching above them, a low, irregular dome, studded with stalactites, rose twenty or thirty yards above a narrow black lake about one hundred yards wide. Because Barbara's gem illuminated only about a quarter mile, they were unable to determine the length of the lake, and even the far shore of the lake was indistinct, lost in the deep gloom of the cavern.

A massive boom behind them reverberated through the cavern as Justin attacked the obstructed break in the wall. Barbara threw a red restraining net around the block Sibyl had slammed back into the opening.

"It won't last long," Barbara said. "Where are the elevators?"

"Well assuming they're still there and haven't been filled in or destroyed by a cave in," Sibyl said facing the far end of the lake, "they're down there. On the other side."

Barbara looked down the shoreline that dwindled into the shadows. Her stomach sank. "Assuming they're still there and haven't caved in, how do we get there?"

A blast echoed through the cavern and Barbara sensed the limestone block weaken. They would be through the wall and on them in minutes.

"We walk when we can, wade when we can't walk, and swim when necessary," Sibyl stated firmly.

Barbara eyed the sullen, flat surface of the lake and felt a tremor of fear sweep through her body. "I'm not swimming in that. There could be something down there. Something I don't want to meet." She shuddered again. "And if it is, it has tentacles."

Another explosion shattered the quiet, and this time chunks of rock flew from the wall and fell at their feet.

"Damn," Jaromir shouted. "Next time they're in. If we don't go now, the only swimming we will do is if Justin decides to drown us."

"And put out that light, girl," Sibyl said.

Barbara wondered how she knew there was a light. "Sure, and blunder around in the dark?"

Sibyl extended her hand to Barbara and Jaromir. "Take my hand. As I said, there is more than one way to see."

Barbara extinguished her flare and they stood once more in total darkness. Sibyl grasped her hand.

"Now take Jaromir's," Sibyl ordered. Barbara reached toward Jaromir blindly and found his outstretched hand. "Close your eyes," Sibyl said, "and follow me."

It wasn't so much walking as floating, Barbara realized as they glided silently along the lake. She sensed the deeper black bulk of boulders on their right as they passed, twisting along a trail that only Sibyl could distinguish. Occasionally they waded in shallow water and then clambered back onto the rocky shore, skimming over an uneven path that wove further into the cavern.

Minutes later they heard a final explosion at the rock wall behind them that blew a gaping hole in the limestone wall. They heard muted shouting, and then a searing white light lit the cavern roof, illuminating a circle of the cavern that ended just a few feet behind them. They moved on silently, protected for the time being by the darkness and shadows beyond the arc of Justin's light.

The noise of their pursuers lessened as they twisted around turns in the lake shore and plunged ever deeper into the grotto. Barbara felt their pace ease, and she opened her eyes. But it made little difference—even with her eyes open, she could see nothing in the inky blackness. They came to a stop.

"Where are we?" Barbara whispered. She realized there was little need to whisper—Justin and his posse knew where they were—but the stifling dark and oppressive silence seemed to call for hushed tones.

"At the end of the lake," Sibyl said.

Jaromir loosened his hand and extended his ring hand. A barely discernible blue haze grew out over the water. Jaromir increased the illumination enough so that they could make out the dark line of the shore on the other side. To their right, the lake tapered sharply into a brooding river that seemed to ooze from a limestone rock face. They had two choices: somehow get across to the other side of the water or retrace their steps toward Justin.

A sudden explosion of white light behind them lit the cavern brightly within a few hundred yards of where they stood.

"Damn it," Jaromir muttered.

"How much time do we have?" Barbara asked.

She sensed Jaromir shrug. "They're moving faster than I thought. Guess they had the advantage of light. Maybe five minutes?"

"Sibyl, how do we get across?" Barbara asked, feeling slightly panicky. "Swim?"

Sibyl said nothing.

Now they could hear shouts ringing behind them in the hollow cavern.

"Sibyl!" Barbara said sharply.

Sibyl kept staring across the lake. "I thought there would be a boat on the far side."

"You *thought* there would be a boat?" Barbara asked incredulously.

Sibyl turned to Barbara and fixed her with her empty eyes. "There you go again, honey. In the notes I found, they wrote that there was a permanent barge docked at the far end of the lake. I could have brought it to our side." She turned back to the far shore. "It's not there."

Barbara whirled as a new flare lit the canyon. This time, there was no escaping it—they were illuminated on the rocky lakeside like deer in a gigantic headlight.

Jaromir took two steps to the water and dipped his hand into the murky lake. In the glare, Barbara could see he had closed his eyes.

"Christ," she mumbled. "This is not the time to check the water temperature."

"Be quiet," Sibyl said softly.

Barbara turned back toward the rough trail they had traveled, expecting to see the posse round the last rocky finger. The three of them would be trapped against the lake and the end of the cavern. She bent down and began untying her runners.

"No," Jaromir called. "We can cross now."

Barbara looked up and saw that the of lake in front of them was now covered in blue ice that extended to the other shore.

She scrambled to her feet and stepped tentatively on the ice. It felt solid and firm underneath her shoes. Sibyl followed, extending her hand to Jaromir, who took it gently and led her onto the ice.

"Nice work, love," she said.

The lake had narrowed as they neared the eastern end, and the distance to the far shore less than fifty yards. They slid rapidly across the smooth, slippery surface, reaching the other side in minutes. In front of them, clearly illuminated by Justin's flare, a rough black opening led from the limestone cavern. They stepped on the rocky shore and heard a roar of fury behind them.

Led by Justin, incongruously dressed in a dark suit and bright red necktie, their pursuers slipped around the rock jutting into the lake and collected on the shore the three of them had just escaped. The light burned even brighter, and Barbara could make out Justin's blazing blue eyes and Elrabol's slicked back black hair. She could see the light glinting off Meijer's round glasses and turning the Berserkers' steel masks dull silver, eight of them forming an arc around Justin and the two agents.

The cavern shook again with a deep shriek from Justin, and she felt the blackness of his rage extend across the cavern. He hesitated at the ice and nodded his head at one of the Berserker officers, who strode forward and stepped onto the frozen surface. They could feel the blaze of hatred from the

Berserker's round eye holes as his long strides took him quickly to the center of the frozen lake. The rest of the party began to rush toward the shoreline, but Justin raised his arms and restrained them.

"My turn," Barbara said. She clasped her jewel in her hand and spread a blanket of red fire across the ice surface.

The Berserker hesitated, and Barbara intensified the heat until the ice cover abruptly disappeared and the Berserker plunged into the cold water, weighed down by this black robe and struggling frantically to stay afloat.

"Come on," Jaromir shouted. "Let's move."

Sibyl smiled. "Just a sec, love."

As the Berserker flailed toward the shoreline, the water erupted around him. Pale tentacles the size of bicycle inner tubes snaked out of the lake and one by one encircled the Berserker. His screams were muffled by his mouthpiece, but it only served to amplify his terror as his oddly flat cries vibrated off the limestone wall. After a few moments of thrashing, the oily water calmed and the Berserker disappeared below the surface.

Barbara turned to Sibyl, her eyes wide. "Did you do that?"

Sibyl's smile widened. "You were right, honey. Strange creatures live in dark, underground lakes."

Ahead of them, Jaromir stood impatiently. "Nice," he said, nodding. "But we need to go now. That'll slow them down, but they will get across."

Barbara glanced back at the ten figures on the far shore, milling about in confusion. There was no time for complacency.

"They'll create a bridge, form stepping stones, refreeze the lake," Jaromir said grimly. "Take my word for it; they will find a way."

They turned away from the lake as Justin extinguished his flare, turning the cavern pitch dark again. Jaromir thrust his hand forward and a pale blue light lit the rocky surface above the lakeshore and the entrance into the mines they had seen. They quickly left the echoing grotto behind and entered the mouth of a broad cave that had been dug out of the limestone.

"We are in the mine," Sibyl said, clinging to Jaromir's hand.

As they drew further from the mine entrance, Jaromir intensified the light from his gem. The mine shaft ran for nearly half a kilometer then veered to the right. All around them puddles of standing water and fallen rock made walking treacherous. They reached the end of the main tunnel and turned right. Sibyl stopped.

"Sibyl," Jaromir said sharply. "We've got to move. Our only chance is to get to the elevator and above ground before they catch us."

Sibyl stood silent at the end of the main tunnel, her head turning slowly. "We should go left," she said at last.

Jaromir shone his light in the direction she was facing. "We can't go left," he said. "It's a solid rock wall. The mine shaft goes to the right." His voice rose in exasperation. "Please, Sibyl. Come on!"

Sibyl said nothing. She focused on the wall to their left for several seconds and then walked toward it.

"Sibyl!" Barbara hissed. "You're going to run into a stone wall!"

Barbara glanced at Jaromir in alarm as they watched Sibyl near the wall, and then walk right through it. Moments later, she reappeared.

"It's as I thought," she said. "It's an illusion. Justin wanted us to go to the right. A dead end." She nodded through the wall. "The elevators are this way."

They rushed forward, Barbara slowing at the wall and closing her eyes as she passed through. Once beyond the illusion, they were in a long, straight tunnel that ran horizontal to the main entry shaft. They hurried along the wide passageway, noticing steel rails embedded in the stone floor. A few hundred feet into the shaft, they stumbled on three abandoned ore cars sitting empty on the rusted rails. Unlike the caves under the castle, the mine tunnel had few turns or curves, and in minutes Jaromir's light revealed a reinforced dome at the end of the shaft cluttered with pipes, tools, broken fencing, rolls of cable and the entrance to two elevator cages. The three broke into a run and stood in front of the rusted elevators, unused in a century.

A blast exploded from the tunnel behind them. "They've collapsed the roof of the right wing of the tunnel," Sibyl said. "When they realize we're not under ten tons of stone, they'll come this way."

Jaromir had been studying the two elevator cages. He grabbed the handle of a folding metal gate across the larger of the two cages and yanked it back. It screeched and grudgingly slid aside a few feet. He reached across to the second car on his right and pulled, the fence sliding several feet. He turned around.

"Take your pick," he said, looking into the blue-lit faces of the two women. "But we do have one small problem." He pointed over his shoulder. "Each car is attached to a cable connected to a drum at the ground level. The drum is operated by an electric motor, which is several hundred feet above us and hasn't run for a hundred years. Any ideas of how we move one of these rusted, creaky old cages from here"—he nodded at the stone floor in front of him and then toward the roof—"to up there?"

Sibyl's head tilted upward, her face tense as she listened intently. She held up her hand, and Jaromir stopped speaking and stared down the tunnel. "They're coming," Sibyl said.

Barbara turned to see a bright light moving up the shaft, silhouetting the ore cars. Next to her, Sibyl nodded abruptly. Suddenly, the ore cars leapt from the track and slid swiftly sideways down the tunnel. Metallic screeching mixed with shouts and screams as the cars slammed into their pursuers. Barbara looked toward the dust and screams halfway down the tunnel and jumped back slightly as the shaft ceiling crashed onto the floor, sealing them off. She glanced admiringly at Sibyl. "Nice work. Again."

"We've slowed them down," Sibyl said, breathing hard. "But that's all." She nodded at the elevators. "Are they frozen solid with rust?" she asked.

Jaromir inspected the cages and rattled the door frame. "Don't think so. They run on vertical rails, but they seem to be loose."

"Which one is lighter?

"One on the right."

Sibyl began walking toward the car. "Let's go."

Let's go, Barbara thought. *Now there is a dandy idea. And exactly how are we going to do that?*

Chapter 31

ZOLTAN, I THINK I'VE GOT something here.

Friesen's message reached Zoltan like an electric shock.

It could be the opening to an old mine shaft.

Zoltan's heart rate quickened. He knew it was still a long shot, but he excitedly passed the message on to the other men and clambered down the hillside from his perch near the antenna, careful not to lose his footing in his impatience. With instructions from Friesen, he made his way down to the narrow trail and slipped through the mossy notch that led to the box canyon. Friesen stood in front of him, studying the rusted iron bars of the entranceway. Zoltan broke into a run. Moments later Kwan and Maphaela burst through the notch quickly followed by Malik.

They stood in a semi-circle staring at the blocked entrance. Zoltan thought about the scene, so similar but so different, when they stood around the impenetrable doorway out of the tunnels, frustrated and trapped.

Zoltan turned and took Friesen's hand. "Thank you," he said. He looked back at the entrance. "She is down there. I feel it."

"Along with Justin and friends," Friesen muttered.

"That is true," Zoltan agreed. "We have focused on getting here." He nodded at the men around him. "And because of you, we have succeeded. But from here we do not know what we will encounter. Even if we find where they are holding Barbara, it will be fortified, possibly impassable. Should we manage to enter, the forces arrayed against us will be beyond our comprehension."

"And your point is?" Friesen asked impatiently.

Zoltan looked around the arc of faces, fixing each with his black eyes. "It is highly unlikely we shall succeed," he said. "And far more likely some of us, possibly all of us will die.

"I have pledged myself to Barbara. My life is forfeit if I fail to help free her." He looked grimly at the men. "But this is not the case with you. Mr. Friesen is correct. We have no plan and little hope. While I have made a vow to find Barbara or die trying, none of you has done the same. Each of you has shown bravery and dedication to get us here. But you have no obligation to go further. I will enter the shaft, but I urge the rest of you to consider seriously whether you wish to accompany me." He nodded at the men. "And because I love each of you, I urge you not to."

Water dripped quietly into a small pool at the base of the canyon wall. Overhead dusk darkened the square of sky they could see from the gorge.

"I thought we'd been through this already," Friesen said in an uncharacteristically soft voice, breaking the silence. "But for Mr. József's sake, can we formalize this and move on?" He drew out his stone. "Mr. József, would you please hold out your hand?"

Zoltan held out his right hand uncertainly, palm up. Friesen placed his glowing purple stone in the outstretched palm. "With my soul, I pledge to stand with you until we free Barbara or until I die." He stepped back and nodded his head in a bow. Instantly the other three men removed their stones and placed them in Zoltan's hand, repeating the same pledge."

Zoltan closed his palm and raised his eyes to the darkening sky. "I am honored," he said solemnly. He opened his hand. "Please."

Each of the men retrieved their stones and stood back, smiling.

"Well," Friesen said, "if we've got that out of the way, can we get to work?"

The old cast iron bars blocking the entranceway yielded quickly to the battering of Friesen's gemstone. He wielded it like a hammer, its thick purple beam smashing against the grill over and over until the bars cracked and then tore out of the limestone, clattering as they struck the floor on the other side of the entrance.

Zoltan led the way, his blue stone held aloft as he ducked through the opening, and the others quickly followed.

"My god," Maphaela said.

The men stood in a square room the size of the interior of a large church. In the weak light provided by Zoltan's stone, they could see two huge wood crosses looming to their right. In front of them a metal cage rose from the dark floor to the high ceiling above them. The far reaches of the room were lost in shadow, but cables stretched along the floor and a hulking motor, mounted to a great wheel wound with cable, squatted in front of them.

"What is it?" Friesen asked, his voice hushed.

"It's a hoistroom," Maphaela said, striding forward. "And look at this," he cried, reaching the motor. "It's a Ward Leonard DC motor! One of the most powerful direct current motors ever built. I've never even seen one of these."

"Jesus, Maphaela, you got a Junior Woodchucks Guide or something?" Malik blinked at Friesen.

"Forget it, Mr. Malik," Kwan said. "It's a Disney thing again."

Malik nodded uncertainly. "It seems odd to me that grown men would still be attached to cartoons."

"Malik," Maphaela broke in. "Can you shine some light over here?"

Malik shone the amber light from the gem mounted in his turban in a broad arch, and Kwan added his pale green beam. The light bathed the room in an eerie yellow glow.

"See?" Maphaela gestured toward the high towers against the right-hand wall. "Those are headframes. Malik, focus on the top of the structure. "He nodded upward. "That's called a sheave wheel at the top. It carries the cable from the drum over there," he said, pointing toward the motor," and then the cable attaches to the skips."

"Pardon my ignorance, Huey, but what the hell is a skip?" Friesen asked.

Maphaela waved his hands impatiently. "You know, like an elevator car."

"Yes," Zoltan said. The other men quieted as Zoltan spoke for the first time since entering. "An elevator to the tunnels where they are holding Barbara."

Maphaela nodded. "Most likely."

Kwan had moved toward the cages in the center of the room and inspected the vertical chutes with his green light. "There is a single shaft with separate cables and entry cages. I can see a hundred feet or so down the shaft and it's empty. Shouldn't there be an elevator car, a skip?"

Maphaela moved toward Kwan. "Probably at the bottom of the shaft. That would eliminate the tension on the cable if they were inactivated."

Silence wrapped around the men as they stared at the empty cages in front of them.

"I don't want to state the obvious," Friesen said at last. "But that's a long way to jump."

Zoltan studied the shaft for a long moment. "Mr. Maphaela, you said the cars would be at the bottom."

"I said probably," Maphaela corrected. "They could be stopped at one of the lower shaft stations. That's where the miners would bring the ore and load it onto the skips. Stations are broad landings where the horizontal tunnels meet the elevator shaft."

"How many would there be?" Friesen asked.

Maphaela shrugged. "Hard to know. Depends on the depth of the overall shaft, the veins of ore they found, the amount of time they worked the deposit. But given the age of the mine, I'd guess two or three in addition to the bottom level."

"So when they closed the mine, they would have simply lowered the cars to the bottom and left them there?"

"Most likely."

"And there is no other way down."

"Not necessarily. The main shafts carry the ore and miners, but secondary compartments are built around the collar." Maphaela pointed to the square of concrete around the cages. "See? Over there behind the right-hand elevator? There's a hatch." He looked above it. "There is a small headframe that would operate the emergency elevator. Once the cars were deactivated and the shaft closed, the last miners probably reached ground level using the emergency chute."

"Well, can't we do the same thing in reverse?" Friesen asked.

"The cable has been cut," Maphaela said, nodding at the cable end dangling from the headframe. "I imagine they severed the cable when they were done. That elevator would be smashed to pieces at the bottom of the shaft."

Silence crept back into the cavernous room.

"And next to that," Zoltan said. "There is a grate, yes?"

"That's right," Maphaela said. "The ventilation shaft."

"And that would run to the bottom of the mine?"

"I imagine," Maphaela nodded. "But it is hardly wide enough for one person. But…" Maphaela paused.

"Yes?" Zoltan prompted.

"Sometimes ladders were built into them in case of total power failure."

Friesen rushed around the elevator cages and kneeled by the grated opening. He shone his purple light down the shaft. "This isn't worth shit," he grumbled. "Can't see a thing. Can someone help out over here?"

Malik moved to his side and directed his light through the gate.

"Goddamn!" Friesen yelled excitedly. "Metal rungs! As far as I can see." He formed his purple beam into a club and began to hammer the iron bars.

"Wait!" Maphaela shouted. "That collar is old. You could collapse the whole thing." He stepped to the side of the grate and pulled out his orange jewel. He fashioned it into a bright flame and began using it like an acetylene torch, cutting through the iron grate, bar by bar. As each one was severed, the men waited anxiously to hear it clang somewhere below them, but they heard nothing.

Finally Maphaela cut through the final bar of the grate, clearing the opening. The men looked down a shaft about the width of a man's shoulders that disappeared into utter blackness.

Friesen turned to lower himself over the edge and looked up. "Well, let's go!"

"Just a moment, Mr. Friesen," Zoltan said. "Let us consider what we are undertaking. If I understand correctly, we will be climbing down cast iron ladder rungs that were set in limestone perhaps more than a hundred years ago." He paused and looked at Maphaela. "Yes?"

Maphaela nodded.

"We do not know how far it is to the bottom. There could be thousands of such treads. Some might be missing. Some might pull out in our hands. The ladder might end in the middle of the shaft."

Friesen looked at Zoltan incredulously. "Are you seriously suggesting that we not try? Of course there is danger! Jesus, we've been in danger since we took these damned jobs; we just didn't know it."

"Again, I appreciate your loyalty and courage, Mr. Friesen. I am in no way suggesting that we not explore this possibility. What I am saying is that there is a very good chance that the person who goes first will fall to the bottom of the shaft and die." He nodded at Friesen. "And so I would like to lead this phase of the expedition, if you please."

Friesen paused for a moment at the edge of the shaft and stared at Zoltan. Even in the semi-darkness the men could see Friesen's eyes sparkle. Then his thin face split in a wide grin and he laughed deeply and loudly until the inside the chamber echoed with his amusement. Everyone smiled except Zoltan.

"What is it?" Zoltan asked.

Friesen shook his head. "Mr. József, you are too much. Now get out of my way so I can get started."

"Please, Mr. Friesen," Zoltan pleaded. "Just a moment please."

Friesen was still crouched on the edge of the ventilation shaft. "I don't want to argue, József."

"It's not that," Zoltan muttered. He took a step back and closed his eyes.

"Mr. József," Malik inquired, concern in his eyes. "What is it?" He directed a soft amber glow to Zoltan's face. For the first time since their encounter with Justin, his lips curved in a smile.

"She's out," he whispered.

Chapter 32

BARBARA WAS DETERMINED TO CLOSE the rusted gate in the mine car as they shuddered slowly upwards. She realized it was irrational. After all, they were being propelled up a shaft that had not seen a cage move in a century by the untried kinesthetic power of a blind woman she hardly knew. She doubted that falling out of the front of the cage was their greatest danger. Still, after much swearing and yanking, she managed to drag the sliding gate across the opening, the gate screeching in protest the entire way. Once she managed to get it closed, she kicked the gate in frustration.

"Good idea," Jaromir said behind her, looking intently upwards and illuminating the ancient shaft with his blue gem. "When something doesn't work, kick it. Doesn't help but makes you feel better."

Barbara managed a self-conscious chuckle as the car drifted slowly upward. She stared worriedly through the latticed bottom of the elevator car. "Is this as fast as we can go?"

Sibyl stood against the back of the cage, her two hands raised and grasping bars shoulder high. Her eyes were closed and her head moved slowly, rhythmically back and forth. "If you've got some jet engines, honey, strap them onto the bottom, okay?"

"Sorry," Barbara said as the car struggled upward. "I just feel so helpless."

"Just cover our rear," Sibyl said quietly. "I'll handle the levitation."

"First floor," Jaromir chanted. "Anyone for the first floor?"

The cage gradually moved above the edge of the landing and they could see a wide loading area cluttered with ore carts and piles of rock. Jaromir's faint light showed a tunnel leading from the far perimeter of the landing. The car glided silently above the landing and they were encased in a stone rectangle again.

"How many landings are there?" Barbara asked, pacing nervously in the small cage.

"According to Sibyl's map, there are two," Jaromir replied. "Two between the bottom and ground level mine opening that is."

"If it's not buried under sixty tons of rock," Barbara muttered. "Or if the shaft is even open that far."

Jaromir yanked his arm down abruptly and shone his beam back down the shaft. "What's that?"

Then Barbara heard it—a slow whir and then a crashing coming from bottom of the shaft. The railings for the second car that ran parallel to theirs began to shudder, flakes of rust and clouds of dust sifting through the bars of their skip.

Without warning, a bright white light exploded below them and a brilliant fireball rushed up the shaft, barely giving Barbara enough time to throw a shield across the bottom mesh of their car. Despite the insulation, the heat burned through the soles of her runners as the ball roared upward around their car and into the darkness above.

"Damn," Jaromir swore. "I thought we had more time."

Barbara continued to stare into the darkness below them. "It appears we don't."

"Two," Jaromir called out quietly as another flat loading space glided slowly by them. "We're at the second landing. The next landing is at ground level."

Sibyl said nothing, but Barbara could see the sweat beading on her forehead and her eyes squeezed tightly shut.

"Barbara," Jaromir yelled, "look left!"

Barbara wheeled in time to see a shadowy shape ascending rapidly toward them. It was the second car, cloaked and nearly invisible. She gripped her jewel and threw a broad blaze at the shape, and immediately the cage was sheathed in red flames. Sparks cascaded into the blackness as the covering burned away. The second car was twenty feet below them and closing rapidly. They could see their pursuers staring up at them through the top bars of their car. Barbara dropped to one knee and directed a red beam at the cable attached to the second car, cutting it cleanly. The bottom section of the cable fell heavily onto the top of approaching car, but it continued upward without hesitating.

"They're not using cables," Jaromir said, kneeling beside her. "I will protect Sibyl, but you have to slow them down." He glanced worriedly at the figure leaning against the bars, rocking wearily. "Don't know how much more she has to give."

As he spoke, great black wings erupted from the pursuing car and beat violently at their cage, buffeting it from side to side, shaking the three occupants so violently that Barbara and Jaromir had to grab onto bars of the skip to keep from being thrown onto the metal floor. Shrill, deafening caws filled the shaft, driving into their ears like knives. Barbara managed to dampen the noise with a red cloak around the old skip, but the beating of the wings had slowed the car. Behind them they heard Sibyl groaning in effort. Jaromir jumped to his feet and stumbled to her side, wrapping the two of them in a dense grey fog.

Elrabol, Barbara thought. *Raven Man.*

Scenes from their encounter at the village swept over her and she shuddered. Barbara closed her eyes and directed a thin, sharp scarlet beam through the bars into the black wings striking at the car. She heard a muffled scream beside them, and Barbara ignited the beam until it flared bright, crimson and searing, illuminating the vertical shaft in blood-red light. She was almost overcome by the stench of burning feathers.

The battering wings withdrew, and Barbara stared at the second car six feet away directly across from her and moving at their speed. *How odd,* she thought, staring into Justin's glittering blue eyes, now level with hers as both cars groaned upwards. *We're in two cages just feet apart, both of us suspended in space.*

Barbara saw Elrabol, crumpled on the floor at Justin's feet, holding his face in his hands and clawing at his eyes. Meijer looked at Barbara through his round glasses and smiled. Behind them was the rank of steel-masked Berserkers.

She had not expected the attack to come from behind, and when the blow struck her heavily between her shoulders, she had no defense. The impact knocked her breathless and slammed her against the car so that her face turned sideways painfully. It was if a giant hand pushed her relentlessly, crushing her against the steel bars. Her hand wrapped around her jewel at her chest, but it was far too late for a shield. What then? As her breath squeezed from her, she saw Justin only a few feet away. His red lips turned up at the corners. She knew she had only moments before blacking out.

The explosion surprised even Barbara. The impact slammed their car against the far rails of the shaft, and as she slumped to her knees, gasping for breath, the blast rang deafeningly in her ears. Clutching her throat and choking, she looked in front of her.

The other car was gone. They continued to rumble slowly up the shaft, but there was only blackness where Justin had stood only moments ago. Barbara pulled herself to her feet, grimacing from the pain in her chest and ribs. Halfway down the shaft, metallic screeching split the heavy air. *Braking*, Barbara thought. *The explosion blew them back down the shaft, but he's stopping the descent.* She looked anxiously over toward Sibyl and Jaromir.

Jaromir thinned the blue-grey cocoon around them and stared at her briefly. "Damn," he smiled. "More there than meets the eye, it seems."

"Not out of the shaft yet," Barbara said. "They've stopped but they'll be heading back up any minute. How much farther to the top?"

She could see Jaromir shake his head in the gloom. "Not sure. The attacks slowed us down."

"How's she doing?"

"Best she can. But she's drained."

Barbara heard a whirring and shaking from below. "Protect her at all costs."

Jaromir nodded, and drew the heavy grey cloak closed again.

This time they made no attempt to hide their ascent. The car below her rose steadily but warily in the shaft beside them. *Cautious*, she thought.

Guess I got their attention.

The blast above them shook the rocky sides of the shaft, twisting the small elevator car like a birdhouse in the wind. *Shit,* Barbara thought. *Why don't I learn? Why don't I expect the unexpected?*

Rocks rained down onto the top of their car, pebbles and dust sifting through the bars and clattering on the steel mesh floor. Barbara could feel the car slow. She threw out a net across the adjoining shaft, but too late. Above them another explosion, this one larger, dislodged boulders the size of soccer balls from the sides of the shaft. They pounded on the bars, bending them as they crashed onto the top of the car in a mounting pile. The car slowed and then came to a stop.

"What is it?" Barbara called.

Jaromir stepped out from the cover and looked at Barbara, fatigue and worry in his eyes. "She's done. The extra weight. She can't lift us any further. God damn it," he spit in frustration. "So close."

Barbara looked down at Justin's car hovering below them. "They're waiting. Like vultures. Waiting for us to plunge to the bottom of the shaft."

Barbara felt the car budge, slipping slightly downward.

"Does she have enough strength to slow our descent?"

Jaromir shrugged. "Maybe. But what good will that do? They'll just wait for us at the bottom."

"That's what they'll expect. What if she lowered us to the last landing we passed. We stop there."

"And then what?"

Barbara shook her head. "I don't know. But there will be a maze of tunnels. We have a chance of losing them there. And if we have to fight, we will choose the battleground."

Jaromir nodded. He thinned the blue veil still covering Sibyl. Barbara stared in shock. Sibyl had ground her forehead into the metal bars until she had opened bleeding wounds that ran into her hair. Blood mingled with sweat and stained her beautiful cheeks and neck. She gasped for breath.

"Sibyl," Barbara said quietly. "You have been magnificent."

Sibyl turned toward Barbara and gave a sad smile. "But not quite magnificent enough," she whispered. "Sorry, honey."

"We're not done yet," Jaromir said. He went to Sibyl's side and rubbed the back of her neck gently. "Can you lower us to the landing we passed?"

Sibyl struggled for breath, and the car jarred downward several feet.

"Sorry," Sibyl said again. "Getting pretty tired."

"Can you lower us?" Jaromir repeated.

Sibyl nodded her bleeding head. "No problem lowering, honey. The trick will be to stop. I can let go," she looked at Jaromir over her shoulder, "but do I have the strength to stop?"

Jaromir wrapped his arms around her neck and kissed her cheek. "If you don't," he said, "you'll die trying."

Sibyl turned back to the bars of the cage. "Along with the two of you," she said. "Get ready."

Barbara's stomach dropped as the car went into freefall then slowed and came to a shuddering stop. Jaromir peered downward. Jeers and laughter floated up from Justin's car, which maintained a safe distance below them.

Jaromir placed his hands over Sibyl's, which were wrapped tightly around the cage bars. "Almost there," he said. "Once more, love."

This time the car descended more slowly, but then Sibyl gave a cry and her face turned upward in agony. The car plummeted. The sides of the shaft rushed by, and Barbara sensed more than saw the landing below them.

"Now!" she yelled. "Brake now!"

Sibyl strained at the bars, Jaromir's hands covering hers, his head buried in her hair. The car slowed, but it kept descending. Barbara watched in agony as the landing slid into view and then slowly by them as they continued to sink downward. She closed her eyes. The car halted, slipped, and then came to a stop.

Barbara was afraid to open her eyes. When she did she saw that they had passed the landing as she had feared, but at the top of the cage there was a narrow space, maybe two feet, between them and the bottom of the landing.

"Can she raise us, just a few feet?" Barbara urged.

"No!" Jaromir shouted. "She is half dead just holding us here."

The damned gate she spent so much time closing. She grasped her jewel and rapidly cut across the top and then sliced downward neatly about three feet and back across to the edge. The section fell clattering onto the car floor, and the gap was clear. Barbara scrambled up the intact section of gate and studied the gap. At the top, her gem gave off a pink glow, enough for her to see the space between the car and the lip of the landing.

She clambered back down.

"Sibyl, there is a narrow gap at the top of the folding gate. There is enough room for us to climb through and onto the landing. Barely. You will have to climb up the gate and through the opening and then crawl onto the landing apron. Can you do that?"

"Think so," Sibyl murmured. "But I can't leave the car and keep it from falling."

"Yes, you can," Barbara said firmly. "You tossed mine carts around like toys. You weren't in those."

"But that was different, honey," Sibyl said, turning her empty eyes toward Barbara. "I am so tired."

"Can't help it," Barbara said curtly. "Jaromir is going to help you through the opening and onto the landing. And I'm staying here until you're out, understand? So you damn well better hold this thing where it is until I get out. You got that, girl?"

Sibyl smiled broadly and nodded. She slowly unclenched her fingers from the bars. They were cramped and curled like talons. The car shook slightly, but she took Jaromir's hand and wobbled toward the skip gate. Barbara held her breath as they crept up the lattice, Jaromir in the lead and holding Sibyl's hand. They made it out of the car and crawled onto the rock surface of the landing. The cage slipped, held, and slipped again. The opening narrowed by the second. Barbara climbed the gate in two or three strides, slithered through the opening, and rolled onto the rocky floor of the landing as the car plunged downward.

Chapter 33

THE CLIMB DOWN THE VENTILATION shaft settled into a sort of waking nightmare. Zoltan clung to the rungs, every inch of his body tense with anxiety. The narrow chute was lit only by the faint amber glow of Malik's jewel set in his turban. He felt for each rung with his right foot before stepping downward, testing the curved iron loop briefly to make sure it was secure. After that he could only hope it wouldn't suddenly tear out of the stone when he put his full weight on the rung and send him plummeting to the shaft bottom. Slowly, they inched downward, the silence only marred by the increasingly labored breathing of the men and their rhythmic shuffle as they followed, foot by careful foot.

Time seemed to have little meaning. The stone sides of the shaft inched by, unchanging in the twilight from Malik's gem. Rusty iron rungs tore at their hands until they were raw and bloody. And still they went down, step after step.

"Maphaela!" Friesen called upward. His words were muffled in the vertical stone chute.

"Yeah?" Maphaela responded, his voice barely audible even though he was only twenty feet above.

"You said there should be loading landings. Where are they?"

"I said there *probably* were landings," Maphaela corrected. "Even if there are, this shaft could be a mile deep. We are moving a few yards a minute. If the first landing was a third of the way down, it would be an hour or more before we get there." He paused. "If it is there at all."

They continued plodding down, the silence broken by an occasional curse as one of the men caught his hand on a splinter of metal or missed a rung with his foot.

"So how long have we been going?" Friesen shouted back up the chute.

"Thirty-seven minutes, Mr. Friesen," Zoltan answered calmly.

"Lie to me," Friesen said wearily. "Tell me it's been an hour and we're almost there."

The slow descent continued. In the lead, Friesen strained his eyes for some opening below, some relief from the endless row of metal bars they clung to. He stopped abruptly. Above him, Malik sensed that Friesen wasn't moving and shouted, "Halt!"

"Mr. Friesen," Zoltan called down anxiously. "Are you all right?"

"Shh," Friesen hushed.

The men quieted and strained to hear.

"Hear it?" Friesen said. "A clattering."

As he spoke, the elevator railing to the right of the plenum began to shake slightly. Below, a low metal muttering became more distinct.

"There is a car coming up the shaft!" Friesen shouted.

Now the other men could hear the noise, and the rail next to them started shuddering more vigorously. Zoltan concentrated and detected more than the metallic scrape and clang below them. He felt her moving upward, her gem ablaze, her soul on fire.

"It's Barbara!" Zoltan called out. "And she's not alone."

"Barbara," Friesen said, looking upward toward Zoltan. "Are you sure?"

Even in the dim light, Friesen could see the smile on Zoltan's lips. "Yes, Mr. Friesen. I am sure."

Friesen looked uncertainly into the abyss below them. "If she's on her way up, should we start climbing back up to the mine head?"

Suddenly the second set of elevator rails began to vibrate. "Looks like she's got friends," Friesen said.

He squinted. Far below them, a tiny spark of white light began to grow. It exploded upwards. "Hold on!" he yelled. "Face the wall and close your eyes."

The fireball rocketed by them. Friesen smelled singed hair. If they had been in the elevator shaft with the fireball, they would have all been incinerated.

"Everyone Okay?" he called, looking up the shaft.

"Maphaela, okay," Maphaela called from above.

"Kwan, lost some hair, but Okay."

"Thanks to you, Mr. Friesen," Zoltan said, "I too am fine."

"Malik?"

"Fine."

The men closed distance until the five of them were almost on top of each other.

"That was an attack on Barbara's car," Zoltan said. "It seems that they avoided it."

"They are driving up shaft one, but the car in shaft two is in pursuit," Friesen said. "So what do we do?"

"Down," Zoltan said firmly. "As quickly as possible. We may be able to help." He paused. "Or we may be too late."

The men continued their downward climb, faster now, less careful, their weariness gone.

The air around them vibrated violently as if a hurricane blew in the shaft below them. A cacophony of high-pitched screams, like the caws of giant crows, shattered the silence. Then a flash of red lowed far below them. Friesen climbed downward quicker, almost recklessly, taking little time to test each rung before stepping onto it. There was a desperation to their descent.

An explosion shook the walls they clung to. A roar of red flame belched upward, and the shaft filled with acrid smoke.

"What the fuck was that?" Friesen called out.

"Barbara," Zoltan said quietly, almost whispering. "She is still alive."

"Malik!" Friesen called excitedly. "Look down shaft one."

Malik's beam couldn't illuminate the full shaft, but they could see movement in the darkness.

"It's a car, not far below us."

Something like joy swept through him. "Yes, yes," Zoltan said. "It is them!"

"Come on, come on," Friesen urged the approaching car. "A little farther and you're there."

Suddenly a blast struck the stone shaft wall about fifty feet below them. The unexpected impact almost blew the men from their precarious perches. They heard rock dislodge and crash onto the mesh top of the ascending elevator cage.

"Explosion in shaft one!" Friesen called out. "Above the car."

A second explosion erupted, stronger than the first, caving in a huge section of the shaft wall. Great chunks of rock sheared away from the shaft and hurtled downward.

"They're using the rock to slow the car in shaft one!" Maphaela yelled.

"And it's working," Friesen muttered, watching the shadowy shape of the car he had spotted, the top now covered in boulders, hesitate, stop, and then begin descending.

"They're heading down. Controlled descent."

"May be trying to get to the landing," Maphaela called. "Can't be far below us."

"Go," Malik ordered.

Now there was no thought of their own safety. Friesen rushed down the rungs, leg after leg, hand over hand, and the men above him followed.

"There!" Kwan yelled. "The landing."

Below them they could make out a gap in the narrow plenum shaft walls, a widening barely visible in the gloom.

"And the elevator car in shaft one—it's docked just below it," he shouted excitedly.

"Heads up!" Friesen called from below. "The plenum shaft is heading into a tunnel. Imagine it will take us to the landing."

The rungs stopped at a small wood platform. Behind it a narrow tunnel mouth opened. Friesen put his foot tentatively on the old wood. Just above him, Kwan grimaced. When was the last time it held two hundred pounds? Friesen released his last handhold and stepped onto the rough timbers.

It held, and he tiptoed across the surface, maybe ten feet, to the tunnel and realized he had started breathing again. The other men followed.

Far below them they heard a muted crash. Zoltan's excitement turned to terror. What the hell was going on?

They had barely started down the tunnel when they heard banging as the second elevator car clashed to a stop at the landing just below them. Shouts and clanging filled the air. Orders were screamed, rattling off the trembling rocks. The blood in Zoltan's veins turned to ice. It was a voice they all recognized.

Zoltan rushed by Friesen and ran forward, bending slightly in the low shaft. Fifty yards into the tunnel, narrow stone steps carved from the rock led downward onto the dusty landing, which was filled with piles of rocks and ore cars standing on abandoned rails. At the bottom of the steps, they clustered around Zoltan. He grasped his gem and squeezed his eyes shut.

"Zoltan," Friesen asked urgently. "What do you make of it? What's going on?"

Zoltan opened his eyes and looked at the men, his face drawn and haggard. "She is alive. I believe they have fled into the mine tunnels. Justin is behind them." He shut his eyes briefly. "He has a force. I don't know how many or who."

Friesen started toward the main tunnel opening.

"Mr. Friesen," Zoltan called. "We must stay together. If we are to defeat Justin, it will require all of our combined strength, yes?"

Friesen stopped and looked back impatiently.

"Barbara's signal is clear," Zoltan went on. "She is not communicating; she does not know we are here. But her jewel, it is so strong. I believe I can follow her path."

"And if we don't move," Friesen said irritably, "by the time we find them Justin and gang will have them as stuffed trophies."

Zoltan nodded grimly and led the men up the main tunnel.

There were fewer forks in the mine than in the caves underneath the Buda Castle, and at junctions Zoltan felt little hesitation as his own jewel tugged him onward.

Led by Zoltan with Malik's jewel lighting the way, the men pushed deeper into the mine, desperately looking for a sliver of light, straining to hear a cry or shout.

After several minutes, Maphaela shouted from behind. "To our right. Noise!"

They had come to a fork in the tunnel. The opening to the smaller shaft to their right was narrow and framed in old timbers. They stood at the entrance and listened intently.

"I smell burnt hair," Malik pronounced, his nose raised slightly.

A shriek erupted from the shaft so hideous, so full of hate, rage, and pain, that it momentarily froze them in horror.

"Go!" yelled Zoltan, sprinting down the shaft, Friesen at his side.

Kwan and Maphaela followed close behind.

"Kill them!" Justin's muffled voice screamed in front of them and to their left. "Now!"

Chapter 34

THEY HAD ONLY MINUTES TO escape from the landing and into the mine tunnels before they heard Justin raging behind them, screaming at the Berserkers. But it gave them a slight head start. While Justin's troop blundered around on the landing, Barbara, Jaromir, and Sibyl hurried deeper into the mine, taking side tunnels and hoping to shake their pursuers. But it was, they realized, only a matter of time. In less than fifteen minutes, they saw lights in the tunnels behind them, and soon they heard voices and shouts.

A timbered tunnel mouth opened in front of them to their right, and Barbara slipped into the darkness of the shaft. The other two followed and pressed themselves against the damp wall. Barbara crept back toward the mouth of the shaft and peered in the direction they had come. In the sharp white light that blazed ahead of Justin, she saw one of the Berserker officers striding toward them.

"They are here!" the Berserker's toneless voice boomed.

Barbara ducked quickly back inside the tunnel mouth. "Jaromir," Barbara called, retreating while facing the entrance, her jewel held in front of her. "Shine down the shaft. What's ahead?"

Jaromir turned and extended his hand into the darkness. "Steady slope downward," he called back. "Goes a ways." He intensified his light and peered down the tunnel.

"Back!" Barbara yelled.

A fireball screeched toward them, exploding against the left upright timber of the entrance frame, setting it aflame. She threw her arm over her eyes against the blinding light and retreated slowly down the slope. Next to her, Sibyl stood facing forward, both arms outstretched. She sensed Jaromir join her on the other side, his ring extended forward.

"Jaromir," she said, breathing hard, "I need a report. How far does the tunnel extend?"

Ahead of them she heard shouting and scuffling.

"Jaromir!" she repeated sharply.

"Leave him alone, honey." Sibyl said. "It goes fifty feet and stops."

Barbara whirled and shone her jewel down the shaft. The red beam lit the space with the glow of a spectacular sunset. Fifty feet behind her, the tunnel ended in a solid rock face.

"Maybe it's an illusion," she said, turning back. "One of Justin's tricks."

"Not this time," Sibyl said beside her.

They were now some twenty feet from the passageway entrance, and they concentrated on the rectangle, still lit by the smoldering fire from the burning timber. They retreated slowly down the slope. The first Berserker peeked around the corner, and Jaromir met him with an ice shaft that entered its neck just below the metal grate covering its mouth and chin. The Berserker lurched backward, and lay twitching on the stone floor, its throat torn out by the shard. To the right of the entrance, they heard Justin's shriek of fury once more, shaking the limestone walls around them.

"Two down," Barbara said, "and six to go."

"Not counting Justin, Meijer, and Elrabol," Jaromir muttered.

The three of them had backed halfway down the slope toward the end of the tunnel. Around them, there were mounds of rocks, several abandoned shovels, and to one side a pile of rusty railroad spikes. Behind them, lying across the tunnel, twenty rails that had never been laid in this dark end of the line were stacked three feet high.

"I can't hold him at the entrance," Barbara said, her jewel glowing in her hand. "He's too strong." She glanced over her shoulder to look at the rails.

As soon as she turned, she knew she had made a mistake. Justin sensed her momentary shift of attention and charged around the timbered opening in the tunnel above them. She hurriedly drew a dense red curtain between them and the approaching men, barely in time to divert a black ball Justin hurled down the shaft that would have crushed them against the stack of steel rails.

Lit by a white fire that grew from his head like some fantastic halo, Justin led his force downward toward the retreating trio. For some reason Barbara recalled that the first principle of warfare was to occupy the high ground in any battle. *Little late for that,* she thought. Even from a distance in the murk of the tunnel, the blue of Justin's eyes burned with a glow so intense Barbara averted her eyes. She thought of Sibyl next to her.

"Back," she called to Sibyl and Jaromir. "Behind the rails. Quickly!"

She drew back, maintaining the gauzy red shield, trying to negotiate the uneven surface while facing a quickly advancing Justin, Meijer and Elrabol on either side of him.

Barbara sensed more than saw Sibyl trip on a loose rock and fall to the mine shaft floor. When she fell, she slid underneath the retreating shield and in that second, Justin slammed a barrier against Barbara's protective net. Sibyl scrambled to her feet, but it was too late—she stood unsteadily beyond the protection of the shield.

Barbara watched in horror as Justin roared in glee, picked Sibyl off the floor like a rag doll, shook her in midair, and then hurled her against the side of the mine shaft. Sibyl's head struck the rock, and she slid unconscious to the floor.

Justin's aura glowed brighter in victory. His scorching gaze swept toward Sibyl. "You bitch!" he screamed at her in fury. "For two years you have taunted me. Two years!" His voice boomed, primal and inhuman. "Finally I have you outside." His red lips drew back in pure hatred. "There is no protection for you here!"

Justin's hand drew back, and Barbara felt Jaromir leap forward. He dashed through both shields, his blue ring blazing at Justin, and threw himself over Sibyl. Jaromir's move caught Justin by surprise, and he flinched as the blue blade Jaromir hurled at him carved a bright red line in in his left cheek.

"Both of you!" screamed Justin. "Both of you die!" He slashed his hand forward, hurtling a yellow-tipped black shaft at Jaromir's back.

The spear struck Jaromir between his shoulder blades, and he twisted in agony as the blade penetrated his body and emerged through his chest.

But Justin's attention had shifted away from Barbara, and his black net barrier thinned as he concentrated on Jaromir. In fury and dread, Barbara flung a wall of fire at Justin fiercer, hotter, more brutal than anything she had conjured before, any flame she had dreamed of. It surged around Justin, and she watched as his halo faded and his hair caught on fire, his dark eyebrows singed to the skin. Behind him, Berserkers were screaming and stripping off flaming hoods and robes. Meijer had been blown to the ground and scrambled on all fours searching for his round glasses among the rocks and debris.

Justin turned toward her, his usual red lips now purple, his handsome face twisted in hatred. Elrabol had been knocked to his knees when the firestorm hit, and now he picked himself up from the smoke and burning rags on the shaft floor. His tunic had been burned off of him and he stood next to Justin, naked and fat.

"She is mine," Elrabol shrieked, rushing forward. "This time, you whore! This time you are mine!"

Fury lit his eyes into red coals, and his blistered nose transformed into a razor-sharp beak as he advanced. Black feathers grew from his forehead and massive black wings assaulted the red barrier between him and Barbara. Again and again they beat against the red web that separated them, folding it inward, collapsing it around Barbara, and still he came, a fetid smell of rotten meat and acid from his open mouth, his beak pecking, slashing, shredding the web faster than Barbara could repair it. He was only inches away, lunging, the beak seeking her throat, trying to strip her face to the bone, to peck out her eyes, to eat them. The raven bill split open in a great cry of conquest.

She had only seconds. She dropped her shield. With the web down, she flipped open the cover of the suicide ring and drove her left hand deep in the Raven Man's open mouth, thrusting hard, oblivious to the pain, driving her fist deeper and deeper into his throat until she could shove no further. She felt the suicide pill slip from the opened ring and into Elrabol's gullet. She withdrew her arm and with her jewel in her right hand, quickly reestablished the barrier.

It had only taken moments. She was vaguely aware of blood streaming down her left arm as she looked through the red gauze at the Raven Man.

His blazing eyes dulled, his beak began to melt, and his fat hands clutched at his throat. He fell back, his belly shuddering, his wide mouth opening and closing slowly. His legs collapsed and he fell, thrashing and gurgling at Justin's feet.

And then it was quiet. Barbara stood erect, gazing at the tall figure in front of her. Justin still had the advantage of elevation, and he stared down at her with the slit eyes of a cat, the eyes of a predator reflecting only the calculating determination of an animal. They were made all the more savage by the missing eyebrows and lashes, singed off in the firestorm. The suit was steaming but more or less intact, while the white shirt underneath had burned away except for a few grey shreds, revealing raw flesh underneath his red tie. Behind him, four of the Berserkers stood in a row, their hoods gone, revealing scorched hairless heads. Little or nothing was left of their clothing, and their muscled arms hung huge and dangerous at their sides. She glanced beyond them and saw two other figures lying lifeless on the floor. *Four down and four to go*, she thought. Meijer had fallen to the floor in the first wave of her fire attack and emerged relatively intact. The back of his bald head glowed scorched red and he held his broken glasses in his hand. The room smelled of singed hair and charred clothing.

Barbara rapidly strengthened her shield, aware that she could not lift her left arm and that she was nearing exhaustion. She squeezed her eyes shut and then opened them wide. She looked at her arm for the first time. Deep slashes ran down her lower arm and wrist. She turned her arm over and realized that a main artery had been sliced open and blood puddled at the feet. Quickly she grasped her jewel and winced as she directed a beam of cauterizing light at the wound.

She looked back at Justin and smiled. "Think you're going to need a new suit." She shook her head. "And that tie's got to go."

Justin's eyes narrowed and then grew large.

The blackness struck so suddenly and with such force that she was pushed back against the pile of rails. She regained her footing, clutching her jewel fiercely in her good hand, and stepped toward Justin.

Barbara noticed a slight motion behind the row of Berserkers, to her right, but Barbara kept her eyes steady on Justin. He held her gaze.

Her heart stuttered. In her peripheral vision, she saw Sibyl stir, gently shake her head, and open her opaque eyes.

"Your nobility is looking pretty tattered right now," Barbara sneered. "You can't stand up to me, even with your zombies behind you, can you?" She spat toward him. "You disgust me."

He turned his glare back at her, and she held it. In seconds, she felt needles poke into her eyes with a stabbing pain that jolted right into her brain. But she did not blink.

Justin leaned forward slightly. "I will blind you," he said in a voice filled with such rage and malice that Barbara recoiled. "And then I will kill you. More slowly and painfully than you can imagine."

Her eyes stung and began to blur, but in front of her, she could see Sibyl slide slowly to a sitting position. Sibyl glanced toward the pile of railroad spikes, and two began to move.

"You never could do shit right, honey," Sibyl called, her voice low and penetrating. "You should have finished me first."

Terror registered in Justin's feral eyes, and he swung his gaze toward Sibyl in panic. As he did, the two spikes flew from the pile and cut through the air like arrows, embedding themselves deeply into Justin's eye sockets. The scream that erupted shook the walls of the cave. Behind her, Barbara heard rocks clatter on the mine floor. The old timbers shifted and shuddered and dust fell from the roof like snow. Justin stumbled backward, clutching at his eyes, crying out in a frenzy of pain and fury, shrieking over and over.

Meijer watched in shock as Justin backed into the cave wall and fell to his knees. He rushed to Justin's side and drew his ring, quickly placing a defensive curtain around the two of them. The four Berserkers stood dumbly, their metal masks hiding any emotion.

"Kill them!" Meier shrieked at the remaining Berserker officer. "Now!"

Barbara began to weave on her feet. She had stopped the blood follow from her arm, but she calculated she had lost a good quart of blood. Faintness rushed through her in waves. She wondered how long she could hold on before blacking out.

The officer motioned at Sibyl, who still sat against the wall with Jaromir's body across her legs, and one of the Berserkers charged across the mine shaft toward her. Sibyl elevated an ancient pick and launched it at the approaching Berserker. Barbara watched helplessly as he knocked it aside with a wave of his hand and continued toward Sibyl.

Barbara fell to one knee, braced herself against the rails, and desperately tried to clear her head.

The sudden shriek from the Berserker sounded like the screech of amp feedback, piercing and constant, like an icepick in the ear. Barbara looked up in time to see the turbaned man, Malik, and the other one—what was his name? Friesen?—dash into the room. She realized that one of them had bludgeoned the Berserker approaching Sibyl in the stomach with a purple rod that looked like a piece of hardened steel. The Berserker fell forward and Barbara heard a distinct snap as Malik stepped on the back of the Berserker's neck.

She slumped down sideways against the rails. Her eyesight had become hazy, but she could make out more figures rushing into the cave, and one in particular. *It's Zoltan*, she thought as she slipped into unconsciousness. *He found me.* Even as she blackness overcame her, her lips curled in a smile.

Chapter 35

ZOLTAN'S EYES SWEPT ACROSS THE scene in front of him. Against the far wall Justin was screaming, clutching at his bleeding eye sockets. Next to him, Meijer crouched low to avoid Justin's flailing arms while monitoring the situation unfolding in front of him. His eyes, squinting through broken glasses perched crookedly on his nose, grew wide as he saw Zoltan enter the shaft. He intensified the black gauze barrier. The three remaining Berserkers stood outside of the protective perimeter, and they turned toward Zoltan, their eyes swiveling uncertainly in the round eyeholes of their masks. To Zoltan's left, a dark-skinned woman sat upright against the other wall, the jewel maker Jaromir unmoving across her legs, a black spear protruding from his back. The woman's head turned toward Zoltan as he entered the shaft and he could see she was blind. An odor of burnt hair and blasted stone hung heavy in the low tunnel.

A yard in front of the woman, a Berserker sprawled face down on the rock floor. Malik stepped off the figure's neck, kicking off its mask, which clattered across the stone, revealing a hairless head, ears and nose removed, metal electrodes extending from the ear holes. Thin red lips parted slightly showing long white teeth filed sharp. Dull eyes stared out of browless sockets.

Friesen and Malik had burst into the shaft first, Friesen turning toward the wailing Justin while Malik advanced forward to a slight figure slumped against a stack of rusting steel rails piled chest high near the end of the shaft. His heart leapt into his mouth. It was Barbara.

Behind Zoltan, Kwan and Maphaela rushed to his side, but he gestured frantically at Barbara propped up against the pile of rails. "Barbara!" He shouted. "Help her."

The two men glanced briefly around them and ran toward the end of the shaft. Malik had eased Barbara upright into a sitting position at the base of the pile of rails and held a flask of water to her lips.

Kwan dropped to one knee and took her wrist.

"How is she?" Maphaela asked.

"Pulse is weak but steady. She's lost a lot of blood." He looked up into the anxious faces of the other two men. "She should be Okay. Keep giving her water, Malik."

Barbara smiled slightly. "Well, it's nice to see you too."

Fighting every impulse to join the three men attending Barbara, Zoltan walked to the center of the mine shaft and stood next to Friesen and turned and faced Justin and Meijer.

"Mr. Friesen," he said quietly, "I would appreciate it deeply if you would go to Barbara."

"But…" Friesen began to protest, looking at Zoltan.

Zoltan turned his head sideways and fixed Friesen with a gaze hardened with hate and wrath. Friesen nodded and backed toward the pile of rails, facing Justin the entire time.

It took Zoltan several moments to realize that Justin was clutching at spikes embedded deep in his eye sockets. In a burst of agony, he yanked them from his face and hurled them to the stone floor. His scream of rage and pain shook the stone walls again, and he began slicing the air blindly. Zoltan ducked as a black scythe swept across the shaft. To his left, even in her weakened condition, Barbara had managed to throw up a frail red curtain, deflecting the blade as it cut through the air.

The Berserker to Justin's left was not so lucky. In his fury, Justin had slashed his arm toward Barbara, catching the Berserker at the waist. It gave a short screech then crumpled to the ground, neatly cut in two, its feet twitching while the upper body lay still.

Justin slashed again, this time to his right, but Zoltan had time to throw up his own shield to protect himself and the woman against the wall behind him. The remaining two Berserkers pitched onto the floor to protect themselves.

Now Justin slashed aimlessly, carving stones into dust, cutting log supports into chunks of broken wood. The Berserkers huddled against the black protective curtain, hoping to escape the fury. At the far end of the mine shaft behind Barbara and the four men, a weakened timber gave way, and stones collapsed in a loud rush as the ceiling gave way. Dust swelled through the mine.

"Stop," Zoltan said. His voice was not loud, hardly loud enough to penetrate Justin's screams and the clattering stones. Nor was it angry or harsh. But the single word echoed in the shaft as if delivered through a bullhorn, and every figure in the room froze. The stillness that followed was marred only by the odd pebble rolling from the collapsed roof.

The men stared in silence. Zoltan had always seemed a rather small man, but now he stood straight, tall, almost towering, his silver hair swept back from a face that was calm and set. White eyebrows overhung jet black eyes behind rimless spectacles. The deep obsidian eyes that had transfixed Barbara when they first met the day he had made her gem. But they were not the eyes she recalled. These were burning coals, the streaks of dark green and blue she remembered from so long ago now flickering like tongues of flame.

Zoltan faced Justin, standing six feet away. Blood dripped from Justin's empty eyes, ran down his cheeks and onto his raw chest. His hairless head swiveled back and forth slightly like an animal trying to identify a scent.

"It is over," Zoltan said.

"Never!" screamed Justin in a guttural snarl. His blistered lips pulled away from perfect white teeth

Zoltan shifted his glance toward Meijer, who still crouched at Justin's feet. Zoltan's eyes narrowed. He fixed Meijer with his gaze, intense as a laser. Meijer cowered, and then whimpering, drew back against the stone wall.

"Justin!" Meijer blurted. "He's right. I see it. You may be able to destroy us, all of us, but you will die as well." He wheezed. "And me, too. You cannot triumph. Not today."

Justin gave a great scream of hatred and slashed viciously at the enemy in front of him. Walls shook and stones clattered nervously from the ceiling.

"Please, Justin!" cried Meijer. "We will all die! He will let us go. We will go back to the Company. You can get medical help for your eyes." Slowly he stood up. "We will retreat and reorganize." His voice became more confident. "We cannot win here, but our ultimate victory is assured."

Justin panted loudly, a dog in searing summer heat.

"Please." Meijer reached out and took Justin's right hand.

Justin ripped it loose and slammed a backhand across Meijer's face. His head jerked back, his glasses skittering across the stony floor. A trickle of blood started from one nostril.

Meijer's pale blue eyes flickered and he held up a platinum ring holding his dark grey jewel. A wire curled from the stone and wound quickly around Justin's neck. Meijer drew his hand back sharply and the garrote tightened. Justin's scream caught in his throat and he clutched desperately at his neck where the sharp wire bit deeply into his skin. It contracted slowly. Blood spewed from the cut as the tautened wire reached the carotid arteries. Justin's mouth opened wide in a gurgling wail, his thin red tongue protruding between white teeth. He stood, thrashing and clawing at the wire tightening around his neck. His struggling slowed and his arms dropped from his neck and fell to his side. He twitched once and slumped slowly onto the stone floor.

Perhaps it only took seconds, a minute at the most, but to the watchers it seemed time had stood still, the final act played out in silence.

"You will take him with you," Zoltan said, breaking the spell.

The bloody garrote uncoiled from around Justin's neck and retracted into Meijer's glowing dark grey jewel. Meijer kicked the remaining Berserker officer, still sprawled on the floor, and produced a rent in the black protective curtain. "Take him," Meijer ordered

The officer jumped to his feet, his gold-trimmed mask contrasting with the charred rags he wore and his blistered skin. The officer entered the gap between barriers and picked Justin up with one hand and slung the body across his massive shoulder and stood at attention. Meijer closed the protective net.

"You will not need that," Zoltan said. "You are free to go. We will not harm you."

Zoltan turned slightly as a commotion broke out behind him.

"Not harm him?" Friesen shouted, his rage and disbelief amplified in the shaft. "We damn well *are* going to harm him!"

Hands grabbed at Friesen as he began to lunge toward Meijer. Malik reached the collar of Friesen's shirt and twisted it. "We're going to *kill* the son of a bitch."

Zoltan faced Friesen, who stopped and became silent.

"I understand your anger, Mr. Friesen. But I have made a deal with Mr. Meijer, and we will honor it."

Friesen remained still. "I don't recall any deal," he said.

"Justin would have killed us all, I assure you. Mr. Meijer was to remove Justin or kill him. He kept his part of the bargain, yes?"

"But he will go back to whatever hellhole they have down there," Friesen shouted, waving toward the shaft entrance, "and it will all go on and on. We've killed Justin. Let's finish the job!"

Zoltan nodded. "Indeed, Mr. Friesen. But it will go on and on whether Justin or Mr. Meijer are there or not. There is always another to take their place." He glanced around the shaft. "I do not see Mr. Garripoli," he said, turning back toward Meijer.

Meijer licked his lips. "He stayed behind at the Company."

"I see, I see. You will return. But perhaps Mr. Garripoli may not be entirely happy to see you, no?"

"That is none of your affair." Meijer eyed Friesen uncertainly. "If you can keep your rabble at bay, we will leave." He looked at Friesen again. "But I will maintain my shield."

"As you wish."

Meijer nodded, a slight smile on his lips. "This is far from over. And I repeat, this may be a setback, but our final victory is assured. You have no idea what you are up against."

Friesen lunged toward Meijer, only snapped to a halt by Malik's iron grip on his collar.

Meijer laughed and looked at Zoltan. "You see, people are stupid. Animals. Packs of animals. So easily led. Bread and games." He shook his head in amusement. "And such games we have! No, in this match I do not envy your position."

Zoltan's face remained set, his eyes hard and black. "Perhaps. But I do believe you will return perhaps a bit weakened, yes? A bit less certain? The Committee will hear your report. They will know there are people watching. Powerful people. This is indeed not over." He nodded up the shaft. "You will get into the elevator and descend."

"Uh, uh, honey," a voice called out behind him.

Zoltan turned toward Sibyl in surprise.

"We've only got one car left, and they can't have it."

Malik had released Friesen's collar, and now Friesen stood glaring at Meijer. "You can climb down into your rat hole," he snarled.

Meijer looked at Zoltan, his smug smile fading. Without his glasses he squinted nearsightedly. "That wasn't the deal," he protested. "You said we could take one of the cars down."

Zoltan arched his eyebrows. "At that point I believed there were two cars. We had heard both in the shaft." He shrugged. "Most regrettable."

"But we can't..." Meijer spluttered. "We can't climb down! There aren't any stairs."

"True," Zoltan nodded. "But it seems there are metal rungs, a ladder, in the stone of the ventilation shaft, yes? It is not comfortable, but you don't have much choice."

"Ladder!" Meijer shouted. "What are you talking about?"

The two remaining Berserkers shuffled their feet uneasily.

"There is no ladder down the damned mine shaft!"

"That is where you are wrong," Zoltan said mildly. "You see that is how we arrived. By ladder."

"So you came this far on some damned ladder," Meijer cried. "But does it go all the way to the bottom of the elevator shaft? Are all the rungs still in place?"

Zoltan shook his head. "Alas, Mr. Meijer, that we have no way of knowing." He nodded toward Malik and Friesen. "Mr. Malik and Mr. Friesen will escort you to the shaft and point out your descent route. You will understand if I do not see you out?" He gave a small bow. "Until we meet again, yes?"

"I look forward to it," Meijer sneered.

Still cloaked in the black mesh shield and facing Zoltan, Meijer slowly made his way up the sloping shaft. The Berserker officer carrying Justin's limp body over his shoulder walked inside the shroud while the other remained outside, ordered to take the brunt of any attack against them as they retreated. Malik joined Friesen and the two followed close behind. In a few moments, they had exited the charred tunnel entrance and disappeared.

Zoltan stared after them briefly, then turned and hurried toward Barbara, who was now sitting against the pile of rails, her legs folded under her. She smiled as Zoltan approached and wearily raised her arms toward him. Zoltan fell to his knees and wrapped his arms around her.

"Easy, sir," Barbara murmured. "I'm still a bit under the weather."

Zoltan leaned back and looked into her face and ran his hand through her red hair, falling in short curls to her chin. "Your hair," he said. "You cut it."

Barbara laughed out loud. "Yes, you idiot. Before we left the Market."

Zoltan smiled. "It is still beautiful. But your eyes, they are not the same."

Barbara's smile faded slightly. "No," she said softly. "I suppose they're not."

"Emerald green now," he went on. "So much darker than when we met, yes?"

Several minutes later, Friesen and Malik rounded the entrance at the top of the shaft slope. "They are gone," Malik proclaimed.

"They didn't get the cage, did they, honey?" Sibyl asked.

Malik smiled. "No, ma'am. I believe if you listen hard you will be able to hear them cursing as they make their way downward, rusty rung by rusty rung." He left the top of the shaft and walked to Sibyl, who had slid slightly to one side. He knelt and took Jaromir's wrist between his thumb and fingers. After a few moments, he looked up and shook his head.

"Ma'am, I have not had the pleasure. My name is Malik." He extended his hand.

Sibyl hesitated and then reached out and took it. She placed her other hand on top. "Such strong hands," she said, opening her eyes. "I am Sibyl."

Malik nodded and looked into her blank eyes, realizing that she could not see. "Thank you. It is a pleasure."

Sibyl sighed. "A pleasure. Honey, you don't know the half of it."

"The man across your legs is dead. He has been killed by a spear that penetrated his back."

Sibyl turned her face away toward the stone wall of the shaft.

Kwan had joined Malik while Zoltan helped Barbara to her feet. Maphaela put his hand under her arm.

"Yes," Sibyl said. "The spear was meant for me. Justin's last triumph." Her blank eyes drifted upward slightly. "He was safe, behind Barbara's shield. He could have stayed there." She paused. "His name is Jaromir."

"We met, at the crypt," Malik replied. "I believe he left with Justin."

Sibyl turned back toward Malik, fixing him with her empty eyes. "He had a change of heart. Or perhaps more accurately, he listened to his heart."

"Sibyl," Kwan said, crouching next to her. "Malik is going to remove Jaromir's body. Can you feel your legs?"

"What I can really feel is a splitting headache," she said.

"Justin hurled her against the rocks," Barbara explained, walking slowly toward the group with help from Zoltan and Maphaela. She fixed her eyes on Sibyl. "I thought you were dead."

Sibyl grinned. "I'm tough, girl. You know that."

"When I saw you move, just the shift of your head…" Barbara stopped, tears forming in her eyes.

"I hear you, honey," Sibyl said, smiling broadly up at Barbara. "I was real glad to wake up too."

Malik put his hands underneath Jaromir's arms and lifted him gently off Sibyl.

She closed her eyes and patted the stone floor next to her. "Put him here."

Malik lifted the body upright. The spear point had just penetrated Jaromir's body, the ugly yellow point extending barely an inch through his tunic.

"Careful," Zoltan ordered. "The point is death. Do not touch it. Pull the shaft back into the body."

Kwan stood and grasped the spear extending from Jaromir's back and pulled. The barbs of the point ripped reluctantly through skin and muscle until it was covered by flesh. A brief red flash burst from Barbara's necklace, neatly cutting the shaft extending from Jaromir's back. It clattered heavily onto the stone. Malik picked up Jaromir and set the body next to Sibyl, his legs extended. Malik released the body and it slid slightly toward Sibyl until their shoulders were touching. His eyes were closed, his face oddly peaceful.

"His ring," Barbara said, nodding toward Jaromir's hand, resting on his outstretched leg. "It contains his gem."

Malik looked uncertainly at Zoltan.

"We will take it," Zoltan said. "Neutralize it."

Barbara shook her head. "No." She knelt beside Jaromir and carefully lifted his hand. The glorious ice-blue gem that had come alive as Jaromir led them through the caverns and battled Justin in the mine shaft was dark. Barbara gently tugged the ring off his finger. Then she reached over and took Sibyl's hand.

"Barbara!" Zoltan said sharply. "What are you doing?"

"I'm putting it where it belongs," she said, lifting Sibyl's right hand.

Zoltan took a step toward her. "You can't, my love. It's *his* soul encrypted in the stone." He reached out his hand to grasp her wrist. "It could be catastrophic, for your friend. Perhaps for all of us."

Barbara stared at Zoltan's hand for a long moment and then fixed him with her dark green eyes. Zoltan hesitated and slowly withdrew his arm.

Barbara slipped the ring onto Sibyl's finger.

There was a quiet beyond silence, and then Sibyl opened her eyes. She stared at them through ice-blue irises and smiled at Barbara. "I just knew you had red hair, girl," she said.

Chapter 36

SIBYL SAT CROSS-LEGGED OUTSIDE the entrance to the mine, her face turned to the sun. Tears ran down her cheeks uncontrollably. Barbara knelt behind her, her arms around Sibyl's shoulders, hugging her tight as she shook gently.

"Sibyl," Barbara whispered. "Maybe you shouldn't look directly into the sun. We don't really know, you know, about your eyes."

"Honey, I have never seen anything more beautiful," she said, but she dropped her eyes to the clearing around them. "And the bushes, the trees. They are so green."

Zoltan crouched In front of them, studying their faces anxiously. He stood and looked at the group.

"We do not know how the Company will react. If the women feel ready, perhaps this is a good time to depart, yes? Mr. Friesen and Maphaela, will you please check to make sure our route out is secure?"

The two men slipped back through the gap in the rocks and surveyed the hillside and surrounding area and returned to the narrow canyon.

"All clear," Friesen announced.

"I could see the van at the bottom of the hill," Maphaela added. "Still there."

"So let's go," Friesen added impatiently.

"Where?" Malik asked. He stood tall a few feet away from Barbara and Sibyl.

"Where?" Friesen asked. "To Zoltan's house. Where else?"

"I'm not sure that's wise," Malik said staring down the trail.

"Wise?" Friesen demanded. "What's not wise is wasting time not getting Barbara and Sibyl medical attention."

"Perhaps," Kwan added from the limestone doorway into the mine. "But I don't think they are in danger. I examined them both in the mine when we exited the elevator. As best I can tell, Sibyl has a severe concussion, but there is not much we can do. She needs rest."

"And Tylenol," Sibyl added. She stood, bracing herself against the rock wall. "Anyone have a Tylenol?" Her eyes drifted downward. "The moss," she said softly. "It's so vibrant, so gorgeous."

"As for Barbara, she has lost blood, but her pulse is strong. She will be weak for some time and needs rest, but she is past the risk of hypovolemic shock."

"Which is…? Friesen asked.

"It can occur when blood and fluid loss keeps the heart from pumping sufficient blood to the body. If that were the case, her pulse would be weak, racing."

"But you said they both need rest. They've been through hell. Let's go back to Zoltan's house and let them rest up, get stronger, for Christ's sake."

"I understand your concern, Mr. Friesen, and share it," Zoltan said, "but I fear Mr. Malik is correct. We can assume the Company will be in disarray, but if they don't know by now that we escaped, they will soon. They would like nothing more than to destroy us, and we are most vulnerable in Budapest."

"But their agents are decimated!" Friesen argued. "Even if they have the capacity to strike, it will be days."

"Perhaps, but make no mistake—they are a formidable force. They have extensive and deadly personnel above ground."

Friesen opened his hands in exasperation. "If not your house, then where?"

"The Market, I believe," Zoltan answered. "I realize we have been focused on escaping and recovering Barbara, but that is now accomplished. We must begin to make longer range plans. The Market is a relatively safe place to do so." He nodded grimly at the entrance to the mine. "I believe we all now know the nature of our adversaries, no?"

"The Market is in New York," Friesen said. "So seven of us—including two who are suffering from major injuries, I might add—all of whom look like we've been dragged behind a semi for several blocks, are just going to hop on over to the airport and catch the next flight to New York City. No danger there."

"Something like that," Zoltan said. "If our cards still work. Please, give me a moment, yes? I will call Madam Jeanine." Zoltan walked to the gap at the edge of the clearing and took the phone he'd picked up in Budapest from a breast pocket in his vest.

"Madam Jeanine?" Friesen asked.

Barbara sat against the wall next to Sibyl. "Yep. Madam Jeanine's Travel. 'We Specialize In Where No One Else Goes.'"

"She's a travel agent?"

Barbara waggled her head. "Sort of. She works out of the Market. She is tattooed with vines and flowers that seem to grow while you are watching them from head to toe. Well, at least the parts I've seen. Her teeth are filed to a point."

"Perfect," Friesen said. "I'll keep that in mind."

Zoltan returned to the group, smiling. "We are good to go. My card is still operative. Madam Jeanine has chartered a plane for us and there will be a nurse on board. It will meet us at the Ferihegy Airport in an hour."

"Ferihegy," Maphaela said. "That's where we flew in, isn't it? Will they be watching it?"

Zoltan sighed. "Hopefully not. I doubt they'll be that organized yet. Still, we must not rule out the possibility, yes?" He motioned down the path. "But please, we must hurry. They airport is a half hour away."

The group made their way out of the grotto onto the trail that wound between rock faces on each side. In a few minutes, they emerged from the gap onto the ridge that curved around the hillside. Far below them they could see the black SUV parked at the barrier.

Friesen looked down the steep scree slope. "I don't recommend sliding down on your ass," he said.

Sibyl stood at the mossy entrance and opened her arms wide, staring at the expanse in front of her. "It's magnificent," she whispered.

Malik was already striding ahead along the path. "This will take us to the old road," he said confidently. "Come."

They followed as the trail traversed the steep hillside and then began to slope downward as they entered a copse of twisted cedars. They rounded a bend and saw that the trail met the rutted abandoned road just a few yards ahead. Slowed by Barbara's weakened pace, the six of them stayed together while Malik hurried onto the road and down to the base of the hill.

"I'm at the barrier!" Malik called below them. "Not far now."

They went more quickly, and after a last bend they saw the yellow arm across the road. Malik had already entered the SUV and had started the engine as they scrambled down the last few feet and into the car.

Malik backed the SUV into a small clearing and turned down the road. "Directions," he barked.

By the time they approached the airport, the skies were transitioning from violet to dark purple. The gate to the airport was open, and Malik drove toward a small brick terminal at the end of a broad drive. He pulled into a handicapped spot next to the terminal entrance and leapt out. He opened the rear door and helped Barbara as the others exited into the growing darkness. Zoltan held the double glass doors open as the other six entered the building. Friesen rushed to the wall of windows that opened onto the tarmac.

"It's here," he called, pointing. An executive jet sat thirty yards away, its stairway down and a pale light glowing from the cabin.

A young man in a dark suit and blue tie stood behind a counter as the group hurried in. He scanned the group and nodded at Zoltan, who approached the counter. "You must be Mr. DeAngelo," he said in a strong Hungarian accent.

"*Így van,*" Zoltan replied in Hungarian. "May we board the plane? We are rather in a hurry."

The agent nodded and fingered a clipboard. "Of course. There are just a few papers to sign."

Zoltan turned to the group. "Please board. I will complete the paperwork and join you. Mr. Malik, will you please instruct the pilot to be ready for takeoff as soon as I am on board?"

Malik nodded and opened the door onto the tarmac. The low whine of the jet engines filled the terminal as the team hurried through the doors, across the runway and climbed the stairs into the cabin.

Zoltan turned to the man at the counter, who was flipping through a sheaf of papers on the clipboard. Suddenly he looked up, staring over Zoltan's shoulder, and his eyes grew wide.

Zoltan sensed the men behind him before he turned around. Instinctively, his right hand drifted to the watch pocket in his vest and folded around his gem.

"What's the hurry, DeAngelo?" O'Brien demanded.

Zoltan turned slowly as the airport agent slid behind the counter. O'Brien stood six feet away. His arms hung at his side, a pistol in his left hand. Paulson stood on his right, pointing a Glock at Zoltan's head. A man Zoltan didn't recognize with long black hair, fidgety brown eyes and an Uzi underneath his coat stood on his left.

Rage built inside Zoltan, exploding like a wildfire. He fixed his eyes on Paulson. "Tired of breaking into apartments, Paulson?"

The man's meaty face was a mask of loathing.

"Just a slight career correction," Paulson sneered. He pointed the pistol at Zoltan's feet. "I'm going to enjoy this," he said, each word wrapped in hatred. "Start with your feet." He moved the gun upward. "Then your knees. Then your balls. If you're not dead by then, straight through your fucking mouth."

The fury uncoiled inside Zoltan like a striking cobra. Through a light blue haze he saw himself plunge a knife deep into Paulson's chest.

The haze abated, and Zoltan realized his hand still grasped his gem. But in front of him, Paulson had collapsed to his knees, clutching at a blue-green blade that thrust out from his shirt. Deep red blood pulsed from the wound. Paulson looked up at Zoltan, a brief bewildered look in his eyes, and fell forward onto the floor.

Zoltan shifted his eyes to O'Brien, who raised his hands shoulder high, his gun dangling from one finger.

"Always hated that son-of-a-bitch," he said.

The other man began to raise his Uzi. "What the fuck, man!" he screamed, his eyes dancing wildly from Paulson's crumpled body to O'Brien.

O'Brien's hand twitched and he gripped his gun. There was a sharp crack and a neat hole appeared in the man's forehead. His head pitched backward, and he fell heavily onto his back, a pool of blood spreading from the back of his head.

"Never liked him much either."

Zoltan glared into O'Brien's face. The fire burned less fiercely inside of him. "Drop the gun. Back out the door, facing me. Get into your car and drive out the gate. Keep driving."

O'Brien flinched at the voice, commanding and inflected with menace. The gun clattered onto the tiled floor and he backed slowly to the glass doors. He pushed them open with his back and walked to a black Mercedes parked next to the SUV. He turned on headlights, pulled out of the parking area and drove down the long drive through the gate. Zoltan followed the taillights until they disappeared.

The airport agent peered fearfully over the countertop. Zoltan turned to him.

"I believe you needed a few signatures, yes?" he asked calmly.

Still crouching beneath the counter, the young man shoved the clipboard across the Formica top. Zoltan scribbled his signature on two sheets and walked out the door to the waiting plane. He climbed the steps and walked down the narrow aisle as the attendant pulled the walkway into the plane and sealed the port. The plane began taxiing down the runway as Zoltan made his way to the back of the plane. He felt the eyes of the others following him as he weaved down the aisle of the moving plane, but he said nothing until he settled into the seat across the aisle from Barbara.

"Christ, Zoltan," she said, staring at him anxiously, "what the hell happened? We heard the gunshot."

Zoltan stared straight ahead. "We no longer need to be concerned with Paulson."

"You shot him?"

"No," Zoltan replied softly. "It would appear that I stabbed him in the heart with a turquoise dagger."

Chapter 37

BARBARA HAD EXPECTED THE MARKET station to be deserted when the train pulled in at 4:21, but instead, it was crowded with people, many in their red and black uniforms, others in work clothes. The seven of them were the only passengers on the train, and when it wheezed to a stop and they disembarked, the crowd pulled backward from the platform. Then the applause began.

At first it was a smattering of clapping, but soon it built into a roar. The group stood looking at the faces in front of them, some smiling, but most grim with respect. Mrs. Harlow emerged from the gathering and walked toward Zoltan. She shook his hand firmly and then turned to the other six as the crowd on the landing quieted.

"Your journey has been reported," she said. She nodded to Sibyl. "We are honored to welcome you all back and to thank you."

Zoltan gazed at the people standing silently along the platform.

"I don't know what to say," he stammered. "We did not expect such a reception."

"Or *any* reception for that matter," Friesen muttered.

"Mr. Friesen," Mrs. Harlow said, "your courage has been noted." She turned to Malik. "And you, sir. You have exhibited steadfast leadership."

Malik bowed from the waist.

"But how…" Zoltan began. "We only left Budapest last night."

"We don't know it all, by any means," Mrs. Harlow said, "but we followed some of your remarkable journey. You see, Mr. DeAngelo, your gem has been transmitting."

Zoltan's eyebrows drew together. "Madam, transmitting to what?"

Samantha stepped forward. "When we inspected the agents' gems, we chemically replicated the molecular receiver in your stones to better analyze it. We used your stone, Mr. DeAngelo, to clone the receiver. It wasn't perfect, but we kept working on it. We were able to refine the construction as we better understood the atomic composition. We made considerable progress."

"You mean you replicated his stone?" Barbara asked.

"No. Just the molecular cluster that acted as the receiver. What we have looks more like a golf ball."

Pierre stood at Samantha's side. "And then a week ago it began to vibrate."

"We were amazed," Pierre said, "but we knew it had to be a transmission from you, Mr. DeAngelo."

"But we could barely receive Zoltan's messages in the caves," Maphaela said. "Just yards away."

"Quite right," Pierre continued. "The receiver we replicated from Mr. DeAngelo's stone is designed to receive transmissions from a distance, thousands of miles."

"Like long wave vs short wave radio," Maphaela said.

"Exactly, but on an even more intense basis. After that first signal, we narrowed the frequency until we could monitor your images on an ongoing basis. Within a few hours, we heard all of your conversations."

"But we were transmitting mentally," Kwan pointed out. "Wouldn't you have only picked up our thoughts rather than our speech?"

"At first that was the case, but as the five of you became more attuned to each other, your mental chatter became dialogue. Any oral message, of course, is simply the vocalization of a mental language construction. We were able to monitor your entire conversation for the last week."

"We initially kept your exploits secret," Mrs. Harlow added. "We suspected there might be agents even in the Market who would have used the information to tip off your adversaries. Only Pierre, Samantha and I monitored your progress." She paused. "With great anxiety and fear for your lives I might add. But we recorded the conversations."

"Jeez," Friesen said, "if I'd known we were going live, I would have deleted more expletives."

"On the contrary," Mrs. Harlow continued, "you were all magnificent. Yesterday, when it was clear that you had safely escaped, we broadcast over the Market emergency sound system edited sections of your ordeal in the castle labyrinth as well as your attempts to locate Barbara."

"You should have heard the shout go up when you received the signal from Barbara," Samantha added.

"For hours people stood or sat and just listened to the broadcast," Mrs. Harlow said. The confrontation in the mine was terrifying. We followed it like an old radio broadcast of a Joe Louis fight." She stopped and looked at the seven men and women. "We have long known of the Company, heard rumours of its activity. We knew some of the gem makers worked for it. But we did not realize the extent or nature of the organization." Her eyes darted to one side. "Or perhaps we just chose not to know. But your courage…" She stopped and swallowed hard. "We were humbled."

The crowd around them nodded in assent.

Zoltan felt his throat close. He had not cried for a very long time. He was not going to start now.

"But you are exhausted," Mrs. Harlow continued. "Let us go to the shop. For tonight we have room for all of you." She glanced at Zoltan. "You and Barbara will stay in your apartment?"

"Only if the door is fixed," Barbara said.

Mrs. Harlow smiled. "Quite intact, I assure you. There have been changes since that incident. But come, we can talk about all of that later. I have scheduled a briefing for tomorrow afternoon with the Market Council, if you don't mind. For all seven of you."

Zoltan raised his eyebrows. Maybe it was just a formality. *Perhaps each of us will be given a key to the Market*, he thought wryly. But from Mrs. Harlow's tone, he suspected there was more to it than that.

"As I said," Mrs. Harlow continued, "significant changes have occurred here while you were away. I look forward to discussing those with you and your team."

The crowd parted as the seven followed Mrs. Harlow.

"Not sure I want to take the elevator up to the apartment," Barbara said as the strode through the Market entrance. "The last time I was in an elevator, rocks were falling on the top."

"Uh, huh," Sibyl agreed. "And I damn near let us plunge to the bottom of the shaft."

Barbara reached over and squeezed her hand. "But you didn't," she said.

The group made their way through another crowd of Market folk, who nodded and whispered to each other as Mrs. Harlow led the group to her shop. Sibyl's eyes darted around the perimeter of the dome and then to the sun embedded in the tiled roof, her face blank with awe.

#   #   #

Relief flooded through Barbara as she entered Mrs. Harlow's shop and heard the familiar tinkling of the bell as the door opened. The welcome smell of waxed wood and dust was somehow comforting. Mrs. Harlow pulled back the curtain that separated the shop space from the workshop in the back. Workers looked up from their tables as the group passed through and entered the door into the hallway. They filed into the conference room where Justin had ordered them to Budapest just a week ago and sank gratefully into chairs around the circular table.

They were silent for several long moments. Then Zoltan leaned forward on his elbows and looked at his companions with sparkling black eyes. "We did well, yes?"

The fatigued faces around him creased in smiles.

"And now," he continued, "so much to talk about. So much. So many questions."

Barbara looked around at the circle of faces. Uncertainty flickered in their eyes. Friesen stared pensively at the ceiling, and Kwan shifted uneasily in his chair.

"All of which can wait until tomorrow," she said softly. "I don't know about the rest of you, but I feel pretty drained." Only Maphaela smiled slightly. She wasn't sure if the pun just wasn't that funny or if everyone was too tired to laugh.

"Of course," Zoltan said. "We are all fatigued, yes?" Heads bobbed wearily. "May I suggest we sleep and reconvene tomorrow?" He looked at their host standing by the door. "And Mrs. Harlow has arranged for a medical team to be present. They will provide each of us with a full examination."

The group exchanged nervous glances.

"But that can wait. In the meantime, Mrs. Harlow has excellent accommodation, I assure you. And breakfast tomorrow, Mrs. Harlow?"

She smiled. "Of course. Catered by Lodde's."

"Best breakfast restaurant in the Market," Zoltan explained, leaning back in his chair. "And then we meet here again? At 1:00? Mrs. Harlow would like to catch all of us up on changes that have occurred in the Market governance in our absence." He looked solemnly at the faces around him. "And then we have been invited, all of us, to meet with the newly constituted Market Council. It seems they would like to hear more about our recent activities and our common adversaries."

There was a long silence as if no one wanted to be the first to move.

Finally Friesen stood. "We are so tired we can't keep our eyes open. But we don't want it to end." He shook his head thoughtfully. "Such friends. Such comrades."

The group rose in assent, and then one by one, the men and women embraced each other, tears welling in their eyes.

"Please, this way," Mrs. Harlow said quietly. "I will show you to your rooms."

Friesen led the five out of the room. Sibyl left last, clutching Barbara's hand and pulling her gently into the hall.

"I'm afraid to let go," she said. "You be here tomorrow, girl," she growled.

Barbara smiled. "I'll be here. Promise."

Sibyl nodded and followed Mrs. Harlow.

Chapter 38

MRS. HARLOW HAD BEEN RIGHT—the carved door to Zoltan's apartment looked like it had never been damaged. Zoltan pushed the code buttons and the lock whirred. He turned the brass knob and they walked into the apartment. Barbara scanned the room. Debris from the blast has been removed, and the desk drawers she had strewn over the maple floor had been replaced. She walked to the leather sofa and lay back against the cushions. The faint smell of old leather made her feel safe.

Zoltan hurried to her side and knelt by the sofa. "I am sorry. You must be so tired."

Barbara turned her head to his face, only a foot away, creased in worry. "I am," she said. "But I feel much better. The IV on the plane did wonders."

Zoltan's face relaxed and he smiled. "I am so glad. So very glad. But you need sleep."

Barbara looked into Zoltan's dark eyes. "May I share your bed tonight?"

A spike of alarm flashed across his face. "Barbara, I…"

She reached out and put a finger to his lips. "I know you have worried about this. I am so sorry. You are afraid, so afraid. Because…because you love so fiercely."

Tears polished his eyes. "It has been so long, Barbara. You need a young man to share your bed. Not me. I am hardly an ideal lover."

"Sir," Barbara said softly. "I am so tired of you telling me what I need and don't need." She smiled mischievously. "And you were a great lover.

I've seen the pictures to prove it."

Zoltan looked over the top of the sofa, his eyes unfocused. "So long ago. So very, very long ago. I am not that man."

"No, you are not." Barbara leaned back against the cushion. "Do you recall when you asked me to look at myself in a mirror?"

He looked back to Barbara. "Of course."

"Do the same for yourself. Not in a mirror, although that's not bad either," she smiled. "But inside. Don't you feel the strength? Where did the courage come from? Yes, and the power? You're right—you're not the frightened, sad, desperate little man I first met only a month ago. Surely you feel it."

Zoltan cocked his head slightly.

"There was always a darkness about you," she continued. "A background of sorrow. But now it is gone. The *Mester's* black stone is gone. It is no longer dripping bleakness, hopelessness, impotence into your soul. It is gone, and you are free."

Zoltan gave a wry grin. "Are any of us truly free?"

Barbara rolled her eyes. "You can be so exasperating."

Zoltan laughed aloud. "Oh, Barbara. You do make me laugh." His face became grave. "And you have brought me joy, something I thought I would never know again."

Barbara took his hand and raised it to her lips and kissed his fingers. "I want to lie with you tonight." She held his hand against her cheek. "No expectations. No requirements." Her green eyes shone. "Well, just two."

Zoltan's face tensed.

"You must love me," Barbara whispered, "and you must hold me."

His face softened and his lips relaxed into a tender smile. He raised his hand and brushed back a curl of red hair from her forehead. His fingers travelled to her ear, and he traced along its edge and down to her chin. He leaned forward and kissed her on the lips.

"The love walked in with you through that door the first night you arrived," he said. "From that moment I was lost." His black eyes looked deeply into hers. "And to hold you, madam, would be one of the great pleasures of my life."

Barbara stood and pulled him gently to his feet. She took his hand and led him to his bedroom.

\#   \#   \#

Barbara awoke to the aroma of frying bacon and percolating coffee. She sank back into the soft down pillows, wondering if she were still dreaming. But as her head cleared, the smells were still there, wafting through the open bedroom door. She rolled out of the bed, slightly surprised that she wore only her jewel, and slipped into the red silk pajamas laid out at the foot of the bed. She smiled as she spotted the red brocade slippers neatly tucked under the chair where her clothes were piled. She slid her feet into them and padded soundlessly down the hallway toward the living room.

As she neared, the smells became stronger, and she followed them through the kitchen doors. Zoltan, wearing a blue robe elaborately embroidered with brightly-colored dragons, slid bacon, crisp and brown, onto a plate covered with a paper towel.

"Bacon in the morning," she commented from the door. "You really do know how to treat a woman."

Zoltan finished transferring the bacon and turned to Barbara. He nodded to an ancient aluminum coffee pot gurgling on the stove. "And coffee," he smiled. "Could be a bit strong since I haven't made it in several decades."

Barbara laughed and walked to him. She put her arms around his neck and kissed him. "I'll take my chances." She stepped back and saw a dozen eggs sitting on the counter. Slices of bread were waiting in a new chromium toaster. "But when did you get all of this?"

"I ordered it while we were at Mrs. Harlow's. It was waiting outside the door when I got up." Zoltan smiled ruefully. "And it is a good thing I did."

Barbara looked at him quizzically.

"My bank account. All the money was withdrawn at 8:15 this morning."

"Oh, no!" Barbara said in shock. "Everything? They cleaned out your entire account?"

Zoltan leaned against the stove. "I had a small amount in a checking account. By the time the Credit Union realized what had happened, they were able to protect that." He shrugged. "But basically, madam, yes, I am broke." He turned to the eggs. "So not only am I eighty years older than you, I have enough money to pay my rent for three months." He glanced over his shoulder and opened his eyes wide. "Quite a catch, yes?"

Zoltan opened the top of the grey cardboard egg carton. "How would you like your eggs, madam?"

Barbara rushed to him and hugged him from behind. She pressed her cheek into his back. "Oh, Zoltan. I am so very sorry," she whispered.

"As am I," Zoltan said.

He had picked up an egg and tapped it on the edge of a beige mixing bowl. The shell remained unbroken, so Zoltan struck it against the bowl more energetically. This time, the shell shattered and half of the egg dripped on the outside of the bowl onto the counter.

Barbara held him around the waist and gently pushed him aside. "I'll do this. You're out of practice, that's all."

Zoltan sighed. "So it would seem. Along with several hundred other aspects of being a normal human being."

Barbara kissed him on the cheek and deftly broke the eggs into the bowl.

"I remember the first time you did this," Zoltan said. "Not so long ago, really. But so very, very long ago. You were almost as beautiful then as you are now."

Barbara felt her face redden. "Well you, sir, are far more handsome." She gestured to the percolator on the stove, which had stopped bubbling and sat quietly on the burner, a thin plume of steam arising from its spout. "Now, would you be so good as to pour us both mugs of coffee while I scramble some eggs to go with that bacon, whose smell is driving me crazy."

Zoltan went to the cupboard and pushed a few plates around. Finally he returned with a couple of ancient tea cups, decorated in gold leaf and colored glazes. The rims were chipped.

"I'm afraid this is the best I can do," he said, putting them on the counter. "We can pick up some mugs at the Market today."

"They'll be fine, but could you rinse out the worst of the dust?"

They sat at the small table in the corner of the kitchen. Barbara sipped her coffee, looking over the rim at Zoltan's face. He raised his head and smiled at her. The sadness that had clouded his eyes had lifted, and his dark eyes, which could blaze with such ferocity, looked at her softly.

"I am so glad," she said.

Zoltan cocked his head slightly.

"Last night. That you felt human again. That in my arms you shed the fears and cautions of so many years. But now, you wonder, what can you offer me?"

She placed her cup on a cracked saucer and reached over to cover his left hand. "Not even a bank account."

Zoltan rolled his eyes upward. "Madam, I do wish you would stop doing that. I feel...naked."

Barbara gave a tiny smile. "You look good naked."

Zoltan looked quickly at his plate. "You know what I mean," he mumbled in embarrassment.

Barbara laughed, and Zoltan looked at her, and he began laughing as well. "That's better," Barbara said, still smiling broadly. "You were looking so serious."

"And reasonably so, yes?"

She gave his hand a squeeze. "Yes. But this you must know and must believe. There is no one in the world I would rather be with and no place in the world I'd rather be. Please, drop that from your list of concerns, okay?"

Zoltan looked at her gratefully.

Barbara raised her hands in exasperation. "Yes, you idiot, I really do mean it, and no I'm not just saying that to make you feel better." She shook her head. "After all we've been through." Now her face became serious. "How can you doubt me?"

Zoltan sat back. "I am sorry. Truly. It is not you I doubt. It is me. I do not know what I have to offer you."

"Do they offer courses in the Market?" Barbara asked.

Zoltan looked puzzled. "Courses? Well, yes, I believe so."

"Anything on self-esteem building? Being your own best friend? Overcoming negative thinking? Being the man your dog thinks you are? That sort of thing?"

"But I don't have a dog."

"It's a figure of speech," Barbara said, rolling her eyes elaborately. "Being the person people who know and love you know you to be."

"Oh, I see," Zoltan replied, abashed. "I see."

"In the meantime, there's a song, from a long time ago. I remember my mother playing it. For some reason, the lyrics always stayed with me." She sang in a soft, resonant voice:

I'll be your mirror
Reflect what you are, in case you don't know
I'll be the wind, the rain and the sunset
The light on your door to show that you're home

I find it hard to believe you don't know the beauty that you are
But if you don't, let me be your eyes
A hand in your darkness, so you won't be afraid

Barbara got up and walked around the table. She sat in Zoltan's lap and hugged him hard around the neck, her cheek wet from the tears that leaked from his eyes.

Chapter 39

THEY ARRIVED AT MRS. HARLOW'S around 12:30, Zoltan lugging his gem making machine in the old oak box into the front room. The bell tinkled, but no one appeared. Finally Zoltan struck a round chromium bell on the counter. The curtains parted, and a young man approached them.

"Mr. DeAngelo," he nodded at Barbara, "Madam. Mrs. Harlow sends her regrets. She has been detained on Syndicate business. She will join you in the conference room just as soon as possible."

"Thank you," Zoltan said. "In the meantime, is it possible to meet with Samantha and Pierre?"

"Yes, of course, "the man said, drawing back the red curtain and holding it open with his arm. "Please. I will take you to their lab."

They were shown down the long corridor to a door with a rectangular pane of glass. Through it, Barbara could see flickering screens, computer terminals that rose to the roof, and various enclosed cubicles.

Mrs. Harlow's assistant knocked, and Pierre opened the door "Mr. DeAngelo, Barbara," he smiled. "So good to see you."

Zoltan nodded. "The pleasure is mine. I am sorry to bother you, but I have a request to make of you and Samantha."

"Of course. Please, step inside."

They walked through the open door, and Zoltan set the box with his gem maker on a black topped table. Samantha turned from a monitor screen and walked toward them, her brown eyes alive with curiosity.

"So, Mr. DeAngelo," she said, eyeing the box. "What new wonder have you brought us today?"

"Doctor," Zoltan nodded in greeting.

"Mr. DeAngelo," she said, her nose raised slightly. "That would be Samantha to you."

"Of course. Samantha," he said somewhat uncomfortably. Zoltan gestured at the box. "You have seen the gems, but not the machine that produces them, yes?"

The physicists nodded.

"That machine is inside this box."

Pierre's eyes flickered to Zoltan's face and then back to the oak case.

"I have a meeting with Mrs. Harlow and my colleagues, but before that there is an issue I wonder if you could help me with?"

"Of course," Samantha replied. "If we can."

"Quite simply, I need to know if it still works."

Samantha glanced up. "If it still makes gems, as before?"

"Yes, but if it does continue to produce gems, are they pure? Are they free of any receiver that would compromise the owner? Or do they still possess the tiny amplifier that enhances the owner's characteristics?"

"I see," Pierre nodded. "It will be a fascinating challenge. Would you please remove the machine from its case? We can then begin to analyze its operation and capacity."

Zoltan unfastened the brass hasps and opened the old box. "I am happy to leave the machine with you to examine." He paused, staring at the brass and wood machine nestled inside. "But I believe we need to go one step further, no? If the machine still works at all, we will need to make a jewel."

Pierre and Samantha exchanged glances.

"That makes sense," Samantha agreed. "It is only that way we can assess the nature of the gem."

Zoltan nodded. "But that will require a volunteer, yes? And I cannot ask anyone to take this risk. We do not know what the outcome will be."

Pierre nodded. "Perhaps we could put out a request for volunteers to the Market. I am sure there are many who would be willing."

"I will do it," Samantha said. "I would be honored to volunteer." She smiled. "As long as you are the gem maker." She glanced at Barbara. "I understand you have considerable skill in adjusting the resulting jewel to maximize the best qualities of the owner."

Zoltan looked anxiously at the physicist. "I do my best, but surely this is entirely different, and very dangerous. You are too important to the program to become a, what is the term? Guinea pig."

"Hm," Samantha commented, "when you put it that way it doesn't sound all that noble or enticing. But you see, Mr. DeAngelo, it is because I am so enmeshed in the project that I wish to volunteer. This is the logical next step," Samantha said, smiling broadly. "I look forward to it."

#   #   #

By the time they reached the conference room, most of the others were already sitting in chairs, chatting animatedly. When they entered, Sibyl rushed up to Barbara and hugged her around the waist, twirling her in a circle.

"Sibyl," Barbara croaked, "I can hardly breathe."

Kwan and Maphaela approached Zoltan and shook his hand warmly. Friesen and Malik stood as Zoltan made his way to round conference table.

"Please, gentlemen," Zoltan said, "do sit down."

The seven took chairs around the table. Tired as they still were, the joy of reconnecting quickly overrode the fatigue and the group talked animatedly until Mrs. Harlow entered the room. She moved to the head of the table and remained standing.

"If you will," she began. "I apologize for keeping you waiting. But issues have transpired since you left that you should know about and which will affect all of you."

Barbara looked curiously at Zoltan, who gave her a small shrug.

"As you will recall, especially those of you who were here at the time," Mrs. Harlow nodded toward Zoltan and Barbara, "we had an ugly incident ten days ago. There was a break-in at the Building, and the security forces, which had been essentially limited to patrolling the perimeter of the station for several years, re-entered the Market. It is not entirely clear who ordered this redeployment, but the sight of the guards, in their uniforms and armed with scimitars, alarmed many of us."

Barbara remembered trying to enter the market and the terror she felt when one of the red-helmeted guards had approached her demanding a pass. Her heart raced again as she recalled looking into the face covered by a black molded mask, the slits for the eyes covered with a clear material. And the voice: the guard's breathing had rasped loudly, inhumanly.

"Berserkers," she murmured to herself.

"Based on your accounts, not quite," Mrs. Harlow responded. "But too close for comfort for many of us. The Market people demanded a public meeting. The Chief of Security Forces has been fired. All but five or six of the guards were also let go. The uniforms have been destroyed." She shook her head slightly. "I melted down those ridiculous scimitars into something useful. And as the criticism escalated, the Market Council resigned." Mrs. Harlow glanced around at the people seated at the table. "And I have had the honor of being named Interim Council Chair."

Her comment was met with silence until Friesen began to clap, and then the whole table erupted in applause.

"Please," Mrs. Harlow said severely, raising her palms. "We are in precarious times. I would greatly prefer to remain in my shop, but we are in a situation where we need to rebuild our security force from the ground up. As well, we realize we can no longer remain in our cloistered cavern here. Evil is afoot, and we have been willfully blind to the threat it poses, not only to the Market but to the world we are, like it or not, still very much a part of." She stopped and leaned on the conference table. "I am telling you this because the Council board has asked that you join our community as we restructure. In different capacities, of course."

There was rustling and whispering around the table.

"The Council has requested a 3:00 meeting where we will go over the details of our offer. But in the meantime, our medical team is here. Some of you have suffered grave wounds," Mrs. Harlow said, looking at Barbara and Sibyl, "and all of you have endured great trauma, both recently and in the past. You will be given a thorough physical and then recommendations for healing." She nodded in conclusion. "If there are no objections, we will reconvene here at 1:55. I will then take you to the Council Chambers." She smiled and nodded at the door, which opened to reveal a cluster of white-coated medical personnel. "Dr. Keller, could you take it from here, please?"

\#　　\#　　\#

The Council chambers were located in a wood-paneled room above the credit union. Each of the eleven Market guilds had one representative on the Council, and many appeared as if they had just left work, which they had. The head of the bakers' guild wore a flour-dusted apron over his red tunic, and the musicians' rep was studying a score of a new production. Madame Jeanine, her tattooed ruby red lips in a broad smile, nodded at the group as they entered.

With Mrs. Harlow as chair, the twelve council members sat in a semi-circle around the table and the seven members of the team took chairs across from them.

The meeting began with Zoltan's summary of recent events and then opened up to questions from the syndicate representatives. As the gem makers shared their personal stories, each filling in blanks and contributing their knowledge and information, the emergence of an operation terrifying in its scope and impact emerged. Zoltan's shared Dezso's story of the rise of the Mester as a crime boss in post-WWI Budapest and the mysterious appearance of Justin. Barbara provided detailed descriptions of her interaction with Justin and her understanding of the Company's operations and intent.

"I think it can be summed up in a quote I came across years ago in a book I found in my father's library," Barbara concluded. "It stuck with me all these years, but now I think I finally really understand it: 'Through clever and constant application of propaganda, people can be made to see paradise as hell, and also the other way round.'"

"The leader of the leatherworkers' syndicate nodded his head grimly. "Hitler, if I'm not mistaken."

"Yes," Barbara nodded. "That is what we are up against."

New to all of them was Sibyl's description of the Company's workings from the inside, including her chilling accounts of the brutality used to maintain discipline inside the compound. Of particular interest to the Council was the composition and the role of the Committee.

"I sat with them many times," she told the group, "but I don't know who they are. When meeting at the Company, they wore masks, black top hats and robes. Their voices were disguised. But they are only monsters in the figurative sense: they are real people—billionaires, heirs to great fortunes. All men of achievement." She paused. "At any cost. But success at its most ruthless rewards psychopathic behavior. These men are shaping our world above ground and below. I know what they are capable of. They must be stopped."

While the discussion about the Company had been expected, Mrs. Harlow's offer of appointments to the seven of them was not.

As Mrs. Harlow had indicated, after the community's reaction to the aggressiveness of the security forces and they all became more aware of the dangers presented by Justin and the Company, the Market board had undertaken a major reorganization over the previous few days, and members of Zoltan's team figured prominently.

Apparently, the Council had interviewed Malik the day before after the meeting at Mrs. Harlow's had ended, and so he was the only one not surprised when he was named Director of the Market security forces. Along with Kwan and Maphaela, he was charged with rebuilding the Security force—and Market confidence in it. Anticipating the extent of the threat presented by the Market, a new intelligence unit had been created that focused on continued investigation and monitoring of the Company with Friesen and Sibyl as directors.

And even though he did not represent a syndicate, Zoltan was made a full member of the Council with Barbara named as a special advisor.

"I'm flattered, Mrs. Harlow," Barbara protested, "but I don't deserve anything. I know nothing about Market affairs."

But Mrs. Harlow remained firm. "We cannot, of course, compel you to work with us in this capacity. But Barbara, you are truly extraordinary, even here.'

Damn it, Barbara thought as she felt the blush warming up her neck and into her face once again.

"Your capacity for empathy and compassion is needed, greatly needed, as we move forward. You do not realize what an asset you are, young lady."

Barbara smiled and nodded mutely in assent.

When the meeting finally ended with vows of friendship and solidarity as they moved forward in a world revealed to be fraught with more evil than any of them had known just a few short weeks earlier, Mrs. Harlow and the team exited the building and made their way to the Market Pub nearby. They sat together around a long wood table in the far corner of the pub.

"Mr. Malik!" Zoltan enthused, cradling a mug of porter. "New Director of the Security Forces. Congratulations, sir."

Malik stood and bowed his head to the group. "I'm immensely honored, of course." He glanced at Mrs. Harlow. "But I do worry that I am not qualified for such a task as I do not know this marvelous place or its ways."

Mrs. Harlow waved her hand dismissively. "Now, Mr. Malik, as I said at your interview yesterday, we have tried using only local personnel and we can all see where that led. We need new ideas, ideas about community policing, communication, citizen engagement. And we did not make this appointment lightly. I took the liberty to look into your background, sir." She stopped and looked respectfully at Malik, still standing. "I am so very sorry about the loss of your daughter, Mr. Malik, and then your wife so soon after. It must have been crushing."

Malik's eyes glistened, but he said nothing.

"But your record in military policing and human rights enforcement is impeccable, outstanding."

Malike nodded in acknowledgment and took his seat.

She turned to Friesen. "We also examined Mr. Friesen's background closely. Mr. Friesen, to have your son die, only days after his birth. Again, my sincerest condolences." She paused respectfully. "Your history is more checkered. A martial arts fighter. Military school graduate. A mercenary..."

"Only for the good guys," Friesen said under his breath.

"An ideal intelligence agent." She looked around the table at the group. "The Market Board met this morning, which is why I was late for our session." She nodded at Zoltan. "Your encounter with the Company has awakened us. We realize we can no longer sit on the sidelines and ignore this threat. We committed to creating a counterintelligence agency with the purpose of monitoring and counteracting activities of the Company with Mr. Friesen and Ms. Sibyl at the helm."

Zoltan nodded at Mrs. Harlow. He remembered the last words of a very brave man as he died in the *Mester's* office*: You were right, Victor,* Zoltan thought. *It was not the end. But at least we now know the enemy and are prepared to fight back.*

Sibyl looked at Mrs. Harlow. "Yes, ma'am. I can see Mr. Friesen in this role perfectly. But how do I fit in? You don't know me." She glanced around the table. "None of you do

"Lady, Sibyl," Friesen said. "You know more about the operation of the Company than any other person alive that doesn't work for them. I wouldn't know where to start without you."

"And as for not knowing you," Barbara said from across the table, "I know you like a sister. Your bravery, determination, grit..."

Sibyl turned to her. "Now girl, you just stop that. I am already blushing from head to foot."

Kwan took a deep swallow of the dark beer in his mug and looked at Malik at the end of the table. "I am honored to be part of your security team, sir, and for the confidence you showed in us by requesting that Maphaela and I act as your deputies."

Malik looked at Kwan and Maphaela, sitting next to each other. "Gentlemen, you learn the character of a person when you fight beside him or her," he said solemnly. "Together we can do more than keep the Market secure; we can help it grow and flourish in the space we safeguard. I am the one that is honored by your acceptance of my offer."

"I am honored, too, of course," Maphaela said. "More than you know. And it also helps answer the question of where the hell I am going to live since my flat in Cape Town was raided. Apparently everything, including my gem maker, was stolen."

Malik stirred in his chair. "Sadly, I just learned that the same has occurred to me. My home was ransacked last night and my gem machine taken."

"I feared this would happen," Kwan said, "but not so soon. I have not yet contacted my caretaker "Given this news, I fear the worst."

"As do I," Friesen added. "I locked the machine securely in a vault, but I have no doubt the Company agents will have little difficulty breaking into it. So these appointments are most timely." He smiled at Mrs. Harlow. "We are between jobs, it seems, and kicked out of our accommodations. Your kind offer—not only of a job but room and board—is most welcome."

A silence settled around the table, dampening the earlier enthusiasm.

Zoltan broke the uneasy quiet. "We still have at least one machine. Mine was safe in the apartment. Security tightened after the last break-in. Even if they tried, they would have been unable to enter. As well, I have used it since our return."

A murmur arose around the table.

"Yes, Dr. Samantha Chambers now joins us as a gem carrier," Zoltan said smiling. "It appears that I will be able to use the machine indefinitely, though Drs. Chambers and Millard are already examining it to better understand its operation and mechanics. As well," Zoltan continued, nodding at Mrs. Harlow. "I have the contact information for all the remaining gem makers. I have messaged them a summary of the recent events. I have recommended that they do everything possible to protect their machines. And, as soon as possible, I will invite them to join us in determining a way forward that is independent of the Company and which will be designed to counter their mission."

"Well, yet more good news," Friesen said, beaming. "I'd say this is an encouraging ending to a job well done."

"May I propose a toast?," Malik said, standing once again, raising his glass of ginger ale. "To our beloved Mr. DeAngelo, our friend and comrade, Zoltan József. Now a member of the Market Council. The first, I understand, to hold that position without being a member of a syndicate for more than fifty years. And," he added, "one of the bravest men I have ever met."

"To Zoltan!" Friesen shouted, lifting his scotch.

"Zoltan!" the group shouted, rising to their feet and applauding.

Zoltan remained seated, staring at his beer in embarrassment.

"Gentlemen, ladies," he said, glancing up from the table. "I thank you." He took a deep breath. "But it is I who should honor you, for without you I would have remained in my quiet, protected and desperate world, frightened and voiceless. The *Mester* would have retained his hold, the depression and hopelessness that immobilized me issuing like poison gas from his stone."

Zoltan paused and he turned his eyes toward Barbara.

"But there was one who would not permit me to wallow in that trough, to remain sad and powerless." He smiled. "No matter how hard I tried. And who inspires all of us to be better men, to revive the compassion and courage we had lost, and to use them to fight the darkness that had deadened us for so many years."

Zoltan stood. "Would you join me in a toast to Barbara."

"To Barbara!" Malik called out solemnly. Everyone rose and turned toward Barbara.

"To Barbara!" the voices repeated in unison, each face radiant with love and respect.

Barbara sank into her chair, her face as red as the hair that tumbled around it.

Chapter 40

"I CAN ALMOST SEE HIS great bald head approaching us across the Market."

Barbara and Zoltan sat at a table near the fence separating the café from the bustling Market floor.

Zoltan stared over the crowd at the clock on the far wall. It was almost 10:00 at night, a week after they had returned from what had become known as the Battle of the Mine, but the artificial sun never set and, it seemed, neither did Market folk.

"A brave man, Caraldo."

Barbara squeezed her eyes shut. "How long ago was that? I can't figure it out. It seems like months, years, but I know it wasn't."

Zoltan took a sip of his espresso thoughtfully. "It was neither. It was exactly thirty days ago."

Barbara looked up to the soaring tiled roof of the Market. "How is that possible?"

He smiled at her. "It has not been uneventful." He took another sip and looked blankly into the crowd. "And now, we face a host of new questions, yes?"

"I know you worry. What will you do? How will you live? What next?" Barbara said, leaning across the table. "I feel it, like you are standing on the edge of a cliff and you know you have to jump, but it's foggy. You can't see the bottom. Are there rocks? A great river? Maybe it doesn't matter. Maybe it's time to hit the reset button."

Zoltan's glance swerved back to Barbara. "Can you stop that?" he asked. "Do you know what it feels like to have no mental privacy? To know I cannot hide a feeling, or even an image?"

Barbara put her hand on his. "I'm sorry. I didn't mean to upset you. You're not always that transparent. Many times you are unavailable to me. But these emotions—they are as vivid and searing as if they were my own. I cannot help it. And I will not allow you to fixate on such negative thoughts."

Zoltan cocked his head, partly in amusement, partly in curiosity. "And how, pray tell, will you stop me?"

"By getting you to notice the positive, to make yourself open to the possibility of joy, hope. I mean look at what came out today. You're healthy as can be. The doctors couldn't believe it. They said you have the physique and health of a forty-year-old."

Zoltan sat back. "But with the disconnect from the *Mester's* stone, it seems that we are now aging. At a more or less normal rate."

"Welcome to the club," Barbara said.

Zoltan laughed. "Of course, you are quite right."

"And Samantha's jewel—perfect."

"Yes," Zoltan agreed wistfully. "Beautiful, was it not? It fit her so well. All golds, yellows, cinnamon, and copper."

"And no transceivers. Just the tiny ochre enhancer at the heart of the stone. You did a magnificent job."

Zoltan waved his hand modestly. "It had little to do with me."

"Maybe, but perhaps more than you give yourself credit for. You feel the soul of each person before you make his or her jewel. Even when you made mine, I knew you were trying to find the best in me, to invest it in the stone." She laughed ruefully. "I'm afraid I didn't give you much to work with."

Zoltan's jet eyes sparkled. "On the contrary, Madam. I knew it was there. It was my job to find it."

Barbara fingered her jewel through her sweatshirt and then leaned across the table and kissed Zoltan hard on the lips. Zoltan rocked back in his chair in surprise, looking around uncomfortably as other customers in the café smiled and nodded at the couple.

"Madam," he said, looking into Barbara's laughing eyes. "Ah," he sighed. "So beautiful." He reached across and brushed her red hair back behind her ears. "Your hair, it is getting longer, yes?"

Barbara clasped her hand against his and kissed it. "Yes, hair does that."

Barbara focused her eyes on Zoltan.

"I want to ask you something about our escape from the Mester's compound."

Zoltan's smile faded. "Seems so long ago."

"I think it's safe to say a lot has happened in a short time," Barbara agreed. "But this is something specific."

"Of course."

"When we fled across the back of the compound and found the gate locked, you summoned the old oak tree. It lowered its branches and carried us to safety.'

"Yes?"

"How did you know it would hear you? Help us?"

Zoltan's smile returned. "The tree and I are old friends. During our annual meetings I fled the *Mester*, the dark confines of his compound, and escaped onto the grounds. That is how I knew about the ladder from the roof. I spent many hours under its leaves." He dropped his eyes. "When things were at their worst, I would hug it. It would comfort me."

"Okay. But you had never spoken before. It had never picked you up."

"No, no. Never."

"But that day you did. It did. Why?"

"I doubt I need to remind you, madam, that our options were severely limited."

"But why did it even occur to you?"

Zoltan sat back thoughtfully. "When we got near the tree I sensed that it was listening. I felt its presence, yes?"

"But then you took out your gem and wrapped your arms around the tree."

Zoltan nodded slowly. "When we were there, when I saw the gate was locked, that there was no way out, I knew my friend would help us. I just knew. All I had to do was ask."

"I see. You spoke with the tree? In words?"

He shook his head slowly. "No. Not in words. But we understood each other. Fortunate, no?"

"I don't think it was just fortunate. I think your gem allowed you to communicate with the old oak on a level impossible before. And we could go on. Your gem was the best at sending and receiving messages. Malik's provided the most light in the caves. Dear Jaromir was able to freeze the lake with his gem. Up to then, I think, it was mainly a party trick. But faced with death, especially of Sibyl, he found his ring had far more power than he had understood."

"And you, your gem has given you the power of fire, yes? And perhaps it has also accelerated your empathic development? Clearly each gem seems to have some special strength, or it elevates a specific power in its owner we may not even know about."

"So why, since you've made hundreds, maybe thousands of gems, aren't those gem owners using their stones as we have? Their potential is enormous."

"But unrecognized, no? And we are talking about gem-makers' rings. We have learned that their architecture is different."

"But not mine."

"No," Zoltan smiled. "But you are."

Barbara's face remained set. "Perhaps, but the point is we have these powerful stones and we don't know how they work. What they can and cannot do. We have little control over the energy they possess."

Zoltan thought back to the confrontation with Paulsen in the terminal, the fury that raged through him. His shock at seeing the razor-sharp turquoise blade driven deep into Paulsen's chest, knowing it was his, that he had somehow created it, unconsciously it seemed. How had it happened? Channeled, what was his stone's potential. Uncontrolled, what damage could it do?

"Yes, but why such urgency?" His face was somber, his dark eyes attentive. "What is it?"

Barbara toyed with the cup in front of her, sliding it slowly around the saucer.

"Barbara, talk to me."

"I've been having visions." Her eyes remained turned to the table. "Nightmares, sort of, except they're not at night. They intrude at odd times. It's like a film clip just suddenly appears in my head. No warning, no trigger."

Zoltan studied her with concern. The empath skills that had advanced so rapidly had gradually made her a seer as well, but her divination skills were still new, demanding and confusing. He saw the strain in her face. He slid his hand across the table and covered hers.

"Go on."

"There is nothing clear. It always starts with a storm, black clouds, claps of thunder, jagged lightning bolts. And then come the images -- berserker faces, charging horses carrying figures in red armor, crying ravens flying in great circles in the grey sky. Black stones, like the Mester's, in the hands of men in black cloaks and top hats." She shook her head and looked at him pleadingly. "Zoltan, they scare me. I don't know what to do with them."

He squeezed her hand softly. "And these visions, they seem important? Not just flashbacks from what you have been through."

She shook her head. "I don't know what they mean, but I know they relate to the future. They're trying to show me something, tell me something, but I don't know what it is." Her eyes glistened with tears of frustration and fear.

Zoltan said nothing and let Barbara settle. She took a deep breath and smiled slightly. "Thanks for listening."

"I am privileged to have a green-eyed oracle on my side, whatever is to come."

"Yes, that's it," Barbara said emphatically. "Something *is* to come, and I can just catch glimpses of it. I see great darkness but also a faint path, and sometimes it even winds past your oak tree. I feel crushing danger, evil that fills me like black ink. But also white seeds that spread and explode into gouts of fire. There *is* a way forward."

The turmoil he saw in Barbara's eyes made Zoltan flinch. "Barbara," he said, "please give me your hands."

Uncertainly, Barbara turned her hands over on the wood table and

Zoltan folded them in his. He gripped her fingers softly, lovingly. "Now, please close your eyes."

He did not know what to expect or even what he was doing. He had none of the empathic powers Barbara had, but he could not stand to see her suffer alone. He closed his own eyes and emptied his mind, concentrating on the warmth where their hands connected. Then it was as if a dam opened and her pain and confusion rippled up his arm and into his heart. He drew it out, sucking the poison as if from a snake bite. The flow slowed and then stopped. The warmth remained but the pain was gone.

He opened his eyes to see Barbara staring at him in wonder and, perhaps love?

"I believe your oracular powers will improve," he said. "The visions will become more clear, and like all our powers, you will learn to control it, let the visions nest when you wish and to fly over your head when you do not."

The were silent for a long moment, still holding hands and looking intently into each other's eyes.

"There are no more like you, are there?" she said at last.

Zoltan looked embarrassed. "Well, I suppose not. And if there were they would have been dead long ago."

Barbara smiled. "There is one thing that is clear to me, that I understand through this jumble of senses visions: Discovering and developing the full powers of our gems is the key to surmounting the forces of the Company, to our survival. That I know. Solving that mystery will be essential. But as to how we do that.." she shrugged. "I have no idea."

"Nor do I," he said, a look of amusement on his face. "But as a famous man once said, 'Perhaps the answer will come like a flash of lightning and in an instant the truth will be revealed!'"

Barbara clapped her hands in delight. "Nicola Tesla!"

He nodded in admiration. "Ah madam. You never cease to amaze me."

"He always appealed to me. A mystic genius."

Zoltan shook his head and smiled. "Of course he did. Did you know he was the Chief Electrician for the Budapest Telephone Exchange?"

"I did not."

Zoltan's smile faded. He stared over Barbara's shoulder pensively.

"I know that look. What are you thinking about?"

His eyes refocused. "Tesla had another famous quotation: 'If you want to find the secrets of the Universe, think in terms of energy, frequency, and vibration.'"

"Huh. I have no idea what that means."

"Nor do I. But is it not curious that those are precisely the elements peculiar to the gems and their ability to receive and transmit?"

Barbara looked at him doubtfully. "You think Tesla is behind the gems?"

Zoltan shrugged. "Probably not. But there is a strange story. I heard it from my father as a child in Budapest. I really never thought much about it."

"Go on."

"Tesla was obsessed with the idea of wireless transmission of both power and communication. Years later he predicted that we would be able to communicate face-to-face anywhere in the world with an instrument that could be carried in a pocket."

"The cellphone."

"And perhaps more? This much is well known. While in Budapest, around 1882, he had an epiphany. He was obsessed with the idea of wireless transmission. He was on the verge of a nervous breakdown. One evening, while walking with a friend in the *Varsoliget* Park, he looked into the setting sun and began reciting a passage from Faust."

"Faust. Like Goethe's Faust?"

"The same. Then it came to him. He feverishly drew a diagram in the sand. It was the basis for the transmission technology he later perfected."

"The answer came like a flash of lightning and in an instant the truth was revealed."

"Exactly."

"But how does that tie him to the gems?"

"Tesla left Budapest suddenly, supposedly after an argument with the owner of the telephone company, Tivadar Puskas, a very wealthy, influential man. Puskas went on to invent the forerunner of the radio, advanced broadcast equipment, switchboards – many innovations that brought him wealth and fame. He represented Edison in Europe for many years."

"Tesla's arch-rival."

"So where did all Puskas' ideas come from? Puskas seized Tesla's papers, claiming they had been developed at his expense. Some were far beyond Puskas' ability, but the papers remained, and they were passed onto his nephew." He stopped speaking and his face grew taut. "Sandor Fejér. Son of Puskas' brother and a disciple of Friedrich Nietzsche."

"Hell of a coincidence. But how do you know all of this?"

When Zoltan turned to her, she saw pain in his black eyes. "I told you that my father was a communist during the White Terror, no?"

"Yes," she said softly. "And that he was executed."

"The White Guard, as they were called. They murdered thousands, and especially Jews." He gave a mirthless laugh. "Especially communist Jews. They had local commanders, informants. In our area it was Sandor Fejér. He identified my father. They took him into the caves and shot him."

"Oh, no. How did he know your father?"

Zoltan's face was fixed in a grim smile. "He and my father were best friends. Neighbors and colleagues. They worked at the university together. They discussed philosophy, Tesla, politics."

Barbara shook her head. "I am so sorry."

"Indeed," Zoltan said, his face brightening. "But that was a long time ago."

"Yeah, but pain like that lingers."

Zoltan shrugged. "More importantly, I'm seeing patterns that eluded me. My father told me that he and Fejer were members of a philosophy club. A club to which he claimed Nietzsche had once belonged. I was too young for that to mean much, but I understood it was important to my father." He paused, looking over Barbara's shoulder. "Az Arany Lelkek Rendje. Yes, that was it. The Order of the Golden Souls."

Barbara looked dubious. "I get it. There are a lot of coincidences there. But with all due respect, Zoltan, I don't see how any of this brings us closer to figuring out how we identify and strengthen the powers of our gems."

Zoltan shrugged. "Nor do I. At least not yet."

They both looked up from the table as Malik strode across the café floor toward them.

"So sorry to interrupt," Malik said, his usually stern face soft and smiling.

"Malik!" Barbara cried, pulling out a chair. "Do join us for a coffee."

He took the chair and sat down. "Nothing I'd rather do," he said, "but I cannot stay." His eyes swept the Market floor. "Such an extraordinary place. The governing model—unlike any I've seen. People don't exactly vote. They are organized into syndicates. They meet and convey their wishes to the Board. And if the Board doesn't listen, well, they revolt it seems."

Zoltan's gaze also travelled around the giant dome. "I have lived here for, well, for longer than I care to remember. And over all those years I seldom visited. Had little to do with this place or its people. A shame, no?"

"That is about to change, I believe," Malik said. "Congratulations, sir, on your appointment to the Market Board."

Zoltan glanced down at this cappuccino. "Well, it was quite a surprise, I must say." He raised his eyebrows. "Hope I am up to the task."

Malik stiffened. "Of that I have no doubt. It is important to keep in mind this new challenge as..." Malik broke off uncomfortably.

Zoltan looked amused. "As I consider my future and whether I should jump off a cliff?"

Malik's face clouded. "I beg you sir, do not. Money is never that important."

Zoltan laughed and shook Malik's hand warmly. "I appreciate your concern, Malik. I genuinely do. But I assure you I am speaking strictly metaphorically."

Malik looked perplexed but nodded. Then he turned his attention to Barbara.

"Madam," he said. "Mr. Friesen and I are free to accompany you as requested."

Barbara smiled. "That is wonderful, Malik. I will contact you with the details in an hour."

Malik nodded again and walked out of the café gate, looking back occasionally until he disappeared into the crowd.

"You must be pleased about your appointment to the Market Board."

"Yes, nice honour indeed. But sadly, my dear, it has no stipend attached.

A voluntary position, yes?"

"So, you think, how do I make a living? But it's obvious isn't it? Now that you know your gem machine works, you make jewels just like you have always done."

"A thought that has occurred to me as well, of course. But madam, Barbara, the machine is—or at least was—only able to make twelve gems a year. And," Zoltan said, his eyes straying to the cooling expresso in front of him on the dark wood table, "I do not have my former customer identification service. You see, I was always informed of a potential client. I know now they were picked out by the staff at the Company." He shrugged. "Though how they were selected I never knew." He sighed. "Or cared."

"But now you choose your own clients!" Barbara enthused. "Good people, whose generosity and humanity is enhanced and not twisted into greed and selfishness. Don't you see? You would be creating a counterforce."

"I appreciate your enthusiasm, truly I do. But I must point out that each jewel I made cost the purchaser between $50,000 and $250,000."

Barbara frowned slightly. "Mine was the cheapest?"

"All the same product, I assure you. No, the charge was based on the owner's wealth. His or her desperation to have such a stone. Most of that money stayed with me and provided a very comfortable, if lonely life. Money I foolishly left in a single account easily hacked by the Company."

"So?"

Zoltan covered both of Barbara's hands with his own. "As you have no doubt noticed, the good and courageous, those with the open hearts and minds, they are usually not in the same income bracket as my former clients."

Barbara leaned back in her chair and looked over the crowd thoughtfully.

"You opened a new account at the Market Credit Union, right?"

Zoltan smiled wanly. "Of course. But it is as they say, yes? I closed the gate after the horse had left the corral."

"Would you mind giving me the account number?"

Zoltan looked puzzled but pulled out a small notebook form his vest. He wrote out the number and tore out the page. He pushed the paper across the table.

"I am afraid it is of little use. There is nothing in it."

"For now," Barbara agreed. She was silent for a few moments. *But perhaps it will fatten up a little once I'm done.*

"Zoltan, I would like to take the train out tomorrow morning."

Shock and this sadness swept across Zoltan's face. He dropped his gaze to the table.

"Of course," he murmured. He folded his hands in his lap. "I understand." He looked up into her face and gave a wry smile. "I knew you would come to your senses. It is the only logical thing for you to do."

Barbara looked up at the glowing ball in the middle of the dome and shook her head. "Oh, my God. You can be such an idiot."

Now Zoltan looked hurt. "Madam?"

Barbara reached back over the table and grabbed his hands fiercely, pulling them back onto the table. "I love you, Zoltan. Haven't I proven that to you over the last weeks?" Her eyes filled with tears. "How can you think I'd just walk away? Take that stupid little train to Grand Central Station and forget all this happened? And you'd just let me go?"

People at the table around them looked uneasily as Barbara's voice rose.

"Look at me," she demanded. "Look me in the eyes."

Zoltan slowly raised his eyes and stared into hers, lost in the emeralds, now swirling with anger and passion.

"Do you love me?" she demanded more loudly. "Do you?"

He leaned forward. "I have never loved another more than you. That I swear."

Light applause broke out and customers beamed at them, clapping. Embarrassment swept over Zoltan, and then it disappeared, replaced by something else. He stood up, still holding one of Barbara's hands, and bowed to the crowd.

Zoltan sat back down, his eyes fixed on the cappuccino and his face red with embarrassment.

"I am not used to public declarations of affection."

Barbara laughed. "I'm not surprised since for the last several decades you have been unable to touch another person or share your name."

Zoltan smiled ruefully. "Excellent point, madam. Perhaps I will get over my reserve, yes?"

"I certainly hope so. Now, back to the train."

"Yes?"

Barbara's face set. "I don't want to go into details now, but I have to resolve my marriage issue. And, I suppose, dispel the murder suspicions."

Zoltan nodded. "I see. You want to meet with your husband, David."

"Don't *want* to, exactly, but I think it's necessary. There are loose ends I need to tie up. And some issues I need to confront."

"I see. Would you like me to accompany you?"

Barbara reached back across the table and covered his hand with hers. "Not this time." She sat back and looked over Zoltan's shoulder. "I need to do this one on my own."

Zoltan looked at his coffee. "Is it safe to confront him on your own? He is a violent man."

Barbara chuckled. "Unlike Justin, the *Mester*, Zhukov…should I go on?"

Zoltan smiled. "All true."

"But if it will make you feel better, I don't plan on meeting him alone. I have asked Mr. Malik and Friesen to accompany me."

"Ah," Zoltan said, his face brighter. "Mr. Malik's message."

Barbara explained that she had already written her husband a letter, demanding that they meet. She had confided in Mrs. Harlow, who had suggested they could use a cooperative apartment building on the Lower East Side where the Market maintained a suite of condominiums and offices for visiting buyers.

"She said once you are inside and engage the security system, the offices are impregnable and soundproof. However, there is a full audio system in each meeting room. Very sensitive. Each word spoken will be recorded."

Zoltan nodded. "Yes, I have heard of it. But when did all if this happen?"

"Four days ago. After the meeting with the Market Council I requested a private meeting with Mrs. Harlow." Barbara smiled. "I think she kind of likes me now. Anyway, she is totally behind my divorce. And it seems that signing contracts is commonly conducted there. In fact, Mrs. Harlow has arranged for a lawyer they use to meet David and me there."

"I see. To finalize a divorce?"

Barbara waggled her head back and forth. "Among other things, yes."

"Other things?"

"Just some of those loose ends I mentioned."

Zoltan looked at her quizzically. "I see. And you wish to do this when?"

"Four o'clock tomorrow morning."

Zoltan's eyebrows drew together. "Such an unusual hour."

"Yeah, I know," Barbara said pensively. "But there is something about 4:00, isn't there? Not night, not morning. An unworldly time. I think David will find it a bit, say, unsettling."

Zoltan shook his head admiringly. "You do have a flare for the dramatic." His face became somber. "You are quite sure you want to go through with this?" His dark eyes searched her face. "You are severing your last ties."

Barbara smiled. "Dear, dear Zoltan. Yes, I am quite sure. I do believe my ties to that world have been severely tattered and frayed already, don't you? Hanging by a thread, I'd say, which I am looking forward to cutting."

"I see. And you are sure he will come?"

Barbara smiled. "I made him an offer, as they say, he couldn't refuse. I used Mrs. Harlow's computer. Untraceable. She even has paper that hold no fingerprints, no DNA. She sent it out by courier yesterday. Would you like to see it?"

"You have a copy?"

Barbara nodded and took a file folder from her backpack. She pulled out a single sheet of paper and slid it across the table to Zoltan.

Attention: David Steubenville

I have proof that your wife, Mrs. Barbara Steubenville, is alive. You will meet me tomorrow morning at 4:00 am at the Grand Street subway station. Once you have disembarked, you will make your way along the landing to the Grand Street and Chrystie Street exit. I will recognize you. At that time two men will approach you and escort you to a nearby office, where you will be given legally admissible evidence that your wife is alive and well. Failure to attend this meeting—or any attempt to approach the police—will result in the release of sensitive documents to the IRS relating to certain offshore holdings. You will come alone. If you are tailed or bugged, we will know, and the meeting will be cancelled and said documents released. You are no doubt aware that the IRS pays whistleblowers 30% of recovered funds hidden in offshore accounts to avoid taxes and awards the fraudster serious jail time.

"Ah, you are a wonder." He smiled, and then his face grew somber. "Good luck, love."

Chapter 41

BARBARA SAT IN THE SWIVEL chair staring out the window, her back to the office door, her black hoodie pulled over her head. Her gem hung down outside of the shirt, but she had dimmed the jewel so that it gave off only the slightest pink glow. Outside it was still dark, but in the eternal light of New York, she could make out the dim outlines of bushes and flowers in the garden just beyond the window. A green glass desk lamp cast a circle of white on the red leather blotter that covered the top of the old oak desk. Papers were stacked in neat piles. She tapped the face of her watch: 4:12. She knew Malik and Friesen had met David and that they were on their way. She checked the heart rate readout on the watch display. It fluctuated between sixty-eight and sixty-nine. Not too bad.

She heard a scuffling outside the office door and then a sharp knock. She continued staring out the darkened window.

"Come in," she said softly.

Reflected in the dark glass, she saw the door open. Friesen stood on one side of the doorway and Malik towered on the other. David, his eyes darting around the room nervously, stood in between.

"What the fuck is this all about?" he demanded.

Friesen clamped his hand on David's arm, and David squealed in pain.

"Mr. Malik, Mr. Friesen," Barbara said. "Thank you for delivering Mr. Steubenville. Please wait outside the door. If I need you I will call. Oh, and if you could ask Ms. Kamatovic to join you now?"

"We will be just outside, ma'am," Malik said.

Friesen gave David a slight push into the dark room and closed the door. Barbara turned slowly in her chair toward him, her face hidden in the darkness and the shadows of her hoodie.

"And who the fuck are you?" David spluttered. "What do you want?" he asked, his voice shaking.

"What do I want, David?" she asked. "What do you think I deserve?" She brightened the gem on her chest and drew back the hood of her sweatshirt. "Surprise."

David's face twisted from terror to rage. His lips drew back, exposing his teeth. "You bitch," he hissed.

"David," she said mildly, "for once, would you please just shut the fuck up and listen?"

"What do you want?" he repeated. "The house? Take it. The car?"

Barbara looked at him in disappointment. "Now, David, why in the world would I want with an empty house that has all of the charm of a cheaply decorated warehouse? Much less a car that costs a thousand dollars to change the oil."

David squirmed. "What then? What do you want?"

"I want to negotiate a fair divorce agreement, David. That's all." She gestured to the chair in front of the desk. "Please, sit down."

David did as he was told, nervously glancing from side to side.

Barbara gave a small rueful smile. "I know I've been away for a while, and I do apologize for not staying in closer touch, but I have followed events following my disappearance. From what I understand, you are under active investigation for my murder."

"I wish I *had* killed you, you bitch," he snarled.

"Now, now. No use dwelling on the past. But you see, here is the thing. After we have our little chat, I am going to disappear once more. You will never see or hear from me again. Without proof that I am alive, that would prove awkward for you, would it not?"

David glared at her but said nothing.

"I think there is a simple solution to what I am sure is a vexing problem for you: a legal divorce."

Barbara leaned forward in her chair and nodded at the papers in front of her. "I have drawn up divorce papers that comply with the requirements of New York Consolidated Statutes, Article 13 of Domestic Relations."

"I doubt they're worth the paper they're printed on," David said contemptuously. "You're no lawyer."

"God, you are such an idiot. Who draws up your contracts, David? Your letters, your divorce papers. You? No, that would be beneath you. Your legal secretaries do the actual work,. That would include me. I assure you, the papers are entirely legal and will withstand any court test."

In the dim light, Barbara could see that David's left eyelid seemed to have developed a tic.

"Now, if we can come to amicable terms, I am prepared to sign a legal divorce agreement witnessed by a lawyer."

"At 5:00 in the morning?"

Barbara glanced at her watch. "4:34 Actually. And yes, unlike you, Ms. Kamatovic is a lawyer who is more committed to her clients than to amassing a fortune." There was a soft knock, and Barbara nodded toward the door. "That would be Ms. Kamatovic. I believe she is waiting in the anteroom with Mr. Malik and Mr. Friesen."

David's tic seemed to get worse.

"Now, with my notarized signature on the divorce papers, you will have proof that I am alive, right?"

David nodded warily. "I suppose."

"So that would let you off the hook on the murder charge and," she smiled at him, "you can go on being your usual asshole self and screwing young secretaries like Elaine."

"And what if I don't agree?" he asked angrily.

"David, David," Barbara sighed. "I don't think you have the right attitude. For starters, as I already said, I am going to disappear again and you, nor anyone you know, will ever see me again. You will continue to be suspected of my murder and, David, I believe the police will scrutinize you and your financial dealings very closely." She shrugged. "I'm afraid the IRS might find some of your more adventurous investments rather interesting, don't you?"

Barbara felt him seething, the tension building inside him like a pressure cooker. She had always wondered if those safety valves really worked.

"So. Let's get back to our discussion. I believe an equitable divorce agreement would be in both of our best interests. Wouldn't you agree?"

He glared at her across the desk but said nothing.

"If you agree to liquidate your assets and transfer half to me via a bank account that even despicable lawyers like you can't discover, I will sign the divorce papers. This morning. Done."

While she had been talking, his eyes flickered like tiny computer screens, adding and subtracting, calculating.

"Okay," he snarled. "You can have half of it. It'll be worth it just to get you out of my life."

"Good. And how much would that be?"

"I have about $50,000 in the checking account. Another $175,000 or so in savings. Maybe another million in an offshore account. That's it."

Barbara began to laugh uncontrollably. "You really did think I am stupid, didn't you? Just stayed at home and read *Vogue*. Watched a little TV. Maybe went for a shopping junket now and then." She sighed. "I tried, at first anyway. I really did."

"I don't know what you're talking about," David said sullenly.

"Oh, I think you do. I am talking about the five offshore accounts you maintain to avoid taxes. Not one, but five. And those are the ones I am aware of. I am actually pretty good with computers and your security wall is very weak. Loading the data on a flash drive was ridiculously easy. I can tell you the locations, account numbers and amount in each slimy little bank: $2.3 million in the Caymans. Just over three million in Nevis. $3.5 million in two accounts in the Bahamas. Do I need to mention the $1.2 in the Channels? Altogether you have $10 million stashed in numbered accounts that I have identified. I suspect there's more, but I don't want to quibble over details."

Anger and hatred in David's eyes gave way to shock. "But you can't…" he spluttered, and then his eyes hardened. "This is a fucking bluff, isn't it? You've got no proof of any of this."

Barbara touched a button on the computer keyboard, which flared up glaringly in the dimly lit room. She tapped a few keys and then turned the screen toward David.

"These are the statements and account information on the two accounts in the Bahamas." She waited a few seconds so David could study the screen and then tapped a key. "This is the account information and balance from your stash in the Caymans. And now…"

"You bitch," he snarled, leaning forward angrily.

Barbara's jewel burst into angry red flames, framing her face. David raised his hands defensively and sat heavily back into his chair.

"Shut up, David," she said calmly. "I promise you, I have all the information the IRS would need to convict you of tax evasion. And do you know what the average sentence is for tax evasion on this scale? I'll spare you the suspense. It's three to five years."

David's eyes were wide with fear. "What was that?" he asked shakily. "That little trick with the flames?"

Barbara smiled and held out her gem, now gently pulsing between her fingers. "Oh, just a little bauble I picked up for $50,000. Lovely isn't it?" *God, I'm enjoying this.*

Barbara pushed the papers across the desk to David. "Now can we get to down to business?"

Chapter 42

"BARBARA, PLEASE," ZOLTAN PLEADED. "I need to know. Where did this money come from?"

"How much so far?"

Barbara and Zoltan sat at in a corner table of the restaurant, which was covered in a cheerful red and white checked tablecloth

"More than four million dollars!" Zoltan whispered sharply.

Barbara's face darkened slightly into a frown. "Weasel. He better come up with the rest."

"Barbara!" Zoltan said, raising his voice slightly.

She shrugged. "Okay. So it's like a settlement, a divorce settlement. Between me and David."

"For four million dollars?"

"Should be closer to five."

"But how…?" Zoltan ran his hands through his silver hair. "This is the outcome of your meeting with your husband? Please, assure me you did not steal it."

Barbara laughed and her green eyes lit up in mirth.

"No, Mr. József, I did not steal it. In my chat with David, I was able to convince him that a fair divorce settlement that divided our estate evenly was in his best interests. He got off cheap given the years I spent with the bastard."

Zoltan took a sip of orange juice and looked over the crowd at Lodde's eating breakfast, his Belgian waffle getting cold. He turned his attention back to Barbara.

"But four million dollars. Where did it come from?"

"My ex-husband was not only a bastard, but he was also a crook. He specialized in concealing assets for the purpose of tax evasion and collected substantial clients' fees in the process. He ran the gamut: offshore bank accounts, credit cards, shell corporations, foreign trusts. And then he stashed his ill-gotten gains in his own personal offshore accounts."

"And you knew all of this about your husband?"

Barbara raised her hand, clutching her fork. "Please. Ex-husband. At best."

"Very well, but how did you convince him to give up this hidden money?"

"You're not the only one with a valuable flash drive, sir. And when I pointed out that in the event he did not comply with divorce statutes and distribute our assets equally these documents would be turned over to the IRS for a whistleblower fee, he saw the wisdom of cooperation." Barbara smiled. "I, sir, am now officially divorced."

"And wealthy, yes?"

"Actually, no. You will notice the money has gone into your account with the Market Credit Union. It is untraceable. Neither one of us needs to be concerned with finances."

"Barbara," Zoltan said, looking at her earnestly. "I cannot let you do this. I do not *want* you to do this. This is your money, not mine."

"It is our money, you big oaf."

Zoltan sighed and poured more maple syrup on his waffle. He cut off a bite and looked at it for several moments. "It is *not* our money. It is yours. And it seems you threatened him to get it, did you not?"

Barbara looked casually at her plate. "Not really. I just reminded him that he is the prime suspect in my murder and that if I disappeared again with no proof that I was not dead, he would remain under suspicion indefinitely, which would probably not be great for business. With a notarized signature on divorce papers that unfortunate pall would be lifted."

Zoltan put the piece of waffle in his mouth and chewed it

slowly. "Blackmail."

"Zoltan," Barbara said, her voice softening. "I have known about David's tax evasion for years. The money he transferred to your account is the profits from money laundering. That's what he did. He worked with drug dealers and organized criminal gangs to clean their money and stash it offshore. He did the same with his profits. Believe me, he will make plenty more."

Zoltan looked uncertain. "Then the money is dirty, yes? Tainted by the suffering of others."

"What money isn't?" she asked pensively. "But more than that, it is money that will cause the suffering of many more. I know David. Left to him, that money will be invested in crooked land deals, fossil fuels, drugs, strip mining. David is the kind of man that sees a forested mountain range and says, 'We could put a pipeline right through there. Make millions.'" She shook her head. "I always knew he was a shallow, venal slimeball, but now I see there is more to him than I realized. He's a shallow, venal, slime ball doing enormous damage."

"Still…" Zoltan began.

"Look at it this way," Barbara said, putting her elbow on the table and resting her chin in her hand. "David put that money in bank accounts to avoid taxes. What he did was illegal, fraudulent, and I have all the proof needed to put him away for a long time. He knows that, and I still have that option if he does not come up with the full amount we agreed to. However, given our current straits, I offered a legal divorce on the basis of a fair agreement that we both signed. No further questions asked. The agreement is fully in line with New York statutes. I have legally and ethically acquired my share of our estate and it will be used to benefit society as a whole."

Zoltan looked up at the ceiling, a lattice covered in grape vines. "Perhaps you should have been a lawyer, yes? I suspect you would have been a very good one." He dropped his gaze and looked at her thoughtfully. "Thank you."

Barbara's eyes twinkled. "It was my pleasure. Really."

"Yes, I do gather you derived a certain amount of satisfaction from the encounter. But it was most courageous of you. Perhaps even a bit foolish? He could have shot you. He could have had thugs waiting for you."

"No chance. Security at the suite was airtight. And as for the thugs, I'd put Malik and Friesen up against any bums he could hire. And we do have our gems."

Zoltan took another bite. "I see. And perhaps one evening you could share the entire story with me over a nice glass of Bordeaux?"

Barbara's smile widened. "I look forward to it." Her face became serious. "You don't know how much I look forward to it."

He slid his left hand across the table and took her hand gently. "Madam, as do I, for you have done something I thought no one could ever do."

"Read your mind?" Barbara asked.

"Ah, perhaps that too."

"There's more?" she grinned.

Zoltan looked into her mischievous green eyes. "Yes, well many things actually. But one in particular."

She looked at him quizzically.

"You see," he said softly, "you made me love again."

Tears leaked from the corners of Barbara's eyes.

"Soon then," she murmured. "But your waffles..." She nodded at the Belgian waffles cooling on his plate. "Perhaps we should attend to our breakfasts first?"

Read on for an excerpt from the next Soul Catcher novel,

Underground

Coming soon from Castle Bridge Media

Chapter 1

BARBARA ENTERED THE COUNCIL CHAMBER slightly out of breath. Zoltan's message had been short and insistent. As always, it was not a voice she heard – just a message she understood, clear and urgent: *Barbara, please come join us in the council. There is an important matter we must discuss.*

It had been nearly a month since they returned to the Market after their escape from the nightmare of Justin and the Company. During that time they had been trying to discover the capacities of their gems. From their battle with Justin in the mines and the flight of Zoltan, Kwan, Maphaela and Friesen in the caves following the encounter with Justin and his cronies deep under the Buda Castle, they recognized that each gem had some special strength. Or perhaps it elevated a specific power in its owner.

Malik's gem provided a blazing beam of amber light. Zoltan was able to communicate over long distances and even converse with trees and possibly other plants and animals. Barbara had discovered early her ability to erect protective barriers and harness fire. And Jaromir had been able to freeze the lake with his gem, halting the pursuit by Justin and his lieutenants and band of Berserkers. Up to then, his ability to freeze water instantly had been mainly a party trick. But faced with death, especially of Sibyl, he found his ring had far more power than he had understood.

While they all knew their gems could provide them with power they were barely aware of, power that could be developed, the identification of what those capabilities were and how to harness them had progressed slowly.

What they had improved was communication via their jewels, a capacity the men had discovered while wandering in the maze of tunnels. Now along with Sibyl, who had inherited Jaromir's jewel after he had been killed by Justin in the caves, the six were able to send messages quickly and clearly to each other.

As she entered, Barbara scanned the room. Maphaela, Kwan, Friesen and Sibyl sat around the oval table. Zoltan leaned on the tabletop, a screen behind him. Malik, in his black and red Market Security uniform and jet-black turban, stood to Zoltan's left at one end of the table. Next to him sat a man she did not recognize. Mrs. Harlow, Chair of the Market Council, sat at the other end.

Uh oh, Barbara thought. *This looks serious.*

Zoltan gave her a tight smile and nodded at an empty chair next to Mrs. Harlow. Barbara glanced at the stranger. He was a tall man, but excruciatingly thin, almost skeletal. His face was so pale his skin seemed almost transparent. A shock of dirty blond hair was shoved under a stained baseball cap with *Mets* written across the front. He wore overalls over a thin t-shirt that might once have been white.

Zoltan ran a hand through his long silver hair and looked at the group through rimless glasses.

"Thank you all for coming," he began. "I know it's short notice and each of you are settling into your work here at the Market." He glanced around the table. "But we have some unexpected news." He paused. "Not so much unexpected, perhaps, as untimely.

"As you know, Mr. Malik was named by the Market Council to the post of Director of the Security Forces. In just a moment I will turn the meeting over to him and his deputies, Mr. Kwan and Mr. Maphaela. But before I do that, I want to remind you of a very brave man."

Zoltan's voice tightened and he stared at the gleaming wood surface for a few seconds before he looked back up at the group.

"I am speaking of Victor Caraldo, who some of you know as the Mester's thug, yes?" There were nods from the agents. "But who in the end was a man who gave his life to save mine and Barbara's and brought down the *Mester's* organization. A man of integrity and courage.

"Though he was lying in a pool of his own blood, dying on the floor of the Mester's office from a knife wound, he thanked me. Yes, and when I said it was us who needed to thank him, he said, 'You don't understand. For the first time in my life, no one has a part of my soul except me.'"

Zoltan paused again and cleared his throat. "'Honor me and go,' he said. 'This is not the end.' And indeed he proved correct. It was, in fact, the beginning, yes?"

The men's faces were set and grim. Sibyl's grey eyes shone. Their emotions swept through Barbara like a howling wind – anger, sadness, loss, suffering, but also resolve, hope and something she couldn't quite identify. Perhaps it was heart.

"We knew that even with the defeat of Justin, the movement he was part of would not disappear. That we would be called to encounter it again. To conquer it, perhaps once and for all." All eyes were focused on Zoltan.

"It appears that confrontation has begun. It seems that our hope to have sufficient time for reconnaissance, to identify allies and plan for an attack, to fully develop the powers of our gems was in vain." Maphaela and Kwan muttered quietly to each other. Sibyl leaned back in her chair and stared at the ceiling.

"What you will hear is not good news, but it is a notice that we cannot ignore. You see, it appears that rather than us taking the battle to the Company, they have brought it to us." He nodded at Malik.

Barbara shifted her gaze to Malik, who stood tall and imposing, his Market security uniform and black turban set with a single amber gem, making him look even more regal than usual. *My god,* she thought admiringly. *I want him on my side.*

Malik gave a slight bow. "As you all now know, the residents of the Market are not the only inhabitants of the New York underground. While it is impossible to know exact numbers, it is likely there are hundreds of people living in the subway system within a few miles of us." He glanced at the disheveled man sitting beside him. "Erik Becker is one of those. By this time you will have learned of the battle that occurred here between the Market and the Gagna." He swept the room with his stern gaze. "Is that correct?"

Even if she hadn't, Barbara would have been too intimidated to admit it. But she recalled Zoltan's account of the event several years before of the raid on the Market by the Gagna, denizens of the vast subway system. Many were mentally ill; all homeless and desperate, people who had escaped the hell of the streets for the eternal dark of abandoned subways stations and unused spur lines where they could not be found. Most had lived below ground for many years, reduced to living on rats and what they could grab during brief ventures above ground. Then they started infiltrating the Market, stealing food and goods they sold to pawn shops. Usually, they lived alone or in small groups, but an enterprising gang organized enough of them to form an armed raiding party.

The Market Security guards were overwhelmed and the mob, armed with guns and knives, forced their way into the Market. But instead of retreating, the people of the Market left their shops and grabbed axes, knives, poles – whatever they could find. A small group of men and women formed a phalanx in the center of the Market using steel trash container lids as shields. They charged, and the terrified Gagna dropped their weapons and fled. A black tile star in the middle of the Market floor commemorated the event.

"Mr. Becker is one of the Gagna who chose to stay with the Market, as did many others, who have become productive Market members. But, along with several of his colleagues, preferred not to live within the Market confines. However, he visited his friends often. When I learned of Mr. Becker, I requested a meeting with him. At our meeting I hired him as an intelligence agent to provide us with information on the Gagna, information that could be vital in the event of another attack."

"But I thought that was impossible," Barbara said. "Isn't that why the Market introduced the sanctuary system? Any attempt at violence would be neutralized."

Malik nodded. "That is true. But as you are aware, even the Market was unable to implement full sanctuary protection for the entire community. A determined band could do a great deal of damage. Possibly override the sanctuary protection system itself."

Malik's usual military bearing became even more pronounced. "In addition, Mr. Becker has brought us new information. I am afraid it alters the situation considerably."

He looked down at the man, who was staring at the table while twisting his hands nervously. Malik normally spoke in firm, commanding tone, but now his voice was soft and low. "Would you like to proceed, Mr. Becker?"

Becker looked up at him, his faced drawn in terror. Whether it was fear at the information he had or the idea of sharing it with the group, Barbara could not be sure. His eyes skittered around the table and refocused on his hands.

Malik smiled kindly. "That is fine, Mr. Becker. Perhaps we could show the video first? And then you could help us understand it?"

Becker looked up again and nodded gratefully.

"When I enlisted Mr. Becker as intelligence agent, I did not know what exactly I wanted him to look for."

"If you know the enemy and know yourself, you need not fear the result of a hundred battles." Everyone turned toward Kwan. "If you know yourself, but not the enemy," he continued, "for every victory gained you will also suffer a defeat. If you know neither the enemy nor yourself, you will succumb in every battle."

Malik bowed toward Kwan. "I am honored to have another student of Sun Tzu at the table. Your perspective on this matter will be invaluable." He looked back at the larger group. "As Mr. Kwan has pointed out, I realized after taking the position of Head of Security that we had no knowledge of local threats to the Market. Or indeed if we had any at all." He nodded toward Mrs. Harlow sitting at the opposite end of the table. "But given past events and with Mrs. Harlow's consent, I enlisted Mr. Becker and provided him with some basic intelligence gathering equipment, including a watch capable of taking video, even in low light conditions."

Barbara couldn't help glance at what appeared to be a perfectly normal wristwatch Becker wore.

"It seems that a man named Aras Heath is reorganizing the Gagna with one specific aim: raiding and taking full control of the Market."

Barbara heard group members shift uneasily in their chairs.

"Promising food, he drew quite a crowd to an abandoned station." He looked at Becker. "The Worth Street station, I believe?"

Becker nodded without looking up.

"But as you will see, all of the attendees were not Gagna. Nor, it appears, is Mr. Heath working alone."

The board room light dimmed, and a video appeared on the screen behind Zoltan. The images were a little jerky, but surprisingly clear, Barbara thought, for being recorded through a pinhole lens on a wristwatch in dim lighting. The walls of the old station were decorated with graffiti lit by four or five LED lanterns. The camera shifted to a long table surrounded by dozens of men and women. Becker had scanned the length of the table, which was loaded with piles of cookies, loaves of bread, several roast turkeys, potatoes, wedges of cheese, bowls of popcorn and boxes of wine. Plates and plastic cups were stacked neatly at the end of the table like a church potluck buffet, but most of the crowd ignored them, ripping chunks from the turkeys, stuffing handfuls of mashed potatoes into their mouths, jamming cookies into their pockets as if they were starving.

Which I guess many of them are, Barbara thought.

The video was taken from the back of the feasters so it was hard to distinguish individual features. But while the Gagna were of different builds and sizes, there was a common greyness that seemed to extend from their worn and filthy clothing to their necks, hair and the skin of their hands and faces.

The camera panned over the heads of the crowd to the far end of the table. A man dressed in black jeans and t-shirt – presumably Aras Heath -- sat in a huge yellow armchair, preposterous in the atmosphere of decay and peeling walls of the abandoned station. His hair was short and dyed bright red. He sat watching the free-for-all in front of him, a slight smile on his wide lips. A thick gold chain with what looked like a dark ruby hung from his neck. Next to him stood a stocky man, his face hidden in the cowl of a long grey or brown robe or possibly a hooded sweatshirt, Barbara could not be sure. The figure next to Heath brushed back the hood from his face whispered something in the other man's ear.

"Oh, my God," Sibyl said in a hushed voice.

Barbara looked more closely and gasped. Standing next to Aras Heath was a squat, sneering figure watching the people scrabbling hungrily at the table through his round glasses.

It was Meijer.

About the Author

DON SAWYER IS AND EDUCATOR and author of a dozen books in a variety of genres, including two Canadian bestsellers. He has worked with youth and adults from many cultural backgrounds and in a variety of locales, including teaching in a small Newfoundland outport, training community workers in West Africa, teaching adults on a First Nations reserve in British Columbia and designing a climate change action course for Jamaican youth. He currently lives in the Niagara region of Ontario with Jan Henig Sawyer.

CASTLE BRIDGE MEDIA RECOMMENDS...

If you liked this book, you might also enjoy reading the following titles from Castle Bridge Media available on Amazon or by order at your favorite book store:

The 23rd Hero
By Rebecca Anne Nguyen

ANIMAL CHARMER
By Rain Nox
Animal Charmer
Magic & Melody

Austinites
By In Churl Yo

Bloodsucker City
By Jim Towns

SOUL CATCHER
By Don Sawyer
The Burning Gem
The Tunnels of Buda

THE CASTLE OF HORROR ANTHOLOGY SERIES
Volume 1
Volume 2: Holiday Horrors
Volume 3: Scary Summer
   Stories
Volume 4: Women Running
   From Houses
Volume 5: Thinly Veiled:
   The 70s
Volume 6: Femme Fatales*
Volume 7: Love Gone Wrong
Volume 8: Thinly Veiled:
   The 80s
Volume 9: Young Adult
Volume 10: Thinly Veiled:
   Saturday Mournings
Volume 11: Revenge
Volume 12: Ripped From
   The Headlines
Edited By Jason Henderson
and In Churl Yo
*Edited By P.J. Hoover

Child of Dark Water
By E..G. Rand

Castle of Horror Podcast Book of Great Horror: Our Favorites, Top Tens and Bizarre Pleasures
Edited By Jason Henderson

Cherry Dark
By R.L. Wilburn

Dream State
By Martin Ott

Dominic
By Lee Guzman

FRENCH DECEPTION
By Janice Nagourney
A Forgery in Paris
A Forgery in Lyon
A Forgery in Marseille

FuturePast Sci-Fi Anthology
Edited by In Churl Yo

GLAZIER'S GAP
Ghosts of the Forbidden
By Leanna Renee Hieber

Hellfall
By Jay Gould

Isonation
By In Churl Yo

JAYU CITY CHRONICLES
By Chris M. Arnone
The Hermes Protocol
Necropolis Alpha

Junk Film: Why Bad Movies Matter
By Katharine Coldiron

MID-LIFE CRISIS THRILLERS
18 Miles From Town
By Jason Henderson
Lost Angel
By Sam Knight
Ties That Kill
By Deven Greene

Nightwalkers: Gothic Horror Movies
By Bruce Lanier Wright

THE PATH
By David Bowles
The Blue-Spangled Blue
The Deepest Green

SURF MYSTIC
By Peyton Douglas
Night of the Book Man
Dark of the Curl

The Thing That Happened When We Were Little
By Caroline Kelly Franklin

Yesterday's Tomorrows: The Golden Age of Science Fiction Movies
By Bruce Lanier Wright

Please remember to leave us your reviews on Amazon and Goodreads!

THANK YOU FOR SUPPORTING INDEPENDENT PUBLISHERS AND AUTHORS!
castlebridgemedia.com